THE GAP DRAGON

While Smash watched the girls escape, the Gap Dragon leaped at him; the huge metal claws of the foremost set of feet raked at his belly. Smash had to fall on his back to avoid them—and the weight of the dragon landed on him.

The sinuous body began moving, bringing another set of legs to bear. These would soon attack the pinned ogre. It would be easy for these long claws to spear through his flesh repeatedly, and sooner or later they would puncture a vital organ. Even ogres could be killed, Smash remembered.

This, Smash decided, was delightful! He hadn't had so much fun since he was almost eaten by a tangle tree when he was very young.

By Piers Anthony
Published by Ballantine Books:

THE MAGIC OF XANTH
   A Spell For Chameleon
   The Source Of Magic
   Castle Roogna
   Centaur Aisle
   Ogre, Ogre
   Night Mare
   Dragon on a Pedestal

THE APPRENTICE ADEPT
   Book One: Split Infinity
   Book Two: Blue Adept
   Book Three: Juxtaposition

INCARNATIONS OF IMMORTALITY
   Book One: On A Pale Horse
   Book Two: Bearing An Hourglass

OGRE, OGRE

Piers Anthony

A Del Rey Book

BALLANTINE BOOKS • NEW YORK

A Del Rey Book
Published by Ballantine Books

Library of Congress Catalog Card Number: 82-6659

ISBN 0-345-33509-0

Manufactured in the United States of America

First Edition: October 1982
Thirteenth Printing: December 1985

Cover art by Darrell K. Sweet

For Cheryl—
my daughter,
whose tantrums really
aren't that bad

Contents

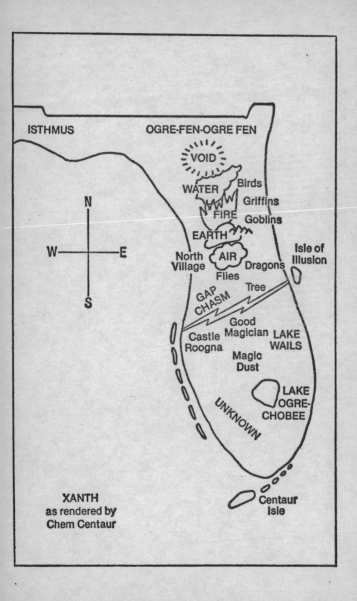

Chapter 1. Nightmare

Tandy tried to sleep, but it was difficult. The demon had never actually entered her private bedroom, but she was afraid that one night he would. This night she was alone; therefore she worried.

Her father Crombie was a rough soldier who had no truck with demons. But he was away most of the time, guarding the King at Castle Roogna. Crombie was fun when he was home, but that was rare. He claimed to hate women, but had married a nymph, and tolerated no interference by other males. Tandy remained a child in his eyes; his hand would have hovered ominously near his sword if he even suspected any demon was bothering her. If only he were here.

Her mother Jewel was on a late mission, planting orange sapphires in a stratum near the surface. It was a long way away, so she rode the Diggle-worm, who could tunnel through rock without leaving a hole. They would be back after midnight. That meant several more hours, and Tandy was afraid.

She turned over, wrapped the candy-striped sheet about her in an uncomfortable tangle, and put the pink pillow over her head. It didn't help; she still feared the demon. His name was Fiant, and he could dematerialize at will. That meant he could walk through walls.

The more Tandy thought about that, the less she trusted the walls of her room. She was afraid that any unwatched wall would permit the demon to pass through. She rolled over, sat up, and peered at the walls. No demon.

She had met Fiant only a few weeks ago, by accident. She had been playing with some large, round, blue rubies, rejects from her mother's barrel—rubies were supposed to be red—and one had rolled down a passage near the demons' rum works. She had run right into a rum wrap a demon was using, tearing it so that it became a bum wrap. She had been afraid the demon would be angry, but instead he had simply looked at her with a half-secret half-smile— and that had been worse. Thereafter that demon had shown up with disturbing frequency, always looking at her as if something demoniacally special was on his mind. She was not so naïve as to be in doubt about the nature of his thought. A nymph would have been flattered—but Tandy was human. She sought no demon lover.

Tandy got up and went to the mirror. The magic lantern brightened as she approached, so that she could see herself. She was nineteen years old, but she looked like a child in her nightie and lady-slippers, her brown tresses mussed from constant squirming, her blue eyes peering out worriedly. She wished she looked more like her mother—but of course no human person could match the pretty faces and fantastic figures of nymphs. That was what nymphdom was all about—to attract men like Crombie who judged the distaff to be good for only one thing. Nymphs were good for that thing. Human girls could be good for it, too, but they really had to work at it; they fouled it up by assigning far more meaning to it than the nymphs did, so were unable to proceed with sheer delighted abandon. They were cursed by their awareness of consequence.

She peered more closely at herself, brushing her tresses back with her hands, rearranging her nightie, standing straighter. She was no child, whatever her father might choose to think. Yet she was not exactly buxom, either. Her human heritage had given her a good mind and a soul, at the expense of voluptuousness. She had a cute face, with a pert, upturned nose and full lips, she decided, but not enough of the rest of it. She couldn't make it as a nymph.

The demon Fiant obviously thought she would do, however. Maybe he didn't realize that her human component made her less of a good thing. Maybe he was slumming, looking for an intriguing change of pace from the dusky demonesses who could assume any form they chose, even animal forms. It was said that sometimes they would change to animal form in the middle of the act of—but no human girl was supposed to be able to imagine anything like that. Tandy couldn't change form, in or out of bed, and certainly she didn't want any demon's attention. If only she could convince him of that!

There was nothing to do but try to sleep again. The demon would come or he wouldn't; since she had no control over that, there was no sense worrying.

She lay down amidst the mess her bed had become and worried. She closed her eyes and remained still, as if sleeping, but remained tensely awake. Maybe after a while her body would be fooled into relaxing.

There was a flicker at the far wall. Tandy spied it through almost-closed eyes and kept her small body frozen. It was the demon; he really had come.

In a moment Fiant solidified inside the room. He was large, muscular, and fat, with squat horns sprouting from his forehead and a short, unkempt beard that made him look like a goat. His hind feet were hooflike, and he had a medium-length tail at his posterior, barbed at the tip. There was a dusky ambience about him that would have betrayed his demonic nature, no matter what form he took. His eyes were like smoky quartz shielding an internal lava flow, emitting a dull red light that brightened when his attention warmed to something. By diabolic standards, he was handsome enough, and many a nymph would have been deliciously happy to be in Tandy's place.

Tandy hoped Fiant would go away, after perceiving her alseep and disordered, but knew he wouldn't. He found her attractive, or at least available, and refused to be repulsed by her negative response. Demons expected rejections; they thrived on them. It was said that, given a choice between rape and seduction, they would always choose the rape. The females, too. Of course, it was impossible to rape that kind; she would simply dematerialize if she didn't like it. Which might be another explanation for Fiant's interest in Tandy; *she* couldn't dematerialize. Rape was possible.

Maybe if she were positive, welcoming him, that would turn him off. He was obviously tired of willing females. But Tandy couldn't bring herself to try that particular ploy. If it didn't work, where would she be?

Fiant approached the bed, grinning evilly. Tandy kept her eyes screwed almost shut. What would she do if he touched her? She was sure that screaming and fighting would only encourage him and make his eyes glow with preternatural lust—but what else was there?

Fiant paused, looming over her, his paunch protruding, the light from his eyes spearing down through slits. "Ah, you lovely little morsel," he murmured, a wisp of smoke curling from his mouth as he spoke. "Be thrilled, you soft, human flesh. Your demon lover is here at last! Let me see more of you." And he snatched the sheet away.

Tandy hurled the pillow at him and bounced off the bed, her terror converting to anger. "Get out of here, foul spirit!" she screamed.

"Ah, the tender morsel wakes, cries welcome! Delightful!" The demon strode toward her, the blue tip of his forked tongue rasping over his thin lips. His tail flicked similarly.

Tandy backed away, her terror/anger intensifying. "I loathe you! Go away!"

"Presently," Fiant said, his tail stiffening as it elevated. "Hone your passion to its height, honey, for I will possess its depth." He reached for her, his horns brightening in the reflected glare of his eyes.

Desperate, Tandy wreaked her ultimate. She threw a tantrum. Her body stiffened, her face turned red, her eyes clenched shut, and she hurled that tantrum right at the demon's fat chest.

It struck with explosive impact. The demon sundered into fragments, his feet, hands, and head flying outward. His tail landed on the bed and lay twitching like a beheaded snake.

Tandy chewed her trembling lip. She really hadn't wanted to do that; her tantrums were devastating, and she wasn't supposed to throw them. Now she had destroyed the demon, and there would be hell to pay. How could she answer to hell for murder?

The pieces of the demon dissolved into smoke. The cloud coalesced—and Fiant formed again, intact. He looked dazed. "Oh, that kiss was a beauty," he said, and staggered through the wall.

Tandy relaxed. Fiant wasn't dead after all, but he was

gone. She had the best of both situations. Or did she? He surely would not stay gone—and now they both knew her tantrums would not stop him. She had only postponed her problem.

Nevertheless, now she was able to sleep. She knew there would be no more trouble this night, and her mother would be home the next few nights. Fiant, for all his boldness when he had his victim isolated, stayed clear when a responsible person was in the neighborhood.

Next day Tandy tried to talk to her mother, though she was pretty sure it wouldn't help. "Mother, you know that demon Fiant, who works at the rum refinery? He—"

"Oh, yes, the demons are such nice people," Jewel said, smelling of mildly toasted sulfur. That was her magic: her odor reflected her mood. "Especially Beauregard, doing his research paper—"

"Which he has been working on since before I was born. He's a nice demon, yes. But Fiant is another kind. He—"

"They never make any trouble for me when I have to set gems in their caves. The demons are such good neighbors." The sulfur was getting stronger, beginning to crinkle the nose; Jewel didn't like to hear criticisms.

"Most are, Mother." Naturally the demons didn't bother Jewel; without her, there would be no gems to find, and the demons were partial to such trinkets. "But this one's different. He—"

"Everyone's different, of course, dear. That's what makes Xanth so interesting." Now she smelled of freshly blooming orange roses.

"Maybe different isn't quite what I mean. He comes to my room at night—"

"Oh, he wouldn't do that! That wouldn't be right." The wrongness of such a thing showed in the smell of an overripe medicine ball; even immature medicine balls smelled unpleasantly of illness, and aging intensified the effect.

"But he *did*! Last night—"

"You must have dreamed it, dear," Jewel said firmly. And the aroma of carrion of a moderately sated dragon showed how distasteful any such notion was to Jewel. "Sometimes those nightmares carry irresponsible dreams."

Tandy saw that her mother did not want to become aware of the truth. Jewel had been a nymph and retained many of her nymphal qualities despite the burden of experience that marriage and motherhood had imposed on her. She had no real understanding of evil. To her, all people and all creatures were basically good neighbors, including demons. And in truth, the demons had been tolerably well behaved, until Fiant had taken his interest in Tandy.

Her father Crombie would understand, though. Crombie was not only human, he was a man of war. Well did he understand the ways of males. But he hardly ever had time off, and she had no way to advise him of her situation, so he couldn't help now.

As she thought of her father, Tandy abruptly realized that Jewel could not afford to lose her faith in people, because then she would have to question Crombie's fidelity. That could only disrupt her life. Evidently Jewel's thoughts were to some extent parallel to Tandy's because now there was the disturbing odor of a burning field of wild oats.

So Tandy couldn't actually talk to her mother about this. It would have to be her father, in private. That meant she had to get to him, since he would not be home in time to deal with the demon. It was said that no man could stand against a demon in combat, but Crombie was more than a man: he was her father. She had to reach him.

That was a problem in itself. Tandy had never been to Castle Roogna. She had never even been to the surface of Xanth. She would be lost in an instant if she ever left the caves. In fact, she was afraid to try. How could she travel all the way to her father's place of employment, alone? She had no good answer.

The demon did not come the following night. The nightmares visited instead. Every time she slept, they trotted in, rearing over her bed, hooves flashing, ears flat back, snorting the scary vapors that were the bad dreams they bore. She woke in justified terror, and they were gone—only to return as she slept again. That was the way of such beasts.

Finally she became so desperate she threw a tantrum at one of them. The tantrum struck it on the flank. The mare squealed with startled pain, her hindsection collapsing, and her companions fled.

Tandy was instantly sorry, as she generally was after throwing a tantrum; she knew the dark horse was only doing its duty and should not be punished. Tandy woke completely, tears in her eyes, determined to help the animal—but of course it was gone. It was almost impossible to catch a nightmare while awake.

She checked where the mare had stood. The floor was scuffled there, and there were a few drops of blood. Tandy hoped the mare had made it safely home; it would be several nights before this one was fit for dream-duty again. It was a terrible thing to lash out at an innocent creature like that, no matter how bothersome it might be, and Tandy resolved not to do that again.

Next time she slept, she watched for the nightmares, trying to identify the one she had hurt. But they were a long time in coming, as if they were now afraid of her, and she could hardly blame them for that. But at last they came, for they were compelled to do their job even when it was dangerous to them. Timidly they approached with their burdens of dreams, and these now related to the harming of equines. They were making her pay for her crime! But she never saw the hurt one, and that made her feel increasingly guilty. She was sure that particular nightmare was forever wary of her, and would not come again. Maybe it was lying in a stall wherever such creatures went by day, suffering. If only she had held her temper!

It was the job of nightmares to carry the unpleasant dreams that sleepers were scheduled to have, just as it was Jewel's job to place the gems people were destined to find. Since the dreams were ugly, they could not be trusted to voluntary participation. Thus nightmares had a bad reputation, in contrast with the invisible daymares who brought in pleasant daydreams. People tried to avoid nightmares, and this made the horses' job more difficult. Tandy wasn't sure what would happen if the bad dreams did not get delivered, but was sure there would be trouble. It was generally best not to interfere with the natural order. She wondered idly what dreams the nightmares themselves had when they slept.

A few days later, when Tandy was settling down, the demon Fiant came again. He walked right through the wall, a lascivious grin on his face. "Open up, cutie; I'm here to fulfill your fondest fancies and delve into your deepest desires." His tail was standing straight up, quivering.

For a moment Tandy froze, unable even to speak. She

had been bothered by this creature before; now she was terrified. Staring-eyed, she watched his confident approach.

Fiant stood over her, as before, his eyes glowing like red stars. "Lie back, spread out, make yourself comfy," he gloated. "I shall exercise your extreme expectations." He reached for her with a long-nailed diabolic hand.

Tandy screamed.

This night, Jewel was home; she rushed in to discover what was the matter. But the demon marched calmly out through the wall before Jewel arrived, and Tandy had to blame her scream on the nightmares. That provided her with a fresh burden of guilt, for of course the mares were innocent.

Tandy knew she had to do something. Fiant was getting bolder, and soon he would catch her alone—and that would be worse than any nightmare. He had proved he could survive one of her tantrums, so Tandy had no protection. She would have to go to her father Crombie—soon. But *how*?

Then she had an inspiration. Why not catch a nightmare and ride her to Castle Roogna? The creature would surely know the way, as the mares had the addresses of all people who slept.

But there were problems. Tandy had no experience riding horses; she had sometimes ridden the Diggle behind her mother, traveling to the far reaches of Xanth to place emeralds and opals and diamonds, but this was different. The Diggle moved slowly and evenly, phasing through the rock as long as someone made a tune it liked. The nightmares, she was sure, moved swiftly and unevenly. How could she catch one—and how could she hold on?

Tandy was an agile girl. She had climbed all over the caverns, swinging across chasms on rope-vines, squeezing through tiny crevices—good thing she was small!—swimming the chill river channels, running fleetly across sloping rockslides, throwing chunks at the occasional goblins who pursued her. If a nightmare got close enough, she was confident she could leap onto its back and hang on to its flowing mane. It would not be a comfortable ride, but she could manage. So all she really had to worry about was the first step—catching her mare.

The problem was, the nightmares came only during a

person's sleep. She might pretend sleep, but she doubted she would fool them—and if she grabbed one while awake, it would surely dissipate like demon-smoke, leaving her with nothing but a fading memory. Nightmares were, after all, a type of demon; they could dematerialize in much the way Fiant did. That was how they passed through walls to reach the most secure sleepers. In fact, she suspected they became material only in the presence of a sleeper.

She would have to ride the nightmare in her sleep. Only that would keep it material, or enable her to dematerialize with it.

Tandy set about her task with determination. It was not that she relished the prospect of such a ride, but that she knew what would happen to her at the hands—or whatever—of the demon if she did not ride. She set up a bolster on two chairs and practiced on it, pretending it was the back of a horse. She lay on her bed, then abruptly bounced off it and leaped astride the bolster, grabbing a tassle where the mane should be and squeezing with her legs. Over and over she did this, drilling the procedure into herself until it became fast and automatic. She got tired and her legs got sore, but she kept on, until she could do it in her sleep—she hoped.

This took several days. She practiced mostly when her mother was out setting jewels, so that there would be no awkward questions. The demon did not bother her by day, fortunately, so she was able to snatch some sleep then, too.

When she was satisfied, and also when she dared delay no longer, because of Fiant's boldness and her mother's upcoming overnight journey to set diamonds in a big kimberlite pipe—a complex job—she acted.

She wrote a note to her mother, explaining that she had gone to visit her father and not to worry. Nymphs tended not to worry much anyway, so it should be all right. She gathered some sleeping pills from the recesses where they slept, put them in her pockets, and lay down. One pill was normally good for several hours before it woke, and she had several; they should keep her in their joint sleep all night.

But as the power of the pills took their magic effect on her body, drawing her into their slumber, Tandy had an alarming thought: suppose no nightmares came tonight?

Suppose Fiant came instead—and she was locked in slumber, unable to resist him? That thought disturbed her so much that the first nightmare rushed to attend to her the moment she slept.

Tandy saw the creature clearly in her dream: a midnight-colored equine with faintly glowing eyes—there was the demon stigma!—set amidst a flaring forelock. The mane was glossy black, and the tail dark ebony; even the hooves were dusky. Yet she was a handsome animal, with fine features and good musculature. The black ears perked forward, the black nostrils flared, and the dark neck arched splendidly. Tandy knew this was an excellent representative of the species.

"I'm asleep," she reminded herself. "This is a dream." Indeed it was. A bad dream, full of deep undertow currents and grotesque surgings and fear and shame and horror, making her miserable. But she fought it back, nerved herself, and leaped for the dark horse.

She made it. Her tedious rehearsals had served her well. She landed on the nightmare's back, clutched the sleek mane, and clasped its powerful body with her legs.

For an instant the mare stood still, too surprised to move. Tandy knew that feeling. Then the creature took off. She galloped through the wall as if it were nothing—and indeed it felt like nothing, for they had dematerialized. The power of the nightmare extended to her rider, just as the sleeping power of the pills extended to their wearer. Tandy remained asleep, in the dream-state, fastened to her steed.

The ride was a terror. Walls shot by like shadows, and open spaces like daylight, as the mare galloped headlong and tailshort. Tandy hung on to the mane, though the strands of it cut cruelly into her hands, because she was afraid to let go. How hard would she fall, where would she be, if she lost purchase now? This was a worse dream than any before—and the sleeping pills prevented her from waking.

They were already far away from her mother's neat apartment. They cruised through rock and caverns, water and fire, and the lairs of large and small monsters. They galloped across the table where six demons were playing poker, and the demons paused a moment as if experiencing some chill doubt without quite seeing the nightmare. They zoomed by a secret conclave of goblins planning foul play, and these, too, hesitated momentarily as the ambience of bad visions touched them. The nightmare plowed through the deepest recess, where the Brain Coral stored the living artifacts of Xanth, and the artifacts stirred restlessly, too, not knowing what moved them. Tandy realized that when a nightmare passed a waking creature, she caused a brief bad thought. Only in sleep did those thoughts have full potency.

Now Tandy had another problem. She had to guide this steed—and she didn't know how. If she had known how, she still wouldn't have known the way to Castle Roogna. Why hadn't she thought of this before?

Well, this was a dream, and it didn't have to make sense. "Take me to Castle Roogna!" she cried. "Then I'll let you go!"

The nightmare neighed and changed course. Was that all there was to it? It occurred to Tandy that the steed was as frightened as Tandy herself was. Such horses weren't meant for riding! So maybe the mare would cooperate, just to be rid of her rider.

They burst out of the caverns and onto the upper surface of Xanth. Tandy was used to strange things in dreams, but was nevertheless awed. Her eyes were open—at least they seemed to be, though this could be merely part of the dream—and she saw the vastness of the surface night. There were spreading trees and huge empty spaces and rivers without cave-canyons, and above was a monstrous ceiling full of pinpoints of light in great patches. She realized that these were stars, which her father had told her about—and she had thought he was making it up, just as he made up tales of the heroic deeds of the men of legendary Xanth's past—and that where there were none was because of clouds. Clouds were like the vapor surrounding waterfalls, loosed to ascend to the heavens. Turn a cloud loose, and naturally it did whatever it wanted.

Then from behind a cloud came a much larger light, surely the fabled sun, the golden ball that tracked across the sky, always in one direction. No, not the sun, for that chose to travel, for reasons of its own, only during the day.

Jewel had told her that, though Tandy wasn't sure Jewel herself had ever seen the sun. When Tandy had asked her father whether it was true, Crombie had just laughed, which she took to be affirmation of the orb's diurnal disposition. Of course things didn't need sensible reasons for what they did. Maybe the sun was merely afraid of the dark, so stayed clear of night.

No, this must be the moon, which was an object of similar size but dimmer because it was made of green cheese that didn't glow so well. Evidently, high-flying dragons had eaten most of it, for only a crescent remained, the merest rind. Still, it was impressive.

The mare pounded on. Tandy's hands grew numb, but her hold was firm. Her body was bruised and chafed by the bouncing; she would be sore for days! But at least she was getting there. Her bad dream slipped into oblivion for a while, as dreams tended to, fading in and out as the run continued.

Abruptly she woke. A dark castle loomed in the fading moonlight. They had arrived!

Barely in time, too, for now dawn was looming behind them. The nightmare could not enter the light of day. In fact, the mare was already fading out, for regardless of dawn, it was no longer bound when Tandy left the dream-state. The sleeping pills must have finished their nap, and Tandy had finished hers with them. No—the stones were mostly gone; they must have bounced out one at a time in the course of the rough ride, and now only one was left, not enough to do the job.

In a moment the mare vanished entirely, freed by circumstance, and Tandy found herself sprawled on the ground, battered and wide-eyed.

She was stiff and sore and tired. It had not been a restful sleep at all. Her legs felt swollen and numb from thigh to ankle. Her hair was plastered to her scalp with the cold sweat of nocturnal fear. It had been a horrendous ordeal. But at least she was in sight of her destination.

She got painfully to her feet and staggered toward the edifice as the blinding sun hefted itself ambitiously above the trees. The Land of Xanth brightened about her, and the creatures of day began to stir. Dew sparkled. It was all strangely pretty.

But as she came to the moat and saw that there was the stirring of some awful creature within it, orienting on her, she had a horrible revelation. She knew what Castle Roogna looked like, from descriptions her father had made. He had told her wonderful stories about it, from the time she was a baby onward, about the orchard with its cherry-bomb trees, bearing cherries a person dared not eat, and shoes of all types growing on shoe trees, and all manner of other wonders too exaggerated to be believed. Only an idiot or a hopeless visionary would believe in the Land of Xanth, anyway! Yet she almost knew the individual monsters of the moat by name, and the same for the guardian zombies who rested in the graveyard, awaiting the day when Xanth needed defense. She knew the spires and turrets and all, and the ghosts who dwelt within them. She had a marvelously detailed mental map of Castle Roogna—and this present castle did not conform.

This was the wrong castle.

Oh, woe! Tandy stood in dull, defeated amazement. All her effort, her last vestige of strength and hope, and her deviously laid plans to reach her father lay in ruins. What was she to do now? She was lost in Xanth, without food or water, so tired she could hardly move, with no way to return home. What would her mother think?

Something stirred within the castle. The drawbridge lowered, coming to rest across the small moat. A lovely woman walked out of the castle, subduing the reaching monster with a trifling gesture of her hand, her voluminous robe blowing in the morning breeze. She saw Tandy and came toward her—and Tandy saw with a new shock of horror that the woman had no face. Her hood contained a writhing mass of snakes, and emptiness where human features should have been. Surely the nightmare had saved the worst dream for last!

"Dear child," the faceless woman said. "Come with me. We have been expecting you."

Tandy stood frozen, unable even to muster the energy for a tantrum. What horrors lay within this dread castle?

"It is all right," the snake-headed woman said reassuringly. "We consider that your phenomenal effort in catching and riding the nightmare constitutes sufficient challenge to reach this castle. You will not be subject to the usual riddles of admission."

They were going to take her inside! Tandy tried to run, but her strength was gone. She was a spunky girl, but she had been through too much this night. She fainted.

Chapter 2. Smash Ogre

Smash tromped through the blackboard jungle of Xanth, looking at the pictures on the blackboards because, like all his kind, he couldn't read the words. He was in a hurry because the foul weather he was enjoying showed signs of abating, and he wanted to get where he was going before it did. When he encountered a fallen beech tree across the path, he simply hurled it out of the way, letting the beech-sand fall in a minor sandstorm. When he discovered that an errant river had jumped its channel and was washing out the path and threatening to clean the grunge off his feet and make his toenails visible for the first time in weeks, he grabbed that stream by its tail and flexed it so hard that it splatted right back into its proper channel and lay there quivering and bubbling in fear. When an ornery bullhorn blocked the way, threatening to ram its horn most awkwardly into the posterior of anyone who distracted it, Smash did more than that. He picked it up by the horn and blew a horrendous blast that nearly turned the creature inside out. Never again would that bullhorn bother travelers on that path; it had been cowed.

This sort of thing was routine for Smash, for he was the most powerful and stupid of all Xanth's vaguely manlike creatures. The ground trembled nervously when he tromped, and the most ferocious monsters thought it prudent to catch errands elsewhere until he was gone. Naturally the errands fled with indecent haste, wanting no part of this. In fact, no creature with any wit at all wanted any part of this. For Smash was an ogre.

He was twice the height of an ordinary man, was broad in proportion, and his knots of hairy muscles stood out like the boles of tormented old trees. Some creatures might have considered him ugly, but these were the less imaginative individuals. Smash was not ugly; he was horrendous. By no stretch of imagination could any ogre be considered less than grotesque, and Smash was an appalling specimen of the breed. There had not been a more revolting creature on this path since a basilisk had crossed it.

Yet Smash, like most powerfully ugly creatures, had a rather sweet interior, hidden deep inside where it would not embarrass him. He had been raised among human beings, had gone on an adventure with Prince Dor and Princess Irene, and had made friends with centaurs. He had, in short, been somewhat civilized by his environment, incredible as this might seem. Most people believed that no ogre was civilizable, and that was certainly the safest belief to hold.

Yet Smash was no ordinary ogre. This meant that he usually did not strike without some faint reason and that his natural passion for violence had been somewhat stifled. This was a sad condition for an ogre, yet he had borne up moderately well. Now he had a mission.

The bad weather cleared. The clouds drew their curtains aside to let lovely shafts of sunlight slant down, making the air sparkle prettily. Birds shook out their feathers and trilled joyfully. Everything was turning clean and pleasant.

Smash snorted with disgust. How could he travel in this? He would have to camp for the afternoon and night and hope the morrow was a worse day.

He was hungry, for it took huge and wasteful quantities of energy to sustain an ogre in proper arrogance. He cast about for something edible and massive enough to sustain him, such as a dead dragon or a vat of spoiling applesauce or a mossy rock-candy boulder, but found nothing. This region had already been scavenged out.

Then he heard the squawk of a contented griffin and he sniffed the aroma of delicious pie. The perceptions of ogres were a-cute rather than a-ugly, oddly; though the griffin was some distance away, Smash located it precisely by sound and odor. He tromped toward it. This must be the creature that had cleaned out all the edibles of this region.

The griffin had captured a monstrous shoefly pie. The winged shoes had been cooked to a turn, the juices of their fine leather suffusing the pie, which massed about as much as the griffin. This was an ideal meal for an ogre.

Smash marched up, not bothering to employ any stealth. The griffin whirled, half spreading its wings, issuing a warning squawk. Nobody in his right mind interfered with a feeding griffin, except a sufficiently large and hungry dragon.

But Smash was not in his right mind. No ogre ever was. There was simply not enough mind there to be right. "Me give he three, leave sight of me," he said. All ogres spoke only in inane rhyme and lacked facility with pronouns, which they took to be edible roots. But ogres generally made themselves plain enough, in their brutish fashion.

The griffin had not had prior experience with an ogre. That was its fortune. There were very few ogres in these parts. The griffin opened its eagle beak wide and screeched a warning challenge.

Smash's bluff had been called. That was unfortunate, because no ogre was smart enough to bluff. With dimwitted joy, he rose to the prospect of mayhem. "One," he said, counting off on his smallest hamfinger. The griffin didn't move.

"Two." After a brief search, he found another finger.

The griffin had had enough of this. It gave a raucous battle cry and charged, which was just as well, for Smash had lost count. This sort of intellectual exercise was horrendously difficult for his kind; his head hurt and his fingers felt numb. But now he was released from the necessity of counting all the way to three, and that was a great relief.

He grabbed the griffin by its bird beak and lion's tail, whirled it around, and hurled it out over the forest in a cloud of small feathers and fur. The griffin, startled by this reception, spread its wings, oriented, circled, decided the event must have been a fluke, and started to come in for another engagement. Ogres did not have a monopoly on stupidity!

Smash faced the lion-bodied bird. "Scram, ham!" he bellowed.

The blast of the bellow tore out half a dozen pinfeathers and two flight feathers, and sent the griffin spinning out of

control. The creature righted itself again, but this time decided to seek its fortune elsewhere. Thus did it finally do
something halfway smart, yielding the stupidity title to the
ogre.

Smash took a flying leap into the center of the shoefly
pie. Leatherlike pastry crust flew up. The ogre grabbed a
big handful of the delicious mess and stuffed it into his
maw. He slurped noisily on a boot, chewed the tongue in
half, and masticated on a pleasantly tough heel. Oh, it was
good! He grabbed two more handfuls, crunching soles and
sucking on laces and spitting the metal eyelets out like
seeds. Soon all the pie was gone. He burped up a few metal
nails, well satisfied.

After gorging, he went to a stream and slurped a few
gallons of shivering cool water. As he lifted his head, he
heard a faint call. "Help! Help!"

Smash looked about, his ears rotating like those of the
animal he was, to orient on the sound. It came from a
nearby brambleberry bush. He parted the foliage with one
gross finger and peered in. There was a tiny manlike creature. "Help, please!" it cried.

Ogres had excellent eyesight, but this person was so
small that Smash had to focus carefully to see him. Her. It
was naked and had—well, it was a tiny female imp. "Who
you?" he inquired politely, his breath almost knocking her
down.

"I'm Quieta the Imp," she cried, rearranging her hair,
which his breath had violently disarrayed. "Oh, ogre,
ogre—my father's trapped and will surely perish if not rescued soon. Please, I beseech you most prettily, help him
escape, and I will reward you in my fashion."

Smash did not care one way or another about imps; they
were too small to eat; anyway, he was for the moment full.
This one was hardly more massive than one of his fingers.
He did, however, like rewards. "Okay, dokay," he agreed.

"My name's Quieta, not Dokay," she said primly. She
led him to a spot under a soapstone boulder. It was, of
course, a very clean place, and the soap had been carved
into interesting formations. There was her father-imp,
caught in an alligator clamp. The alligator's jaws were
slowly chewing off his little leg.

"This is my father Ortant," Quieta said, introducing them. "This is big ugly ogre."

"Pleased to meet you, Bigugly Ogre," Imp Ortant said as politely as the pain in his leg permitted.

Smash reached down, but his hamfingers were far too big and clumsy to pry open the tiny clamp. "Queer ear," he told the imps, and obediently both covered their minuscule ears with minature hands.

Smash let out a small roar. The alligator clamp yiped and let go, scrambling back to the farthest reach of its anchor-chain, where it cowered. The imp was free.

"Oh, thank you, thank you so much, ogre!" Quieta exclaimed. "Here is your reward." She held out a tiny disk.

Smash accepted it, balancing it on the tip of one finger, his gross brow furrowing like a newly plowed field.

"It's a disposable reflector," Quieta explained proudly. Then, seeing that he did not comprehend: "A mirror, made from a film of soap-bubble. That's what we imps do. We make pretty, iridescent bubbles for the fairies, and lenses for sunbeams, and sparkles for the morning dew. Each item works only once, so we are constantly busy, I can tell you. We call it planned obsolescence. So now you have a nice little mirror. But remember—you can use it only one time."

Smash tucked the mirror into his bag, vaguely disappointed. Somehow, for no good reason, he had expected more.

"Well, you saved my father only once," Quieta said defensively. "He's not very big, either. It's a perfect mirror, you know."

Smash nodded, realizing that small creatures gave small rewards. He wasn't quite sure what use the mirror would be to him, since ogres did not look at their own ugly faces very much, because their reflections tended to break mirrors and curdle the surfaces of calm lakes; in any event, this mirror was far too small and frail to sustain his image. Since it could be used only once, he would save it for an important occasion. Then he tromped to a pillow bush, pounded it almost flat and lumpy, and snored himself to sleep while the jungle trembled.

* * *

The weather was unconscionably fair the next day, but Smash tromped on regardless until he reached the castle of the Good Magician Humfrey. It was not particularly imposing. There was a small moat he could wade through, and an outer wall he could bash through—practically an open invitation.

But Smash had learned at Castle Roogna that it was best to be polite around Magicians, and not to bash too carelessly into someone's castle. So he opened his bag of belongings and donned his finest apparel: an orange jacket and steely gauntlets, given to him four years ago by the centaurs of Centaur Isle. The jacket was invulnerable to penetration by a weapon, and the gauntlets protected his hamfists from the consequence of their own power. He had not worn these things before because he didn't want them to get dirty. They were special.

Now, properly dressed, he cupped his mug and bellowed politely: "Some creep asleep?" Just in case the Good Magician wasn't up yet.

There was no response. Smash tried again. "Me Smash. Me bash." That was letting the Magician know, delicately, that he was coming in.

Still no answer. It seemed Humfrey was not paying attention. Having exhausted his knowledge of the requirements of human etiquette as he understood them, Smash proceeded to act. He waded into the water of the moat with a great and satisfying splash. Washing was un-ogrish, but splashing wasn't. In a moment the spume dimmed the sunlight and caused the entire castle to shine with moisture.

A sea monster swam to intercept him. Mostly that kind did not frequent rivers or moats, but the Good Magician had an affinity for the unusual. "Hi, fly," Smash said affably, removing a gauntlet and raising a hairy hamfist in greeting. He generally got along all right with monsters, if they were ugly enough.

The monster stared cross-eyed for a moment at the huge fist under its snout, noting the calluses, scars, and barnaclelike encrustations of gristle. Then the creature turned tail and swam hastily away. Smash's greetings sometimes affected other creatures like that; he wasn't sure why.

He redonned the gauntlet and forged on out of the moat, reaching a brief embankment from which the wall rose. He lifted one gauntleted hamfist to bash a convenient hole—and spied something on the stone. It was a small lizard, dingy blah in color, with medium sandpaper skin, inefficient legs, a truncated tail, and a pungent smell. Its mean little head swiveled around to fix on the ogre.

Smash's gauntleted hand snapped out, covering the lizard, blocking its head off from view. Ogres were stupid but not suicidal. This little monster was no ordinary lizard; it was a basilisk! Its direct glance was fatal, even to an ogre.

What was he to do? Soon the creature's poisonous body would corrode the metal of the gauntlet, and Smash would be in trouble. He couldn't remain this way!

He remembered that Prince Dor had had a problem with a basilisk that was a cockatrice. Dor had sent news of a baleful henatrice, and the cock-lizard had hurried off at a swift crawl to find her. But Smash had no such resource; he didn't know where a hen might be, and realized that this one might even *be* a henatrice. It was hard to look closely enough to ascertain the sexual status of such a creature without getting one's eyeballs stoned. And if he had happened to know where a basilisk of the opposite sex might be, how could he tell that news to this one? He didn't speak the language. For that he needed the assistance of his friend Grundy the Golem, who could speak any language at all.

Then he remembered the imp's disposable reflector. He fished in his bag with his left mitt and, after several clumsy tries, brought it out. He stuck it to the tip of his gauntleted finger and poked it toward the region where the basilisk's head should be.

Carefully he withdrew his right hand, averting his gaze. This was delicate work! If he aimed the mirror wrong, or if it fell off his finger, or if the basilisk didn't look—

There was a plop on the ground at his feet. Oh, no! The mirror had fallen! Dismayed, he looked.

The basilisk lay stunned. It had seen its own reflection in the mirror and suffered the natural consequence. It would recover after a while—but by then Smash would be out of its range.

The mirror had not dropped. It had shattered under the impact of the basilisk's glare. But it had done its job. Quieta's little reward had proved worthwhile.

Smash scooped out a handful of dirt and dumped it over the body of the basilisk so that he would not accidentally look at it. As long as that mound was intact, he would know he was safe.

Now he hefted his right fist and smashed it into the stone wall. Sand fragments flew outward from the impact with satisfying force. This was sheer joy; only when exercising the prerogative of his name did Smash feel truly happy. Smash! Smash! Smash! Dust filled the air, and a pile of rubble formed about him as the hole deepened.

Soon he was inside the castle. There was a second wall, an arm's reach inside the first. Oh, goody! This one was a lattice of bars, not nearly as substantial as the first, but much better than nothing.

For variety, Smash used his left fist this time. After all, it needed fun and exercise, too. He smashed it into the bars.

The fist stopped short. Oooh, ouch! Only the gauntlet preserved it from injury, but it still smarted. This was much tougher stuff than stone or metal!

Smash took hold of the bars with both hands and heaved. His power should have launched the entire wall toward the clouds, but there was nary a budge. This was the strongest stuff he had encountered!

Smash paused to consider. What material could resist the might of an ogre?

Thinking was hard for his kind. His skull heated up uncomfortably, causing the resident fleas to jump off with hot feet. But in due course he concluded that there was only one thing as tough as an ogre, and that was another ogre. He peered at the bars. Sure enough—these were ogres' bones, lashed together with ogres' sinews. No wonder he had found them impervious!

This was a formidable barrier. He could not bash blithely through it—nor would he wish to, for the bones of ogres were sacred to ogres. Little else was.

Smash pondered some more. His brain was already sweating from the prior effort; now there was a scorched smell as the fur of his head grew hot. Ogres were creatures of action, not cerebration! But again his valiant and painful effort was rewarded; he rammed through a notion.

"Oh, ogres' bones," he said. "Me know zones of deep, deep ground where can't be found."

The wall of bones quivered. All bad ogres craved indecent burial after death; it was one of their occasional links with the species of man. The best interment was in a garbage dump or toxic landfill for the disposal of poisonous plants and animals, but ordinary ground would do if properly cursed and tromped down sufficiently hard.

"Me pound in mound with round of sound," Smash continued, arguing his case with extraordinary eloquence.

That did it. The wall collapsed into an expectant pile. Smash picked up a bone, set it endwise against the ground, and, with a single blow of his gauntleted fist, drove it so deep in the earth that it disappeared. He took another and did the same. "Me flail he nail," he grunted, invoking an ogrish ritual of disposal. He was nailing the ground.

Soon all the bones were gone. "Me fling he string," he said, poking the tendons down after the bones with his finger and scooping dirt over the holes. Then he stomped the mound, his big flat feet making the entire region reverberate boomingly. Stray stones fell from the walls of the castle, and the monster of the moat fled to the deepest muck.

At last it was time for the concluding benediction. "Bone dark as ink, me think he stink!" he roared, and there was a final swirl of dust and grit. The site had been cursed, and the burial was done.

But now a new hazard manifested. This was a kind of linear fountain, the orange liquid shooting up high and falling back to flow into a channel like a small moat. It was rather pretty—but when Smash started to push through it, he drew back his hand with a grunt. That was not water—it was firewater!

He tried to walk around it, but the ring of fire surrounded the inner castle. He tried to jump over, but the flames leaped gleefully higher than he could, licking up to toast his fur. Ogres could not be hurt by much, but they did feel pain when burned. This was awkward.

He tried to pound out a tunnel under the fire, but the water flowed immediately into it and roasted him some more. It danced with flickering delight, with evilly glittering eyes forming within its substance, winking, mocking him, and fingers of flame elevating in obscene gestures. This was in fact a firewater elemental, one of the most formidable of spirits.

Smash pondered again. The effort gave him a splitting headache. He held his face together with his two paws, forcing the split back together, squeezing his skull until the bone fused firm, and hurried back to the moat to soak his head.

The cool shock of water not only got his head back together, it gave him an idea. Ideas were rare things for ogres, and not too valuable. But this one seemed good. Water not only cooled heads, it quenched fire. Maybe he could use the moat to break through the wall of fire.

He formed his paw into a flipper and scooped a splash through the hole in the outer wall toward the firewall. The splash scored—but the fire did not abate. It leaped higher, crackling mirthfully. He scooped again, wetting the whole region, but with no better effect. The firewall danced unharmed, mocking him with foul-smelling noises.

Ogres were slow to anger, because they lacked the wit to know when they were being insulted. But Smash was getting there. He scooped harder, his paw moving like a crude paddle, hurling a steady stream of moatwater at the wall. Still the fire danced, though the water flooded the region. Smash labored yet harder, feeling the exhilaration of challenge and violence, until the level of the moat lowered and the entire cavity between the outer wall and the firewall surged with muddy fluid. The sea monster's tail was exposed by the draining water; it hastily squiggled deeper. Still the fire danced, humming a hymn of victory; it could not be quenched. Water was as much its element as fire. It merely flickered on the surface, spreading wider, reaching toward Smash. Was there no way to defeat it?

"Hooo!" Smash exclaimed, frustrated. But the blast of his breath only made the flame bow concavely and leap yet higher. It liked hot air as well as cool water.

Smash couldn't think of anything better to do, so he kept shoveling water. The flood level rose and backwater coursed out through the gap. Smash tried to dam it up with rubble, but the level was too high. The fire still flickered merrily on the surface, humming a tune about an old flame.

Then the ogre had one more smart notion, a prohibitively rare occurrence for his kind. He dived forward, spread his arms, and swam under the fire. It couldn't reach him *below* the moatwater. He came up beyond it, the last hurdle navigated.

"Ccurrssess!" the firewater hissed furiously, and flickered out.

Now Smash stood within a cluttered room. Books overflowed shelves and piled up on the floor. Bottles and boxes perched everywhere, interspersed with assorted statuettes and amulets and papers. In the middle of it all, like another item of clutter, hunched over a similarly crowded wooden desk, was a little gnome of a man. Smash recognized him—the Good Magician Humfrey, the man who knew everything.

Humfrey glanced up from his tome. "Don't drip on my books, Smash," he said.

Smash fidgeted, trying not to drip on the books. There was hardly room for him to stand upright, and hardly a spot without a book, volume, or tome. He started to drip on an amulet, but it crackled ominously and he edged away. "Me no stir, Magician sir," he mumbled, wondering how the Good Magician knew his name. Smash knew of Humfrey by description and reputation, but this was the first time the two had met.

"Well, out with it, ogre," the Magician snapped irritably. "What's your Question?"

Now Smash felt more awkward than ever. The truth was, he did not know what to ask. He had thought his life would be complete when he achieved his full growth, but somehow he found it wasn't. Something was missing—and he didn't know what. Yet he could not rest until the missing element was satisfied. So he had tromped to see the Good Magician, because that was what creatures with seemingly insoluble problems did—but he lacked the intellect to formulate the Question. He had hoped to work it out during the journey; but, with typical ogrish wit, he had forgotten all about it until this moment. There was no getting around it; there were some few occasions when an ogre was too stupid for his own good. "No know," he confessed, standing on one of his own feet.

Humfrey scowled. He was a very old gnome, and it was

quite a scowl. "You came here to serve a year's service for an Answer—and you don't have a Question?"

Smash had a Question, he was sure; he just didn't know how to formulate it. So he stood silent, dripping on stray artifacts, like the unsmart oaf he was.

Humfrey sighed. "Even if you asked it, it wouldn't be the right Question," he said. "People are forever asking the wrong Questions, and wasting their efforts. I remember not long ago a girl came to ask how to change her nature. Chameleon, her name was, except she wasn't called that then. Her nature was just fine; it was her attitude that needed changing." He shook his head.

As it happened, Smash knew Chameleon. She was Prince Dor's mother, and she changed constantly from smart to stupid and from beautiful to ugly. Humfrey was right: her nature was just fine. Smash liked to talk with her when she was down at his own level of idiocy, and to look at her when she was at his level of ugliness. But the two never came together, unfortunately. Still, she was a fairly nice person, considering that she was human.

"Very well," Humfrey said in a not-very-well voice. "We are about to have a first: an Answer without a Question. Are you sure you wish to pay the fee?"

Smash wasn't sure, but did not know how to formulate that uncertainty, either. So he just nodded affirmatively, his shaggy face scaring a cuckoo bird that had been about to signal the hour. The bird signaled the hour with a terrified dropping instead of a song, and retreated into its cubby.

"So be it," the Magician said, shrugging. "You will discover what you need among the Ancestral Ogres." Then he got up and marched to the door. "Come on; my effaced wife will see about your service."

Numbly, Smash followed. Now he had his Answer—and he didn't understand it.

They went downstairs—apparently, somehow, in a manner that might have been intelligible to a creature of greater wit, Smash had gotten upstairs in the process of swimming under the firewall and emerging in the Good Magician's study—where Humfrey's wife awaited them. This was the lovely, faceless Gorgon—faceless because if her face were allowed to show, it would turn men instantly

to stone. Even faceless, she was said to have a somewhat
petrifying effect. "Here he is," Humfrey said, as if delivering a bag of bad apples.

The Gorgon looked Smash up and down—or seemed to.
Several of the little serpents that substituted for her hair
hissed. "He certainly looks like an ogre," she remarked. "Is
he housebroken?"

"Of course he's not housebroken!" Humfrey snapped.
"He dripped all over my study! Where's the girl?"

"Tandy!" the Gorgon called.

A small girl appeared, rather pretty in a human way,
with brown tresses and blue eyes and a spunky, turned-up
nose. "Yes'm?"

"Tandy, you have completed your year's service this
date," the Gorgon said. "Now you will have your Answer."

The little girl's eyes brightened like noontime patches of
clear sky. She squiggled with excitement. "Oh, thank you,
Gorgon. I'm almost sorry to leave, but I really should return home. My mother is getting tired of only seeing me in
the magic mirror. What is my Answer?"

The Gorgon nudged Humfrey, her voluptuous body rip-
pling as she moved. "The Answer, spouse."

"Oh. Yes," the Good Magician agreed, as if this had not
before occurred to him. He cleared his throat, considering.

"Also say, what me pay," Smash said, not realizing that
he was interrupting an important cogitation.

"The two of you travel together," Humfrey said.

Smash stared down at the tiny girl, and Tandy stared up
at the hulking ogre. Each was more dismayed than the
other. The ogre stood two and a half times the height of the
girl, and that was the least of the contrast between them.

"But I didn't ask—" Tandy protested.

"What me task?" Smash said simultaneously. Had he
been more alert, he might have thought to marvel that even
this overlapping response rhymed.

The Gorgon seemed to smile. "Sometimes my husband's
pronouncements need a little interpretation," she said. "He
knows so much more than the rest of us, he fails to make
proper allowance for our ignorance." She pinched Humfrey's cheek in a remarkably familiar manner. "He means
this: the two of you, Smash and Tandy, are to travel
through the wilds of Xanth together, fending off hazards

together. That is the ogre's service in lieu of a year's labor
at this castle—protecting his companion. It is also the girl's
Answer, for which she has already paid."

"That's exactly what I said," Humfrey grumped.

"You certainly did, dear," the Gorgon agreed, planting a
faceless kiss on the top of his head.

"But it doesn't make sense!" Tandy protested.

"It doesn't have to make sense," the Gorgon explained.
"It's an Answer."

Oh. Now Smash understood, as far as he was able.

"May I go back to my tome?" the Good Magician asked
petulantly.

"Why, of course you may," the Gorgon replied gra-
ciously, patting his backside as he turned. The Good Magician climbed back up toward his study. Smash knew the
man had lost valuable working time, but somehow the Magician did not seem unhappy. Naturally the nuances of human interrelations were beyond the comprehension of a
mere ogre.

The Gorgon returned her attention to them. "He's such a
darling," she remarked. "I really don't know how he survived a century without me." She focused, seemingly, on
Tandy. "And you might, if you would, do me a favor on
the way," the Gorgon said. "I used to live on an island near
the Magic Dust Village, which I think is right on your
route to Lake Ogre-Chobee. I fear I caused some mischief
for that village in my youth; I know I am not welcome
there. But my sister the Siren remains in the area, and if
you would convey my greetings to her—"

"But how can I travel with an ogre?" Tandy protested.
"That's not an Answer; that's a punishment! He'll gobble
me up the first time he gets hungry!"

"Not necessarily so," the Gorgon demurred. "Smash is
no ordinary ogre. He's honest and halfway civilized. He
will perform his service correctly, to the best of his limited
understanding. He will not permit any harm to come to
you. In fact, you could hardly have a better guardian while
traversing the jungles of Xanth."

"But how does this solve my problem, even if I'm not
gobbled up?" Tandy persisted. Smash saw that her spunky
nose was a correct indication of her character; she had a

fighting spirit despite her inadequate size. "Traveling won't solve a thing! There's nowhere I can go to—"

The Gorgon touched the girl's lips with a forefinger. "Let your problem be private for now, dear. Just accept my assurance. If my husband says traveling will solve your problem, then traveling will solve it. Humfrey knew an ogre would be coming here at this time, and knew you needed that sort of protection, since you have so little familiarity with the outside world. Believe me, it will turn out for the best."

"But I don't have anywhere to go!"

"Yes, but Smash does. He is seeking the Ancestral Ogres."

"A whole tribe of ogres? I'm absolutely doomed!"

The Gorgon's expression was facelessly reproving. "Naturally you do not have to follow the advice you paid for, dear. But the Good Magician Humfrey really does know best."

"I think he's getting old," Tandy said rebelliously. "Maybe he doesn't know as much as he used to."

"He likes to claim that he's forgotten more than he ever knew," the Gorgon said. "Perhaps that is so. But do not underestimate him. And don't misjudge this ogre."

Tandy pouted. "Oh, all right! I'll go with the monster. But if he gobbles me up, you'll be responsible! I'll never speak to you again."

"I accept the responsibility," the Gorgon agreed. "Now Smash is hungry." She turned to him. "Come to the kitchen, ogre, for a peck or two of raw potatoes. They haven't been cleaned, and some have worms; you'll like them."

"You're joking!" Tandy said. Then she looked again at Smash, who was licking his chops. "You're *not* joking!"

"Well spoke; no joke," Smash agreed, hoping there would also be a few barrels of dirty dishwater to glug down with the potatoes. Tandy grimaced.

Chapter 3. Eye Queue

They traveled together, but it was no pleasure for either. Smash had to take tiny slow steps to enable the girl to keep up, and Tandy made it plain she considered the ogre to be a monstrous lout. She refused to let him carry her, as he could readily have done; despite the Gorgon's assurances, she was afraid of getting gobbled. She seemed to have a thing about monsters, and male monsters in particular; she hated them. So they wended their tedious way south toward Lake Ogre-Chobee—a journey that should have taken Smash alone a single day, but promised to take several days with Tandy. The Good Magician had certainly come up with a bad chore in lieu of his year's service for an Answer! And Smash still didn't know what Question had been answered.

The scenery was varied. At first they crossed rolling hills; it took some time for Tandy to get the hang of walking on a hill that rolled, and she took several tumbles. Fortunately, the hills were covered with soft, green turf, so that the girl could roll with the punches, head over feet without much damage. Smash did note, as a point of disinterest, that his companion was not the child she seemed. She was very small even for her kind, but in the course of her tumbles she displayed well-formed limbs and torso. She was a little woman, complete in every small detail. Smash knew about such details because he had once traveled to Mundania with Prince Dor and Princess Irene, and that girl Irene had somehow managed to show off every salient feature of her sex in the course of the adventure, all the while protesting that she wanted no one to see. Tandy had less of each, but was definitely of a similar overall configuration. And her exposures, it seemed, were genuinely unintentional, rather than artful. She evidently had no notion of what to wear on such a trip. In fact, she seemed amazingly ignorant of Xanth terrain. It was as if she had never been here before—which, of course, was nonsense. Every citizen of Xanth had lived in Xanth, as had even the zombies and ghosts, who no longer lived, but remained active.

After they passed the rolling hills they came to a more stable area, where a tangle tree held sway. Tanglers were like dragons and ogres in this respect: no sensible creature tangled voluntarily with one. Smash didn't even think about it; he just stepped around it, letting it sway alone.

But Tandy walked straight down the neat, clear path that always led to such trees, innocently sniffing the pleasant fragrance of the evil plant. She was almost within its quiveringly hungry embrace before Smash realized that she really didn't know what it was.

Smash dived for the girl, trying to snatch her out of the grasp of the twitching tentacles. "No go!" he bellowed.

Tandy saw him. "Eeek! The monster's going to gobble me!" she cried. But it was Smash she meant, not the real menace. She scooted on inside the canopy of the dread tree.

With a gleeful swish, the hanging tentacles pounced. Five of them caught her legs, arms, and head. The girl was hauled up and carried toward the slavering wooden orifice in the base of the trunk. She screamed foolishly, as was her kind's wont in such circumstances.

Smash took only a moment to assess the situation. Thought with his brain was tedious and fatiguing and none too effective, but thought with his muscles was swift and sure. He saw Tandy in midair, wearing a pretty red print dress and matching red slippers; tentacles were grabbing at these, assuming them to be edible portions. One tentacle was tugging at her hair, dislodging the red ribbon in it. In a moment the tree would realize that the red was only the wrapping, and would tear that away and get down to serious business.

Smash could handle a small tangler; he was, after all, an ogre. But this was a big tangler. It had a hundred or more pythonlike tentacles, and a personality to match its strength. There was no way to negotiate or to reason with it; Smash had to fight.

The ogre charged in. That wasn't hard; tanglers wanted creatures to enter their turf. It was the getting out again that was difficult. He grabbed the mass of tentacles that had wrapped around the terrified and struggling girl. "Tree let be," he grunted, hauling the works back away from the sap-drooling orifice.

Now, tanglers were ferocious, but not unduly stupid. This tree was full-sized—but so was the ogre. Very few things cared to cross an ogre. The tree hesitated, and its coils about the girl loosened.

Then the tree decided that it could, after all, handle this challenge and gain a respectable meal in the bargain. It attacked Smash with its remaining tentacles.

Smash had been wary of this, but was stuck for it. He grabbed a tentacle in each hand and yanked—but the material was flexible and stretchable, and moved with him. He lacked the leverage to rip the tentacles out. Meanwhile, Tandy was being carried back to the orifice, trailing torn swatches of red cloth.

Smash tried a new tactic: he squeezed. Now the tree keened in vegetable pain as its two tentacles were constricted into jelly, dripped and spurted juice, and finally were lopped off. But the thing expected to take some losses, and it could always grow new tentacles; Tandy was almost at the glistening maw. A limber fiber tongue was tasting the red fabric. By the time Smash could truncate all the tentacles, the girl would be long digested.

Smash hurled himself at the orifice. He smashed his gauntleted fists into it, breaking off the wooden teeth. Sap splashed, burning his fur where it struck. The tree roared with a sound like sundering timber, but the tentacles kept coming.

The ogre braced himself before the orifice, blocking the entry of the girl. She banged into him before the tree realized this, and he was able to grab a couple more tentacles and pinch them off. Now the tree could not consume her until it dealt with him—and he was turning out to be tougher than it had anticipated. In fact, he was turning out tougher than *he* had anticipated; he had thought the tree had the advantage, but he was faring pretty well.

It was a bad thing in Xanth when a predator misjudged its foe. The tree was now in trouble, but had to fight on. As new tentacles converged, Smash caught them, twisted several together, and tied their tips into a great raveled knot that he shoved into the orifice in the trunk. The maw closed automatically, squirting digestive sap—and the tree suffered a most unpleasant surprise. The keening of agony magnified piercingly.

During this distraction, Smash unwrapped the girl, squeezing each tentacle until it let go. Soon Tandy stood on the ground, disheveled, shaken, but intact. "So—go," Smash said, catching other questing tentacles to clear her escape.

The girl scooted out. She might be small and ignorant, but she didn't freeze long in a crisis! Now Smash retreated cautiously, glaring at hovering tentacles to discourage renewed attack. But the tree had had enough; the ogre had defeated it. There was no further aggression.

Smash stepped out, privately surprised. How was it he had been able to foil a tangler this size? He concentrated, with effort, and managed to come to a conclusion; he had grown since the last time he had tangled with a tangler. Before, he would not have been strong enough to handle it; now, with his larger mass and the gauntlets, he had the advantage. His self-image had not kept pace with his physical condition. He knew his father Crunch could have handled this tree; he, Smash, was now as powerful as that.

Tandy was waiting for him down the path. She was sadly bedraggled, her dress in tatters, and bruises on her body, but her spirit remained spunky. "I guess I have to apologize to you, Smash," she said. "I thought—never mind what I thought. You risked your life to save me from my folly. I was being childish; you were mature."

"Sure—mature," Smash agreed, uncertain what she was getting at. People did not apologize to ogres, so he had no basis for comprehension.

"Well, next time you tell me 'no go,' I'll pay better attention," she concluded.

He shrugged amenably. That would make things easier.

The day was getting on, and they were tired. Battling tangle trees tended to have that effect. Smash located a muffin bush with a number of fresh ripe muffins, and used his finger to punch a hole in a lime-soda tree so they could drink. Then he found a deserted harpy nest in a tree, long since weathered out, so that the filth and smell were gone. He harvested a blanket from a blanket bush and used it to line the nest. This was for Tandy to sleep in. It took her some time to catch on, but as darkness loomed across the land in the grim way it had in the wilderness, and the nocturnal noises began, she was glad enough to clamber to it and curl up in it. He noted that she was good at climbing, though she hardly seemed to know what a tree was. He settled down below, on guard.

Tandy did not sleep immediately. Curled in her nest, she talked. Apparently this was a human trait. "You know, Smash, I've never been out on the surface of Xanth on foot before. I was raised in the caverns, and then I rode a nightmare to the Good Magician's castle. That was an accident; I really wanted to go to Castle Roogna to see my father, Crombie. But dawn came too soon, and I was out of sleeping pills, and—well, I sort of had to ask a Question so as to have a nice place to stay until I figured out what to do. I spent a whole year working inside the castle; I never even set foot beyond the moat, because I was afraid a certain party would be lurking for me. So it's not surprising I don't know about things like rolling hills and tangle trees."

That explained a lot. Smash realized he would have to watch her more closely, to be sure she did not walk into a lethal trap. The Magician's rationale for having her travel with him was making more sense. She certainly could not safely travel alone.

"I'm sorry I distrusted you, Smash," she continued in her talkative way. "You see, I was raised near demons, and in some ways you resemble a demon. Big and strong and dusky. I was prejudiced."

Smash grunted noncommittally. He had not met many demons, but doubted they could powder rock in the manner of ogres.

"I certainly have a lot to learn, don't I?" she continued ruefully. "I thought trees were sweet plants and ogres were bad brutes, and now I know they aren't."

Oops. "Ogre. No—grrr!" Smash exclaimed emphatically. Tandy was quick to catch on; she had the ready intelligence of her kind. "You mean I shouldn't trust all ogres? That they really do gobble people?"

"Ogres prone to crunch bone," Smash agreed.

"But you didn't—I— mean—" she grew doubtful.

"Smash work hard, girl to guard."

"Oh, you mean because the Good Magician charged you with my protection," she said, relieved. "Your service for your Answer. So ogres do gobble people and crunch bones, but they also honor their obligations."

Smash didn't follow all of the vocabulary, but it sounded about right, so he grunted assent.

"Very well, Smash," she concluded. "I'll trust you, but will be wary of all other ogres. And all other things of Xanth, too, especially if they seem too nice to be true."

That was indeed best. They lapsed into sleep.

No one bothered them in the night. After all, the nightmares had to be wary of Tandy, after she had ridden one of them, and he wasn't sure whether the mares knew how to climb trees. As for himself—it was always the best policy to let a sleeping ogre lie.

They breakfasted on sugar sand and cocoa-nut milk. Tandy had never before drunk cocoa and was intrigued by the novelty. She was also amazed by the way Smash literally shoveled the sugar into his mouth, hardly pausing to chew, and crunched up whole cocoa-nuts, husks and all. "You really are a monster," she said, half admiringly, and Smash grunted agreement, pleased.

Then they resumed their trek south, encountering only routine creatures. A toady was hopping north, looking for some important person to advise; when told that Castle Roogna was many days of hopping distant, it contorted its broad and warty mouth into a scowl. "I hope I don't croak before I get there," it said, and moved on. Croaking, it seemed, was bad form for toadies.

Then there was the quack, with a wide bill and webbed feet and a bag of special magic medicines. He was, he explained, looking for a suitable practice, where his marvelous remedies would be properly appreciated. Meanwhile, did they happen to knew where Pete was? Pete was a bog, very good for delving. Since Pete wasn't north, where

Tandy and Smash had come from, and probably wasn't
south, where the Magic Dust Village was supposed to be,
and wasn't west, where the quack had come from, it had to
be east, by elimination. The quack coughed and, his mind
jogged by the term, deposited some genuine fresh birdlime
on the ground. Flies instantly materialized, having a taste
for lime, and Smash and Tandy moved on.

By noon they were in rougher territory. Sweaters
swarmed about them, causing them to perspire, until
Smash got fed up and issued a bellowing roar that blew
them all away. Unfortunately, it also blew the leaves off
the nearest trees, and several more tatters from Tandy's
dress.

Then they encountered a region of curse-burrs—little
balls of irritation that clung tenaciously to any portion of
the body they encountered. Smash's face lit up in a horrendous smile. "Me remember here!" he cried. "Me whelped
near."

"You were born here? Amidst these awful burrs?"
Tandy smiled ruefully. "I should have known."

Smash laughed. It sounded like a rockslide in a canyon.
"Me sire Crunch, best of bunch." He looked avidly about,
whelphood memories filtering back into his thick skull. Later, his family had moved to the vicinity of Castle Roogna,
because his lovely mother, whose hair was like nettles and
whose face would make a zombie blush, had felt their cub
should have some slight exposure to civilization. Crunch,
the slave of love, had acceded to this un-ogrish notion; who
could resist the blandishments of such a mushface as
Smash's mother?

"Oh, this is awful!" Tandy protested. "These burrs are
getting in my hair." It seemed human girls were sensitive
to that sort of thing.

"Could be worse," Smash said helpfully. "She make
curse."

"Curse?" she asked blankly.

Smash demonstrated. "Burr—grrr!" he growled. A burr
dropped lifelessly off his gross nose.

"I don't think I can make such rhymes," Tandy said.
Then a burr stuck her finger. "Get away, you awful
thing!" she exploded.

The burr dropped off. Tandy looked at it, comprehending. She was certainly intelligent! "Oh, I see. You just have to curse them away!"

Even so, it was not easy, for Tandy had been raised as a nice girl and did not know many curses. They hurried out of the burr region.

Now they came to a dead forest. The trees stood gaunt, petrified in place. "I'd like to know how that happened," Tandy remarked. Smash knew, but it was a long story involving the romantic meeting of his parents, and it was hard for him to formulate it properly, so he let it go.

In the afternoon they came to a region of brambles. These were aggressive plants with glistening spikes. Smash could wade through them imperviously, for his skin was so tough he hardly felt the few thorns they dared to stick him with. It was quite another matter for Tandy, who had delicate and sweet-smelling skin, the kind that was made to be tormented by thorns.

There were neatly cleared paths through the brambles that Tandy was inclined to use, but Smash cautioned her against this. "Lion, ant, between plant."

Her small brow wrinkled. "I don't see anything."

Then an ant-lion appeared. It had the head of a lion and the body of an ant, and massed about as much as the girl did; it was, of course, ten times as ferocious as anything a nice girl could imagine. It roared when it spied her, striding forward aggressively.

Smash roared back. The ant-lion hastily reversed course; it had been so distracted by the luscious prey that it had not before seen the unluscious guardian. But Smash knew that soon many more would arrive and would swarm over the intruders. This was no safe place, even for the likes of himself.

"Now I understand," Tandy said, turning pale. "Smash, let's get out of here!"

But already there were rustlings behind them. The ant-lions had surrounded them. There would be no easy escape.

"Me know path, avoid ant wrath," Smash said, looking upward. How fortunate that he had been raised in this vicinity, so that useful details of geography were coming back to his slow memory!

"Oh, I couldn't swing from branch to branch through the

trees the way I'm sure you can," Tandy said. "I'm agile, but not that agile. I'd be sure to fall."

But the ant-lions were closing in, a full pride of them. Smash had to pick Tandy up to get her out of their reach. Thus burdened, he was unable to fight effectively. Realizing this, the ants grew bolder, closing in, growling and snapping. The situation was getting awkward.

Then Smash spied what he was looking for—the aereal path. "Take care. Go there," he said, boosting the girl up by her pert bottom.

"But it's sidewise!" she protested, peering at the path with dismay. "I'd fall off!"

"Stand tall. No fall," he insisted.

Tandy obviously didn't believe him. But an ant-lion leaped for her, jaws gaping, large front pincers snapping, so she reached up to grab for the high path.

Suddenly she landed on it—sidewise. "I'm level!" she cried, amazed. "The world has turned!" She stood up, or rather sidewise, her body parallel to the ground.

Smash didn't worry about it. He knew the properties of the path, having played on it as a cub. It was always level—to the person on it. He was now far too massive to use it himself, since the aereal path was getting old and brittle, but he didn't need to. He was now unencumbered, free to deal with the lions his own way.

The lions, angered at the escape of the lesser prey, pounced on the greater prey. That was foolish of them. Smash emitted a battle bellow that tore their whiskers back and clogged their pincers with debris, then began stomping and pounding. Lions yowled as the gauntleted fists connected, and screeched as the hairy feet found flesh. Then Smash picked up two ants by their narrow waists and hurled them into the nettles. He took a moment to rip a small hemlock tree out of the ground, shaking the locks from its hem, and bit off its top, forming a fair club from the remaining trunk. Soon the path was clear; the ant-lions, like the tangle tree, had learned new respect for ogres.

"You're really quite something, Smash!" Tandy called, clapping her hands. "You're a real terror when you get worked up. I'll bet there's nothing more formidable than an angry ogre!" She had an excellent view of the proceedings from the elevated path, dodging when an ant flew past. Ant-lions did not normally fly; this was a consequence of being hurled out of the way. Ants were now stuck in a number of the jungle trees.

"Me know who," Smash grunted, pleased. "Ogres two."

She laughed. "That figures. The only thing tougher than one ogre is two ogres." She was now standing inverted, her brown tresses hanging naturally about her shoulders as if she were upright. She looked about, from her vantage. "The ants aren't gone, just backed off, Smash," she reported. "Can you come up here?"

Smash shook his head no. But he wasn't worried. He could use the ant paths. If the ants wanted a little more ogre-type fun, he would gladly accommodate them.

They proceeded south, Tandy tilting with the orientation of the aereal path, sometimes upright, sometimes not, enjoying the experience. "There is nothing much in the caverns like this!" she commented.

Smash tromped along the ant highways, tearing through nettles when he needed to change paths. Soon the nettles and ants were left behind, but the high path continued, so Tandy stayed on it. Smash knew it terminated at the Magic Dust Village, and since they had to pass there anyway, this was convenient. According to Castle Roogna information, the Magic Dusters had once had a population problem, not being able to hold on to their males, so they had constructed the skyway to encourage immigration. Now there were plenty of people at the village, so the path didn't matter, but no one had bothered to take it down. Smash and Tandy made excellent progress.

Now they passed a region of hanging vines. They were twined, almost braided, like queues, and seemed to have eyes looking out from their recesses. Smash distrusted unfamiliar things in general and dangling vines in particular, so he avoided the Eye Queues. They could be harmless, or they could be bloodsuckers. This was beyond the region of his cubhood familiarity, and anyway, things could have changed in the interim. One could never take magic for granted.

He also kept an eye on Tandy, above, to make sure she did not brush against any vines. As a result, he didn't pay close enough attention to his big feet—and stumbled over a minor boulder that was damming a streamlet, much to the streamlet's annoyance.

The boulder dam shattered, of course; it was only stone. The streamlet gladly flowed through, with a burble of thanks to its deliverer. But Smash suffered a momentary loss of balance, his feet sinking into the sodden riverbed, and he lurched headlong into a hanging vine.

The thing wrapped disgustingly around his head. He snatched at it, but already it was sinking into his fur and his flesh and hurting terribly when he tried to scrape it loose. Since an ogre's course was generally that of most resistance, Smash put both hands to his scalp and scraped—and the burgeoning agony made him reel.

"Stop, Smash, stop!" Tandy screamed from above. "You'll rip off your head!"

Smash stopped. "I concur. There is no sense in that."

Tandy stared down at him. "What did you say?"

"I said there is no sense in mortifying my flesh, since the queue does not appear to have seriously incapacitated me."

"Smash—you're not rhyming!"

"Why—so I am not!" he agreed, startled. "That must be the curse of the Eye Queue; it has disrupted my natural mechanism of communication."

"It's done more than that!" Tandy exclaimed. "Smash, you sound smart!"

"That must be a fallacious impression. No ogre is unduly intelligent."

"Well, you sure *sound* smart!" she insisted. "That Eye Queue, as you call it, must have added some brains to your head."

"That seems reasonable," he agreed, after cogitating momentarily without effort. "The effect manifested concurrently with my contact with that object. Probability suggests a causal connection. This, of course, is much worse than any purely physical attack would have been; it has temporarily un-ogred me. I must expunge it from my system!"

"Oh, no, don't do that," she protested. "It's sort of interesting, really. I don't mind you being smart, Smash. It's much easier to talk with you."

"In any event, I seem unable for the moment to deactivate it," Smash said. "It seems I must tolerate this curse for the time being. But I assure you I shall be alert for an antidote."

"Okay," she said. "If that's the way you feel."

"Indubitably."

They went on—and now Smash noted things that hadn't interested him before. He saw how erosion had caused rifts in the land, and how the forest stratified itself, with light-indifferent vegetation and fungi at the nether levels and bright, broad leaves above to catch the descending light of the sun. The entire jungle was a cohesive unit, functioning compatibly with its environment. All over Xanth, things were integrating—in his new awareness. How blind he had been to the wonders of magic, all his life!

As dusk closed, the aereal path descended to the ground, and they arrived at the Magic Dust Village. A troll came forth to meet them. "Ogre, do you come in peace or mayhem?" the creature inquired, standing poised for flight while other villagers hastily manned the fortifications and cleared children and the aged from the region.

"In peace!" Tandy said quickly. "I am Tandy; this is Smash, who is protecting me from monsters."

The troll's eyes gaped. This was an unusual expression, even for this type of creature. "Protecting you from—?"

"Yes."

"Now, we have no prejudice against monsters here," the troll said, scratching his long and horny nose with a discolored claw. "I'm a monster myself, and some of my best friends are monsters. But only a fool trusts an ogre."

"Well, I'm a fool," Tandy said. "This ogre fought a tangle tree to save me."

"Are you sure you aren't a kidnap victim? You certainly do look good enough to eat."

Smash did not appreciate the implication, which would have passed him by had he not suffered the curse of the Eye Queue vine. "My father is Crunch, the vegetarian ogre," he said gruffly. "My family has not kidnapped anyone in years."

The troll looked at him, startled. "You certainly don't sound like an ogre! Did the Transformer-King transform you to this shape?"

"I was whelped an ogre!" Smash insisted, the first traces of roar coming into his voice.

Then the troll made a connection. "Ah, yes. Crunch married a curse-fiend actress. You have human lineage; that must account for your language."

"It must," Smash agreed drolly. He found he didn't care to advertise his misadventure with the vine. He would be laughed out of the village if its inhabitants learned he was intelligent. "But I should advise you, purely in the interest of amity, that I have been known to take exception to the appellation 'half-breed.' I am a true ogre." He picked up a nearby knot of green wood and squeezed it in one hand. The green juice dripped as the wood pulped, until at last there was a pool of green on the ground and the knot had become a lump of coal.

"Yes, indeed," the troll agreed hastily. "No one here would think of using that term. Welcome to our table for supper; you are surely hungry."

"We are only passing through," Tandy said. "We're going to Lake Ogre-Chobee."

"You can't get there from here," the troll said. "The Region of Madness intervenes."

"Madness?" Tandy asked, alarmed.

"From the airborne magic dust we process. Magic is very potent here, and too much of it leads to alarming effects. You will have to go around."

They did not argue the case. Smash's inordinate intelligence, coupled with his memories of this region, corroborated the information; he knew it would be impossible for him to protect Tandy in the Region of Madness. There were tales of the constellations of the night coming to life, and of reality changing dangerously. In Xanth, things were mostly what they seemed to be, so that illusion was often reality. But illusion could be taken too far in the heightened magic of the Madness. Smash was now too smart to risk it.

They joined the villagers' supper. Creatures of every type came forth to feed, all well behaved: elves, gnomes, goblins, a manticore, fauns, nymphs, fairies, human beings, centaurs, griffins, and assorted other creatures. The hostess was the troll's mate, Trolla. "It is much easier to arrive than to depart," she explained as she served up helpings of smashed potatoes and poured out goblets of mead. "We have never had opportunity to construct an exit ramp, and our work mining the source of magic is important, so we stay. You may choose to remain also: we labor hard, but it is by no means a bad life."

Smash exchanged a glance with Tandy, since it occurred to him that this might be the sort of situation she was looking for. But she was negative. "We have a message from the sister of a neighbor of yours. We must get on and deliver it."

"A neighbor?" Trolla asked.

"She is called the Siren."

There was a sudden hush.

"You know," Tandy said. "The sister of the Gorgon."

"You are friend to the Gorgon?" Trolla asked coldly.

"I hardly know her," Smash said quickly, remembering that this village had suffered at the Gorgon's hands—or rather, her face, having had all the men turned to stone. Fortunately, that mischief had been undone at the time of the loss of magic, when all Xanth had become as drear as Mundania, briefly. Numerous spells had been aborted in that period, changing Xanth in ways that were still unraveling. "I had to see Good Magician Humfrey, and she's his wife. She asked us to say hello to the Siren."

"Oh, I see." Trolla relaxed, and the others followed her example. There were murmurs of amazement and awe. "The Good Magician's wife! And she turned *him* to stone?"

"Not anywhere we could see," Tandy said, then blushed. "Uh, that is—"

Trolla smiled. "He's probably too old for such enchantment anyway, so the sight of her merely stiffens his spine, or whatever." She gulped a goblet of mead. "The Siren no longer lures people, since a smart centaur broke her magic dulcimer. She is not a bad neighbor, but we really don't associate with her."

They finished their repast, Smash happily consuming all the refuse left after the others were done. The villagers set them up with rooms for the night. Smash knew these were honest, well-meaning folk, so he didn't worry about Tandy's safety here.

As he lay on his pile of straw, Smash thought about the

place of the Magic Dust Village in the scheme of Xanth. Stray references to it bubbled to the surface of his memory—things he had heard at different times in his life and thought nothing of, since ogres thought nothing of everything. From these suddenly assimilating fragments he was now able to piece together the role of this village, geologically. Here it was that the magic dust welled to the surface from the mysterious depths. The villagers pulverized it and employed a captive roc-bird to flap its wings and waft huge clouds of the dust into the air, where it caused madness close by, technicolor hailstorms farther distant, and magic for the rest of Xanth as it diluted to natural background intensity. If the villagers did not perform this service, the magic dust would tend to clump, and the magic would be unevenly distributed, causing all manner of problems.

Certainly the Magic Dusters believed all this, and labored most diligently to facilitate the proper and even spreading of the dust. Yet Smash's Eye Queue-infected brain obnoxiously conjured caveats, questioning the realities the villagers lived by.

If the magic really came from the dust, it should endure as long as the dust did, fading only slowly as the dust wore out. Yet at the Time of No Magic, all Xanth had been rendered Mundane instantly. That had happened just before Smash himself had been whelped, but his parents had told him all about it. They had considered it rather romantic, perhaps even a signal of their love. Crunch had lost his great strength in that time, but other creatures had been affected far more, and many had died. Then the magic had returned, as suddenly as it had departed, and Xanth had been as it was before. There had been no great movements of dust then, no dust storms. That suggested that the magic of Xanth was independent of the dust.

The dust came from below, and if it brought the magic, the nether regions must be more magical than the surface. Tandy had lived below, yet she seemed normal. She did not even appear to have a magic talent. So how could the magic be concentrated below?

But Smash decided not to raise these questions openly, as they would only make things awkward for the villagers. And perhaps the belief of the Dusters was right and his vine-sponsored objections were wrong. After all, what could a Queue of Eyes understand of the basic nature of Xanth?

His thought turned to a bypath. A magic talent—that must be what Tandy was questing for! He, as an ogre, was fortunate; ogres had strength as their talent. When Smash had gone to Mundania, outside the magic ambience of Xanth, he had lost his strength and his rhyme, distressingly. Now he had lost his rhymes and his naïveté, but not his strength.

Was the infliction of the curse of the Eye Queue really so bad? There were indeed pleasures in the insights this artificial intelligence afforded him. Yet ogres were supposed to be stupid; he felt sadly out of place.

Smash decided to keep quiet, most of the time, and let Tandy do the talking. He might no longer be a proper ogre in outlook, but at least he could *seem* like an ogre. If he generated an illusion of continuing stupidity, perhaps in time he would achieve it again. Certainly this was worth the hope. Meanwhile, his shame would remain mostly secret.

Chapter 4. Catastrophe

In the morning they walked along an old ground-bound path to the small lake that contained the Siren's isle. It was pretty country, with few immediate hazards, and so Smash found it dull, while Tandy liked it very well.

The Siren turned out to be a mature mermaid who had probably been stunning in her youth and was not too far from it even now. She evidently survived by fishing and seemed satisfied with her lot, or more correctly, her pond.

"We bring greetings from your sister the Gorgon," Tandy called as they crossed the path over the water to the island.

Immediately the mermaid was interested. She emerged from the water and changed to human form—her fish-tail simply split into two well-formed legs—and came to meet them, still changing. She had been nude in the water, but it hardly mattered since she was a fish below the waist. But as she dried, the scales that had covered her tail converted to a scale-sequin dress that nudged up to cover the upper portion of her torso. For a reason that had never been clear to Smash, it was all right for a mermaid to show her breasts, but not all right for a human woman to do the same. The finny part of her flukes became small shoes. It was minor but convenient magic; after all, Smash thought, she might otherwise get cold feet. "My sister!" she exclaimed, her newly covered bosom heaving. "How is she doing?"

"Well, she's married to the Good Magician Humfrey—"

"Oh, yes, I had news of that! But how is she recently?"

"Recently?" Tandy's brow furrowed.

Smash caught on to the nature of the Siren's question. "She wants to know whether the Gorgon is pregnant," he murmured.

Tandy was startled. "Oh—I don't know about that. I don't think so. But she does seem happy, and so does the Magician."

The Siren frowned. "I'm so glad she found hers. I wish I had found mine." And Smash now perceived, from this close range and the magnification of his interpretive intellect, that the Siren was not happy at all. She had lost her compelling magic twenty years ago and had very little left.

Such things had not before been concerns of Smash's. Ogres hardly cared about the nuances of the lifestyles of nymphal creatures. Now, thanks to the curse of the Eye Queue, Smash felt the Siren's problem, and felt the need to alleviate it. "We are going to Lake Ogre-Chobee. Perhaps if you went there, you would find yours."

The Siren brightened. "That's possible."

"But we are having trouble finding the way," he said. "The Madness intercedes."

"It's a nuisance," the Siren agreed. "But there are ways around it."

"We would like to know of one."

"Well, there's the catapult. Yet you have to pay the cat's price."

"What is the cat's price?" Tandy asked warily. "If it's a kind of demon, we might not like it."

"It likes catnip—and that's not easy to get."

"Smash could get it," Tandy said brightly. "He fought a tangle tree and a pride of ant-lions."

"Well, he's an ogre," the Siren agreed matter-of-factly. "That sort of thing is routine for them."

"Why don't you come with us and show us where the catnip is?" Tandy suggested. "Then we can all go to the catapult and on to Lake Ogre-Chobee."

The Siren considered. "I admit I don't seem to be accomplishing much here. I never thought I'd travel with an ogre!" She faced Smash. "Are you tame? I've heard some bad things about ogres—"

"They're all true!" Smash agreed. "Ogres are the worst brutes on two legs. But I was raised in the environs of Castle Roogna, so am relatively civilized."

"He's really very nice, when you get to know him," Tandy said. "He doesn't crunch the bones of friends."

"I'll risk it," the Siren decided. "I'll lead you to the catnip." She adjusted her dress, packed a few fish for nibbling on the way, and set off, leading them east of the lake.

The catnip grew in a section of the jungle separated by a fiercely flowing stream. They had to use a narrow catwalk past a cataract that was guarded by a catamount. "Don't fall into the water," the Siren warned. "It's a catalyst that will give you catarrh, catatonia, and catalepsy."

"I don't understand," Tandy said nervously. "Is that bad?"

"A catalyst is a substance that facilitates change," Smash explained, drawing on his new Eye Queue intellect. "In the case of our living flesh, this is likely to mean deterioration and decay such as catarrh, which is severe inflammation inside the nose, catatonia, which is stupor, and catalepsy, which is loss of motion and speechlessness. We had better stay out of this water; it is unlikely to be healthy."

"Yes, unlikely," Tandy agreed faintly. "But the catamount is on the catwalk! It will throw us off."

"Oh, I wouldn't be concerned about that," Smash said. He strode out on the catwalk. It dipped and swayed under his mass, but he had the sure balance of his primitive kind and proceeded with confidence.

"No violence!" Tandy pleaded.

The catamount was a large reddish feline with long whiskers and big paws. It snarled and stalked toward Smash, its tail swishing back and forth.

No violence?

A fright would have been fun, but Smash realized now that the girls would worry, so he used his intellect to ponder on a peaceful option. What about the one he had used on the moat-monster at the Good Magician's castle? "I want to show you something, kitty," he said. He leaned forward and held out his right hand. The catamount paused distrustfully.

Smash carefully closed his gauntleted hamfingers into a huge, gleaming fist. Shafts of sunlight struck down to elicit new gleams as Smash slowly rotated his fist. It was amazing how each shaft knew exactly where to go!

Smash nudged this metallic hamfist under the catamount's nose. "Now kitty," he said quietly. "if you do not vacate this path expeditiously, you are apt to have a closer encounter with this extremity. Does this eventuality meet with your approval?"

The feline's ears twitched as if it suffered indigestion; it seemed to have a problem with the vocabulary. It considered the extremity. The fist sent another barrage of glints of reflected sunlight out, seeming to grow larger. The ogre stood perfectly balanced and at ease, muscles bulging only slightly, fur lying almost unruffled. After a moment, snarling ungraciously, the catamount decided not to dispute the path this time. It backed away.

Well, well, Smash thought. His bluff had worked—now that he had the wit to bluff. Of course, it would have been fun to hurl the catamount into the water below and see what happened to it, but that pleasure was not to be, this time.

A catbird sailed down out of the sky. It had the body of a crow and the head of a cat. "Meow!" it scolded the catamount, and issued a resounding catcall. Then it wheeled on Smash, claws extended cat-as-catch-can.

The ogre's mitt moved swiftly. The hamfingers caught the catbird, who screeched piteously. Smash brought it down, pulled out one large tailfeather, and lofted the creature away. The catbird flew awkwardly, its rudder malfunctioning. The fight had been taken out of it, along with much of the flight.

A catfish protested from below. It lifted its cat-head from the flowing water and yowled. Its voice had a nasal quality; the creature did indeed seem to be suffering from catarrh and perhaps catalepsy, though probably it had built up a certain immunity to the curses of the water. Smash hurled the feather down into its mouth. The catfish choked and sneezed, disappearing.

Now Smash, Tandy, and the Siren crossed without impediment. "Sometimes it's really handy having an ogre along," Tandy remarked. She seemed to have swung from absolute distrust to absolute support, and Smash was not displeased.

The path led through a field of cattails growing in catsup where cattle grazed, fattening up in case some cataclysm came. It terminated at a catacomb. "The catnip grows in there," the Siren said, pointing to the teeth of the comb that barred the entrance. "But it's dangerous to enter, because if the cataclysm comes, the cattle will stampede into it."

"Then I will go alone," Smash said. He brushed the comb aside and marched on down. The way soon became dark, but ogres had good night vision, so he wasn't much bothered.

"Don't invite catastrophe!" the Siren called after him.

"I certainly hope not," Smash called back, though in truth he wouldn't have minded a little of that to make things interesting. "I will be pusillanimously careful."

Deep inside the cave, he found a garden of pleasantly scented, mintlike plants with felinely furry leaves. Each had a spike of blue flowers. These must be the catnips.

Smash took hold of one and pulled it up by the roots, being uncertain which part of the plant he needed, and stuffed it into his bag. The flowers nipped at him, but lacked the power even to be annoying. He grabbed and crammed more plants, until he felt he had enough.

He turned to depart—and spied a dimly glowing object. It was set in the cave wall beside the exit, framed in stone set with yellow cat's-eye gems. It was a furry hump with a tail descending from it: evidently the posterior of some sort of feline. A pussy-willow? No, too large for that. Smash recalled reference to one of the barbarian customs of the Mundanes, in which they killed animals and mounted their heads on walls. That was stupid—perfectly edible heads going to waste! Someone must have done the same for this cat's rear.

Smash considered, then decided to take the trophy along. It certainly wasn't doing any good here in the dark. Perhaps the girls would like to see it. Smash realized that it was a measure of the degradation foisted on him by the Eye Queue that he even thought of showing something interesting to others, but he was stuck with it.

He reached out to grab the stone frame. The cat's-eyes blinked warningly. The thing was firmly set, so he applied force. The frame ripped out of the wall—and the roof collapsed.

Puzzled, Smash put one fist up over his head. The rock fell on this and cracked apart, piling up on either side.

Smash climbed up through the rubble, toting his bag of plants, but was unable to bring the posterior-trophy. In a moment he reached daylight.

"Oh, you're all right!" Tandy cried. "I was so afraid—"

"Rockfalls can't hurt ogres," Smash said. "I tried to take a trophy, but the roof fell in." He dusted himself off.

"A trophy?" Tandy asked blankly.

"The rear end of some kind of cat, mounted in the wall."

"That was the catastrophe!" the Siren cried. "I told you not to invite it!"

Catastrophe—a trophy of the rear of a cat. Now Smash understood. He had not properly applied his new intelligence, and had done considerable damage to the catnip garden as a result. He would try to be more careful in the future. As long as he was cursed with intellect, he might as well use it.

"I had better clear the rocks out of the garden," Smash said. This, too, was an un-ogrish sentiment, but the Eye Queue and the presence of the girls seemed to have that effect on him.

"No, don't bother," the Siren said. "You wouldn't know how to set it right. The caterpillar will take care of that after we leave. It likes to push rocks around."

They crossed the catwalk past the cataract again and proceeded to the catapult. This was a feline creature the size of a small sphinx, crouched in a clearing. Its tail expanded into a kind of netting at the end, large enough for a boulder to rest on. There was a basket nearby, just that size.

The Siren approached the catapult. "Will you hurl us to Lake Ogre-Chobee, please?" she asked. "We have some catnip for you."

The cat brightened. It nodded its whiskered head. They laid the catnip plants down before it, then moved the basket to the expanded tail. The three of them climbed in and drew the wicker lid over, enclosing themselves.

The cat sniffed the catnip. Its tail stiffened ecstatically. Then it nipped the catnip. As the potent stuff took effect, the tail suddenly sprang up, carrying the basket along. Suddenly the party of three was flying.

They looked out between the slats. Xanth was cruising by beneath them, all green and blue and yellow. There were scattered, low-hanging clouds around them, white below, all other colors above, where they couldn't be seen from the ground. Some were rainclouds, shaped like pools, brimming with water. Stray birds were taking baths in them, and flying fish were taking breathers there, too. The basket clipped the edge of one of these rainclouds and tore a hole in it; the water poured out in a horrendous leak. There was an angry uproar from below as the unscheduled deluge splashed on the forest. But this was the Region of Madness anyway; no one would be able to prove the difference.

Now it occurred to Smash to wonder about their descent. They had risen smoothly enough, but the fall might be less comfortable.

Then some sort of material popped out of the lid of the basket. It spread into a huge canopy that caught the air magically and held back the basket. The descent became slow, and they landed by the shore of Lake Ogre-Chobee.

They opened the basket and stepped out. "That was fun!" Tandy exclaimed girlishly. "But how will the catapult get its basket back?"

An orange creature hurried up, vaguely catlike. "I'll take that," it said.

"Who are you?" Tandy asked.

"I am the agent of this region. It is my job to see that things get where they belong. The catapult has a contract for the return of its baskets."

"Oh. Then you had better take it. But I don't know how you'll be able to carry that big basket through that thick jungle, or past the Region of Madness."

"No problem. I'm half mad already." The orange agent picked up the basket and trotted north. The vegetation wilted and died in the creature's vicinity, making a clear path.

"Oh—that's its magic talent," Tandy said. "Agent Orange kills plants."

They turned to Lake Ogre-Chobee. It was a fine blue expanse of water with a whirlpool in the center. "Don't go there," the Siren cautioned. "The curse-fiends live there."

"What is wrong with the curse-fiends?" Smash asked. "My mother was one."

The Siren turned her gaze on him, startled. "Oh—I understood you were an ogre. The curse-fiends are of human derivation. I didn't mean to—"

"My mother is an actress. She had to play the part of an ogress in an adaptation of *Prince Charming*, a Mundane tale. Naturally she was the ingénue."

"Naturally," the Siren agreed faintly.

"But my father Crunch happened onto the set, innocently looking for bones to crunch, and spied her and was instantly smitten by her horribleness and carried her away. Naturally she married him."

"Yes, of course," the Siren agreed, looking wan. "I am jealous of her fortune. I'm of human derivation myself."

"The curse-fiends fired off a great curse that killed a huge forest," Smash continued. "But my parents escaped the curse by becoming vegetarians. Most ogres crunch bones, so this confused the curse and caused it to misfire."

"You were raised in a non-bone-crunching home!" Tandy exclaimed.

"I'm still an ogre," he said defensively.

"I'm glad it worked out so well," the Siren said. "But I think it would be wise to avoid the curse-fiends. They might not appreciate your position."

"I suppose so," Smash admitted. "But they are excellent actors. No one ever confused my mother for a human being."

"I'm sure they didn't," the Siren agreed. "I saw one of the curse-fiends' plays once. It was very well done. But it can be awkward associating with someone who throws a curse when aggravated."

Smash laughed. "It certainly can be! I acted un-ogrish once, letting a wyvern back me off from an emerald I had found—"

"My mother set that emerald in place!" Tandy exclaimed.

"And my mother threw a curse at me," he continued. "It scorched the ground at my feet and knocked me on my head. I never let any monster back me off again!"

"That was cruel," Tandy said. "She shouldn't have cursed you."

"Cruel? Of course not. It was ogre love, the only kind our kind understands. She cursed my father once, and it was two days before he recovered, and the smile never left his face."

"Well, I don't know," Tandy said, and she seemed unusually sober. Did she have some connection to the curse-fiends? Smash filed the notion for future reference.

They walked around a portion of Lake Ogre-Chobee, trying not to attract attention. There were no ogres in evidence, and no traces of their presence—no broken-off trees or fragmented boulders or flat-stomped ground.

There seemed to be no threats, either; the entire lake was girded, as far as they could see, by a pleasant little beach, and the water was clear and free of monsters. Evidently the curse-fiends had driven away anything dangerous.

"Look at the noses!" Tandy cried, pointing across the water. Smash looked. There were scores of nostrils swimming in pairs toward the shore, making little waves. As they drew near, he saw that the nostrils were the visible tips of more extensive snouts, which continued on into long reptilian bodies.

"Oh—the chobees," the Siren said, relaxing. "They're mostly harmless. Chobees aren't related to other kinds of bees; they don't sting. Once in a while one strays up to my lake."

"But what big teeth they have!" Tandy said.

"They're imitation teeth, soft as pillows."

A chobee scrambled out onto the beach. It had short, fat, green legs and a green corrugated skin. The Siren petted it on the head, and the chobee grinned. She touched one of its teeth, and the tooth bent like rubber, snapping back into place when released.

But Smash had a nagging doubt. "I remember something my father said about the chobees. Most of them are innocent, but some—"

"Oh, yes, that's right," the Siren agreed. "A few, a very few, have real teeth. Those kind are dangerous."

"Let's stay away from the bad ones, then," Tandy said. "What do they look like?"

"I don't know," the Siren admitted.

"They look just like the nice ones," Smash said slowly, dredging his memory.

"But then any of these could be a bad one," Tandy said, alarmed.

"True," Smash agreed. "Unless the curse-fiends got rid of them."

"How could the curse-fiends tell the difference, if we can't?" Tandy asked.

"If a chobee eats a curse-fiend, it's probably a bad one," the Siren said, smiling obscurely.

"Do we need to tell the chobees apart the same way?" Tandy asked worriedly.

The Siren laughed musically. Her voice was only a shadow of what it must have been when she had her luring magic, but it remained evocative. "Of course not, dear. Let's avoid them all." That seemed easy enough to do, as the three of them could walk faster than the reptiles could. Soon the chobees gave up the chase and nosed back into the water, where they buzzed away toward the deeper portions of the lake. Tandy watched the wakes their nostrils left with relief.

At one point the lake become irregular, branching out into a satellite lake that was especially pretty. A partial causeway crossed the narrow connection between the large and small lakes. "I'll wade across!" Smash said, delighting in the chance to indulge in some splashing.

"I don't know," Tandy said. "The nice paths can be dangerous." She had learned from her experience with the tangler and the ant-lions; now she distrusted all the easy ways.

"I will explore the water," the Siren said. "I will be able to tell very quickly whether there are dangerous water creatures near. Besides, I'm hungry; I need to catch some fish." She slid into the small lake, her legs converting to the sleekly scaled tail, her dress fading out.

"If you find a monster, send it my way," Smash called. "I'm hungry, too!"

She smiled and dived below the surface, a bare-breasted mernymph swimming with marvelous facility. In a moment her head popped up, tresses glistening. "No monsters here!" she called. "Not even any chobees. I believe that causeway is safe; I find no pitfalls there."

That was all Smash needed. "Too bad," he muttered. He waded in, sending a huge splay of water to either side.

But Tandy remained hesitant. "I think I'll just walk around it," she said.

"Good enough!" Smash agreed, and forged on into deeper water. The causeway dropped lower, but never deeper than chest height on him. He conjectured that it might have been constructed by the curse-fiends to prevent large sea monsters from passing; they preferred deep water and avoided shallows. Maybe the smaller lake had been developed as a resort region. This suggested that there could be monsters in Lake Ogre-Chobee; they just happened to be elsewhere at the moment. Maybe they represented an additional protection for the fiends, converting the whole of the large lake into a kind of moat. It really didn't matter, since he had no business with the curse-fiends. After all, they had not let his mother go willingly to marry his father. She had had no further contact with her people after she had taken up with Crunch the Ogre, and it occurred to Smash that this could not have made her feel good. So his attitude toward the fiends was guarded; he would not try to avoid them, but neither would he try to seek them out. Neutrality was the watchword. He had never thought this out before—but he had not suffered the curse of the Eye Queue before, either. He still hoped to find some way to be rid of it, as these frequent efforts of thought were not conducive to proper ogrish behavior.

He glanced across the water of the little lake. Tandy was picking her way along the beach, looking very small. He felt un-ogrishly protective toward her—but, of course, this was his service to the Good Magician. Ogres were gross and violent, but they kept their word. Also, the Eye Queue curse lent him an additional perception of the virtue of an ethical standard. It was a bit like physical strength; the ideal was to be strong in all respects, ethical as well as physical. And Tandy certainly needed protection. Besides which, she was a nice girl. He wondered what she was looking for in life and how it related to his journey to seek the Ancestral Ogres. Had old Magician Humfrey finally lost his magic, and had to foist Tandy off on an ogre in lieu of a genuine Answer? Smash hoped not, but he had to entertain the possibility. Suppose there was in fact no Answer for Tandy—or for himself?

Smash had no ready answer for that, even with his un-

wanted new intelligence, so had to let the thought lapse.
But it was disquieting. High intelligence, it seemed, posed
as many questions as it answered; being smart was not necessarily any solution to life's problems. It was much easier
to be strong and stupid, bashing things out of the way without concern for the consequences. Disquiet was no proper
feeling for an ogre.

Now he got down in the water and splashed with all
limbs. *This* was proper ogre fun! The spray went up in a
great cloud, surrounding the sun and causing its light to
fragment into a magic halo. The whole effect was so lovely
that he continued splashing violently until pleasantly
winded. When he stopped, he discovered that the water
level of the small lake had dropped substantially, and the
sun was hastening across the sky to get out of the way,
severely dimmed by all the water that had splashed on it.

But his thorough washing did not clear the Eye Queue
from the fur of his head. Somehow the Queue had sunk
into his brain, and the braided Eyes were providing him
new visions of many kinds. It would be hard indeed to get
those Eyes out again.

At last he waded out at the far side. The Siren swam up,
converted her tail to legs, and joined him on the warm
beach. "You made quite a splash, Smash," she said. "Had I
not known better, I would have supposed a thunderstorm
was forming."

"That good!" he agreed, well satisfied. Of course it
wasn't all good; he was now unconscionably clean. But a
few good rolls in the dirt would take care of that.

"That bad," the Siren said with a smile.

He studied her as she gleamed wetly, her scale-suit
creeping up to cover the fullness of her front. She seemed
to be turning younger, though this might be inconsequential
illusion. "I think the swim was good for you, too, Siren.
You look splendid." Privately, he was amazed at his words;
she did look splendid, and her affinity to the voluptuous Gorgon was increasingly evident, but no ordinary ogre would
have noticed, let alone complimented her in the fashion of
a human being. The curse of the Queue was still spreading!

"I do feel better," she agreed. "But it's not just the swim.
It's the companionship. I have lived alone for too long; now

that I have company, however temporarily, my youth and health are returning."

So that explained it! People of human stock had need for the association of other people. This was one of the ways in which ogres differed from human beings. Ogres needed nobody, not even other ogres. Except to marry.

He looked again at the Siren. Her nymphlike beauty would have dazzled a man and led him to thoughts of moonlight and gallivanting. Smash, however, was an ogre; full breasts and smoothly fleshed limbs appealed to him only aesthetically—and even that was a mere product of the Eye Queue. An uncursed ogre would simply have become hungry at the sight of such flesh.

Which reminded him—he needed something to eat. He checked around for edibles and spied some ripe banana peppers. He stuffed handfuls of them into his mouth.

Something nagged him as he chewed. Flesh—female—hunger—ah, now he had it. A girl in danger of being eaten. "Where's Tandy?" he asked.

"I haven't seen her, Smash," the Siren said, her fair brow furrowing. "She should be here by now, shouldn't she? We had better go look for her, in case—well, let's just see. I'll swim; you check the beach."

"Agreed." Smash crammed another double fistful of peppers into his face and started around the beach, concerned. He blamed himself now for his selfish carelessness. He knew that Tandy was unfamiliar with the surface of Xanth, liable to fall into the simplest trap. If something had happened to her—

"I find nothing here," the Siren called from the water. "Maybe she went off the beach for a matter of hygiene."

Good notion. Smash checked the tangled vines beyond the beach—and there, in due course, he found Tandy. "Hiho!" he called to her, waving a hamhand.

Tandy did not respond. She was kneeling on the turf, looking at something. "Are you all right?" Smash asked, worry building up like a sudden storm. But the girl neither moved nor answered.

The Siren came out of the water, dripping and changing in the effective way she had, and joined Smash. "Oh—she's fallen prey to a hypnogourd."

A hypnogourd. Smash remembered encountering that fruit before. Anyone who peeked in the peephole of such a gourd remained mesmerized until some third party broke the connection. Naturally Tandy had not been aware of this. So she had peeked, being girlishly curious—and remained frozen there.

Gently, the Siren removed the gourd, breaking the connection. Tandy blinked and shook her head. But her eyes did not quite focus. Her features coalesced into an expression of vacant, continuing horror.

"Hey, come out of it, dear," the Siren said. "The bad vision is over. It ended when you lost contact with the gourd. Everything's all right."

Yet the girl seemed numb. The Siren shook her, but still Tandy did not respond.

"Maybe it's like the Eye Queue," Smash said. "It stays in the mind until removed."

"The gourds aren't usually that way," the Siren said, perplexed. "Of course, I have not had much personal experience with them, since I have lived alone; there's no one to break the trance for me, so I have stayed clear. But I met a man once, a Mundane, back when I was able to lure men with my music. He said the gourds were like computer games—that seems to be something he knew about in Mundania, one of their forms of magic—only more compelling. He said some people got hooked worse than others."

"Tandy was raised in the caves. She has no experience with most of Xanth. She must be susceptible. Whatever she saw in there maintains its grip on her mind."

"That must be it. Usually people have no memory of what they see inside, but maybe that varies also. That same Mundane spoke of acidheads, which I think are creatures whose heads—well, I can't quite visualize that. But it seems they suffered flashbacks of their mad dreams after their heads were back in normal shape. Maybe Tandy is—"

"I'll go into that gourd and destroy whatever is bothering her," Smash said. "Then she'll be free."

"Smash, you may not have your body in there! I have never looked into a gourd, but I don't think the same rules apply as those we know. You could get caught there, too. It could be catastrophe."

"I will be more careful to avoid that trophy, this time," Smash said with an ogrish grimace. He applied his eye to the peephole.

He was in a world of black and white. He stood before a black wooden door set in a white house. There was no sound at all, and the air was chill. Faintly ominous vibrations wafted in from the near distance. There was the diffuse odor of spoiling carrion.

Smash licked his lips. Carrion always made him hungry. But he did not trust this situation. Tandy was not here, of course, and he saw nothing that could account for her condition. Nothing to frighten or horrify a person. He decided to leave.

However, he perceived no way out. He had arrived full-formed within this scene; there was no obvious exit. He was locked into this vision—unless he had entered through this door and turned about to face it without realizing, and could depart through it. Doors generally did lead from one place to another.

He took hold of the black metal doorknob. The thing zapped him with a small bolt of lightning. He tried to let go, but his hand was locked on. He wore no gauntlets; evidently he had left them behind. The electric pain pulsed through his fingers, locking the muscles clenched with its special magic. There was a wash of pain, literally; his black hand was now glowing with red color, in stark contrast with the monochrome of the rest of the scene.

Smash yanked hard on the knob. The entire door ripped off its hinges. The pain stopped, the red color faded, his fingers relaxed at last, and he hurled the door away behind him.

Before him was a long, blank hall penetrating the somber house. From the depths of it came a horrendous groan. This did not seem to be the way out; he was sure he had not walked any great distance inside the gourd. But it did seem pleasant enough, and was the only way that offered. Smash stepped inside.

A chill draft rustled the fur on his legs. The odor of putrefaction intensified. The floor shuddered as it took his weight. There was another groan.

Smash strode forward, impatient to get out of this interestingly drear but pointless place, worried about Tandy. He needed to consult with the Siren, to work out some strategy by which he might find whatever had scared Tandy and deal with it. Otherwise he would have felt free to enjoy the further entertainments of this house. Had he realized what kind of scene was inside the gourd, he would have entered it years ago.

Something flickered before him. Smash squinted, and saw it was a ghost. "You trapped, too?" he asked sympathetically, and walked through it.

The ghost made an angry moan and flickered to his frontside again. "Boooooo!" it boooooooed.

Smash paused. Was this creature trying to tell him something? He had known very few ghosts, as they did not ordinarily associate with ogres. There were several at Castle Roogna, attending to routine hauntings. "Do I know you?" he asked. "Do we have any mutual acquaintances?"

"Yoowwell!" the ghost yoweled, its hollow eyes flashing darkness.

"I'd help you if I could, but I'm lost myself," Smash said apologetically, and brushed on through it again. The ghost, disgusted for some obscure reason, faded away.

The passage narrowed. This was no illusion; the walls were closing on either side, squeezing together. Smash didn't like to be crowded, so he put one hamhand on each wall and pushed outward, exerting ogre force. Something snapped; then the walls slid apart and lay tilted at slightly odd angles. It would probably be a long time before they tried to push another ogre around!

At the end of the hall was a rickety staircase leading up. Smash pressed one hairy bare foot on the lowest step and shoved down, testing it. The step bowed and squeaked piteously, but supported his weight. Smash took another step—and suddenly the entire stairway began to move, carrying him upward. Magic stairs! What would this enjoyable place think of next?

The stairs accelerated. Faster and faster they went, making the dank air breeze past Smash's face. At the top of the flight they ended abruptly, and he went sailing out into blank space.

Ogres liked lots of violent things, but were not phenomenally partial to falling. However, they weren't unduly concerned about it, either. Smash stiffened his legs. In a moment he landed on hard concrete. Naturally it fractured under the impact of his feet. He stepped out of the rubble and looked about.

He seemed to be in some sort of deep well, or oubliette. The circular wall narrowed above, making climbing out difficult. Then a shape appeared in silhouette, holding a big stone over its head. The figure had horns and looked like a demon. Smash was not especially partial to demons, but he greeted this one courteously enough. "Up yours, devil!" he called.

The demon dropped the stone down the well. Smash saw the dark shape looming, but had no room to step out of the way.

Then light flared. Smash blinked. It was broad daylight in the forest of Xanth. "Are you all right?" the Siren asked. "I didn't dare let you stay out too long."

"I am all right," Smash said. "How is Tandy?"

"Unchanged, I'm afraid. Smash, I don't think you *can* destroy what is bothering her, because the horror is now in her mind. We could smash the gourd and it still wouldn't help her."

Smash considered. His skull no longer heated up when he did that. "I believe you are correct. I saw nothing really alarming in there. Perhaps I should go into the gourd with her and show her that it's not so bad."

The Siren frowned. "I suspect ogres have different definitions of bad. Just what happened in there?"

"Only a haunted house. Shocking doorknob. Ghost. Squeezing walls—I suppose those could have been awkward for a human person. Moving stairs. A demon dropping a rock down a well."

"Why would a demon do that?"

"I don't know. I happened to be below at the time. Maybe it didn't like my greeting."

Tandy stirred. Her eyes swung loosely about. Her lips pursed flaccidly. She looked disturbingly like a ghost. "No, no house, no demon. A graveyard . . ." She lapsed into staring, her mouth beginning to drool.

"Evidently you had separate visions," the Siren said, using a puff from a puffball growing nearby to clean up the girl's face. "That complicates it."

"Maybe if we go in together, we'll share a vision," Smash conjectured.

"But there is only one peephole."

Smash poked his littlest hamfinger into the rind of the gourd. "Two, now."

"You ogres are so practical!"

They set the gourd before Tandy, who immediately peered into the first peephole. Then Smash squatted so that he could peer into the second.

He was back in the well. The rock was plunging at his head. Hastily he raised a fist, since he didn't want a headache. The rock shattered on the fist, falling around him in the form of fragments, pebbles, and gravel. So much for that. If the demon would just drop a few more stones down, Smash would soon have this well filled up with rubble and could step out.

But the demon did not reappear. Too bad. Smash looked around the gloom. Tandy was not with him. He was in the same vision he had left, picking it up in the same moment he had left it. He was using a different peephole, but that didn't seem to matter. Probably Tandy was back in her original vision, at the same point it had been interrupted, getting scared by whatever had scared her before. It seemed the gourd programmed each vision separately.

However, it was all the same gourd. Tandy had to be somewhere in here, and he intended to find her, rescue her from her horror, and smash that horror into a quivering pulp so it wouldn't bother her again. All he had to do was make a sufficient search.

He took hold of a stone in the wall of the well and yanked it out. Three more stones fell out with it. Smash took another; this time five more fell. This old well was not well constructed! He stood on these and drew out more stones. The well filled in beneath him steadily, and before long he was back at the surface. There was no sign whatsoever of the demon who had dropped the first rock on him. That was just as well, for Smash might have treated that demon a trifle unkindly, perhaps snapping its tail like a rubber band and launching the creature on a flight to the moon. The least that demon could have done was to stay around long enough to drop a few more useful boulders down the well.

Now he stood in a chamber surrounded by doors. He heard a faint, despairing scream. Tandy!

He went to the nearest door and grasped the knob. It shocked him, so he ripped the door out of its socket and threw it away. The room inside was a bare chamber: a false lead. He tried the next door, got shocked again, and ripped it out, too. Another bare chamber. He went to the third door—and it didn't shock him. The doors were learning! He opened this one gently. But it led only to another decoy chamber.

Finally he opened one that showed an outdoor walk. He hurried down this, hurdling a square that he recognized as a covered pitfall—ogres naturally knew about such things, having had centuries of ancestral experience avoiding such traps set for them by foolish men—and emerged into a windy graveyard.

Battered gravestones were all around, marking sunken graves. Some stones tilted forward precariously, as if trying to peer into the cavities they demarked. It occurred to Smash that the buried bodies might have climbed out and gone elsewhere, accounting for the sunkenness of the graves and the suspicions of the headstones, but this was not his concern.

The odor of carrion was stronger out here. Maybe some of the corpses had not been buried deep enough. A wind came up, cutting around the stone edges with dismal howling. Smash breathed deeply, appreciating it, then concentrated on the business at hand. "Tandy!" he called. "Where are you?" For she had said she was in a graveyard, and this must be the place.

He heard a faint sobbing. Carefully he traced down the source. It was slow work, because the sound was carried by the wind, and the wind curved around the gravestones in cold blue streams, searching out the best edges for making moaning tunes. But at last he found the huddled figure, cowering behind a white stone crypt.

"Tandy!" he repeated. "It's I. Smash, the tame ogre. Let me take you away from all this."

She looked up, pale with fright, as if hardly daring to recognize him. Her mouth opened, but only drool came out.

He reached out to take her arm, to help her to her feet.

But she was as limp as a rag doll and would not rise. She just continued sobbing. She seemed little different from her Xanth self. Something was missing.

Smash considered. For once he was thankful for the Eye Queue, because now he could ponder without pain. What would account for the girl's lethargy and misery? He had thought it was fear, but now that he was here, she should have no further cause for that. It was as if she had lost something vital, like eyesight or—

Or her soul. Suddenly Smash remembered how vulnerable souls could be, and knew that if anyone were likely to blunder into a soul-hazardous situation, Tandy was the one. She knew so little of the ways of Xanth! No wonder she was desolate and empty.

"Your soul, Tandy," he said, holding her so that she had to look into his face. "Where is it?"

Listlessly she nodded toward the crypt. Smash saw that it had a heavy, tight stone door. Scrape marks on the dank ground indicated it had recently been opened. She must have gone inside, perhaps trying to escape the graveyard—and had been ejected without her soul.

"I will recover it," he said.

Now she bestirred herself enough to react. "No, no," she moaned. "I am lost. Save yourself."

"I agreed to protect you," he reminded her. "I shall do it." He set her gently aside and addressed the crypt. The door had no handle, but he knew how to deal with that. He elevated his huge bare fist and smashed it brutally forward into the stone.

Ouch! Without his gauntlets, his hands were more tender. He could not safely apply his full force. But his blow had accomplished its purpose; the stone door had cracked marginally and jogged a smidgen outward. He applied his horny fingernails and hauled the door unwillingly open.

A dark hole faced him. As his eyes adjusted, he saw a white outline. It was the skeleton of a man. It reached for him with bone-fingers.

Smash realized where the bodies in the sunken graves had gone. They had been recruited for guard duty and were walking about this crypt. But he was not in the mood for nuisance. He grabbed the skeleton by the bones of its

arm and hauled it violently out of the crypt. The thing
flew through the air and landed as a jumble of bones. The
ogre proceeded on into the hole.

Other skeletons appeared, clustering about him, their
connections rattling. Smash treated them as he had the
first, disconnecting their foot-bones from their leg-bones
and other bones, causing the bonepile to grow rapidly. Soon
the remaining skeletons reconsidered, not wishing to have
him roll their bones, and left him alone.

Deep in the ground the ogre came to a dark coffin. The
smell was mouth-wateringly awful; something really rotten
was in there. Was Tandy's soul in there, too? He picked up
the box and shook it.

"All right, all *right!*" a muffled voice came from the
coffin. "You made your point, ogre. You aren't afraid of
anything. What do you want?"

"Give back Tandy's soul," Smash said grimly.

"I can't do that, ogre," the box protested. "We made a
deal. Her freedom for her soul. I let her out of this world; I
keep her soul. That's the way we deal here; souls are the
currency of this medium."

"The Siren let her out by removing the gourd," Smash
argued. "She never had to pay."

"Coincidence. I permitted it, once the deal was struck.
The negotiation is sealed."

Smash had lived and thought like an ogre a lot longer
than he had lived and thought intelligently. Now he reverted to convenient old habits. He roared, picked up the
coffin, and hurled it against the wall. The box fell to the
floor, somewhat sprung, and several ceiling stones dropped
on it. Nauseating goo dribbled from a crack in it. Dirt
sifted down from the chamber wall to smooth the outlines.

"Maybe further negotiation is possible after all," the
voice from the coffin said, somewhat shaken. "Would you
consider trading souls?"

Smash readied his hamfist again. "Wait!" the voice
cried, alarmed. It evidently wasn't used to dealing with real
brutes. "I merely collect souls; I don't have the authority to
give them back. If you want the girl's soul now, your only
option is to trade."

The ogre considered. He might smash the coffin and its
occupant to pieces, but that would not necessarily recover

the soul. If Tandy's soul were in there, it could get hurt in the battering. So maybe it was better to bargain. "Trade what?"

"Another soul, of course. How about yours?"

This box thought he was a typically stupid ogre. "No."

"Well, someone else's. What about that buxom mature nymph out in Xanth, with the sometime fish-tail? She probably has a luscious, bouncy, juicy soul."

Smash considered again. He decided, with an un-ogrish precision of ethics, that he could not make any commitments on behalf of the Siren. "Not her soul. And not mine."

"Then the girl's soul must remain."

Smash got another whiff of the stench from the coffin and knew that Tandy's soul could not be allowed to rot there. He still did not consider the deal by which the coffin had gotten Tandy's soul to be valid. He stooped to pick up the battered coffin again.

"Wait!" the voice cried. "There is one other option. You could accede to a lien."

The ogre paused. "Explain."

"A lien is a claim on the property of another as security for a debt," the coffin explained. "A lien on your soul would mean that you agree to replace the girl's soul with another soul—and if you don't, then your own soul is forfeit. But you keep your soul in the interim, or most of it."

It did seem to make sense. "How long an interim?"

"Shall we say thirty days?"

"Six months," Smash said. "You think I'm stupid?"

"I did think that," the coffin confessed. "After all, you are an ogre, and it is well known that the brains of ogres are mostly in their muscles. In fact, their brains *are* mostly muscles."

"Not true," Smash said. "An ogre's skull is filled with bone, not muscle."

"I stand corrected. *My* skull is filled with necrosis. How about sixty days?"

"Four months."

"Split the difference: ninety days."

"Okay," Smash agreed. "But I don't agree you are entitled to keep *any* soul, just because you tricked an innocent girl into trading it off for nothing."

"Are you sure you're an ogre? You don't sound like one."

"I'm an ogre," Smash affirmed. "Would you like me to throw you around some more to prove it?"

"That won't be necessary," the coffin said quickly. "If you disagree with the assessment, you must deal with the boss: the Night Stallion. He makes decisions of policy."

"The Dark Horse?"

"Close enough; some do call him that. He governs the herd of nightmares."

It began to fall into place. "This is where the nightmares live? By day, when they're not out delivering bad dreams to sleepers?"

"Exactly. All the bad dreams are generated here in the gourd, from the raw material of people's fundamental fears—loss, pain, death, shame, and the unknown. The Stallion decides where the dreams go, and the mares take them there. Your girlfriend abused a mare, so it took a lien on her soul, and when she came here, that lien was called due. So her soul is forfeit, and now we have it, and only the Night Stallion can change that. Why don't we set you up for an appointment with the Stallion, and you can settle this directly with him?"

"An appointment? When?"

"Well, he has a full calendar. Bad dreams aren't light fancies, you know. There's a lot of evil in the world that needs recognition. It's a lot of work to craft each dream correctly and designate it for exactly the right person at the right time. So the Stallion is quite busy. The first opening is six months hence."

"But my lien expires in three months!"

"You're smarter than the average ogre, for sure! You might force an earlier audience, but you'd have to find the Stallion first. He certainly won't come to you within three months. I really wouldn't recommend the effort of locating him."

Smash considered again. It seemed to him that this coffin protested too profusely. Something was being concealed here. Time for the ogre act again. "Perhaps so," he said. "There is therefore no point in restraining my natural inclination for violence." He picked up a rock and crumpled it to chips and sand with one hand. He eyed the coffin.

"But I'm sure you can find him!" the box said quickly. "All you have to do is seek the path of most resistance. That's all I can tell you, honest!"

Smash decided that he had gotten as much as he could from the coffin. "Good enough. Give me the girl's soul, and I'll leave my three-month lien and meet the Stallion when I find him."

"Do you think a soul is something you can just carry in your hand?" the coffin demanded derisively.

"Yes," Smash said. He contemplated his hand, slowly closing it into a brutishly ugly fist that hovered menacingly over the coffin.

"Quite," the coffin agreed nervously, sweating another blob of stinking goo. The soul floated up, a luminescent globe that passed right through the wood. Smash cupped it carefully in his hand and tromped from the gloomy chamber. Neither coffin nor skeletons opposed him.

Tandy sat where she had been, the picture of hopeless girlish misery. "Here is your soul," Smash said, and held out the glowing globe.

Unbelievingly, she reached for it. The globe expanded at her touch, becoming a ghost-shape that quickly overlapped her body and merged. For an instant her entire body glowed, right through the tattered red dress; then she was her normal self. "Oh, Smash, you did it!" she exclaimed. "I love you! You recovered my soul from that awful corpse!"

"I promised to protect you," he said gruffly.

"How can I reward you?" She was actually pinching herself, amazed by her restoration. Smash, too, was amazed; he had not before appreciated how much difference a person's soul made.

"No reward," he insisted. "It's part of my job, my service for my Answer."

She considered. "Yes, I suppose. But how ever did you do it? I thought there was no way—"

"I had to indulge my natural propensities slightly," he admitted, glancing at the pile of bones he had made. The bones shuddered and settled lower, eager to avoid his attention.

"Oh. I guess you were more terrible than the skeletons were," she said.

"Naturally. That is the nature of ogres. We're worse

than anything." Smash thought it best not to inform her of the actual nature of his deal. "Let's get out of here."

"Oh, yes! But how?"

That was another problem. He could bash through walls, but the force holding Tandy and himself inside the gourd was intangible. "I think we'll have to wait for the Siren to free us. All she has to do is move the gourd so we can't look into it any more, but she doesn't know when we'll be finished in here."

"Oh, I don't want to stay another minute in this horrible place! If I had known what would happen when I peeked into that funny little hole—"

"It's not a bad place, this," Smash said, trying to cheer her. "It can even be fun."

"Fun? In this awful graveyard?"

"Like this." Smash had spied a skeleton poking around a grave, perhaps looking for a new convert. He sneaked up behind it. Ogres didn't have to shake the earth when they walked; they did it because they enjoyed it. "BOOO!" he bellowed.

The skeleton leaped right out of its foot-bones and stumbled away, terrified. Tandy had to smile. "You're pretty scary, all right, Smash," she agreed.

They settled down against a large gravestone. Tandy huddled within the protection of the ogre's huge, hairy arm. It was the only place the poor little girl felt safe in this region.

Chapter 5. Prints of Wails

The Siren greeted them anxiously as they woke to the outer afternoon of Xanth. "I gave you an hour this time, Smash; I just didn't dare wait longer," she said. "Are you all right?"

"I have my soul back!" Tandy said brightly. "Smash got it for me!"

The Siren had been looking her age, for her human stock caused her to be less than immortal. Now relief was visibly restoring her youthfulness. "That's wonderful, dear," she said, hugging her. Then, looking at Smash, the Siren sobered again. "But usually souls can't be recovered without hell to pay—ah, that is, some sort of quid pro quo. Are you sure—"

"I've got mine," Smash said jovially. "Such as it is. Ogres do have souls, don't they?"

"As far as I know, only people of human derivation have souls," the Siren said. "But all of those do, even if their human ancestor was many generations ago, and so we three qualify. I'm sure yours is as good as any, Smash, and perhaps better than some."

"It must be stronger and stupider, anyway," he said.

"I'm so glad it's all right," the Siren said, seeming not entirely convinced. She evidently suspected something, but chose not to make an issue of it at this time. Older females tended to be less innocent than young ones, he realized, but also more discreet.

They considered their situation. There seemed to be no ogres and no merfolk at Lake Ogre-Chobee, despite its name.

"Now I remember," Smash said. "The curse-fiends drove the ogres away. They migrated north to the Ogre-fen-Ogre Fen. I don't know why I didn't think of that before!"

"Because you weren't cursed by the Eye Queue before, silly," Tandy said. "You weren't very smart. But that's all right; we'll just go up to the Ogre Fen and find your tribe."

"But that's the entire length of Xanth!" the Siren protested. "Who knows what horrors lie along the way?"

"Yes, fun," Smash said.

"Funny, the Good Magician didn't remind you about the ogres' change of residence," the Siren said. "Well, there's certainly not much doing here. I would like to travel with you a little longer, if I may, at least until I find a lake inhabited by merfolk."

"Sure, come along, we like your company," Tandy said immediately, and Smash shrugged. It really made little difference to him. He was partially preoccupied by his problem with the lien on his soul. He would soon have to find a pretext to go back into the gourd to search for the Night Stallion and fight for his soul.

"But first, let's abolish this menace once and for all," the Siren said. She picked up the hypnogourd and lifted it high overhead, throwing it violently to the ground.

"No!" Smash cried. But before he could move, the gourd had smashed to earth. It fragmented into pinkish pulp, black seeds, and translucent juice. There was no sign of the world he and Tandy had toured within it; the magic was gone.

The ogre stood staring at the ruin. Now, how could he return to that world to settle his account? Somehow he knew his lien had not been abated by the destruction of the gourd; his avenue to that world had merely been closed. It would take time to manifest, but he knew he was in very bad trouble.

"Is something wrong?" the Siren asked. "Did you leave something in there?"

"It doesn't matter," Smash said brusquely. After all, she had meant well, and there was nothing to be done now. No point in upsetting the girls, no matter how privately satisfying it might have been to rant and rave and stomp, ogre-

style, until the whole forest and lake trembled and roiled
with reaction to the violence.

They trekked north through the variegated jungle and
tundra and intemperate zones of Xanth. Most of the local
flora and fauna left the party alone, wisely not wishing to
antagonize an ogre. Upon occasion, some gnarled old bull-
spruce would paw the earth with a branch-hoof and poke a
limb-horn into the way, but a short, sharp blow with
Smash's gauntleted fist taught such trees manners. Progress
was good.

They were just considering where to spend the night
when they heard something. There was a thin, barely audi-
ble screaming, and a cacophony of ugly pantings, breath-
ings, and raspings. "Something unpleasant is going on," the
Siren said.

"I'll investigate," Smash said, glad for the chance for a
little relaxing violence. He tromped toward the commotion.

A crowd of multilegged things was chasing a little fairy
lass, who seemed to have hurt one of her gossamer wings.
She was running this way and that, but wherever she went,
creatures like squished caterpillars with tentacles moved to
block the way, dribbling hungry drool. The fairy was
screaming with fright and horror, and the pursuers were
reveling in her discomfort, playing cruelly with her before
closing for the kill.

"What's this?" Smash demanded.

One of the creatures turned toward him, though it was
hard to tell which side was its front. "Stay out of what does
not concern you, trashface," it said insolently.

Now, Smash normally did not involve himself in what
did not concern him, but his recent experience with Tandy
in the gourd had sensitized him to the plight of small,
pretty females in distress. Also, he did not like being told to
stay out, despite the compliment to his face. Therefore he
reacted with polite force. "Get out of here, you ghastly par-
ody."

"Oho! the ghastly cried. "So the dumb brute needs a lesson, too!"

Immediately the creatures oriented on Smash. From a
distance they were repulsive; from up close, they were
worse. They launched purple spittle at him, belched ob-

scenely all over their bodies, and scratched at him with dirty claws. But several still chased the hapless fairy lass.

Smash became moderately perturbed. Now it seemed the reputation of ogres was on the line. He picked up a ghastly. It defecated on his paw. He heaved it into the forest. It scurried back. He pounded another into the ground—but it merely squished flat, then rebounded. He tore one apart, but it just stretched impossibly, and snapped back to its normal shapelessness when he let go, leaving a slug of smelly slime on his fingers.

Now the fairy screamed louder. The ghastlies had almost caught her. Smash had to act quickly or he would be too late to help her. But what would stop these creatures?

Fortunately, his new intelligence assisted. If throwing, pounding, and stretching didn't work, maybe tying would. He grabbed two ghastlies and squeezed and squished them together, tying a knot in their infinitely stretchable limbs. Then he tied in a third, and a fourth, and a fifth. Soon he had a huge ball of tied ghastlies, since they kept coming stupidly at him. Their rebounding and stretching didn't do them much good; it merely tightened the knots. In due course, all the ghastlies were balled together, spitting, hissing, scratching, and pooping on each other constantly.

Smash dropped the ball, wiped himself off on some towel-leaves, and checked on the fairy. She was as frightened of him as she had been of the ghastlies. He did not chase her; he had only wanted to make sure she was not too badly hurt.

When the fairy saw him stop, she stopped. She was a tiny thing, hardly half the height of Tandy, a nude girl form with sparklingly mussed hair and thin, iridescent wings with scenic patterns. "You aren't chasing me, ogre?"

"No. Go your way in peace, fairy."

"But why did you tie all the ghastlies in a knot, if you didn't want to gobble me up?"

"To help you escape."

She had difficulty assimilating this. "I thought you were an ogre, but you neither sound nor act like one."

"We all have our off days," Smash said apologetically.

Tandy and the Siren arrived. "He's a gentle ogre," the Siren explained. "He helps the helpless." She introduced the three of them.

"I'm John," the fairy said. Then, before they could react, she continued. "I know, I know it's not a proper name for the like of me, but my father was away when I was born, and the message got garbled, and I was stuck with it. So now I'm on a quest for my proper name. But I got tossed by a gust and hurt my wing, and then the ghastlies—"

"Why don't you travel with us?" Tandy asked. "Until your wing gets better. Monsters don't bother us much. We have one of our own." She gripped Smash's dangling ham-hand possessively.

John considered, evidently uncertain about traveling with a monster. Then the ball of ghastlies began working loose, and she decided. "Yes, I will go with you. It should take only a day or so for my wing to mend."

Smash did not comment. He had not asked for any companions, but Tandy had been forced on him, and she had a propensity for inviting others. Perhaps it was because Xanth was so new to her that she felt the company of others who were more familiar with it would improve things. Maybe she was right; the Siren had certainly helped them get out of the gourd. It didn't really matter; Smash could travel with three as well as with one.

Now night came. Smash foraged for food and found a patch of spaghetti just ripening near a spice tree. He harvested several great handfuls, shook the spice on them, and proffered this for their repast. The girls seemed a trifle doubtful at first, but all were hungry, and soon they were consuming the delicious, slippery stuff, ogre-style, by the handful and slurpful. Then they found a basket palm with enough stout hanging baskets for all, and spent a reasonably comfortable night.

But before they slept, the Siren questioned John about the kind of name she was looking for. "Why don't you just take any name you like and use it?"

"Oh, I couldn't," John said. "I can answer only to the name I was given. Since I was given the wrong one, I must keep it until I recover the right one."

"How can you be sure there *is* a right one? If your father was misinformed—"

"Oh, no, he knew who I was. He sent back a good name, but somehow it got lost, and the wrong name arrived instead. By the time he got home, it was too late to fix it."

Smash understood the Siren's perplexity. He, like her, had not been aware that names were so intricately tagged.

"Does that mean that someone else got your name?" the Siren asked.

"Of course. Some male fairy got my name, and must be as unhappy with it as I am with his. But if I find him, we can exchange them. Then everything will be just fine."

"I see," the Siren said. "I hope you find him soon."

In the morning they breakfasted on honeydew that had formed on the leaves of the basket tree, then resumed the trek north. John buzzed her healing wing every so often, and the pattern on it seemed to come alive in a three-dimensional image, like flowers blooming, but she could not yet fly. She had to be content to walk. She was a cheery little thing, good company, and full of cute anecdotes about life among the fairies. It seemed the Fairy Kingdom was a large one, with many principalities and interstate commerce between groups, and internecine trade wars.

They started to climb. None of them was familiar with this section of Xanth, which was east of the Region of Madness, so they merely proceeded directly north. With luck, it wouldn't be too bad.

But it was bad. The mountain became so steep it was impossible to climb normally. They could not go around it, because the sides of the channel they traveled had risen even more steeply. They had either to proceed forward or to retreat all the way to the base and try another approach. None was willing to retreat.

Smash used his gauntleted fists to break out sections of rock, making crude steps for the others. Fortunately, the really steep part was not extensive, and by noon they stood at the top.

It was a lake, hardly on the scale of Ogre-Chobee but impressive enough, brimful with sparkling water. "This must be an old volcano," John said. "I have flown over similar ones, though not this big. We must beware; water dragons like such lakes, especially if they are hot on the bottom."

Smash grimaced. He didn't like water dragons, because they tended to be too much for an honest ogre to handle.

But he saw no sign of such a creature here. No droppings, no piles of bones, no discarded old scales or teeth.

"What are those?" Tandy inquired, pointing.

There were marks on the surface of the water. They were roughly circular indentations, with smaller indentations on one side of each large one. "They look like prints," the Siren said. "As if some creature walked on the water. Is that possible?"

Smash put one foot on the water. It sank through. The ripples moved across the prints, erasing them. "Not possible," he decided.

Still, they decided to stay clear of the water until they knew more about it. Seemingly minor mysteries could be hazardous to their health in Xanth. They walked around the west side of the lake, following one of those suspiciously convenient paths because there was no other route between the deep water and the clifflike outer face of the mountain.

But as they bore north, following the curve of the cone, they encountered an outcropping of spongy rock. "Magma," Smash conjectured, forcing another subterranean memory to the surface, slightly heated.

"I don't care who it is, it's in our way," Tandy complained. Indeed, the rock blotted out the path, forcing them to attempt a hazardous scramble.

"I shall remove it," Smash decided. He readied his hamfist and pounded one good pound on the magma.

The rock responded with a deafening reverberation. They all clapped their hands over their ears while the mountain shook and the lake made waves.

Finally the awful noise died away. "That magma comes loud!" the Siren said.

"Magma cum laude," the ogre agreed, not hearing well yet.

"It sure is some sound," Tandy said, looking dizzy. The fairy agreed.

They decided they didn't like the sound of it, and would try the other side of the lake, where the way might be quieter. As they walked the path back, an awful moan slid across the water. "What is that?" Tandy demanded anxiously.

"The wailing of whatever made the prints," the Siren conjectured.

"Oh. So these are the prints of wails."

"Close enough." The Siren grimaced. "I hope we don't meet the wail, though. I've had some experience with music on water, and this makes me nervous."

"Yes, you ought to know," Tandy agreed. "My father said you could bring any man to you from afar, if he heard you."

"Yes, when I had my magic," she said sadly. "Those days are gone, and perhaps it is just as well, but I do get lonely."

They approached the east side of the lake. But here they encountered more trouble. An ugly head lifted on a serpentine neck. It was not exactly a dragon's head, and not exactly a sea monster's head, but it had affinities with both. It was not large as monster heads went, but it hissed viciously enough.

Smash was tired of being balked. He did not mess with this minor monster; he reached out with one hand and caught the neck between gauntleted thumb and forefinger.

Immediately another head appeared, similar to the first and just as aggressive. Smash caught this one in his other glove.

Then a third came. This was getting awkward! Had he stumbled onto a whole nest of serpents? Hastily Smash smashed the first two heads together, crushing both, and reached for the third.

"They all connect!" the Siren exclaimed. "It's a many-headed serpent!"

Indeed it was! Four more heads rose up, making seven in all. Smash crushed two more, but had to move quickly to prevent the remaining three from burying their fangs in his limbs. He rose to the need, however, by catching one under his feet and the last two in his hands. In a moment all had been crushed, and he relaxed.

"Smash, look out!" Tandy cried. "More heads!"

Apparently a couple of the ones he had dealt with had not been completely destroyed, and had revived. This was unusual; things seldom recovered from the impact of ogre force. He grabbed these—and discovered they sprouted from the same neck. Their junction formed a neat Y. He was sure he hadn't encountered this configuration before.

"More heads!" Tandy screamed.

"Now there were six more, in three pairs. New heads were growing from the old ones!

"It's a hydra!" the Siren cried. "Each lost head generates two more! You can never get ahead of it!"

"I've got too many heads of it!" Smash muttered, stepping back. The hydra was generating a small forest of hissing heads, each lunging and snapping at anything in range. Two were squaring off at each other.

"You can't kill a hydra," the Siren continued. "Its essence is immortal. It draws its strength from the water."

"Then I shall remove the water," Smash said. "It will be easy to bash a hole in this rim and let the lake out."

"Oh, please don't do that!" the Siren protested. "I'm a creature of water, and I hate to see it mistreated. You would ruin a perfectly lovely lake, and drown many innocent creatures below, and kill many innocent lake denizens. There is an entire ecology in any such body—"

Was the mermaid becoming the conscience of the group? Smash hesitated.

"That's true," John admitted. "Pretty lakes should be left alone. Most of them have much more good than evil in them."

Smash looked at Tandy. "I agree," she said. "We don't want to harm others, and this water *is* nice."

The ogre shrugged. He didn't want trouble with his friends. As he thought about it, with his amplified Eye Queue intelligence—which remained a nuisance—he realized they were right. Wanton destruction could only beget a deterioration of the environment of Xanth, and that would, in the long run, damage the prospects of ogres. "No harm to others," he agreed gruffly. If any other ogres ever heard of this, he would be in trouble! Imagine *not* destroying something!

"Oh, I could kiss you," Tandy said. "But I can't reach you."

Smash chuckled. "Good thing. Now we'll have to swim across the lake. Do all of you know how to swim?"

"Oh, I couldn't swim," John said. "My wings would break."

"Maybe you can fly now," the Siren suggested.

"Maybe." The fairy tried, buzzing her pretty wings, making the flower-pattern blossoms again. She seemed to lighten as the downdraft of air dusted dirt out from the ridge, but she did not quite take off. Then she jumped. A gust of wind passed at that moment, carrying her out over the rim. She agitated her wings furiously, but could not sustain elevation and began to fall.

Smash reached out and caught her before she crashed into the rocky slope. She screamed, then realized he was helping her, not attacking her. He set her carefully back on the ledge, where she stood panting prettily and quivering with reaction.

"Not yet, it seems," the Siren said. "But you might sit on Smash's back while he swims."

"I suppose," the fairy agreed faintly. Her little bare bosom was heaving. It occurred to Smash that the loss of the ability to fly might be quite disturbing to a creature whose natural mode of travel was flight. He might react similarly if he lost his ogre strength.

They entered the water. Tandy could swim well enough, and, of course, the Siren converted to mermaid form and was completely at home. John perched nervously on Smash's head and was so light he hardly felt her weight. He began stroking across the lake, careful not to splash enough to cause trouble, despite his pleasure in splashing. Some sacrifices were necessary when one traveled in company.

The Siren led the way, easily outdistancing the others. That creature certainly could swim; she was in her element.

Then something loomed from the north. It was huge and dark, like a low-flying thundercloud, scooting across the water. Simultaneously the awful wailing came again, and now Smash realized it came from the cloud-thing. There was also a pattering drumbeat punctuating the wails.

The Siren paused in place. "I don't like this," she said. "That thing is trotting on the surface of the water; I feel the vibrations of its footfalls. And it's headed for us. I could outdistance it, I think; but Tandy can't, and Smash can't do much without imperiling John. We had better get out of the water."

"It's coming too fast," John said. "It will catch us before we get back to shore."

She was right. The monster loomed rapidly onward, casting a dark shadow. It was not actually a cloud, but was composed of gray-blue foam, with a number of holes through which the wailing passed, and hundreds of little feet that touched the water. When it moved to one side, they saw the prints left on the surface, just like the ones they had seen before. The prints of wails.

"Oh, we are doomed!" John cried. "Save yourself, Smash; dive under the water, hide from it!"

An ogre hide from a monster? Little did the fairy grasp the magnitude of the insult she had innocently rendered. "No," Smash said. "I'll fight it."

"It's too big to fight!"

"It probably smothers its prey by surrounding it," Tandy said. She was being practical. She seemed much less afraid of things since having discovered the ultimate nature of fear inside the gourd. Monsters were only monsters, when one's soul was intact. "You can't fight fog or jelly."

Smash realized she was probably right. These assorted girls were making more sense than he would have thought before he came to know them. In the water, with a delicate and flightless fairy on his head, he could not fight efficiently anyway—and if there was nothing really solid to punch out, his fists would be of little use. It galled him to concede that there were monsters that an ogre couldn't handle, but in this case it seemed to be so. Curse this Eye Queue that made him see reason!

"I'll lead it away!" the Siren cried. She was hovering in the water, her powerful tail elevating her body, so that it was as if she stood only waist-deep. She would have been a considerable sight, that way, for a human male. It seemed to Smash that she should have no trouble attracting a merman, at such time as she found one. "You swim on across the lake," the Siren continued. She set off toward the west, moving with amazing velocity. She was like a bird in flight across the surface of the lake.

When she was a fair distance away, she paused and began to sing. She had a beautiful voice, with an eerie quality, a little like the wailing of the monster. Perhaps she was deliberately imitating it.

The monster paused. Then it rotated grandly and ran toward the Siren, its little feet striking the water without splashing, leaving the prints. That mystery had been

solved, though Smash did not understand how the prints
remained after the wailing monster moved on. But, of
course, the effects of magic did not need any explanation.

Once the monster had cleared the area, lured away by
the Siren, Smash and Tandy swam on across. It was a fair
distance, and Tandy tired, slowing them; it seemed there
were not many lakes this big in the underworld. Finally
Smash told her to grab hold of one of his feet so he could
tow her. The truth was, he was getting tired himself; he
would have preferred to wade, but the water was far too
deep for that. It would have been un-ogrish to confess any
weakness, however.

They made it safely to the north lip. They drew themselves out and rested, hoping the Siren was all right.

Soon she appeared, swimming deep below the surface.
Her tail gave her a tremendous forward thrust, and she
was a thing of genuine beauty as she slid through the water, her hair streaming back like bright seaweed, her body
as sleek and glossy as that of a healthy fish. Then she came
up, her head bursting the surface, her hands rising automatically to brush back her wet tresses, mermaidlike. "My,
that was interesting!" she said, flipping out of the water to
sit on the rim, her tail hidden in the water, so that now she
most resembled a healthy nymph.

"The monster was friendly?" Tandy asked doubtfully.

"No, it tried to consume me. But it couldn't reach below
the water because its magic prints keep it above. It tried to
lure me close, but I'm an experienced hand at luring creatures, and was too careful to be taken in."

"Then you were in real danger!" Tandy was now very
sensitive to danger from monsters that lured their victims,
whether by an easy access path or a convenient peephole.

"No danger for me," the Siren said, flinging her damp
hair out as she changed to human legs and climbed the rest
of the way from the water. "Few creatures can catch my
kind in our element. Not that there are many quite like
me; most merfolk can't make legs. That's my human heritage. Of course, my sister the Gorgon never was able to
make a tail; it was her face that changed. Magical heredity
is funny stuff! But I talked briefly with the monster. He
considers himself a whale."

"A whale of a what?" Smash asked.

"Just a whale."

"Isn't that a Mundane monster?" John asked. It was generally known in Xanth that the worst monsters were Mundane, as were the worst people.

"Yes. But this one claims some whales migrated to Xanth, grew legs so they could cross to inland waters, and then kept the legs for lake-running. Some find small lakes; they're puddle-jumpers. Some find pools of rum; they're rum-runners. He says he's of the first water, a royal monster, a Prince of his kind."

"A Prince of Whales," Tandy said. "Is he really?"

"I don't think so. That's why he wails."

"Life is hard all over," Smash said without much sympathy. "Let's get down off this mountain."

Indeed, the sun was losing strength and starting to fall, as it did each day, never learning to conserve its energy so that it could stay aloft longer. They needed to get to a comfortable place before night. Fortunately, the slope on this side was not as steep, so they were able to slide down it fairly readily.

As they neared the northern base, where the forest resumed, a nymph came out to meet them. She was a delicate brown in color, with green hair fringed with red. Her torso, though slender and full in the manner of her kind, was gently corrugated like the bark of a young tree, and her toes were rootlike. She approached Tandy, who was the most human of the group. "Please—do you know where Castle Roogna is?"

"I tried to reach Castle Roogna a year ago," Tandy said. "But I got lost. I think Smash knows, though."

"Oh, I wouldn't ask an ogre!" the nymph exclaimed.

"He's a halfway tame ogre," Tandy assured her. "He doesn't eat many nymphs."

Smash was getting used to these slights. He waited patiently for the nymph to gain confidence, then answered her question as well as he could. "I have been to Castle Roogna. But I'm not going there at the moment, and the way is difficult. It is roughly west of here."

"I'll find it somehow," the nymph said. "I've got to." She faced west.

"Now wait," Tandy protested, as Smash had suspected she would. The girl had sympathy enough to overflow all

Xanth! "You can't get there alone! You could easily get
lost or gobbled up. Why don't you travel with us until we
find someone else who is going there?"

"But you're going north!" the nymph protested.

"Yes. But we travel safely, because of Smash." Tandy
indicated him again. "Nobody bothers an ogre."

"There is that," the nymph agreed. "I don't want to
bother him myself." She considered, seeming somewhat
tired. "I could help you find food and water. I'm good at
that sort of thing. I'm a hamadryad."

"Oh, a tree-nymph!" the Siren exclaimed. "I should have
realized. What are you doing out of your tree?"

"It's a short story. Let me find you a place to eat and
rest, and I will tell it."

The dryad kept her promise. Soon they were ensconced in
a glade beside a large eggplant whose ripe eggs had been
hard-boiled by the sun. Nearby was a sodapond that sparkled effervescently. They sat in a circle cracking open
eggs, using the shells to dip out sodawater. Proper introductions were made, and the dryad turned out to be named
Fireoak, after her tree.

She was, despite her seeming youth, over a century old.
All her life had been spent with her fireoak tree, which
had sprouted from a fireacorn the year she came into
being. She had grown with it, as hamadryads did, protecting it and being protected by it. Then a human village had
set up nearby, and villagers had come out to cut down the
tree to build a firehouse. Fireoak made fine fire-resistant
wood, the dryad explained; its own appearance of burning
was related to Saint Elmo's fire, an illusion of burning that
made it stand out beautifully and discouraged predatory
bugs except for fireants. In vain had the dryad protested
that the cutting of the oak would kill both it and her; the
villagers wanted the wood. So she had taken advantage of
the full moon that night to weave a lunatic fringe that
shrouded the tree, hiding it from them. But that would last
only a few days; when the moon shrank to a crescent, so
would the fringe, betraying the tree's location. She had to
accomplish her mission before then.

"But how can a trip to Castle Roogna help?" John
asked. "They use wood there, too, don't they?"

"The King is there!" Fireoak replied. "I understand he is an environmentalist. He protects special trees."

"It is true," Smash agreed. "He protects rare monsters, too." Now for the first time he realized the probable basis for King Trent's tolerance of an ogre family near Castle Roogna: they were rare wilderness specimens. "He always looks for the solution of least ecological damage."

The dryad looked at him curiously. "You certainly don't talk like an ogre!"

"He blundered into an Eye Queue vine," Tandy explained. "It cursed him with smartness."

"How are you able to survive away from your tree?" the Siren asked. "I thought no hamadryad could leave for more than a moment."

"That's what I thought," Fireoak said. "But when death threatened my tree, desperation gave me extraordinary strength. For my tree I can do what I must. I feel terribly insecure, however. My soul is the tree."

Tandy and Smash jumped. The analogy was too close for comfort. It was no easy thing to be separated from one's soul.

"I know the feeling," the Siren said. "I lived all my life in one lake. But I suddenly realized that it had become a desolate place for a lone mermaid. So I am looking for a better lake. But I do miss my original lake, for it contains all my life's experience, and I wonder whether it misses me, too."

"How will you know the new lake won't be desolate for you, too?" Fireoak asked.

"It won't be if it has the right merman in it."

The dryad blushed, her face for an instant showing the color of the fire of her tree. "Oh."

"You're a hundred years old—and you have no experience with men?" Tandy asked.

"Well, I'm a dryad," Fireoak said defensively. "We just don't have much to do with men—only with trees."

"What sort of experience have you had?" the Siren asked Tandy.

"A demon—he—I'd rather not discuss it." It was Tandy's turn to blush. "Anyway, my father is a man."

"Most fathers are," the Siren said.

"Mine isn't!" Smash protested. "My father is an ogre."

She ignored that. "I inherited my legs from my father, my tail from my mother. She was not a true woman, but he was a true man."

"You mean human men really do have, uh, dealings with mermaids?" Tandy asked.

"Human men have dealings with any maid they can catch," the Siren said with a wry smile. "I understand my mother wasn't hard to catch; my father was a very handsome man. But he had to leave when my sister the Gorgon was born."

After a pause, Fireoak resumed her story. "So if I can just talk to the King and get him to save my tree, everything will be all right."

"What about the other trees?" John asked.

Fireoak looked blank. "Other trees?"

"The other ones the villagers are cutting down. Maybe they don't have dryads to speak for them, but they don't deserve destruction."

"I never thought of that," Fireoak said. "I suppose I should put in a word at Castle Roogna for them, too. It would be no bad thing to lobby for the trees."

They found good locations in the trees and settled down for the night. Smash spread himself out on the glade ground; no one would bother him. His head was near the liquidly flowing trunk of a water oak Fireoak had chosen; he overheard the hamadryad's muted sobbing. Evidently her separation from her beloved home tree was harder on her than she showed by day, and the threat to that tree was no distant concern. Smash hoped he could find a way to help her. If he had to, he could go and stand guard over her tree himself. But he didn't know how long that would take. He didn't want to delay his own mission too long, lest the time for the Good Magician's Answer should run out. There was also the matter of the gourd-coffin's lien on his soul; anything he had to do, he had better get done within three months. Already he felt not quite up to snuff, as if part of his soul had been leached away, taking some of his strength with it.

Next day the five of them marched north. The land leveled out, but hazards remained. Tandy blundered into a chokecherry bush, and Smash had to rip the entire plant out of the ground before its vines stopped choking her. Farther along they encountered a power plant, whose branches swelled out into strange angular configurations and hummed with power; woe betide the creature who blundered into that!

Around midday they discovered a lovely vegetable tree, on whose branches grew cabbages, beans, carrots, tomatoes, and turnips, all in fine states of ripeness. Here were all the ingredients for an excellent salad! But as Smash approached it, Tandy grew nervous. "I smell a rat," she said, sniffing the air. "There are big rats down in the caves where I live; I know their odor well. They always mean trouble."

Smash sniffed. Sure enough, there was the faint aroma of rats. What were they doing here?

"I smell it, too," John said. "I hate rats. But where are they?"

The Siren was walking around the tree. "Somewhere in or near the vegetable tree," she announced. "I fear this plant is not entirely what it appears."

Fireoak approached it. "Let me check. I'm good with trees." She was showing no sign of the agony of her separation from her tree, but Smash knew it remained. Her night in a tree must have restored her somewhat, though of course it wasn't *her* tree.

The hamadryad stood close to the vegetable tree. Slowly she touched a leaf. "This is a normal leaf," she said. Then she touched a potato—and one of its eyes blinked. "Get away from here!" Fireoak screamed. "It's a rat!"

Then the fruits and vegetables exploded into action. Each one sprouted legs, tail, and snout and dropped to the ground. A major swarm of rats had camouflaged itself by masquerading as vegetables, luring the unwary into contact—but the smell had given them away. Once a rat, always a rat, by the smell of it.

The Siren, Tandy, and John scurried back in time to avoid the first surge of the rat-race. But Fireoak stood too close. The beasties swarmed around her, biting at her legs, causing her to trip and fall.

Smash leaped across, swooping down with one hand to lift the hamadryad clear of the ground. Several rats came up with her, chewing savagely at her barklike skin. She screamed and tried to brush them off, but they clung tenaciously and bit at her hands.

Smash shook her, but hesitated to do it vigorously enough to fling away the rats, lest it hurt her. As it was, bits of bark and leaf were flying off. Smash had to pinch the rats off one by one, and their claws and teeth left scratches on the dryad's body. By the time the last was gone, she was in an awful state, oozing sap from several scrapes. The swarm of rats surrounded Smash and tried to bite his feet and climb his hairy legs.

Smash stomped ferociously, shaking the glade and crushing several rats with each stomp. But there were hundreds of the little monsters, coming at him from every direction, moving rapidly. They threatened to get on him no matter how fast he stomped. He didn't dare set the dryad down, lest the same fate befall her. His great strength hardly availed against these relatively puny enemies.

"Get away from him!" Tandy screamed from a safe distance. "Leave him alone, you rats!" She seemed really angry. It was almost as if she were trying to defend him from the enemy; that, of course, was a ludicrous reversal of their situation, yet it touched him oddly.

Smash stomped away from the tree, but the rats stayed with him. In order to run he would have to do two things: move the dryad back and forth as his arms pumped and flee a known danger. The one seemed physically hazardous to another person, while the other was emotionally distasteful. So he moved slowly, stamping, while the rats began climbing his legs.

Then Tandy's arm shot out as if hurling a rock. Her face was red, her teeth bared, her body rigid, as if she were in a state of absolute fury—but there was no rock in her hand. She was throwing nothing.

Something exploded at Smash's feet. He was knocked off them, barely catching his balance. All around him the rats turned belly-up, stunned.

He stared at the carnage, standing still because his legs were numb. He set down the hamadryad, who stepped daintily over the bodies. "What happened?"

Tandy sounded abashed. "I threw a tantrum."

Smash left the twitching rats and went to join her. His

feet felt as if they were nothing but bones, with the flesh
melted off, though this was not the case. "That's a spell?"

"That's bad temper, my talent," she said, eyes downcast.
"When I get mad, I throw a tantrum. Sometimes it does a
lot of damage. I'm sorry; I should have controlled my emo-
tion."

"Sorry?" Smash said, bewildered, looking back at the
ruin of the rat-swarm. "That's a wonderful talent!"

"Oh, sure," she replied with irony.

"My mother had a similar talent. Of course, she was a
curse-fiend; they all throw curses."

"Maybe I have curse-fiend ancestry," Tandy said sourly.
"My father Crombie came from a long line of soldiers, and
they do get around quite a bit."

Now the others came up. "You did that, Tandy?" Fireoak asked. "You saved me a lot of misery! If Smash had
put me down amidst those awful rats, or if they had
climbed up him and gotten to me, as they were trying to—"
She winced, feeling her wounds. She was obviously in
considerable discomfort.

"That's an extremely useful talent for the jungles of
Xanth," the Siren said.

"You really think so?" Tandy asked, brightening. "I always understood it wasn't nice to be destructive."

"It isn't?" Smash asked, surprised.

Then they all laughed. "Sometimes perhaps it is," the
Siren concluded.

They found some genuine vegetables for lunch, then resumed the march. But soon they heard a ferocious snuf-
fling and snorting ahead, low to the ground. "Oh, that
might be a dragon with a cold," John said worriedly. "I
can't say I really like dragons; they're too hot."

"I will go see," Smash said. He discovered he was rather
enjoying this journey. Violence was a natural part of his nature—but now he had people to protect, so there was a
certain added justification to it. It was more meaningful to
bash a dragon to save a collection of pretty little lasses than
it was to do it merely for its own sake. The Eye Queue
caused him to ponder the meaning of the things he did,
and so it helped to have at least a little meaning present. At
such time as he got free of the curse, he could forget about
these inconvenient considerations.

He rounded a brush-bush and faced the snorting monster, hamfists at the ready—and paused, dismayed.

It was no dragon. It was a small oink, with a squared-off snout and a curled-up tail. But it snorted like a huge fire-breathing monster.

Smash sighed. He picked up the oink by the tail and tossed it into the brush. "All clear," he called.

The others appeared. "It's gone?" Tandy asked. "But we didn't hear any battle."

"It was only a short snort," the ogre said, disgusted. He had so looked forward to a good fight!

"Another person might have represented it as the most tremendous of dragons," the Siren said.

"Why?"

"To make it seem he had done a most valiant deed."

"Why do that?" Smash asked, perplexed.

She smiled. "Obviously you don't suffer from that syndrome."

"I suffer from the Eye Queue curse."

"Cheer up, Smash," Tandy said. "We're bound to encounter a real dragon sometime."

"Yes," the ogre agreed, cheering as directed. After all, the thing to do with disappointments was to rise above them. The Eye Queue told him that.

"Speaking of dragons," John said, "there is a story that circulates among fairies about dragons and their parts, and I've always wondered whether it was true."

"I've met some dragons," Smash said. "What's the story?"

"That if a dragon's ear is taken off, you can listen to it and hear wondrous things."

Smash scratched his head. Several fleas jumped off, startled. Since his skull no longer heated much when he tried to think, the fleas had no natural control. "I never tried that."

"It must be sort of hard to get a dragon's ear," Tandy remarked. "I doubt they part with them willingly."

Fireoak considered. "There are stories the mockingbirds tell, to mock the ignorant. They would nest in my tree sometimes and talk of marvelous things, and I never knew how much to believe. One did once mention such a quality of a dragon's ear. It said the ear would twitch when anything of interest to the holder was spoken anywhere, so one would know to listen. But often the news was not pleasant, for dragons have ears for bad news. And as Tandy says, dragons' ears are very hard for normal people to come by."

"Next dragon I slay, I will save an ear," Smash said, intrigued.

They continued north till dusk, with only minor adventures, avoiding tangle trees, clinging vines, and strangler figs, scaring off tiger lilies and dogwood, and ignoring the trickly illusions spawned by assorted other plants. Swarms of biting bugs converged, but Smash blew them away in his usual fashion with selected roars. By nightfall the party was close to something significant, but Smash couldn't remember what.

They located a forest of black, blue, and white ash trees whose shedding ashes covered the forest floor. Any recent footprints showed; and, because each color of tree spread its ashes at a different hour, it was possible to know how recently any creature had passed. White prints were the most recent, blue prints were older and somehow more intricate, with maplike traceries on them, and black prints dated from the night. Some ashes had been hauled, but no dragons or other dangerous creatures had been here in the past few hours.

Amidst this forest was a handsome cottonwood that provided cotton for beds for them all. "I always thought camping out would be uncomfortable," Tandy remarked. "But this is getting to be fun. Now if only I knew where I was going!"

"You don't know?" the Siren asked, surprised.

"Good Magician Humfrey answered my Question by telling me to travel with Smash," Tandy said. "So I'm traveling. It's a pretty good trip, and I'm learning a lot and meeting nice new people, but that's not my Answer. Smash is looking for the Ancestral Ogres, but I doubt that's what I'm looking for."

"I understand the Good Magician is getting old," the Siren said.

"He's pretty old," Tandy agreed. "But he knows an awful lot, and your sister the Gorgon is making him young again."

"She would," the Siren said. "I am jealous of her power

over men. In my heyday I used to summon men to my isle, but she always took them away, and, of course, they never looked at other women after she was through with them."

Because they had turned to stone, Smash knew. The fact was, the Gorgon had been as lonely as the Siren, despite her devastating power. The Gorgon had been smitten by the first man who could nullify her talent, Magician Humfrey, so she had gone to him with a Question: would he marry her? He had made her serve a year as housemaid and guardian in his castle before giving her his Answer: he would. Evidently that was the sort of man it required to capture the heart of the Gorgon. Smash understood that their wedding, officiated by Prince Dor when he was temporary King, had been the most remarkable occasion of the year, attended by all the best monsters. Smash's father Crunch had been there, and Tandy's mother Jewel. By all accounts, the marriage was a reasonably happy one, considering the special nature of its parties.

"I wonder what it is like to be with a man?" Fireoak said, in a half-wistful question. Her injuries of the day had fatigued her greatly, perhaps making her depressed. Evidently their conversation of the preceding night had remained on her mind.

"My friends always told me men were difficult to get along with," John said. "A girl can't live with them, and she can't live without them."

"Well, I've tried living without," the Siren said. "I'm ready to try with. Good and ready! At least it shouldn't be dull. First pool I find with an available merman, watch out!"

"Poor merman!" the fairy said.

"Oh, I'm sure he'll deserve whatever I give him. I don't think he'll have cause to complain, any more than Magician Humfrey has with my sister. We draw on similar lore."

"All girls do. But it seems terribly original to each innocent man." There was general laughing agreement.

"You speak as if no man is here," Tandy said, sounding faintly aggrieved.

"There's a man here, listening to our secrets?" Fireoak cried, alarmed.

"Smash."

There was another general titter. "Don't be silly," John said. "He's an ogre."

"Can't an ogre also be a man?"

The tittering subsided. "Yes, of course, dear," the Siren said reassuringly. "And a good one, too. We take Smash too much for granted. None of us could travel freely here without his formidable protection. We ought to thank him, instead of imposing on him."

Smash lay still. He had not intended to feign sleep, but thought it best not to join in this conversation. It was interesting enough without his participation. He had not known about this conspiracy of the females of Xanth, but now he could remember how he had seen it in action when Princess Irene snared Prince Dor, and even when his mother pacified his father. It did seem that the distaff knew things that the males did not and used them cleverly to achieve their desires.

"What's a lady ogre like?" Tandy asked.

"One passed my tree once," Fireoak said. "She was huge and hairy and had a face like a bowl of overcooked mush someone had sat on. I never saw anything so ugly in all my life."

"Well, she was an ogress," the Siren said. "They have different standards of beauty. You can bet they know what bull-ogres like, though! I suppose an ogre wants a wife who can knock down her own trees for firewood—no offense, Fireoak—and kill her own griffins for stew so he doesn't have to interrupt his dragon hunting for trifles."

They laughed again, and their chatter meandered across other femalish subjects, recipes, prettifying spells, jungle gossip, and such, until they all drifted off to sleep. But the images they had conjured enchanted Smash's imagination. An ogress who could knock down her own trees and slay her own griffins—what an ideal mate! And a face like squashed mush—what sheerest beauty! How wonderful it would be to encounter such a creature!

But the only ogress he had met was his mother—who wasn't really an ogress, but a curse-fiend acting the part. She acted very well, but when she forgot her makeup, her face no longer looked like mush. Smash had always pretended not to notice how distressingly fair her face and form became in those unguarded moments, so as not to embarrass her. The truth was, had his mother the actress chosen to pass among females like these Smash now traveled with, she could have done so without causing alarm. And, of course, as soon as she prepared herself, she was the compleat ogress again, as brutish and mean as any ogre could ask for. Certainly his father Crunch loved her and would move mountains for her, despite her secret shame of an un-ogrish origin. One of those mountains had been moved to rest near their home so that she could climb it and look out across Xanth when the mood took her.

At last Smash slept. He still wasn't used to doing so much thinking, and it tired him despite the amplification the Eye Queue provided. He had never had to work things out so rationally before, or to see the interrelationships among diverse things. Well, one day he would win free of the curse and be a true brute of an ogre again. He slept.

Chapter 6. Dire Strait

Next morning they came up against the barrier Smash had been unable to remember. It was a huge crevice in the earth, a valley so deep and steep that they shrank back from it. It extended east and west; there seemed to be no end to it, no way around.

"How can we go north?" Tandy asked plaintively. "This awful cleft is impossible!"

"Now I remember it," Smash said. "It crosses all of Xanth. Down near Castle Roogna there are magic bridges."

"Castle Roogna?" Fireoak asked. She looked wan, as if she had not been eating well, though she had been provided with all she wanted. Smash suspected her absence from her beloved tree was like an ordinary person's need for water. She would have to return to it soon, or die. She was suffering from deprivation of soul, and would soon become as Tandy had been within the gourd, if not helped. Her rat wounds only aggravated the condition, hastening the process.

"That's right," Tandy said brightly. "If this crack passes near Castle Roogna, you can follow it there! Your problem is solved."

"Yes, solved," the hamadryad agreed wanly.

Now the Siren noticed her condition. "Dear, are you well?"

"As well as I can be," the dryad replied gamely. "The rest of you must go on across the chasm; I will find my own way to Castle Roogna."

"I think you have been away from your tree too long," the Siren said. "You had better return to it, to restore your strength, before attempting the long trip to Castle Roogna."

"But there is not time!" Fireoak protested. "The moon is waning, night by night; soon the lunatic fringe will sunder, and my tree will be exposed."

"Yet if you perish on the way to see the King, you can do your tree no good," the Siren pointed out.

"It is indeed a dire strait," the dryad agreed, sinking to the ground.

The Siren looked at Smash. "Where is your tree, dear?" she asked Fireoak.

"North of the chasm. I had forgotten about—"

"But how did you cross?"

"A firebird helped me. Because I am associated with a fireoak. But the bird is long gone now."

"I think we must nevertheless cross over soon and return you to your tree," the Siren said. Again she looked meaningfully at Smash.

"We will go with you, to guard your tree," Smash said, catching on.

Tandy clapped her hands. "Oh, how wonderful to think of that, Smash! We can help her!"

Smash said nothing. The Siren had really thought of it, but he was amenable. They couldn't let Fireoak perish from neglect—and she surely would, otherwise. They could certainly guard her tree from harm; no one would come near an ogre.

But first they had to get to the tree—and that meant crossing the chasm—in a hurry. How were they going to do that?

"You chipped steps in the prints-of-wails mountain," Tandy suggested.

"But that was slow," the Siren said. "It could take several days. We must cross today."

They stared into the chasm, baffled. There seemed to be no way to cross it rapidly—yet they had to, somehow. For now all could see how the hamadryad was failing. Fireoak's surface had turned from lightly corrugated skin to deeply serrated bark, from young nymph to old tree trunk. Her green hair was wilting, and the tinge of red was turning black. Her fire would soon be out.

"There must be a path," John said. "If we just spread out and look, surely we'll find it."

That was a positive idea. They commenced their search for the path.

There was the sound of galloping hooves from the west. The group ran back together, and Smash faced the sound, ready for whatever might come.

Two centaurs appeared, moving rapidly. One was male, the other female. Centaurs could be good news or bad, depending. Smash was conscious of his orange jacket and steel gauntlets, gifts of the centaurs of Centaur Isle, but knew that there could be rogue centaurs in this wilderness. What were these two doing here?

Then Smash recognized them. "Chet! Chem!" he exclaimed.

The two drew up, panting, a light sheen of sweat on their human and equine portions. Smash embraced each in turn, then turned to make introductions. "These are friends of mine from the Castle Roogna region." He faced the other way. "And these are friends of mine from all over Xanth."

"Smash!" the filly centaur exclaimed. "What happened to your rhymes?"

"I'm cursed with intelligence, among other things."

"Yes, I can see the other things," Chet said, contemplating the assorted females. "I never knew you were interested."

"We sort of imposed on him," Tandy said.

"Yes, Smash is impose-able," Chem agreed. She was young, so lacked the imposing proportions of her mother; the last time Smash had seen her, she had been playing children's galloping games. In another year or so she would be looking for a mate. He wondered why she was not still in centaur-schooling, as her mother was very strict about education. "We came here to do the same."

"The same?" Smash asked. "We're traveling north."

"Yes," Chem said. "Good Magician Humfrey told me where to intercept you. You see, I'm doing a thesis on the geography of uncharted Xanth, completing my education, but my folks won't let me travel alone through that region, so—"

"And so I escorted my little sister this far," Chet finished. He was a handsome centaur, with noble features, a fine coat, and excellent muscles on both his human and equine portions. But a purple scar marred his left shoulder, where a wyvern had once bitten him, causing serious illness. "I know she'll be safe with you, Smash. You're a big ogre now."

"Safe? We're about to try to cross this gulf!" Smash protested. "And we don't know how."

"Oh, yes. The Gap Chasm. I brought you a rope." Chet presented a neat coil. "Humfrey said you would need it."

"A rope!" Suddenly their way down into the chasm was clear. Centaur rope was always strong enough for its purpose.

"I'll help get you down," Chet said. "But I'm not supposed to go myself. I have to return immediately to Castle Roogna with a message or two. What's the message?"

Smash's curse of intelligence enabled him to catch on. "A village is about to cut down a fireoak tree for timber. The tree's hamadryad will die. The King must save the tree."

"I'll tell him," Chet agreed. "Where is it?"

Smash turned to Fireoak, who sat listlessly on the ground. "Where is your tree?"

The hamadryad made a feeble motion with her hand.

"This is no good," Chet said. "Chem, let's use your map."

The filly walked over to Fireoak. "Show me on my picture," she said.

An image formed between them. It was a contour map of the Land of Xanth, a long peninsula with the Gap Chasm across its center and the ocean around it. "Show me where the tree is," Chem repeated.

Fireoak looked, slowly orienting on the scene. "There," she said, pointing to a region near the northern rim of the Gap.

Chem nodded. "There is a human village there, just setting up. That's already on my chart." She looked at her brother. "Got it, Chet?"

"Got it, Chem," the male centaur replied. "You always do make the scene. Smash, the moment you're down in the Gap, I'll gallop back and tell the King. I'm sure he'll handle the business about the tree. But it will take me a couple days to get there, so you'll have to protect the tree until then." He glanced about. "Was there any other message? It seems there should be more than one."

The people looked around at each other. Finally Tandy said, "I'd like to send a greeting to my father Crombie, if that's all right."

Chet tapped his head, making a mental note. "One greeting to Crombie from daughter. Got it." He looked more carefully at Tandy. "He always bragged he had a cute daughter. I see he was correct."

Tandy blushed. She hadn't known her father had said that about her.

They tied the rope to the trunk of a steelwood tree. Chem insisted on going down first. "That will prove the rope is safe," she explained. "Even Smash doesn't weigh more than I do." Of course she was correct, for though her human portion was girlishly slender, her equine portion was as solid as a horse.

She backed down, her four hooves bracing against the steep side of the chasm. The rope looped once about her small human waist, just below her moderate bosom, and she used her hands to give herself slack by stages. When she got down to where the slope leveled out enough to enable her to stand, she released the rope.

The Siren went down next, having less trouble because she had so much less mass. Then Tandy, followed by the fairy, who fluttered her wings to make herself even lighter than she was. Smash then made a harness out of the end of the rope, set Fireoak in it, and stood on the brink to lower her carefully to Chem's waiting arms.

Finally Smash himself descended, merely applying one gauntlet to the rope and sliding rapidly down. Chet undid the upper end from the steelwood tree and dropped it into the chasm. They would need the rope again on the north slope.

"I'm on my way with one and a half messages," Chet called, and galloped off. "Remember: two days."

The slope continued to level, until they stood at the base. Here grass grew, but no trees. It was pleasant enough, and the north slope was visible a short distance away. They walked across, studying the rise for the most suitable place to ascend.

It certainly wasn't good for climbing with a party of girls. The ground sloped gently up to a corner; from there the cliff went almost straight up a dizzying height, beyond the reach of the rope, even if there were any place or way to anchor it.

"We must do what we started to do before," the Siren said. "Spread out and look for a suitable place to climb."

"I believe there are paths here and there," Chem said. "I don't have them on my map, because few people remember the Gap Chasm; it has an enduring forget-spell on it. But there has been enough travel in Xanth so that people have to have crossed it, and not just at the magic bridges."

"A forget-spell," the Siren said. "How interesting. That accounts for Fireoak's forgetting it. And I'm sure Smash has been here before, too. I hope that's the extent of the spell."

"What do you mean?" Tandy asked.

"Oh, I'm just a worrier over nothing."

"I don't think so," Tandy said. "If there's any danger, you should warn us."

The Siren sighed. "You're right. Yet if there is danger here, it's too late for us to avoid it, since we're already here. It's only that once I heard something about a big dragon in a chasm—and this is a chasm. It would be hard to escape a monster here. But of course that's far-fetched."

"Let's look for good hiding places, too," Tandy said. "Just in case."

"Just in case," John agreed, overhearing. "Oh, suddenly I don't really like this place!"

"So we must try to get out of this chasm as fast as we can," Smash said, though the prospect of danger did not bother him. There really had not been much violence on this journey.

Chem trotted east, while Smash lumbered west, since these were the two fastest movers of the group. The girl, Siren, and fairy spread out in between. They left the hamadryad in the shade of a bush, since she was now too weak to walk.

The cliff face changed, sloping at different angles and different heights, but Smash found nothing that would really help. It looked as if he would have to bash out a stairway of sorts, tedious as that would be. But could he get the party up that way within two days, let alone in time to save the hamadryad and her tree?

There was a commotion to the east. Chem was galloping back, her lovely brown hair-mane flinging out, tail swishing nervously. "Dragon! Dragon!" she cried breathlessly.

The Siren's concern had been justified! "I'll stop it," Smash said enthusiastically, charging east.

"No! It's big. It's the Gap Dragon!"

Now Smash remembered. The Gap Dragon ranged the Gap Chasm, trapping and consuming any creatures foolish enough to stray here. The forget-spell had deceived him again. The monster really profited from that spell, since no one remembered the danger. But it was coming back to him now. This was a formidable menace.

The Siren, Tandy, and John were running west. Behind them whomped the monster. It was long and low, with a triple pair of stubby legs. Its scales were metallic, glistening in the sunlight, and clouds of steam puffed out of its nostrils. Its body was the thickness of a good-sized tree trunk, but exceedingly limber. It moved by elevating one section and whomping it forward, then following through with another, because its legs were too short for true running. But the clumsy-seeming mechanism sufficed for considerable velocity. In a moment the Gap Dragon would overtake the Siren.

Smash lumbered to the fray. He stood much taller than the dragon, but it reached much longer than he. Thus they did not come together with a satisfying crash. The dragon scooted right under Smash, intent on the nymphlike morsel before it.

The ogre screeched to a stop, literally, his calloused hamfeet churning up mounds of rubble. He bent forward and grabbed the dragon's tail as it slid westward. He lifted it up, holding it tightly in both hands. This would halt the monster!

Alas, he had underestimated the dragon. The creature whomped onward. The tail lost its slack—but such was the mass and impetus of the monster that it wrenched the ogre into a somersault. He flipped right over, hanging on to that tail, and landed with a whomp of his own on his back—on the dragon's tail.

But Smash's own mass was not inconsiderable. The

shock of his landing traveled along the body of the dragon
in a ripple. When the ripple passed a set of legs, they were
wrenched momentarily off the ground; when it arrived at
the head, the mouth snapped violently. The jaws, reaching
close to the desperately fleeing Siren, fell short.

Now Smash had the Gap Dragon's baleful attention. The
dragon let out a yowl of discomfort and whipped its head
around. Its tail, pinned under the ogre, thrashed about, so
that Smash had trouble regaining his feet.

The dragon's neck curved in a sharp U-turn, bonelessly
supple. The head traveled smoothly back along the length
of the body. The monster hardly needed its legs for this
sort of maneuver. In a moment the spreading jaws were at
Smash's own head, ready to take it in.

The ogre, still flat on his back, stabbed upward with a
gauntleted fist. The jaws closed on it, but the fist continued
inexorably, punching past the slurp-wet tongue and into the
back of the throat. The dragon's head was so large that
Smash's whole arm was engulfed—but that strike in the
throat caused the monster to gag, and the jaws parted
again. Smash recovered his arm before it got chomped.

The ogre sat up, but remained in the midst of the coils
of the dragon. The two grotesque heads of ogre and dragon
faced each other, snout to snout. Smash realized that this
time he had gotten himself into an encounter whose outcome he could not know. The Gap Dragon was his match.

Delightful! For the first time since attaining his full
strength, Smash could test his ultimate. But at the moment
they were all tangled up in an ineffective configuration,
unable to fight decisively.

Smash made a face, bulging his eyes and stretching his
mouth wide open. "Yyrwll!" he yyrwlled.

The Gap Dragon made a face back, wrinkling up its
snout horrendously and crossing its eyes so far that the
pupils exchanged places. "Rrooarw!" it rrooarwed.

Smash made a worse face, swallowing his nose and part
of his low forehead. "Ggrummf!" he ggrummffed.

The dragon went him one better, perhaps two better,
swallowing its snout up past the ears and partway down its
neck. "Ssstth!" it ssstthed.

The monster was outdoing him. Petulantly, Smash bit
into a rock and spit out a stream of gravel. The dragon's

teeth were pointed, so it could not match that. Instead, it hoisted a petard of steam at him, the greasy ball of vapor curling the hairs of his face and clogging his nostrils.

So much for the niceties. Now the real action commenced. Smash threw himself into the sheer joy of combat, the fundamental delight of every true ogre. It had been some time since he had crunched bones in earnest. Of course, this dragon was mostly boneless, but the principle remained.

He punched the dragon in the snoot. This sort of punch could put a fist-sized hole in an ironwood tree, but the dragon merely gave way before the force of it and was only slightly bloodied. Then the dragon struck back, snapping sidewise at Smash's arm. That sort of bite could lop a mouthful of flesh from a behemoth, but the gauntlet extended back far enough to catch the edge of the bite and strike sparks from the teeth.

Then Smash boxed the dragon's right ear with his left fist—and the ear squirted right off the skull and flew out of sight. The dragon winced; that smarted! But the monster hardly needed that ear, and came back with a blast of steam that cooked the outer layer of the ogre's head. Smash's thick skull stopped the heat from penetrating to the Eye Queue-corrupted brain—more was the pity, he thought.

So much for the second exchange of amenities. Smash had had slightly the better of it this time, but the fight was only warming up. Now the pace intensified.

Smash took hold of the dragon's upper jaw with one hand, the lower jaw with another, and slowly forced the two apart. The dragon resisted, and its jaw muscles were mighty, well leveraged, and experienced, but it could not directly withstand the full brute force of a concentrating ogre. Slowly the jaws separated.

The dragon whipped its body about. In a moment the sinuous length of it was wrapped about the ogre's torso, engulfing him anew. While Smash forced open the jaws, the dragon tightened its coils, constricting him.

All this was in slow motion, yet it was a race. Would Smash rip the head apart first, or would the dragon squeeze the juice out of him? The answer was uncertain. Smash was having trouble breathing; he was beginning to lose strength. It seemed to him that this should not be happening, or at least not this fast. But the dragon's jaws were now quite far apart, and should soon break.

Neither ogre nor dragon would give. They remained, their strength in balance. The jaws were on the verge of breaking, the torso on the verge of smothering. Who would succumb first? It occurred to Smash that he might break open the dragon's jaw, but be unable to extricate himself from its convulsed coils and smother because he couldn't breathe. Or the dragon might crush him—but suffer a broken jaw in Smash's dying effort. Both could lose this encounter.

In the good old days before the Eye Queue vine had fallen on him, Smash would not have wasted tedious thought on such a thing; he would merely have bashed on through, to kill and/or be killed, hardly caring which. Now he was cursed with the notion of meaning. To what point was this violence if neither participant survived?

It was discomfiting and un-ogrish, but Smash found he had to change his tactic. This one had little promise of success, since it would not free him from the serpent's toils. He was in a dire strait, and bulling ahead would only worsen it.

He drew the dragon's head forward, toward his own face. The dragon thought this meant Smash was weakening, and went forward eagerly. In a moment, the dragon believed, it could chomp the ogre's face off. Its breath steamed out, its woodsmoke fragrance toasting Smash's skin. He tried to sneeze, but was unable to inhale because of the constriction in which he was held.

Sure of victory now, the dragon cranked its jaws marginally closer together and lunged. Smash deflected the thrust as much as he could and jerked his head to the side. The dragon's head plunged down as Smash's hands let go—and the huge wedge-teeth chomped savagely on the uppermost coil. This was a device Smash had used on the tangle tree with good effect.

It took the Gap Dragon a moment to catch on. Meanwhile, it chewed. It surely felt the bite, but did not yet realize that this was its own doing, or that its teeth had not contacted ogre flesh. It took a while for the difference in taste to register. The dragon wrenched its supposed prey

upward, driving the teeth in deeper. The coil loosened, giving Smash half a gasp of breath.

Then at last the dragon realized what it was doing. Its
jaws began to open, to free itself from its own bite and to
emit a honk of sheer pain and frustration—but Smash's
two gauntleted hamhands came down on either side of it,
clasping the snout, pressing it firmly closed on the meat.
The jaw muscles were weaker this way; the dragon could
not release its bite. Still, the ogre could not use his hands
for further attack, for the moment he let go, the jaws
would open. It was another position of stalemate.

Blood welled out around the dragon's lower fangs and
dripped off its chin, coating Smash's gauntlet. The fluid
was a deep purple hue, thick and gooey, smelling of ashes
and carrion. It probably had caustic properties, but the
gauntlet protected Smash's flesh, as it had when he held
the basilisk. The centaur gifts were serving him well.

Now it was the dragon's turn to scheme. Dragons were
not the brightest creatures of Xanth; but, as with ogres,
their brains were largely in their muscles, and they were
cunning fighters. The dragon knew it could get nowhere
unless it freed itself from its own bite, and knew that its
own coils anchored the ogre in place so that he could put
his clamp on that bite. By and by, it realized that if it
released the ogre, the ogre would lack anchorage and could
then be thrown off. So the dragon began laboriously uncoil-
ing.

Smash held on, gasping more deeply as the constriction
abated. His strategy was getting him free—but it would
free the dragon, too. This fight was a long way from over!

At last the coils were gone. The dragon wrenched its
forward section away—and Smash's lower hand slipped on
the blood coating it, and he lost his hold.

Now they faced each other again, the dragon with bloodied jaw and little jets of purple goo spurting from the deep
fang-holes in its body, the ogre panting heavily from sore
ribs. On the surface Smash had had the better of this
round, but inside he doubted it. His rib cage was made of
ogre's bones; nevertheless, it was hurting. Something had
been bent if not broken. He was no longer in top fighting
condition.

The dragon evidently had found the ogre to be stiffer

competition than anticipated. It made a feint at Smash, and
Smash raised a fist. Then the dragon dived abruptly back,
as if fleeing. Suspicious, Smash paused—then saw that the
dragon was going after Fireoak the Hamadryad, who was
still lying helplessly on the ground.

This was very bad form. It suggested that Smash was no
longer worth noticing as an opponent. His temper heated
and bent toward the snapping point.

Chem Centaur leaped to Fireoak's defense, intercepting
the dragon before Smash reoriented. She reared, her fore-
hooves flashing in the air, striking at the dragon's snout.
But she could not hope to balk such a monster for long.
The Siren and John were running up to help, but Smash
knew they could only get themselves in trouble.

He grabbed the dragon's tail again, this time bracing
himself firmly against the rocky ground so as not to be
flipped over. The moving body took up the slack again
with a heavy shock that transmitted straight to the ogre's
braced feet. The feet plowed into the ground, throwing up
wakes of dirt and stones, then driving down deeper. When
the dragon finally halted, Smash was braced knee-deep at
an angle in the ground. He was strong, but the dragon had
mass that mere strength couldn't halt instantly.

The dragon's nose had stopped a short distance from the
hamadryad. Infuriated at this balk, the creature turned
again, lunging at the ogre.

Smash exploded out of the ground, kicking dirt in the
dragon's snoot. He reached for the jaws, but this time the
dragon was wise enough to keep its mouth shut; it wanted
no more prying open! It drove at the ogre with sealed jaws,
trying to knock him down before taking a bite.

Smash boxed at the head, denting the metal scales here
and there and rebloodying the smashed ear-socket, but
could do no real damage. The dragon weaved and bobbed,
presenting a tricky target, while gathering itself for some
devastating strike.

The ogre looked toward the assembled girls. "Get away
from here!" he bellowed. He wanted no more distractions
from the main event; one of them was sure to get inciden-
tally gobbled by the dragon.

From the other side Tandy called, "I've found a ledge!

It's out of reach of the dragon! We can use the rope to climb to it while Smash destroys the dragon!"

She had boundless confidence in his prowess! Smash knew he was in the toughest encounter of his life. But he could proceed with greater confidence the moment he knew the girls were safe. He looked where Tandy pointed and saw the ledge, about halfway up the steep slope. There was a pining tree on it, its mournful branches drooping greenly, the sad needles hanging down. They would be able to loop the rope about the trunk of this tree and haul themselves up to it.

Then the dragon, taking advantage of Smash's distraction, leaped at him. The ogre ducked, throwing up a fist in his standard defensive ploy, but the dragon's mass bore him down. The huge metal claws of the foremost set of feet raked at his belly, attempting to dismember him. Smash had to fall on his back to avoid them—and the weight of the dragon landed on him. Now the stubby legs reached out on either side, the claws clutching the earth, anchoring the long body. Smash was pinned.

He tried to get up, but lacked leverage. He reached out to grab a leg, but the dragon cunningly moved it out of reach. Meanwhile, the sinuous body was moving elsewhere along its line, bringing another set of legs to bear. These would soon attack the pinned ogre. It would be easy for these free claws to spear through his flesh repeatedly, and sooner or later they would puncture a vital organ.

But Smash had resources of his own. He reached up to embrace the serpentine segment. He was just able to complet the circuit, his fingers linking above it. Now he had his leverage. He squeezed.

Ogres were notorious for several things: the manner in which their teeth crunched bones into toothpicks, the way their fists pulverized rocks, and the power of their battle embrace. A rock-maple tree would have gasped under the pressure Smash now applied. So did the Gap Dragon. It let out a steam-whistle of anguish.

But its body was flexible and compressible. When it had been squeezed down to half its original diameter, Smash could force it no farther without taking a new grip—and the moment he released his present one, the body would

spring out again. His compression was not enough. The
dragon was in pain, but still able to function; now it was
again bringing its other claws into play. That would be
trouble, for the outsides of Smash's arms were exposed.
They could be clawed to pieces.

He drew on another weapon—his teeth. They did not
compare with those of the dragon, but they were formidable enough in their own fashion. He pretended the under-
belly before him was a huge, tasty bone and started in.

The first chomp netted him only a mouthful of scales.
He spit them out and bit again. This time he reached the
underlayer of reptilian skin, still pretty tough, but no
match for an ogre's teeth. He ripped out a section, exposing
the muscular layer beneath. He sank his teeth into that.

Again the monster whistled with pain. It struggled to
draw back—but Smash's embrace held it firm. The compression made it worse; the ogre's teeth could take in twice
as much actual flesh with each bite.

The dragon's claws ripped out of the ground. It humped
its midsection, lifting Smash into the air. The huge head
swung around, blasting forth steam. Now the ogre had to
let go, for the back of his neck could not withstand much
steam-cooking. He dropped off, spitting out a muscle. It
would have been nice to chew the thing up and swallow it,
but he needed his teeth clear for business, not pleasure.

The dragon was doubly bloodied now, yet still full of
fight. It snorted a voluminous and slightly blood-flecked
cloud of steam, charged Smash—and sheered off at the
last moment, leaving the ogre smiting air with his fists.
The serpentine torso whizzed by faster and faster, until the
tail struck with a hard crack against Smash's chest.

It was quite a smack. Smash was rocked back. But his
orange centaur jacket was made to protect him from physical attack and it withstood the lash of the sharp tail. Otherwise Smash could have been badly gashed, or even cut in
half. The tail, at its extremity, was long and thin, like a
whip, with edges like a feathered blade. Smash wanted no
more of that.

He spied a boulder half buried in the ground. He ripped
it from its mooring and hurled it at the dragon. The dragon
dodged, but Smash threw another, and a third. Eventually
he was bound to score, and the dragon knew it.

The dragon ducked behind a small ridge of rock and disappeared. Smash lobbed a boulder at it without effect. Cautiously he moved up and peered behind the ridge—and found nothing. The dragon was gone.

He bent to study the ground. Ah—there was a hole slanting down—a tunnel the diameter of the dragon. The monster had fled underground!

He dislodged a larger boulder and rolled it to cover the hole. That would seal in the dragon, at least until Tandy and the others could vacate the Gap Chasm. It was too bad he hadn't been able to finish the fight, but it had been an excellent one, and such ironies did occur in the wilds of Xanth.

Then two sets of claws came down from behind him. The dragon had emerged from another hole and ambushed him from the rear! That was what came of getting careless in the enemy's home territory.

Smash tried to turn, but the claws landed on his shoulder and hauled him backward to the opening jaws. This time he could not attack those jaws with his hands; he could not reach them. He was abruptly doomed.

Tandy appeared beside the boulder. "Look out, Smash!" she cried unnecessarily.

"Get away from here!" Smash shouted as he felt the dragon's steam on the back of his neck.

But Tandy's face was all twisted up in terror or horror or anger; her eyes were squeezed almost shut, and her body was stiff. She paid no attention to him. Then her arm moved as she threw something invisible. Smash, realizing her intent almost too late, dropped to his knees, though the talons dug cruelly into his shoulder.

The tantrum brushed over his head, making his fur stand on end. The dragon caught the full brunt of it in the snoot and froze in place, half a jet of steam stuck in one nostril.

Smash turned and stood. The Gap Dragon's eyes were glazed. The monster had been stunned by the tantrum. "Quick, run!" Tandy cried. "It won't hold that dragon long!"

Run? That was hardly the way of an ogre! "You run; I shall bind the dragon."

"You lunkhead!" she protested. "Nothing will hold it long!"

Smash picked up the dragon's whiplike tail. He threaded the tip of it into the smash-ruined ear, through the head, and out the other ear, drawing a length of it through. Then he used a finger to poke a hole in the boulder, and a second hole angling in to meet the first inside the stone. He passed the tail tip in one hole and out the other, exactly as if this were another dragon-head. Then he fashioned an ogre hangknot and tied the tail to itself. "Now I'll go," he said, satisfied.

They walked to the cliff face. Behind them the Gap Dragon revived. It shook its head to clear itself of confusion—and discovered it was tied. It tried to draw back—and the tail pulled taut against the boulder.

"A little puzzle for the dragon," Smash explained. Privately, he was nettled because he had had to have help to nullify the monster; that was not an ogre's way. But the infernal common sense foisted on him by the Eye Queue reminded him that without an ogre the girls would have very little chance to survive and the hamadryad's tree would be cut down. So he beat down his stupid pride and proceeded to the next challenge.

Chem, John, Fireoak, and the Siren rested on the ledge. The rope dangled down carelessly.

"All right, girls, it's over," Tandy called. "Ready for us to come up?"

No one answered. It was as if they were asleep.

"Hey, wake up!" Tandy cried, irritated. "We have to be on our way, and there's a long climb ahead!"

The Siren stirred. "What does it matter?" she asked dolefully.

Smash and Tandy exchanged glances, one cute girl glance for one brute ogre glance. What was this?

"Are you all right, Siren?" Smash called.

The Siren got to her feet, standing precariously near the edge of the ledge. "I'm so sad," she said, wiping a tear. "Life has no joy."

"No joy?" Tandy asked, bewildered. "Smash tied the dragon. We can go on now. That's wonderful!"

"That's nothing," the Siren said. "I will end it all." And she stepped off the ledge.

Tandy screamed. Smash leaped to catch the Siren. Fortunately, she was coming right toward him; all he had to do was intercept her fall and swing her about and set her safely on her feet.

"She tried to kill herself!" Tandy cried, appalled.

Something was definitely wrong. Smash looked up at the pining tree. The other three sat drooping, like the tree itself.

Then he caught on. "The pining tree! It makes people pine!"

"Oh, no!" Tandy lamented. "They've been there too long, getting sadder and sadder. Now they're suicidal!"

"We must get them down from there," Smash said.

The Siren stirred. "Oh, my—I was so sad!"

"You were near the pining tree," Tandy informed her. "We didn't realize what it did."

The Siren mopped up her tear-stained face. "So that was it! That's a crying shame."

"I'll climb up and carry them down," Smash said.

"Then *you'll* get sad," Tandy said. "We don't need a suicidal ogre falling on our heads."

"It does take a while for full effect," the Siren said. "The longer I sat, the sadder I got. It didn't strike all at once."

"That's our answer," Tandy said. "I'll go up and push people off the ledge, and Smash can catch them. Quickly, before I get too sad myself."

"What about Chem?" the Siren asked. "She's too heavy for Smash to catch safely."

"We'll have to lower her on the rope."

They decided to try it. Tandy climbed the rope, picked up the weeping John, and threw her down. Smash caught the fairy with one hand, avoiding contact with her delicate wings. Then Tandy pushed Fireoak off the ledge. Finally she tied the end of the rope about the centaur's waist, passed the rope behind the tree, and forced her to back down while Smash played out the other end of the rope gradually. It was slow, but it worked.

Except for one thing. Tandy remained beside the tree, since the rope was now taken up by the centaur, and the tree was getting to her. She wandered precariously near the edge, her tears flowing. Then she stepped off.

If Smash moved to catch her, he would let Chem fall. If he did not—

He figured it out physically before solving it mentally. He held the rope in his right hand while jumping and reaching out with his left hand. He caught Tandy by her small waist and drew her in to his furry body without letting Chem slip.

Tandy buried her face in his pelt and cried with abandon. He knew it was only the effect of the pining tree, but he felt sorry for her misery. All he could do was hold her.

"That was a nice maneuver, Smash," the Siren said, coming up to take the girl from his arm.

"I couldn't let her fall," he said gruffly.

"Of course you couldn't." But the Siren seemed thoughtful. It was as if she understood something he didn't.

Now they were all down and safe—but unfortunately at the bottom of the Gap Chasm. The Gap Dragon was still twitching, trying to discover a way to free itself without pulling out either its brains or its tail. Which was more important wasn't clear.

John revived. "Oh, my, that was awful!" she exclaimed. "Now I feel so much better, I could just fly!" And she took off, flying in a loop.

"Well, *she* can get out of the chasm," the Siren said.

Smash looked at the fairy, and at the dragon, and at the pining tree. There was a small ironwood tree splitting the difference between the pining tree and the top of the cliff wall. He had an idea. "John, can you fly to the top of the chasm carrying the rope?"

The fairy looked at the rope. "Way too heavy for me."

"Could you catch it and hold it if I hurl the end up to you?"

She inspected it again. "Maybe, if I had something to anchor me," she said doubtfully. "I'm not very strong."

"That ironwood tree."

"I could try."

Smash tied an end of the rope to a rock, then hurled the rock up past the ironwood tree. John flew up and held the rope at the tree. Now Smash walked over to the Gap Dragon, which was still trying to free itself from the boulder without hurting its head or its tail in the process. Smash knocked it on the head with a fist, and it quieted down; the dragon was no longer in fighting condition and couldn't roll with the punch.

Smash untied the tail, disconnected it from the boulder, unthreaded the head, and tied the tip of the tail to the nether end of the rope. Then he dragged the inert dragon to the base of the chasm wall and placed its tail so that it reached well up toward the top.

"Now drop that stone." he called.

The fairy did so. The rock pulled the slack rope up and around the ironwood trunk. When it began to draw on the dragon's tail, the weight of the rope wasn't enough. The fairy flew down and sat on the rock, adding weight, and it dropped down farther. Finally Smash was able to jump and catch hold of it.

John flew back to the ground while Smash hauled the dragon up by the tail. But soon the weight was too much; instead of hauling the dragon up, Smash found himself dangling. This was a matter of mass, not strength.

"We can solve that," Chem said, shaking off her remaining melancholy. She had received a worse dose of pining than the others, perhaps because of her size and because she had been closest to the tree. "Use the boulder for ballast."

Smash rolled the boulder over. He hooked a toe in the hole he had punched in it, then drew on the rope again. This anchorage enabled him to drag the dragon farther up the slope. When it got to the point where both ogre and boulder were dangling in the air, Chem added her considerable weight to the effort by balancing on the boulder and clinging to Smash. "I'll bet you've never been hugged like this before," she remarked.

Smash pondered that while he hauled on the rope, trying to get the dragon up. Actually, he had embraced his friend Chet, her older brother, and Arnolde the Archivist, the middle-aged centaur who was now in charge of liaisons with Mundania. But those had been males, and his recent company had attuned him somewhat more to the difference of females. Chem was not of his species, of course, but she was clinging to him with extraordinary constriction because it was hard for her human arms to support her equine body. She was pleasant to be close to; her present hug was almost like that of an ogress.

All these girls were pleasant to be close to, he realized as the Eye Queue curse enabled him to think the matter through. Each had her separate female fashion, sort of rounded and soft, structured for holding. But it seemed best not to let them know that he noticed. They allowed themselves to get close to him only because they regarded him as a woolly monster who had no perception of their nonedible attributes.

He hauled on the rope, bringing the dragon up another notch. Now Smash was approaching the limit of his strength, for the dragon was a heavy monster and there was a long way to haul. When the job got near the end, ogre, boulder, and centaur were all getting light; any more and they would be swinging in the air.

But at last it was done. Now the Gap Dragon was suspended by its tail from the ironwood tree, its snout just touching the level ground at the base of the chasm. Smash climbed the rope to the tree, caught the trailing tip of the dragon's tail, and knotted it about the tree. Then, clinging to the tree, he untied the rope and flung it upward over the tip of the cliff. He had had the foresight to leave Chem and the boulder anchoring the rope at ground level before doing this.

John flew up and caught the rope. She dragged the end to a tree beyond the chasm and tied it firmly with a fairy knot. Smash climbed the rest of the way up and stood at last on the northern side of the Gap Chasm. Now they had their escape route.

"Climb the dragon, climb the rope," he called down. His voice echoboomed back and forth across the chasm, but finally settled down to the bottom, where they could hear it.

Tandy came up, placing her feet carefully against the dragon's metal scales, which tended to fold outward because of its inverted position, making the footing better. The Siren followed, not quite as agile.

Chem and Fireoak were more of a problem. The centaur had let herself down readily enough, but lacked the muscle either to climb the dragon vertically or to haul herself up along the rope to the top. And the hamadryad was too weak even to make the attempt.

Smash could handle that. He slid down the rope and

dragon, picked up the dryad, and carried her to the top.
Then he returned for the centaur. He had her hold on to
him again, circling her arms about his waist while he
hauled himself up by hands and feet. Progress was slow,
for her hooves could not grip the dragon's scales comfortably, but eventually they made it to the ironwood tree.

At this point the nature of the problem changed. The
rope went straight up to the overhanging lip, and Smash
doubted Chem could hold on to him while he climbed that.
Also, he was tiring, and might be unable to haul himself
and her up, using only his arms. So he parked her,
wedged between the ironwood trunk and the cliff, while he
rested and considered.

But he was not provided much time for either. The Gap
Dragon, quiescent until now, stirred. It was a tough animal, and even a punch in the head by the fist of an ogre
could not put it to sleep indefinitely. It twisted about,
trying to discover what was happening.

"I think you had better climb back up your rope now,"
Chem said.

"Tie the end about your waist; I will draw you up from
above."

"I will make a harness," she decided. She looped the
rope around her body in various places. "This way I can
defend myself."

Smash clambered up the taut rope while the dragon
thrashed about with increasing vigor. As Smash crossed the
cliff lip, he saw the dragon's head coming back up along
its body, toward the centaur filly. That could certainly be
trouble!

Atop the cliff, Smash took hold of the rope and drew it
up. The weight was great, but the rope was magically
strong. He had to brace carefully, lest he be pulled back
over the cliff. Again he was reminded that strength alone
was not sufficient; anchorage was at times more important. He solved the problem by looping the rope about his
own waist so that he could not be drawn away from the
tree and could exert his full force.

John was hovering near the lip. "That dragon has spotted Chem," she announced with alarm. "It's reaching up. I
don't know whether it can . . ."

Smash kept on hauling. He could go only so fast, since

he had to take a fresh grip each time and tense for the renewed effort. He hated to admit it, even to himself, but he was tiring more rapidly. What had become of his ogre endurance?

"Yes, the dragon can reach her," John reported. "It's lunging, snapping. She's fending it off neatly with her hooves, but she's swinging around without much leverage. She can't really hurt it. It's trying again—you'd better lift her up higher, Smash!"

Smash was trying, but now his best efforts yielded only small, slow gains. His giant ogre muscles were solidifying with fatigue.

"Now the dragon is trying to climb its own tail, to get higher, so it can chomp the rope apart or something," the fairy said. "This time she won't be able to stop it. Pull her up quickly!"

But try as he might, Smash could not. The rope began to slip through his exhausted hands.

The Siren leaped up. "I have a knife!" she cried. "I'll go down and cut off the dragon's tail so it will drop to the bottom of the chasm, out of reach!"

"No!" Tandy protested. "You'll have no way to get up again!"

"I'll do it!" John said. "Quick—give me the knife!"

The Siren gave her the knife. The fairy dropped out of sight beyond the ledge. Smash tried to rouse himself to resume hauling on the rope, but his body was frozen into a deathlike rigor. He could only listen.

The Siren lay on the bank, her head over the cliff, looking down. "The dragon's head is almost there," she reported. "John is down near the tree. She's afraid of that monster; I can tell by the way she skirts it. But she's approaching the tied tail. Now she's sawing on it with the knife. She's not very strong, and those scales are tough. The dragon doesn't see her; it's orienting on Chem. Oops—now it sees John. That knife is beginning to hurt it as she digs through the scales. It's slow work! The dragon is turning its head about, opening its jaws. Chem is slipping down farther. She's kicking at the dragon's neck with her forefeet, trying to distract it. Now she's throwing dirt at it from the chasm wall. John is still sawing at the tail. I think she's down to real flesh now. The dragon is really angry. It's blasting out steam—Oh!" She paused, horrified.

"What happened?" Tandy demanded, her face pale with strain.

"The steam—John—" The Siren took a ragged breath. "The steam shriveled her wings, both of them. They're just tatters. John's clinging to the tree trunk. Still sawing at the tail. What awful courage she has! She must be in excruciating pain."

The fairy had lost her newly recovered wings and was suffering terribly—because of Smash's failure. In an agony of remorse, he forced strength through his frozen muscles and hauled again on the rope. Now it came up, its burden seeming lighter, and soon the centaur was over the lip of the chasm and scrambling to safety. But what of John?

"There goes the dragon!" the Siren cried. "She did it! She cut through the tail! There's dragon blood all over her and she's lost the knife, but the dragon's bouncing down the slope in a cloud of dust and steam. Now the monster's rolling at the base. It's galumphing away!"

"What of John?" Tandy cried.

"She's sitting there by the ironwood tree. Her eyes are closed. I don't think she quite comprehends what has happened. Her wings—"

Tandy was fashioning the rope into a smaller harness. "Lower this to her. We'll draw her up!"

Smash merely stood where he was, listening. His brief surge of strength had been exhausted; now he could do nothing. He felt ashamed for his weakness and the horrible consequence of it, but had no further resource. John had thought she would be safe in the company of an ogre!

Chem drew the fairy up. Smash saw John huddled in the harness. Her once-lovely wings, with the blossoming flower patterns, were now melted amorphous husks, useless for flying. Would they ever grow back? It seemed unlikely.

"Well, we crossed the chasm," Tandy said. She was not happy. None of them was. One of their number had lost her invaluable wings, another was too wasted to stand, and Smash was too tired to move. If this was typical of the hazards they faced, traversing central Xanth, how would they ever make it the rest of the way?

"Well, now," a new voice declared.

Smash turned his head dully to view the speaker. It was a gnarled, ugly goblin—at the head of a fair-sized troop of goblins.

Goblins hated people of any type. The strait had become yet more dire.

Chapter 7. Lunatic Fringe

If you fight, we'll shove you all over the brink without your rope," the goblin leader said. He was a stunted black creature about John's height, with a huge head, hands, and feet. His short limbs seemed twisted, as if the bones had been broken and reset many times, and his face was similarly uneven, with one eye squinting, the other round, the nose bulbous, and the mouth crooked. By goblin standards, he was handsome.

The goblins spread out to surround the party. They peered at the ogre, centaur, hamadryad, fairy, Siren, and girl as if all were supreme curiosities. "You crossed the Gap?" the leader asked.

Tandy took it upon herself to answer. "What right have you to question us? I know your kind from the caves. You don't have any useful business with civilized folk."

The leader considered her. "Whom do you know in the caves, girl-thing?"

"Everybody who is anybody," she retorted. "The demons, the Diggle-worm, the Brain Coral—"

The leader seemed fazed. "Who are you?"

"I am Tandy, daughter of Crombie the Soldier and Jewel the Nymph. You know who sets out those black opals you goblins steal to give to your goblin girls! My mother, that's who. Without her there wouldn't be any gems of any kind to find anywhere."

There was a muttering commotion. "You have adequate connections," the goblin leader grudged. "Very well, we won't eat you. You may go, girl-thing."

"What of my friends?" Tandy asked suspiciously.

"They have no such connections. Their mothers don't plant gems in the rocks. We'll cook them tonight."

"Oh, no, you won't! My friends go with me!"

"If that's the way you want it," the goblin said indifferently.

"That's the way I want it."

"Come this way, then. You'll all go in the pot together."

"That's not what I meant!" Tandy cried.

"It isn't?" The goblin seemed surprised. "You said you wanted to be with your friends."

"But not in the pot!"

The goblin shook his head in confusion. "Females change their minds a lot. Exactly what do you want?"

"I want us all to continue our trip north through Xanth," Tandy said, enunciating clearly. "I can't do it alone. I don't know anything about surface Xanth. I need the ogre to protect me. If he weren't worn out from fighting the Gap Dragon and hauling us all up out of the Gap, he'd be cramming all of *you* into the pot!"

"Nonsense. Ogres don't use pots."

Tandy huffed herself up into the resemblance of a tantrum. But before she completed the process, a goblin lieutenant sidled up to whisper in the leader's ear. The leader nodded. "Maybe so," he agreed. He turned back to Tandy. "You are five females, guarded by the tired ogre?"

"Yes," Tandy agreed guardedly.

"How many others has he eaten?"

"None!" Tandy responded indignantly. "He doesn't eat friends!"

"He can't be much of an ogre, then."

"He beat up the Gap Dragon!"

The goblin considered. "There is that." He came to a decision. "My name is Gorbage Goblin. I control this section of the Rim. But I have a daughter, and we are exogamous."

"What?" Tandy asked, bewildered.

"Exogamous, twit. Girls must marry outside their home tribes. But there is no contiguous goblin tribe; we are apart from the main nation of goblins. The dragons extended their territory recently, cutting us off." He scowled. "The other goblins keep forgetting us, the slugbrains. I don't know why."

Smash knew why. It was the forget-spell laid on the Gap Chasm. These goblins lived too close to it, so suffered a peripheral effect.

"So my daughter Goldy Goblin must cross to another tribe," Gorbage grumbled. "But travel beyond our territory is now hazardous to the health. She needs a guard."

Tandy's face lighted with eventual comprehension. "You want us to take your daughter with us?"

"To the next goblin tribe, north of here. Beyond the dragons, in the midst of the five forbidden regions, near the firewall. Yes."

Five forbidden regions? Firewall? Smash wondered about that. It didn't sound like the sort of territory to take five or six delicate girls through.

"You will let us go if we do that?" Tandy asked.

"You and the ogre."

Tandy's face set. She was a very stubborn girl at times. "*All* of us."

The goblin leader wavered. "That's a lot to ask. We haven't had fresh meat in several days."

"I don't care if you never have fresh meat again!" the girl flared. "You can cook up zombies if you get hungry. I want all my friends."

"It's only one daughter you're taking north, after all."

"Remember the feminine wiles," the Siren murmured.

Tandy considered. "The ogre can't do all the guarding," she said reasonably. "When he fights off a big dragon or a tangle tree or something, he gets tired. Then he has to rest, and someone else stands guard, like the centaur. If we cross a lake, the Siren scouts it out first. We never know whose skill will be useful." She paused, then with an effort turned on extra charm. "If you really want your daughter to travel safely—"

Gorbage capitulated with bad grace. "Oh, very well. All of you go. It's a bad deal for me, but Goldy will slaughter me if I don't get her matched soon. She's a cussheaded lass, like all her kind."

Smash was amazed. Tandy had, with a little timely advice from the Siren, talked them out of disaster and gotten them all free passage through goblin-infested territory. Already his own strength was filtering back; all he needed was a little rest. But there was no longer any need for violence.

Goldy Goblin turned out to be a petite, amazingly pretty lass. The goblin females were as lovely as the goblin males were ugly. "Thank you so much for taking me," she said politely. "Is there anything I can do in return?"

Tandy had the grace to take this seriously. "We have to stop by a fireoak tree in this vicinity. If you could show us the best route to it—"

"Certainly. There's only one fireoak hereabouts, with a resident hamadryad nymph—" Goldy paused, spying Fireoak. "Isn't that she?"

"Yes. She's trying to save her tree. We must get her back to it as soon as possible."

"I know the way. But the path to it goes by a hypnogourd patch. So you have to be careful."

"I don't want to go near the gourds!" Tandy cried, horrified.

But Smash remembered his contact with the coffin inside the other gourd. Was it possible that—? "I want a gourd," he said.

The Siren was perplexed. "Why would you want a terrible thing like that?"

"Something I may have forgotten in there."

The Siren frowned but dropped the subject.

They trekked on, Smash carrying the hamadryad. He tried not to show it, but his strength had returned only partially. Fireoak was light, the kind of burden he could normally balance on his little finger without effort, but now he had to control his breathing, lest he pant so loudly he call attention to himself. He would be no help at all if they happened on another dragon. Maybe he just needed a good meal and a night's sleep. Yet it had never before taken him so long to recover from exertion. He suspected something was wrong, but he didn't know what.

They came to the region of hypnogourds. The vines sprawled abundantly, and gourds were all about. Smash stared at them, half mesmerized. He had thought his soul lost when the Siren smashed the other gourd—but was it possible that the gourd had been a mere window on the otherworld reality? His Eye Queue was crazy enough to think this was so. Could he use another gourd to return to that world and fight for his soul?

He felt small hands on his arm. "What is it, Smash?" Tandy asked. "I'm deathly afraid of those things, but you seem fascinated. What's with you and those awful gourds?"

He answered, not fully conscious of his situation. "I must go fight the Night Stallion."

"A Dark Horse?"

"The ruler of the nightmares. He has a lien on my soul."

"Oh, no! Is that how you rescued my soul?"

Smash snapped out of it. He hadn't meant to say anything about the lien to Tandy. "I'm gibbering. Ignore it."

"So that's why you wanted another gourd," the Siren said. "You had unfinished business there! I didn't realize . . ."

Now the goblin girl approached. "The ogre's been into a gourd? I've seen that happen before. Some people escape unscathed; some lose their souls; some get only halfway free. We lost a lot of goblins before we caught on. Now we use those gourds as punishment. Thieves are set at a peephole for an hour; they usually escape with a bad scare and never thieve again. Murderers are set there for a day; they often lose their souls. It varies; some people are cleverer than others, and some luckier. The lien is like a delayed sentence; a month or two and it's all over."

"A lien!" the Siren said. "How long for you, Smash?"

"Three months," he replied glumly.

"And you said nothing!" she cried indignantly. "What kind of a creature are you?" But she answered herself immediately. "A self-sacrificing one. Smash, you should have told us."

"Yes," Tandy agreed faintly. "I never realized—"

"How can a person nullify such a lien?" the Siren asked, getting practical.

"He has to go back in and fight," Goldy said. "If he doesn't, he just gets weaker, bit by bit, as the Stallion calls in the soul. It's too late to fight, once the lien is due. He has to do it early, while he has most of his strength."

"But a person can redeem himself if he goes in early?" the Siren asked.

"Sometimes," the goblin girl said. "Maybe one out of ten. One of our old goblins is supposed to have done it a long time ago in his youth. We're not sure we believe him. He mumbles about trials of fear and pain and pride and such-like, making no sense at all. But it is theoretically possible to win."

"So that's why Smash has gotten so weak," the Siren said. "He was using his strength as if he had plenty to spare, but he has an illness of the soul."

"I know about that," Fireoak breathed.

"I didn't know!" Tandy said, clouding up. "Oh, it's all my fault! I never would have taken my soul back if—"

"I didn't know, either," the Siren said, calming her. "But I should have suspected. Maybe I did suspect; I just didn't pursue the thought fast enough. I forgot that Smash is no longer a simple-minded ogre; he has the devious Eye Queue contamination, making him react more like human folk."

"The curse of human intellect, replacing the primeval beastly innocence," Tandy agreed. "I, too, should have realized—"

"Tandy, we've got to help Smash destroy that lien!"

"Yes!" Tandy agreed emphatically. "We can't leave him to the law of the lien."

Smash almost smiled, despite the seriousness of the situation. During his travels with Prince Dor, he had encountered the law of the loin; was this related?

"I'll help," Goldy said.

The Siren frowned. "What is your interest? Your tribe was going to eat us all."

"How can I get to another goblin tribe if I don't have a strong ogre to clear the way? I do know a little bit about the matter."

"I suppose you do have a practical interest," the Siren agreed. "We all need the ogre, until we find our own individual situations. What do you know about the gourds that might help?"

"Our people have reported details of the gourd geography. It's the same for every gourd; they're all identical inside. But each person enters at a different place, and it's possible to get lost. So it is best to carry a line of string to mark the way."

"But a person is out the moment his contact with the peephole is broken! How can he get lost?"

"It's not that sort of lost," Goldy said. "There's a lot of territory in there, and some pretty strange effects. Some talk of graves, others of mirrors. A person always returns to the spot he left, and the time he left, no matter how long he's been away from it; a break in the sequence is only an interruption, not a change. If he's lost in gourdland, he's still lost when he returns there, even if he's been a long time out of his gourd. He doesn't know where he's going because he doesn't know where he's been. But if he strings the string, it'll mark where he's been, and he'll know the moment he crosses his trail. And that's the secret."

Smash was getting quite interested. He had been out of his gourd for some time, but apparently could still return. "What secret?"

"The Night Stallion is always in the last place a person looks, in the gourd," the goblin girl explained. "So all you have to do to reach him is always look in a new place—never in a place you've been before; that's a waste of time and effort. You are apt to get caught in an endless loop, and then you are really lost. You may never find him if you rehash your old route."

"You *do* know something about it!" Tandy agreed. "But suppose Smash threads the maze, finds the Night Stallion—and is too weak to fight him?"

"Oh, it's not that sort of strength he needs," the goblin girl said. "We've had physically strong goblins go in, and physically weak ones, and the weak ones do just as well. All kinds lose in the gourd. Physical strength may even be a liability. Destroying the facilities does not destroy the commitment. Only defeating the Stallion does that, on the Stallion's own terms."

"What are the Stallion's terms?"

Goldy shrugged. "No one knows. Our one surviving goblin refuses to tell, assuming he knows. He just sort of turns a little grayer. I think there is no way to find out except to face the creature."

"I think we have enough to go on," Tandy said. "Let's take a gourd along. We have to get to the fireoak tree before the lunatic-fringe-spell gives out." She went to harvest a gourd, her concern for Smash overriding her fear of the thing.

"I think the peephole is a lunatic fringe," the Siren muttered.

They moved on. Smash pondered what the goblin girl had said. If physical strength was not important in the struggle with the Night Stallion, why was it important to join this contest early, before weakness progressed too far? Was that a contradiction or merely a confusion? He concluded that it was the latter. There was weakness of the body and of the spirit; both might fade together, but they were not identical. Smash was physically weak now because he had overextended himself; otherwise it should have taken him three months to fade. His soul had probably suffered relatively little so far. But if he waited till the end of the lien term to meet the Stallion, then his soul would be weak, and he would lose the nonphysical contest. Yes, that seemed to make sense. Things didn't have to make sense, with magic, but it helped.

They arrived at a pleasant glade. Within it was a crazy sort of shimmer that made Smash feel a little crazy himself; he turned his eyes away.

"My tree!" the hamadryad cried, suddenly reviving.

Smash set her down. "Where?"

"There! Behind the lunatic fringe!" She seemed to grow stronger instant by instant and in a moment pranced into the glade. Her body wavered and vanished.

"I guess the spell is still holding," Tandy said. She followed Fireoak, carrying the gourd, and disappeared similarly. The others went the same route.

When Smash contacted the fringe, he felt a momentary surge of dizziness; then he was through. There before him was the tree, a medium-large fireoak, its leaves blazing in the late afternoon sunlight. The hamadryad was hugging its trunk in ecstasy, her body almost indistinguishable from it, and her color was returning. She had rejoined her soul. The tree, too, seemed to be glowing, and leaves that had been wilting were now forging back into health. Evidently it had missed her also. There was something very touching about the love of nymph and tree for each other.

Tandy approached him, her blue eyes soulful. "Smash, if I had known—" She choked up. She shoved the gourd at him.

"We'll let you go into it until the lunatic fringe fades and the people attack this tree," the Siren said. "Maybe you'll have time to conquer the Night Stallion and regain your full strength." She produced a ball of string that the hamadryad must have stored in her tree. "Use this so you won't get lost in there."

"But first eat something," Chem said, bringing an armful of fruits. "And get a night's sleep."

"No. I want to settle this now," Smash said.

"Oh, please do at least eat something!" Tandy pleaded. "You can eat a lot in a hurry."

True words—and he was hungry. Ogres were usually hungry. So he crammed a bushel of whole fruits into his mouth and gulped them down, ogre-fashion, and drank a long pull of water from the spring at the base of the tree.

As the sun dropped down behind the forest, singeing the distant tips of trees, Smash took leave of the six females as if setting out on a long and hazardous trek. Then he settled down against the trunk of the tree, put the gourd in his lap, and applied his right eye to the peephole.

Instantly he was back in the gourd world. He stood before the crypt, having just gotten up from his snooze. Tandy was not there; for a moment he had feared that she would be locked into this adventure with him, since she had been here before, but of course she was free now.

A chill wind cut around the stonework, ruffling his fur. The landscape was bleak: all gravestones and dying weeds and dismal dark sky. "Beautiful!" he exclaimed. "I would like to stay here forever."

Then his Eye Queue, in its annoying fashion, forced him to amend his statement mentally. He would like to stay here forever after he rescued his soul from the lien and regained his full strength and saved the hamadryad's tree and had gotten Tandy and all the others to wherever they were going and found his Answer from the Good Magician. After these details, then this paradise of the gourd would be a nice retirement spot.

He had been afraid he would find himself somewhere else and be unable, after all, to pursue his quest to its close. Despite what the goblin girl had said, this was a different gourd, and might not know where his adventure in the last gourd had ended. Now he was reassured, and confident that he could locate the Night Stallion and abate the lien. After all, he was an ogre, wasn't he?

He held his ball of string, since he had willed it to accompany him, but again he had forgotten to bring his gauntlets or orange jacket. He backtracked to the back of the haunted house and anchored one end of the string to a post, then crossed the graveyard to the far gate, letting the string unravel behind. It was a good-sized ball, so he was confident he would have plenty to mark his way.

A skeleton came out to see what was going on; Smash made a horrendous face at it, and the thing fled so fast its bones rattled. Yes, the bone-folk remembered him here!

Beyond the gate was a broad, bleak, open plain illuminated by ghastly, pale white moonlight. Black, ugly clouds scudded horrendously across the dismal sky, forming dark picture-shapes that resembled trolls, goblins, and ogres. Naturally the other creatures were fleeing before the ogre-shapes. Smash was delighted; this was an even better scene than the last! Whoever had set up this gourd world had had ogre tastes in mind.

Where should he go now? It was not his purpose to dally amidst the delights of the terrain, but to locate the Night Stallion. Yet he knew that he would have to cover a lot of territory before he reached the last place to look. So he had better move rapidly anywhere, getting the ground covered.

He tromped forth, straight across the beautifully barren plain. The cracked ground shuddered pleasantly under the impact of his feet. He was regaining his strength. Yet now he knew, thanks to the goblin girl, that physical strength was not necessarily what it took to prevail here. He had used it to cow the voice in the coffin, forcing it to release Tandy's soul—but had suffered the compromise of his own soul. Probably the coffin had given him nothing that had not already been allocated; he had fooled himself, thinking an ogre's power would scare the dead. The curse of the Eye Queue was making him see uncomfortable truths!

Yet perhaps he should not take this revelation on faith, either. He could go back and rattle the coffin some more, and determine just how much it feared his violence. After all, the skeletons now fled from him. No—that was a temptation to be avoided, for it would cause him to backtrack his own trail, the one thing he needed to avoid doing. Smash continued resolutely forward.

Black dots appeared on the bleak horizon. Quickly they expanded, racing toward him on beating hooves. The nightmares! This was where they stayed by day—here, where night was eternal.

The mares were handsome animals, absolutely black, with flaring manes, flying tails, and darkly glowing eyes. Their limbs were sleekly muscular, and they moved with the velocity of thought. In moments they surrounded him, galloping around him in a circle, squealing warningly. They did not want him going the way he was going. But since the Night Stallion did not seem to be among them, he had to proceed.

Smash ignored their warning. He tromped onward—and their circle stayed with him despite his speed. Experimentally he dodged to one side, and the circle remained centered on him. He leaped, and the circle leaped with him. Just as he had thought, these were magical creatures, orienting magically; the feet of a dream-horse had no essential connection with the ground. Prince Dor had once mentioned escaping the nightmares by sleeping on a cloud, beyond their reach, but probably Prince Dor had not had any bad dreams scheduled that night. The mares could go anywhere, and Smash could not escape their circle by running.

Not that he wantd to. He liked these fine, healthy animals. They were an ogre's type of creature. He remembered how one of them had given Tandy a ride to the Good Magician's castle—which had perhaps been a better destination for her than the one she had sought. The Good Magician had provided Tandy a home for a year, and a solution to her problem—maybe. Her father Crombie, the soldier at Castle Roogna, might not have been much help. Smash knew the man casually. Crombie was getting old, no longer the fighter he used to be. He was also a woman hater who might not have taken his daughter's problem seriously. But if he had taken it seriously—what could he have done, without leaving his post at Castle Roogna?

And the nightmares—one had helped Tandy travel, but then had put in for a lien on her soul, causing her awful grief. Some help that had been! Maybe these nightmares needed to feel the weight of an ogre's displeasure.

Still he did not know enough to act. What was Tandy's problem that the Magician had answered? She had never quite said. Did it relate to that nightmare lien on her soul? But she had incurred that lien in order to reach the Good Magician. That hardly seemed profitable. Also, she had not been aware of the lien, so she would not have put a Question about it.

How would traveling with an ogre abate her problem? Had it been the Magician's intent that Smash redeem that girl's lost soul with his own? That was possible—but his understanding of the Magician's mode of operations argued against it. Humfrey did not need to fool people about the nature of their payments for their Answers. He should not pretend the service was merely protection duty when, in fact, it was soul substitution. So that, too, remained an enigma.

So far, Tandy had recruited fellow travelers with abandon, and now there were six females in the party. That was probably as unlikely a group as existed at the moment in Xanth. Normally such maidens fled ogres, and for good reason—ogres consumed such morsels. Were it not for Smash's commitment not to indulge his natural appetites because of the service he owed the Good Magician—

He shook his head, flinging loose a few angry fleas. No, he could not be sure of his motive there. His father Crunch was a vegetarian ogre, married to a female of human derivation, so Smash had been raised in an atypical ogre home. His folks had been permitted to associate with the people of Castle Roogna as long as they honored human customs. Smash himself had not operated under the restriction of oath or of human taste—but had always known he would be banished from human company if he ever reverted to the wild state. Anyone who made trouble for King Trent ran the risk of being transformed to a toad or a stinkbug, for Trent was the great transformer. It had been easy to conform. So Smash had not actually crunched many human bones, and had carried away no delicious human maidens. Perhaps he had been missing something vital— but he remained unwilling to gamble that one good meal would be more satisfying than the human friendships he had maintained. So perhaps it was more than the Good Magician's service that protected Tandy and the others.

Ogres weren't supposed to need companionship, but the curse of the Eye Queue showed him that he was, to that extent, atypical of his kind. Like the Siren, he now knew he would be lonely alone.

Smash suddenly realized that the ring of mares was only half the diameter it had been. While he tromped forward, thinking his slew of un-ogrish thoughts, they had been constricting their loop. Soon they would be almost within reach of him.

And if they closed on him all the way—what then? Mere horses could hardly hurt an ogre. Each weighed about as much as he did, but they were only mares, with the foreparts of sea horses and the rear parts of centaurs. They were basically pretty and gentle. True, their ears were flat back against their skulls, and their manes flared like dangerous spikes, their tails flicked like weapons, their teeth showed white in the moonlight, and their eyes stared slantwise at him as if he were prey instead of monster—but he knew he could throw any of them far out across the plain, if he chose, when he had his normal ogre strength. Why should they want to come within his reach?

In a moment he had the answer. These were standard nightmares, used to carry bad dreams to their proper dreamers. They had not been cursed with the Eye Queue; they had no super-equine intelligence. They were giving him the standard treatment, crowding him, trying to scare him—

Smash burst out laughing. Imagine anything scaring an ogre!

The mares broke ranks, startled. This was not S. O. P. The victim was not supposed to laugh. What was wrong?

Smash was sorry. "I didn't mean to mess up your act, mares," he said apologetically. "Circle me again, and I'll pretend to be frightened. I don't want you to get in trouble with your Stallion. In fact, I'd like to meet him myself. I don't suppose you could take me to him?"

Still the mares milled about. Their formation was in a shambles. They were not here to play a game, but to terrify. Since that had failed, they had other business to attend to. After all, night had been drawing nigh when he entered the gourd. The group began breaking up. Probably they would be all over Xanth within the next hour, bearing their burdensome dreams.

"Wait!" Smash cried. "Which of you gave Tandy a ride?"

One mare hesitated, as if trying to remember. "A year ago," Smash said. "A small human girl, brown hair, throws tantrums."

The black ears perked forward. The mare remembered!

"She sends her thanks," Smash said. "You really helped her."

The mare nickered, seeming interested. Did these creatures really care about the welfare of those on whom they visited the bad dreams? Yet his Eye Queue warned him that it was not safe to judge any creature by his or her job. Some ogres did not crunch bones; some mares might not hate girls.

"Did you mean to destroy her?" he asked. "By taking a lien on her soul?"

The mare's head lifted back, nostrils flaring.

"You didn't know?" Smash asked. "When she wandered into the gourd, the coffin-creep stole her soul, on the pretext she owed it for the ride."

The mare snorted. She hadn't known. That made Smash feel better. Life was a jungle inside the gourd as well as in Xanth, with creatures and things grasping whatever they could get from the unwary. But some were innocent.

"She might visit here again," he continued. "You might see her following my string." He pointed to the line he had laid out behind him. "If you like, you could give her another ride and sort of explain things to her. It would help her catch up to me quickly. But no more liens!"

The mare snorted and pawed the ground. She was not interested in giving rides.

"Maybe I can make a deal with you," Smash said. "I don't want Tandy getting in trouble in here." Not at the risk of her soul, certainly! "Is there anything I can do for you, outside?"

The mare considered. Then she brightened. She licked her lips.

"Something to eat?" Smash asked, and the mare nodded. "Something nice?" She agreed again. "Rock candy?" She neighed nay.

Smash played the guessing game, but could not quite come up with the correct item. All the other mares had departed, and this one was fidgeting; he could not hold her longer. "Well, if I find it, maybe I'll know it," Smash said. "Maybe Tandy will know, and bring it with her, if she comes. You keep in touch, okay?"

The nightmare nodded, then turned and trotted off. No doubt she was going to pick up her load of unpleasant dreams for delivery to her clientele of sleepers. Maybe some of them were his friends at the fireoak tree. "Good luck!" Smash called after her, and she flicked her tail in acknowledgment.

Alone again, he wondered whether he had been foolish. What business did he have with nightmares? What would a nightmare want from a person, that the mare could not pick up for herself on her rounds? He was an ogre who loved violence and horror, and he was here on a personal mission. Yet somehow he felt it was best to get along with any creature he could; perhaps something would come of it.

This confounded Eye Queue! Not only did it set him to trying un-ogrish things, it rendered him confused about the meaning of these things and full of uncomfortable self-doubt. What a curse it was!

He faced resolutely forward and resumed his tromping. He saw something new on the horizon and proceeded toward it. Soon it manifested as a building—no, as a castle—no, larger yet, an entire city, enclosed by a forbidding wall.

As he drew close, he discovered the city was solid gold. Every part of it scintillated in the moonlight, shades of deep yellow. But when he drew closer yet, he found that it was not gold but brass—just as shiny, but not nearly as precious. Still it was a marvel.

The outer wall was unbroken, riveted metal, gleaming at every angle. The front gate was the same, so large it dwarfed even Smash's monstrous proportions. This was the sort of city giants would inhabit!

Smash considered that. The little knobs of the haunted house had shocked him; how much worse would this one be? He was not at all sure he could rip this door from its moorings; it was big and strong, and he was now relatively weak. This was not a situation he liked to admit, but he was no longer properly stupid about such things.

He pondered, drawing on the full curse of the Eye

Queue. What he needed was insulation—something to protect him from shock. But there was nothing near; the city
wall rose out of sand. He might use his orange jacket—but
he was not wearing it, here in the gourd. All he had was
the string, and that wasn't suitable.

No help for it. He would have to touch the metal. Actually, there might be a metal floor inside that he would
have to walk on; if he were going to get shocked, it would
happen with every step. Might as well find out now. He
extended a hamfinger and touched the knob.

There was no shock. He grasped and turned the knob. It
clicked, and the door swung inward. It wasn't locked!

There was a bright metal hall leading from the gate into
the city. Smash walked down it, half expecting the door to
slam shut behind him. It did not. He continued through the
hall, his bare, furry soles thumping on the cool metal.

He emerged into an open court with a paving of brass,
the moonlight bearing down preternaturally. All was silent.
No creatures roamed the city.

"Ho!" Smash bellowed, loud enough to disturb the dead,
as seemed appropriate in this realm.

No dead were disturbed. If they heard, they were ignoring him. The city seemed to be empty. There was an eerie
quality to this that Smash liked. But he wondered who had
made this city and where those people had gone. It seemed
like far too interesting a place to desert. If ogres built cit-
ies, this was the sort of city they would build. But of
course no ogre was smart enough to build a single building,
let alone a city, certainly not a lovely city of brass.

He tromped through it, his big, flat feet generating a
muted booming on the metal street. Brass buildings rose on
either side, their walls making blank brass faces at precise
right angles to the street. He looked up and saw that the
tops were squared off, too. There were no windows or
doors. Of course that didn't matter to the average ogre; he
could always bash out any windows when and where he
wanted. All was mirror-shiny; he could see his appalling
reflection in every surface that faced him. Brass ogres
paced him to either side, and another walked upside down
under the street.

Smash remembered the story his father Crunch had told
of entering a sleeping city and discovering the lovely mush-

faced ogress who had become Smash's mother. This city of
brass was pleasantly reminiscent of that. Was there an
ogress here for him? That was an exciting prospect, though
he hoped she wasn't made of brass.

He traversed the city, but found no entrance to any
building. If an ogress was sleeping here, she was locked
away where he couldn't reach her. Smash banged on a
wall, making it reverberate; but though the sound boomed
pleasantly throughout the city, no one stirred. He punched
harder, trying to break a hole in the wall. It was no good;
he was too weak, the brass was too strong, and he lacked
his protective gauntlets. His fist smarted, so he stuck it in
his mouth.

Smash was beginning to be bothered. Before there had
been halfway interesting things like walking skeletons, elec-
trified doors, and nightmares. Now there was just brass.
What could he accomplish here?

He invoked the curse of the Eye Queue yet again and
did some solid thinking. So far, each little adventure within
the gourd had been a kind of riddle; he had to overcome
some barrier or beat some sort of threat before he could
continue to the next event. So it was probably not enough
just to enter this empty city and depart; that might not
count. He had to solve the riddle, thus narrowing the options, reducing the remaining places for the Night Stallion
to hide. Straight physical action did not seem to be the re-
quirement here. What, then, was?

There must be a nonphysical way to deal with this im-
passive place, perhaps to bring it to life so it could be conquered. Maybe a magical spell. But Smash did not know
any spells, and somehow this city seemed too alien to be
magical. What else, then?

He paced the streets, still unreeling his string, careful
never to cross his own path. And, in a little private square
directly under the moon, he discovered a pedestal. Significant things were usually mounted on pedestals directly under the moon, he remembered. So he marched up to it and
looked.

He was disappointed. There was only a brass button
there. Nothing to do except to press it. There might be
serious consequences, but no self-respecting ogre worried
about that sort of thing. He turned his big hamthumb down

and mashed the button. With luck, all hell would break loose.

As it happened, luck was with him. Most of hell broke loose.

There was a pleasantly deafening klaxon alarm noise that filled all this limited universe with vibrations. Then the metal buildings began shifting about, moving along the floor of the city, squeezing the streets and the court. In a moment there would be no place remaining for him to stand.

This was more like it! At first Smash planned to brace himself and halt the encroaching buildings by brute ogre strength. But he lacked his full power now, and anyway, it was better to use his brain. Perhaps the Eye Queue was gradually subverting him, causing him to endorse its nature; already it seemed like less of a curse, and he knew—because, ironically, of the intelligence it provided him—that this was a significant signal of corruption. Mental power tended to corrupt, and absolute intelligence tended to corrupt absolutely, until the victim eschewed violence entirely in favor of smart solutions to stupid problems. Smash hoped he could fight off the curse before it ever ruined him to that extent! If he stopped being stupid, brutal, and violent, he would no longer be a true ogre.

Nevertheless, the expedience of the moment forced him to utilize his mind. He knew that a block that moved one way had to leave a space behind it, unless it happened to be expanding rapidly. He zipped between buildings, emerging from the narrowing aisle just before the two clanged together. Sure enough, there was a new space where a building had stood. It was perfectly smooth brass except for a cubic hole where the center of the building had been. Probably that was the anchoring place, like part of a lock mechanism; a heavy bolt would drop down from the building to wedge in that hole and keep the building from sliding about when it wasn't supposed to. When he had pressed the brass button, the lock bolts had lifted, freeing the buildings. Buildings, like clouds, bashed about all over the place when given the freedom to do so. The klaxon had sounded to warn all crushable parties that motion was commencing, so they could either get out of the way or pick their favorite squishing-spot. It all made a sort of violent sense, his

Eye Queue informed him. He liked this city better than ever.

Now the building blocks were bouncing back, converging on him. Smash moved again, avoiding what could be a crushing experience. He found himself in a new open space, with another anchorage slot.

But the blocks were moving more quickly now, as if getting warmed up. Because they were big, he needed a certain amount of time to run between them. If they speeded up much more, he would not have time to clear before they clanged. That could be awkward.

"Well, brain, what do you say to this?" he asked challengingly. "Can you outsmart two buildings that plan to catch me and squish me flat?"

His vine-corrupted brain, thus challenged, rose to the occasion. "Get in the pit," it told him.

Smash thought this was crazy. But already the brass was moving, sounding off with its tune of compression, and he had to act. He leaped into the pit as the blank metal face of the building charged him.

Too late, it occurred to him, or to his Eye Queue—it became difficult at times to distinguish ogre-mind from vine-mind—that he could be crushed when the bolt dropped down to anchor the building. But that should happen only when the building was finished traveling and wanted to settle down for a rest. He would try to be out by then. If he failed—well, squishing was an ogrish kind of demise.

It was dark there as the metal underbody of the building slid across. He felt slightly claustrophobic—another weakness of intelligence, since a true ogre never worried about danger or consequence. What would happen if the building did not move off?

Then light flashed down from above. Smash blinked and discovered that the center of the building was hollow, glowing from the inner walls. He had found his way inside!

He scrambled up and stood on the floor, still holding his ball of string. The building was still moving, but there was no way it could crush him now. The building floor covered everything except the square where the anchorage hole would be when it lay at anchor, so he could simply ride along with it.

He looked about—and spied an army of brass men and women, each individual fully formed, complete with brass facial features, hair, and clothing—the men fully clothed, the women less so. But they were statues, erected on platforms that, like the floor, moved with the building. Nothing here was of interest to an ogre. He knew brass wasn't good to eat.

Then he spied another brass button.

Well, why not? Maybe this one would make the building stop moving. Of course, if this one stopped and the other buildings did not, there would be a horrendous crash. Smash jammed his thumb down on the button.

Instantly the brass statues animated. The metal people spied the ogre and converged on him. And Smash—

Found himself leaning against the fireoak tree. Tandy stood before him, holding the gourd. She had broken his line of vision to the peephole. "Are you all right, Smash?" she asked with her cute concern.

"Certainly!" he grumped. "Why did you interrupt me? It was just getting interesting."

"The lunatic fringe is tearing," she said worriedly. "The human villagers are in the area and will soon discover the tree."

"Well, bring me back when they do," Smash said. "I have metal men to fight inside."

"Metal men?"

"And women. Solid brass."

"Oh," she said, uncomprehending. "Remember, you're in there to fight for your soul. I worry about you, Smash."

He guffawed. "You worry about me! You're human; I'm an ogre!"

"Yes," she agreed, but her face remained drawn. "I know what it's like in there. You put your soul in peril for me. I can't forget that, Smash."

"You don't like it in there," he pointed out. "I do. And I agreed to protect you. This is merely another aspect." He took the gourd back and applied his eye to the peephole.

The brass people were converging, exactly where they had been when he left. They seemed not even to be aware of his brief absence. The building was moving, too—but it had not moved in the interim. His Eye Queue-cursed brain found all this interesting, but Smash had no time for that nonsense at the moment. The brassies were almost on him.

The first one struck at him. The man was only half Smash's height, but the metal made him solid. Smash hauled him up by the brassard and threw him aside. Smash still lacked the strength to do real damage, but at least he could fight weakly. In his strength he would have hurled the brass man right through the brass wall of the building.

A female grabbed at him. Smash hooked a forefinger into her brassiere and hauled her up to his eye level. "Why are you attacking me?" he asked, curious rather than angry.

"We're only following our program," she said, kicking at him with a pretty brass foot.

"But if you fight me, I shall have to fight you," he pointed out. "And I happen to be a monster."

"Don't try to reason with me, you big hunk of flesh; I'm too brassy for that." She swung at him with a metal fist. But he was holding her at his arm's length, so she could not reach him.

Something was knocking at his knee. Smash looked down. A man was striking at him with his brass knuckles. Smash dropped the brass girl on the brass man's brass hat, and the two crashed to the floor in a shower of brass tacks. They cried out with the sound of brass winds.

Now a half-dozen brassies were grabbing at Smash's legs, and he lacked the strength to throw them all off at once. So he reached down to pluck them off one at a time—

He was under the tree again. He saw the problem immediately. Half a dozen brassies—no, these were men and women of the human village—were converging on the tree, bearing wicked-looking axes. The hamadryad was screaming.

Smash had no patience with this. He stood up, towering over the villagers, ogre-fashion. He roared a fine ogre roar.

The villagers turned and fled. They didn't know Smash was short of strength at the moment. Otherwise they could have attacked him and perhaps put him in difficulty, in the same way the brassies were doing in the gourd. He had replaced the illusion of the lunatic fringe with the illusion of his own formidability.

The hamadryad dropped from her tree, her hair glowing like fire, catching him about the neck. She was now a vibrant, healthy creature. "You great big wonderful brute of a creature!" she exclaimed, kissing his furry ear. Smash was oddly moved; as the centaur had noted, ogres were seldom embraced or kissed by nymphs.

He handed the hamadryad back into her tree, then settled down for another session in the gourd. None of them had anywhere to go until the King got the news and acted to protect the tree permanently, and he wanted to wrap up this gourd business.

"Wake me at need," he said, noting that the shimmer of the lunatic fringe was now almost gone. If trees had ogres to protect them instead of cute but helpless hamadryads, very few trees would be destroyed. Of course, ogres themselves were prime destroyers of trees, using them to make toothpicks and such, so he was in no position to criticize. He applied his left eye to the peephole this time, giving his right orb a rest.

He stood in an alley between buildings. What was this? The sequence was supposed to pick up exactly where it had left off. What had gone wrong?

The two buildings slid toward him, forcing him to scoot out of the way. Smash emerged into a new space—and saw his line of string. He was about to cross his own path! But he couldn't retreat; the buildings were clanging behind him.

Still, his cursed Eye Queue wouldn't let him leave well enough alone. It wanted to know why the gourd scene had slipped a notch. Was the gourd getting old, beginning to rot, breaking down its system? He didn't want to be trapped in a rotting gourd.

The buildings separated, starting to converge on a new spot. The alley reopened, the string he had just set out running down its length—and stopping.

Smash ran to the end of it. The string had been severed cleanly; it ended at the point he had re-entered the vision.

But as the buildings separated, Smash saw another cut end of string. That must be where he had been before, just a little distance away. He had jumped no farther than he could have bounded by foot. But he hadn't jumped physically; he had left the scene, then returned to it slightly displaced. Why?

The buildings reversed course and closed on him again. They certainly wasted no time pondering questions! Smash ran back, his mind working. And suddenly it came to him—he had switched eyes! His left eye was a little apart from his right eye—and though that distance was small in the real world of Xanth, it was larger in the tiny world of the gourd. So there had been a shift, and a break in his string.

Well, that had freed him of the brass folk. But Smash couldn't accept that. He didn't want to escape, he wanted to win, to conquer this setting and go on to the next, knowing he had narrowed the Night Stallion's options. He wanted to do his job right, leaving no possible loophole for the loss of his soul. So he had to go back to the place he had left off, and resume there.

He followed his prior line, dragging his new line behind him. He found the square pit as the building moved off it, and he got down into it. The building swung back, and the interior light came on. Smash climbed out and ran to the end of his string.

The brass folk saw him and came charging in. Smash tied the two ends of string together, making his line complete, then stood as half a dozen people grabbed him. This was where he had left off; now it was all right.

He resumed plucking individual brass folk off. One of them was the girl in the brassiere. "You again?" he inquired, holding her up by one finger, as he had done before. It was really the best place, since she was flailing all her limbs wildly. "Do I have to drop you again?"

"Don't you dare drop me again!" she flashed, her brass surface glinting with ire. She took an angry breath—which almost dislodged her, for she had a full brassiere and his purchase on it was slight. "I have a dent and three scratches from the last time, you monster!" She pointed at her arms. "There's a scratch. There's another. But I won't show you the dent."

"Well, you did kick at me," Smash said reasonably, wondering where the dent was.

"I told you! We have to—"

Then he was back in Xanth again. Smash saw the problem immediately; a cockatrice was approaching the tree. The baby basilisk had evidently been recently hatched and was wandering aimlessly—but remained deadly dangerous.

"Put me down, you lunk!"

Startled, Smash looked at the source of the voice. He was still holding the brass girl, dangling by her brassiere hooked on his finger. She had been brought out of the gourd with him!

Hastily Smash set her down, carefully so she would not dent. He had a more immediate matter to attend to. How could he get rid of the cockatrice?

"Oh, look," the brass girl said. "What a cute chick!" She stepped over to the terrible infant, reaching down.

"Don't touch it!" the Siren cried. "Don't even look at it!"

Too late. The brass girl picked up the baby monster. "Oh, aren't you a sweet one," she cooed, turning it in her hand so she could look it in the snoot.

"No!" several voices cried.

Again they were too late. The brass girl stared deeply into the monster's baleful eyes. "Oh, I wish I could keep you for my very own pet, along with my other pets," she said, touching her pert nose to its hideous schnozzle. "I don't have anything like you in my collection."

The chick hissed and bit—but its tiny teeth were ineffective against the brass. "Oh, how nice," the girl said. "You like me, don't you!"

Apparently the little monster's powers were harmless against the metal girl. She was already harder than stone.

"Uh, miss—" the Siren said.

"I'm called Blyght," the brass girl said. "Of Building Four, in the City of Brass. Who are you?"

"I'm called the Siren," the Siren said. "Blythe, we would appreciate it if—"

"Blyght," the girl corrected her brassily.

"Sorry. I misheard. Blyght. If you would—"

"But I think I like Blythe better. This place is so much softer than I'm used to. So you can use that, Sirn."

"Siren. Two syllables."

"That's all right. I prefer one syllable, Sirn."

"You can change names at will?" John asked incredulously.

"Of course. All brassies can. Can't you?"

"No," the fairy said enviously.

"Blythe, that animal—" the Siren broke in. "It's deadly to us. So if you would—"

Smash had been looking around to see if there were any other dangers. At this point his eye fell on the gourd—and even from a distance his consciousness was drawn into the peephole, and he was back among the brassies. This time he stood within the building, but apart from the crowd, and his string had been interrupted again. He was using his right eye.

The brass folk spied him and charged. This was getting pointless. "Wait!" he bellowed.

They paused, taken aback. "Why?" one inquired.

"Because I accidentally took one of your number out of the gourd, and if anything happens to me, she'll be forever stranded there."

They were appalled, almost galvanized. "That would be a fate worse than death!" one cried. "That would be—" He paused, balking at the awful concept.

"That would be—*life*," another brass man whispered. There was a sudden hush of dread.

"Yes," Smash agreed cruelly. "So I have to fetch her back. And I will. But you'll have to help me."

"Anything," the man said, his brass face tarnishing.

"Tell me how to get out of here, on my own."

"That's easy. Take the ship."

"The ship? But there's no water here!"

Several brassies smiled metallically. "It's not that kind of ship. It's the Luna-fringe-shuttle. You catch it at the Luna triptych building."

"Show me to it," Smash said.

They showed him to a brass door that opened to the outside. "You can't miss it," they assured him. "It's the biggest block in the city."

Smash thanked them and stepped out. The buildings were still moving, but now he had the experience and confidence to travel by their retreating sides, avoiding collisions. He glanced back at the building he had left and saw the number 4 inscribed on the side, but there was no sign of the door he had exited by. Apparently it was a one-way door that didn't exist from this side.

Soon he spied a building twice the size of the others. That had to be the one. He ducked into an anchor hole as the building approached, and in a moment was inside.

There was the fringe-shuttle, like a monstrous arrowhead standing on its tail. It had a porthole in the side big enough to admit him, so he climbed in.

He found himself in a tight cockpit that the cock seemed to have vacated. There was only one place to sit comfortably, a kind of padded chair before a panel full of dinguses. So he sat there, knowing he could bash the dinguses out of the way if they bothered him. There was another brass button on the panel, and he punched it with his thumb.

The porthole clanged closed. A wheel spun itself about. Air hissed. Straps rose up from the chair and wrapped themselves around his body. A magic mirror lit up before his face. An alarm klaxon sounded. The ship shuddered, then launched upward like a shot from a catapult, punching through the roof.

In moments the mirror showed clouds falling away ahead. Then the moon came into view, growing larger and brighter each moment. It was now a half-circle. Of course—that was why the lunatic fringe no longer shrouded the fireoak tree—not enough moon left to sustain it. But the half that remained seemed solid enough, except for the round holes in it. Of course, cheese did have holes; that was its nature.

Now it occurred to him that the brassies might have misconstrued his request. They had shown him the way out of the City of Brass—but not out of the gourd. Well, nothing to do now but carry this through. Maybe the ship could get him back to the fireoak tree.

He didn't really want to go to the moon, though the view of all that fresh cheese made him hungry. After all, it had been at least an hour since he had eaten that bushel of fruit. So he checked the panel before him and found a couple of projecting brass sticks. He grabbed them, wiggling them about.

The moon veered out of the mirror-picture, and Smash was flung about in his chair as if tossed by a storm. Fortunately, the straps held him pretty much in place. He let go of the sticks—and after a moment the moon swung back into view. Evidently he had messed up the ship's program. His Eye Queue curse caused him to ponder this, and he concluded that the sticks controlled the ship. When they were not in use, the ship sailed where it wanted, which was evidently a hole in the cheese of the moon. Maybe this Luna shuttle was the mechanism by which the moon's cheese was brought to Xanth, though he wasn't sure what use metal people would have for cheese.

Smash took hold of the sticks again and wiggled more cautiously. Ogres were clumsy only when it suited them to be so; they could perform delicate tasks when no one was watching. The moon danced about but did not leave the screen. He experimented some more, and soon was able to steer the ship where he wanted and to make it go at any speed he wanted.

Fine—now he would take it back to Xanth and land beside the fireoak tree. Then he could turn it over to Blythe Brassie so she could fly back to her city and building.

Then blips appeared on the screen. They were shaped like little curse-burrs and were hurtling toward him. What did they want?

Then flashes of light came near him. The ship shook. The screen flared red for a moment, as if it had been knocked half silly. Smash understood this sort of thing. It was like getting knocked in the snoot by a fist and having stars and planets fly out from one's head. The entire night sky was filled with the stars flung out from people's heads in the course of prior fights, but Smash didn't care to have his own lights punched out. The thing to do was to hit back and destroy the enemy.

He checked the panel again, enjoying the prospect of a new type of violence. There was a big button he hadn't noticed before. Naturally he thumbed it.

A flash of light shot toward the blips, evidently from his own ship. It was throwing its sort of rocks when he told it to. Very well, in this strange gourd world, he could accept the notion of a fist made of light. But it wasn't aimed well, and missed the blips. It lanced on to blast a chunk of cheese out of the moon. Grated cheese puffed out into space in a diffuse cloud, where some of the blips went after it; no doubt they were hungry, too.

Smash pressed the button again, sending out another fist of light. This one missed both blips and moon. But he was getting the feel of it; he had to have his target in the very center of the mirror, where there was a faint intersection of lines like the center of a spider web. Funny place for a spider to work; maybe it had been trying to catch stray stars or blips or bits of blasted cheese.

To center the target, he had to work the two sticks in a coordinated fashion. He did so, after glancing nervously about to make quite sure no one was near to see him being so well coordinated. Of course, it took more than strength to balance his whole body on a single hamfinger or to smash a rock into a particular grade of gravel with one blow, but that was an ogre secret. It was fashionable to appear clumsy.

When he had a blip centered, he pushed the button with his big left toe so he wouldn't have to stop maneuvering. This time his aim was good; the beam speared out and struck the blip, which exploded with lovely violence and pretty colors.

This was fun! Not as much fun as physical bashing would be, but excellent vicarious mayhem. Ogres could appreciate beauty, too—the splendor of bursting bodies or of blips flying apart, forming intricate and changing patterns in the sky. He oriented on another blip, but it took evasive action.

Meanwhile, all the other blips were nearer, and their light-fists were striking closer. He had to dodge them, and that interfered with his own strikes.

Well, he was not an ogre for nothing! He licked his chops, worked his sticks, looped about, oriented, fired, dodged, and oriented again. Two more blips exploded beautifully.

Then the fight intensified. But Smash loved combat of any kind and was good at it; he didn't have to use physical fists. He almost liked this form of fighting better, because it was less familiar and therefore more of a challenge. He knocked out blip after blip, and after a while the remaining blips turned tail and fled past the moon. He had won the battle of the Luna fringe!

He was tempted to pursue the blips, so as to continue the pleasure of the fight a little longer, but realized that if he wiped them all out at this time, they would not have a chance to regenerate and return for future battles. Better to let them go, for the sake of more fun on future days. Also, he had other business.

He turned the ship about and headed for Xanth—which resembled a small disk from this vantage, like a greenish pie. That made him hungry again. Well, he would be careful not to miss it. He accelerated, zooming happily onward.

Chapter 8. Dragon's Ear

He was back in Xanth. "Smash, something else is coming!" Tandy cried.

"That's all right," he said. "I've won another battle. I feel stronger." And he did; he knew he was winning the gourd campaign, getting closer to the Night Stallion, and recovering physical strength in the process. It had been in large part his former hopelessness that had weakened him. He had believed his soul was doomed, until learning that he could fight for it in another gourd.

Blythe Brassie was still here. Now he wondered—how had she been carried out with him, when he had not been physically *in* the gourd?

His Eye Queue curse provided him with the answer to a question any normal ogre would not even have thought of. Blythe was here in spirit, just as he had been inside the gourd in spirit. It was very hard to tell such spirit from reality, but each person knew his own reality and was not fooled. No doubt Blythe Spirit's real body remained in the gourd, in a trance-state; since the brassies spent much of their time as statues anyway, waiting for someone to come push their button, no one had noticed the difference. Or rather, they had noticed, and been alarmed because she remained a statue while they were animate. So they knew that her vital element, her soul, was elsewhere. Yes, it all made sense. Everything in Xanth made sense, once a person penetrated the seeming nonsense that masked it. Different things made different sorts of sense for different people.

He would have to take the brass girl back. His curse not

only forced intelligence on him, it forced un-ogrish moral awareness. At the moment he wasn't even certain that such awareness was a bad thing, inconvenient as it might be when there was mayhem to be wreaked.

But the tree-chopping attack party was coming again. Smash oriented on the group as it galloped just beyond view. The villagers must have gotten reinforcements. The individuals were larger than basilisks—evidently Blythe had deposited the chickatrice safely elsewhere—but smaller than sphinxes. They were hoofed. In fact—

"That's my brother!" Chem exclaimed. "Now I recognize his hoofbeat. But there's something with him—not a centaur."

Smash braced himself for what could be a complicated situation. If some monster were riding herd on his friend Chet . . .

They hove into view. "Holey cow!" the Siren breathed.

That was exactly what it was—a cow as full of holes as any big cheese. She had holes in her body every which way through which daylight showed. She was worse than the moon! A big one was in her head, about where her brain should have been; evidently that didn't impede her much. Even her horns and tail had little holes. Her legs were so holey they seemed ready to collapse, yet she functioned perfectly well.

In fact, she carried two human riders who braced their hands and feet in her holes. She was a big cow, and her gait was bumpy, so these handholds and footholds were essential.

Now Smash recognized the riders. "Dor! Irene!" he cried happily.

"*Prince* Dor?" the Siren asked. "And his fiancée?"

"Yes, they are taking forever about working up to marriage," Chem murmured with a certain equine snideness. "It's been four years now . . ."

"And Grundy the Golem!" Smash added, spying the tiny figure perched on the back of the centaur. "All my friends!"

"We're your friends, too," Tandy said, nettled.

The party drew abreast of the fireoak tree. "What's this?" the golem cried. "Snow White and the Seven Dwarves?"

Smash stood among the damsels, towering over them, not comprehending the reference. But the Eye Queue curse soon clarified it, obnoxiously. Some of the Mundane settlers in Xanth had a story by that title, and, compared with Smash the Ogre, the seven females were dwarvishly short, as was even Chem the Centaur.

"It seems you have a way with women, Smash," Prince Dor said, dismounting from the holey cow and coming to greet him. "What's your secret?"

"I only agreed not to eat them," Smash said.

"To think how much simpler my life would have been if I had known that," Dor said. "I thought girls had to be courted."

"You never courted me!" Princess Irene exclaimed. She was a striking beauty by human standards, nineteen years old. The other girls all took jealously deep breaths, watching her. "I courted you! But you never would marry me."

"You never would set the date!" Dor retorted.

Her mouth opened in a pretty O of indignation. "*You* never set the date! I've been trying to—"

"They've been fighting about the date since before there was anything to date," Grundy remarked. "He doesn't even know what color her panties are."

"I don't think she knows herself," Dor retorted.

"I do, too!" Irene flashed. "They're—" She paused, then hiked up her skirt to look. "Green."

"It's only a pretext to show off her legs," Smash explained to the others.

"So I see," Tandy said enviously.

"And her panties," John said. She, like Fireoak, the Siren, and Chem, didn't wear panties, so couldn't show them off. Blythe's panties were copper-bottoms.

"You creatures are getting too smart," Irene complained. Then she did a double take, turning to Smash. "What happened to your rhymes?"

"I got cursed by the vine," the ogre explained. "It deprived me of both rhyme and stupidity in one swell foop."

"In a foop? Oh, you poor thing," she said sympathetically.

"Now that incorrigible ogre charm is working on Irene, too," Prince Dor muttered.

"Of course it is, idiot," she retorted. "All women have a

secret passion for ogres." She turned to Smash. "Now you had better introduce us all."

Smash did so with dispatch. "Tandy, Siren, John, Fireoak, Chem, Goldy, and Blythe—these are Dor, Irene, Grundy, and Chet, and vice versa."

"Moooo!" lowed the holey cow, each O with a big round hole in it.

"And the Holey Cow," Smash amended. Satisfied, the bovine swished her tattered tail and began to graze. The cropped grass fell out the holes in her neck as fast as she swallowed it, but she didn't seem to mind.

"I delivered your message," Chet said. "King Trent has declared this tree a protected species, and all the other trees in sight of it, and sent Prince Dor to inform the village. There will be no more trouble about that."

"Oh, wonderful!" the hamadryad cried. "I'm so happy!" She danced a little jig in air, hanging by one hand from a branch. The tree's leaves seemed to catch fire, harmlessly. Both nymph and tree were fully recovered from the indisposition of their recent separation. "I could just kiss the King!"

"Kiss me instead," Dor said. "I'm the messenger."

"Oh, no, you don't!" Irene flashed, taking him firmly by the ear.

"Kiss me instead of Dor," Chet offered. "There's no shrew guarding me."

The hamadryad dropped from her branch, flung her arms about the centaur, and kissed him. "Maybe I have been missing something," she commented. "But I don't think there are any males of my species."

"You could take up with one of the woodland fauns," Princess Irene suggested. "You do have pretty hair." The hamadryad's hair, under its red fringe, was green—as was Irene's hair.

"I'll consider it," Fireoak agreed.

"How did you gather such a bevy?" Prince Dor asked Smash. "They certainly seem affectionate, unlike some I have known." He moved with agility to avoid Irene's swift kick.

"I just picked them up along the way," the ogre said. "Each has her mission. John needs her correct name, the Siren needs a better lake—"

"They all need men," the golem put in.

"I need to go home," Blythe said.

"Oh. I'll take you there now." Smash reached for the gourd.

"She's from a hypnogourd?" Princess Irene asked. "This should be interesting. I always wondered what was inside one of those things."

Smash hooked his finger into Blythe's brassiere and lifted her high.

"Well, that's one way to pick up a girl," Dor remarked. "I'll have to try that sometime."

"Won't work," Irene said. "I don't wear a—"

"Not even a green one?" Tandy asked, brightening.

Smash looked into the gourd's peephole.

The two of them were in the brass spaceship, descending rapidly toward Xanth.

"Oh!" Blythe exclaimed, terrified. She flung her brass arms about Smash. "I'll fall! I'll fall! Save me, ogre!"

"But I have to bring it down to return to your building," Smash said. He was having difficulty because there was hardly room for two. He grabbed for a control stick, jerked it around—and the brass girl jumped.

"What are you doing with my knee?" she cried.

Oh. Smash saw now that he had hold of the wrong thing. But it was almost impossible to operate the controls with her limbs in the way. The ship veered crazily, which set Blythe off again. Her nerves certainly were not made of steel! The more she kicked and screamed, the worse the ship spun, and the more frightened she became. They were now plunging precipitously toward ground.

Then they were back under the fireoak tree. "We thought you had enough time to drop her off," Tandy said. Then she paused, frowning.

Blythe was wrapped around Smash, her metal arms hugging his neck desperately, her legs clasping his side. He had firm hold of one of her knees.

"I think we interrupted something," Princess Irene remarked sardonically.

Blythe's complexion converted from brass to copper. Smash suspected his own was doing much the same, as his Eye Queue now made him conscious of un-ogrish propri-

eties. The two disengaged, and Smash set the brass girl
down on the ground, where she sat and sobbed brass tears.
"We were crashing," Smash explained lamely.

"Oh—Mundane slang," Chet said. "But I think she
wasn't quite ready for it."

"It's really no business of ours what you call it," Grundy
said, smirking.

"Oh, don't be cruel!" the Siren said. "This poor girl is
terrified, and we know Smash wouldn't hurt her. Something is wrong in the gourd."

In due course they worked it out. Smash would have to
return to the brass building first, then come back for
Blythe, who, it seemed, was afraid of interplanetary
heights.

But now dawn was coming, and other business was
pressing. They had to inform the local village of the protected status of the tree and its environs, and then Chet
and his party had to return to Castle Roogna. In addition,
Blythe was no longer so eager to jump into the gourd, with
or without the ogre. If she went alone, she might find herself crashing in the ship, and have no way to get back outside, since she was not an outside creature. It would be
better to send her back later, once things were more settled.

"Oh," Chet said. "Almost forgot. I gave Tandy's message
to Crombie, and he made a pointing—that's his talent, you
know, pointing out things—and he concluded that if you
went north, you'd face great danger and lose three things
of value. But when he did a pointing back where you came
from, there was something else you'd lose that was even
more important. He couldn't figure out what any of the
things were, but thought you'd better be advised. He says
you're a spunky girl who will probably win through in the
manner of your kind."

Tandy laughed. "That's my father, all right! He hates
women, and he knows I'm growing up, so he's starting to
hate me, too. But I'm glad to have his advice."

"What's back at your home that's worse than the jungle
of Xanth?" Chet asked.

Tandy remembered the demon Fiant. "Never mind. I'm
not going home until that danger is nullified. I'll just take
my chances with the three things I'll lose in the jungle."

But she found the message disquieting. She had no things to lose—but she knew her father never made a mistake when he pointed something out.

Princess Irene's talent was growing plants. She grew a fine, big, mixed-fruit bush, and they dined on red, green, blue, yellow, and black berries, all juicy and luscious. Smash had always liked Irene, because no one remained hungry in her presence, and she did have excellent legs. Not that an ogre should notice, of course—yet it was hard not to imagine how delicious such firmly fleshed limbs would taste.

"Uh, before you go," the Siren said. "I understand you have a way with the inanimate, Prince Dor."

"Whatever gave you that idiotic notion, fish-tail?" a rock beside the Prince inquired. The Siren was sitting next to a bucket of water and was soaking her tail; she got uncomfortable when she spent too long out of the water.

"I picked up something, and I think it may be magical," the Siren continued. "But I'm not sure in what way, and don't want to experiment foolishly." She brought out a bedraggled, half-metallic thing.

"What are you?" Prince Dor asked the thing.

"I am the Gap Dragon's Ear," it answered. "The confounded ogre bashed me off the dragon's head."

Smash was surprised. "How did you get that?"

"I picked it up during the fight, then forgot about it, what with the pining tree and all," the Siren explained.

"The Gap Chasm does have a forgetful property," Irene said. "I understand that's Dor's fault."

"But the Gap's been forgotten for centuries, hasn't it?" the Siren asked. "We can only remember it now because we're still quite close to it; we'll forget it again when we go on north. How can Dor possibly be responsible?"

"Oh, he gets around," Irene said, giving the Prince a dark look. "He's been places none of us would believe. He even used to live with Millie, the sex-appeal maid."

"She was my governess when I was a child!" Dor protested. "Besides, she was eight hundred years old."

"And looked seventeen," Irene retorted. "You weren't conscious of that?"

Dor concentrated on the Ear. "What is your property?" he asked it.

"I hear anything relevant," it said. "I twitch when my possessor should listen. That's how the Gap Dragon always knew when prey was in the Gap. I heard it for him."

"Well, the Gap Dragon still has one ear to hear with," Dor said. "How can *we* hear what you hear?"

"Just listen to me, dummy!" the Ear said. "What else do you do with an ear?"

"That's a mighty impolite item," Tandy said, bothered.

"Can we test it?" the Siren asked. "Before you go, Prince Dor?"

"Oh, let me try," John said. She seemed much recovered, though her wings remained nubs. It would be long before she flew again, if ever.

The Siren gave her the Ear. John held it to her own tiny ear. She listened intently, her face showing puzzlement. "It's a rushing sound, maybe like water flowing," she reported. "Is that relevant?"

"Well, I didn't twitch," the Ear grumped. "You take your chances when there's nothing much on."

"How is that rushing noise relevant?" Dor asked the Ear.

"Obvious, stupid," the Ear said. "That's the sound of the waterfall where the fairy she wants is staying."

"It *is*?" John demanded, so excited that her wing-stubs fluttered. "The one with my name?"

"That's what I said, twerp."

"Do you tolerate insults from the inanimate?" the Siren asked the Prince.

"Only stupid things insult others gratuitously," Dor said.

"That's for sure, you moron," the rock agreed. Then it reconsidered. "Hey—"

The Siren laughed. "Now I understand. You have to consider the source."

Prince Dor smiled. "You resemble your sister. Of course, I've never seen her face."

"The rest will do," the Siren said, flattered. "Do only smart people compliment others gratuitously?"

"Perhaps," he agreed. "Or observant ones. But I do obtain much useful information from the inanimate. Now we must go talk with the villagers and head back to Castle Roogna. It has been nice to meet all of you, and I hope you all find what you wish."

There was a chorus of thank-yous. Prince Dor and

Princess Irene remounted the holey cow. Chet kissed Chem good-bye, and Grundy the Golem scrambled onto his back. "Get moving, horsetail!" Then Grundy paused thoughtfully, exactly as the rock had. They moved off toward the village.

"Dor will make a fine King one day," the Siren remarked.

"But Irene will run the show," Chem said. "I know them well."

"No harm in that," the Siren said, and the other girls laughed, agreeing.

"We'd better get started north," Tandy said. "Now that the tree is safe."

"How can I ever thank you?" Fireoak exclaimed. "You saved my life, my tree's life. Same thing."

"Some things are simply worth doing for themselves, dear," the Siren said. "I learned that when Chem's father Chester destroyed my dulcimer, so I couldn't lure men any more." Her sunshine hair clouded momentarily.

"My father did that?" Chem asked, surprised. "I didn't know!"

"It stopped me from being a menace to navigation," the Siren said. "I was doing a lot of damage, uncaringly. It was a necessary thing. Likewise it was necessary to save the fireoak tree."

"Yes," Chem agreed. But she seemed shaken.

They bade farewell to the hamadryad, promising to visit her any time any of them happened to be in the vicinity, and started north.

At first they passed through normal Xanth countryside—carnivorous grasses, teakettle serpents whose hisses were worse than their fires, poisonous springs, tangle trees, sundry spells, and the usual ravines, mountains, river rapids, slow and quicksand bogs, illusions, and a few normally foul-mouthed harpies, but nothing serious occurred. They foraged along the way for edible things and took turns listening to the Gap Dragon's Ear, though it was not twitching; this became more helpful as they gradually learned to interpret it. The Siren heard a kind of splashing, as of someone swimming. She took this to be the merman she wanted to find. Goldy heard the sounds of a goblin settlement in operation: where she was going. Smash heard the rhyming grunts of ogres. Blythe, persuaded to try it, jumped as the Ear twitched in her hands, and she actually heard herself mentioned. The brassies missed her and feared the ogre had betrayed their trust. "I must go back!" she cried. "As soon as I recover enough of my courage. My nerves aren't iron, you know."

But when Chem tried it, her face sobered. "It must be out of order. All I get is a faint buzzing."

The Siren took back the Ear. "That's funny. I get the buzzing, too, now."

They passed the Ear around. Everyone heard the same thing, and it twitched for none of them.

Smash applied his Eye Queue curse to the Ear. "Either it is malfunctioning," he decided, "or the buzzing is somehow relevant to all of us, without being specific to any of us. No one is talking about us, no one is lurking for us, so it is just something we should know about."

"Let's assume it's not malfunctioning," Tandy said. "The last thing we need is a glitching Ear, especially when my father says there is danger ahead. So we'd better watch out for something that buzzes. It seems to be getting louder as we go."

Indeed it was. Now there were variations in it, louder buzzes in front of background ones, an elevating and lowering of pitch. It was, in fact, a whole collection of buzzes, sounding three-dimensional, as some pitches became louder and clearer, while others faded back and some faded out entirely. What did it mean?

They came across a wall made from paper. It traveled roughly east/west and reached up to the top level of the trees, too high for Smash to surmount. It was opaque; he could not see through it at all.

However, a wall of paper could hardly impede an ogre. He readied a good punch.

"Careful!" John cried. "That looks like—"

Smash's fist punched through the wall. The paper separated readily, but glued itself to his arm.

"Flypaper," the fairy concluded.

Smash tried to pull the sticky stuff off, but it stuck to his other hand when he touched it. The more he worked at it, the more places it adhered to. Soon he was covered with the stuff.

"Slow down, Smash," Chem said. "I'm sure hot water will clean that off. I saw a hotspring a short distance back."

She took him to the hotspring and washed him off, and it did clean him up. Her hands were efficient yet gentle; Smash discovered he liked having a female attend to him this way. But of course he couldn't admit it; he was an ogre. "Next time use a stick to poke through that paper," the centaur advised.

But when they returned to the wall, they found the others had already thought of that. They had poked and peeled a hole big enough for anyone to pass through. "But there's one thing," Tandy warned. "There are swarms of flies over there."

So that was what the Ear had warned them of. They were going to pass through a region of flies.

That didn't bother Smash; he normally ignored flies. Blythe was also unworried; no fly could sting brass. But Tandy, Chem, Goldy, John, and the Siren were concerned. They didn't want stinging flies raising welts on their pretty skins. "If only we had some repellent," Tandy said. "In the caves there are some substances that drive them off—"

"Some repellent bushes do grow in these parts," Goldy said. "Let me look." She scouted about and soon located one. "The only problem is, they smell awful." She held out the leaves she had plucked.

She had not overstated the case. The stench was appalling. No wonder the flies stayed clear of it!

They discussed the matter and decided it was better to stink than to suffer too great a detour in their route north. They held their breath and rubbed the foul leaves over their bodies. Then, reeking of repellent, they stepped through the rent in the flypaper and proceeded north.

There was a sound behind them. Marching along the paper wall was a monstrous fly in coveralls, toting a cart. It stopped at the rent, unrolled a big patch of paper, and set it in place, sealing it over with stickum. Then the flypaper hanger moved on to the east, following the wall.

"We're sealed in," Tandy muttered.

A dense swarm of stingflies spotted them and zoomed in—only to bank off in dismay as the awful odor smote it. Good enough; Smash's nose was already acclimating or getting deadened to the smell, which wasn't much worse than that of another ogre, after all.

They walked on, watching the flies. There were many varieties, and some were beautiful with brightly colored, patterned wings and furry bodies. John became very quiet; obviously she missed her own patterned wings. There were deerflies and horseflies and dragonflies, looking like winged miniatures of their species; the deerflies nibbled blades of grass, the horseflies kicked up their heels as they galloped, and the dragonflies even jetted small lances of fire. At one spot there was music; fiddler flies were playing for damselflies to dance. It seemed to be a real fly ball.

This became a pleasant trip, since there seemed to be no dangerous creatures here; the flies had driven them all away. But then the sky clouded and rain fell. It was a light fall—but it washed away their repellent. Suddenly they were in trouble, having failed to take immediate shelter.

The first flies to discover this were sweat-gnats. Soon a cloud of them hovered about each person except Blythe, causing everyone to sweat uncomfortably. Smash inhaled deeply and blew the gnats away, but as soon as the turbulence ebbed, they were back worse than ever. Other flies saw the clouds and, in turn, converged. Some of these were itchers, causing intolerable itches; others were bleeders, causing blood to flow from painless bites. But the worst, as it turned out, were the fly-bys, because they flew by, observed, and carried the news of new prey to all corners of the Kingdom of the Flies. After that, the very sky was darkened by the mass of the converging swarms. There seemed to be no effective way to fight them, for there were far too many to swat or shoo away.

Then the swarms drew off a little, and a pair of shoe-flies marched up. A formation of bowflies sent a fly arrow shooting in the direction Smash's party was supposed to go. It seemed better to obey, rather than fight, for there were sawflies and hammerflies and screwdriverflies that could be most awkward to fend off.

They marched, and the swarms paced them, buzzing out

a tune that sounded like a requiem. Smash had not imagined that so many flies existed in Xanth. They coated the
trees, they popped out of myriad holes in the ground, they
formed clouds in the sky that rained droppings.

The party arrived at a palace fashioned of flypaper
coated with fly ash. Here, surrounded by a cluster of fawn-
ing damselflies, perched the Lord of the Flies—a huge, demonic figure with multiple-faceted eyes. He was reading
the flyleaf of a book titled *The Sting* by Wasp.

"Bzzzzzz?" the Fly Lord inquired, looking up with several facets.

The query seemed to be directed at Smash, but he did
not comprehend fly talk. He grunted noncommittally.

"Bzzzzzz!" the Fly repeated angrily.

Smash had an idea. He lifted the Gap Dragon's Ear to
his own. Maybe that would provide a translation.

All he heard was the roaring and hissing of dragons. No
help there.

The Fly buzzed again, angry light glinting from quite a
number of facets. Giant guardflies swarmed up to grab the
Ear. "Don't fight them, Smash!" Tandy cried, alarmed.

The ogre didn't like it, but realized they could all be
bitten and stung to death if he made trouble. It was the
curse of the Eye Queue again, making him react intelligently. He let the flies take the Ear.

They dragged it to the Fly Lord, who cocked his head in
order to listen to it. And the Ear twitched, almost knocking
the Fly off his perch. "Bzzzzzz!" he buzzed angrily, and
there was a flutter of alarm among the damselflies. It
seemed the Lord had used very strong language. But he got
back up to listen. "Bzzzzzz!" and the guardflies hovered in
military readiness. "BZZZZZZ!" and the surrounding
swarms retreated.

The Fly Lord angled a few facets at Smash, as if pondering a suitable action. Then he buzzed out another command. Instantly the guardflies closed on Smash's party
again, and the bowflies fired off another arrow pointing
the way.

"I don't know whether the Gap Dragon's Ear has provided us with doom or reprieve," Chem said. "But we'd
better go along."

They went along. The arrows pointed them to the east. Soon they arrived at the flypaper wall. At this point a squadron of big spearflies charged, threatening to run every member of the party through.

They got the message. They all plunged through the wall. They got terribly stuck-up with flypaper, but the flies let them be. It seemed they had been banished from Flyland.

They staggered around, looking for another hotspring for washing. But before they found one, a small flying dragon spied them. It winged rapidly east.

"I fear this is dragon country," the Siren said. "Look at the dragonclaw marks on the trees."

Smash saw that all the trees were marked, and the scratches were definitely those of dragons. The largest and deepest scrapes were also the highest; the biggest monsters set the most imposing signatures. "We had better move," he said. In his present state he could not adequately protect this party against a pack of dragons, annoying as it was to admit that fact even privately.

But they couldn't move very well, tangled in flypaper. It was collecting dirt and leaves and stray bugs, making each member of the party resemble a harpy dipped in glue. Long before they found a hotspring, they heard the heavy tread of the feet of a land dragon.

"You know what?" the Siren said angrily. "The flies offered us up to the dragons!"

"And the Ear, too," John cried, spying the Gap Dragon's Ear on the ground.

"That's to frame us," Goldy said. "The dragons will think we killed one of their number, and they'll really chomp us."

Smash braced himself. "I'll try to hold them off."

"You haven't yet recovered enough strength," the Siren said. "And many big dragons are coming. Don't try to fight." She took the Ear from John and listened to it. It twitched in her hand. "Someone's talking about us! An ogre, a centaur, and five nymphs."

"That won't do us much good if the dragons eat us," Tandy muttered.

"What's it like to be eaten?" Blythe asked. Clothed in

paper, she looked just like the others, with hardly any of her metal showing.

"That's right—you have had even less experience in regular Xanth than I have," Tandy said. "But I doubt you'll ever be eaten. Your body is brass."

"Well, everything is brass where I come from," Blythe replied. "My pet bird is brass, my sheep is brass, even my ass is brass. That's the way it is in the City of Brass. What does that have to do with being eaten?"

"Monsters don't eat brass here," Tandy explained.

"I can't be eaten?" Blythe asked, sounding disappointed.

"Oh, you could try," John said. "When the first dragon comes, you could volunteer to be the first eaten. But I think you alone among us are secure from that fate."

"I wonder," the brassie said thoughtfully.

Already the first dragon was arriving. It was a huge eight-legged land rover, snorting smoke. Smash strode forward to meet it, knowing it would have been too much for him even when he had his full strength. It wasn't the dragon's size so much as its heat; it could roast him long before he hurt it. But the dragon would attack regardless of whether he fought, and it was an ogre's way to fight. Maybe he could hurl some boulders at it and score a lucky conk on its noggin.

Then Blythe ran past him, intercepting the dragon. The dragon exhaled, bathing her in flame, but brief heat could not hurt her. She continued right on up to its huge snout. "Eat me first, dragon!" she cried.

The dragon did not squat on ceremony. It opened its monstrous jaws and took her in in one bite.

And broke half a dozen teeth on her hard metal.

Blythe frowned amidst the smoke and piled fragments of teeth. "You can do better than that, dragon!" she urged indignantly.

The dragon tried again—and broke six more teeth.

"Come on, creature!" Blythe taunted. "Show your mettle on my metal. I've received worse dents just from being dropped—but I won't say where."

Now several more dragons arrived. They paused, curious about the holdup. Another snatched Blythe away, crunching down hard on her body—and it, too, lost six teeth.

The brass girl was insulted. "Is that all there is to it? What kind of experience is that? Here I visit this great big, soft, slushy, living world at great inconvenience, and you monsters aren't doing a thing!"

Abashed, the dragons stared at her. She still looked like a clothed flesh person. Finally a third one tried—and lost its quota of teeth.

"If you dumb dragons can't eat one little girl when she's cooperating, what good are you?" Blythe demanded, disgusted. She shook tooth fragments off her body, marched up to one of the largest monsters, and yanked at a whisker. "You—eat me or else!"

The dragon exhaled a horrendous belch of flame. It burned Blythe's remaining flypaper to ashes, but didn't hurt her. Seeing that, the monster backed off, dismayed. If a thing couldn't be chomped or scorched, it couldn't be handled.

"You know, I think we have had a stroke of luck," the Siren said. "The dragons naturally assume we are all like that."

"Luck?" John asked. "Blythe knows what she's doing! She knows she needs us to get her back to her world. She's helping us get out of a fix."

Smash's Eye Queue operated. "Maybe we can benefit further. We need a nice, steady stream of steam to melt off the flypaper."

"A steam bath," the Siren agreed. "But very gentle."

Blythe tried it. She approached a big steam-turbine dragon. "Bathe me, monster, or I'll make you eat me," she said imperiously.

Cowed, the dragon obeyed. It jetted out a wash of rich white steam and vapor. In a moment the brass girl stood shining clean, well polished, the fly ash all sogged off.

"Now my friends," Blythe ordered. "A little lower on the heat; they're tougher than I am and don't need so much."

She was playing it cool! Nervously the others stood in place while the dragon sent forth a cooler blast. Smash and the girls stepped into it. The vapor was as hot as John could stand, but since she had already lost her wings, it didn't hurt her. The others had no trouble. All the flypaper was steamed off.

Smash also became aware that his fleas were gone. Now that he thought about it, he realized that he hadn't been scratching since entering the Kingdom of the Flies. Those fly-repellent leaves must have driven off the fleas, too!

Now a dragon approached with an elf on a leash. "Do any of you freaks speak human?" the elf asked.

Smash exchanged glances with the others. Blythe Brassie had been speaking to these monsters all along, and they had understood. Didn't this elf know that? Better to play it stupid. "Me freak, some speak," he said, emulating his former ogre mode.

The elf considered him. The little man's expression ran a brief gamut from fear of a monster to contempt for the monster's wit. "What are you doing here with these six females?"

"Me anticipate girls taste great," Smash said, slurping his tongue over his chops.

Again the fearful contempt. "I *know* ogres eat people. But what are you doing here in Dragonland?"

Smash scratched his hairy head as if confused. "Me criticize buzzing flies."

"Oh. They booted you." The elf made crude growls at his dragon, and Smash realized he was translating, much as Grundy the Golem did for the King of Xanth. Maybe Blythe had gotten through to the dragons mainly by force of personality.

The dragon growled back. "You'll have to check in with the Dragon Lady."

"Dragon Lady not afraidy?" Smash asked stupidly.

The elf sneered. "Of the like of you? Hardly. Come on now, ignoramus."

Ignoramus? Smash smiled inwardly. Not while he remained cursed with the Eye Queue! But he shuffled behind the dragon, gesturing the girls to follow.

The Siren fell in beside Smash as they walked. "I've been listening to the Ear," she murmured. "The voice that talked about us before was the elf's; the Dragon Lady knows about us already. Now the Ear is roaring like a terrible storm. I don't know what that means."

"Maybe we have to get to that storm," Smash whispered. Then the elf turned, hearing him talk, and the conversation had to end.

They came to a huge tent fashioned of dragonet. Inside the net was the Dragon Lady—a scintillatingly regal Queen of her species. She reclined, half supine, in her huge nest of glittering diamonds; whenever she twitched, the precious stones turned up new facets, like the eyes of the Lord of the Flies, reflecting spots of light dazzlingly. She switched her barbed, blue tail about restlessly, growling, and arched her bright red neck. It was really quite impressive. She had been reading a book of Monster Comics, and seemed not too pleased to be interrupted.

"Her Majesty the Illustrious Dragon Lady demands further information, oaf," the elf said, becoming imperious in the reflected glory of his mistress.

Oaf, eh? Smash played stupider than ever. "Me slow, no know," he mumbled.

"Is it true you are impossible to eat?"

Smash held out a gauntleted fist. The Dragon Lady reached delicately forward with her snout and took a careful nip. The metal balked her gold-tinted teeth, and she quickly desisted. She growled.

"If you aren't edible, what use are you, Her Majesty wants to know?" the elf demanded.

"What a question!" Tandy cried indignantly. "People-creatures rule Xanth!"

"*Dragon*-creatures rule Xanth," the elf retorted. "Dragons tolerate other creatures only as prey." Nonetheless, the Dragon Lady's growl was muted. Smash suspected that she was not eager to incite a war with the Transformer-King of the human folk.

In response to another growl from his mistress, the elf turned again to Smash. "What are we to do with you?" he demanded.

Smash shrugged. "Me only distrust place where me rust." Actually, neither his stainless steel gauntlets nor Blythe's brass rusted; water was more likely to cause trouble with the fires of the dragons. But he was mindful of

the Ear's storm-signal; if he could trick the Dragon Lady
into casting them into the storm, their chances should be
better than they were here.

"Metal—rust," the elf mused as the Dragon Lady
growled. "True, our iron-scaled dragons do have a problem
in inclement weather." He glanced suspiciously at Smash.
"I don't suppose you could be fooling us?"

"Me ghoul, big fool," Smash said amiably.

"Obviously," the elf agreed with open contempt.

So the Dragon Lady ordered the inedible party dumped
into the Region of Air, since the Region of Water did not
border Dragonland. An abrupt demarcation established the
border; the near side was green turf and trees, the far side
a mass of roiling stormcloud. Smash didn't like this, for he
knew the others could not endure as much punishment as
he could. But now they were committed, and it did seem
better than staying among the dragons. They took the pre-
caution of roping themselves together with Chem's rope so
that no one would blow away.

They stepped across the line. Instantly they were in the
heart of the wind, choking on dust. It was a dust storm, not
a rainstorm! The flying sand cut cruelly into their skins.
Smash picked up several girls and hunched his gross body
over them, protecting them somewhat as he staggered forward. Then he tripped, for he could not see his own flat
feet in this blinding sand, and fell and rolled, holding himself rigid so as not to crush the girls.

He fetched up in a valley formed in the lee of a boulder.
Chem thumped to a stop beside them. Here the sand by-
passed the party, mostly, and it was possible for each person to pry open an eye or two. Thanks to the rope, all were
present, though battered.

"What do we do now?" Tandy asked, frightened.

The Siren sat up and put the Ear to her ear. "Nothing
here," she reported. "But maybe the noise of this sandstorm is drowning it out."

Smash took the Ear and listened. "I hear the brass spaceship," he said.

Blythe took it. "I hear my own folk! They're playing the
brass band! I must be ready to go home!"

"Are you sure?" the Siren asked.

"Yes, I think I am now," the brass girl said. "I have experienced enough of your world to know I like mine better. You are all nice enough people, but you just aren't brass."

"All too true," the Siren agreed. "We must find another gourd so Smash can take you back. We might all prefer your world at this moment."

"Maybe that's the silence you heard," Tandy said. "A gourd."

"No, there's lots of noise in the gourd," Smash said. "It's an ogrishly fun place."

"Let's find that gourd!" Blythe exclaimed. She was hardly bothered by the sand; she was merely homesick.

"Not until this storm dies down," the Siren said firmly. "Gourds don't grow in this weather."

"But this is the Region of Air; the wind will never die," Blythe protested.

Chem nodded agreement. "I have, as you know, been mapping the inner wilds of Xanth; that's why I'm here. My preliminary research, augmented by certain references along the way, suggests that there are five major elemental regions in Unknown Xanth: those of Air, Earth, Fire, Water, and the Void. This certainly seems to be Air—and probably the storm never stops here. We'll just have to plow on out of it."

"I can plow!" Blythe said eagerly. She milled her brass hands and began tunneling through the mounded sand. In moments she had started a tunnel.

"Good idea!" Tandy exclaimed. "I'll help!" She shook sand out of her hair and fell in behind the brass girl, scooping the sand farther back. Soon the others were helping, too, for as the tunnel progressed, the sand had longer to go before it cleared.

Finally they were all doing it, in a line, with Smash at the tail end packing the sand into a lengthening passage behind. Progress was slow but relatively comfortable. Periodically Blythe would tunnel to the surface to verify that the storm was still there. When they came to a sheltering cliff, they emerged and made better time on the surface. The landscape was bleak: all sand and more sand. There were dunes and valleys, but no vegetation and no water.

The wind was indefatigable. It howled and roared and whistled. It formed clouds and swirls and funnels, doing its peculiar sculpture in the sky. Every so often a funnel would swoop in near the cliff, trying to suck them into its circular maw, but it could not maintain itself so close to the stone. Smash was aware that this must be a great frustration to the funnels, which were rather like ogres in their way—all violence and brainlessness.

Then they came to another demarcation. As they stepped across it, the winds abruptly ceased. The air cleared miraculously. But this was no improvement, for the violence of the air was replaced by the violence of the land. The ground shuddered, and not by any ogre's tread. It was an earthquake!

"Oh, I don't like this!" Chem said. "I've always been accustomed to the firmness of ground beneath my hooves."

Smash glanced at her. The centaur girl was standing with her forelegs braced awkwardly in different directions, her brown coat dulled by the recent sand-scouring, her tail all atremble, and her human breasts dancing rather appealingly. "Maybe the ground is firmer farther north," he suggested.

They turned north—and encountered an active volcano. Red-hot lava boiled out of it and flowed down the slope toward them. "Oh, this is worse yet!" Chem complained, slapping at a spark that landed in her pretty tail. She was really shaken; this was just not her type of terrain.

The Siren listened to the Gap Dragon's Ear again. "Say!" she said. "The sounds differ, depending on which way I face!" She rotated, listening intently. "To the north, it's a horrendous crashing; that's the volcano we see. I can hear the sound as I see it belch. To the south, it's the roaring of winds. We've already been there. To the west, a sustained rumble—the main part of the earthquake. To the east—" She smiled beautifically. "A lovely, quiet, still silence."

"Graves are silent," Tandy said with a shudder.

"Better a graveyard than this," Chem said. "We can walk on through a cemetery."

"Sometimes," Tandy agreed.

They turned east. The ground shifted constantly beneath

them as if trying to prevent progress, but they were determined to get free of this region.

As the sun set tiredly beyond the volcano, fortunately not landing inside it, they reached another demarcation of zones. Just beyond it was a patch of hypnogourds. The silence was not of the grave, but of a garden area.

"I never thought I'd be glad to see a patch of those," Tandy said grimly.

"This is where we spend the night," the Siren said. "While we're at it, let's find out whether those gourds are edible."

"Save one! Save one!" Blythe cried.

"Of course, dear. Try this one." The Siren handed the brass girl a nice big gourd.

Blythe hesitated, then looked into the peephole. She looked back up. "There's nothing there," she said.

"Nothing there?" It had not occurred to Smash that any of the gourds could be inoperative. He took the gourd from Blythe and looked in.

And found himself in the spaceship, spinning toward the ground. Hastily he grabbed the controls and tilted it back to equilibrium. Without the brass girl entangling him, he could manage just fine.

In moments he brought the ship back to the City of Brass and to the launching building. He managed to turn it around and land fairly neatly. Then he got out and made his way through the moving buildings to the one where Blythe lived, Number Four, following his string back. He wondered idly whether he had left a trail of string strewn all over the sky, near the moon. He had lost that string in Xanth, but retained it here. Good enough.

The brassies clustered around him. "Where is Blyght?" they demanded. "We're rehearsing with our brass band, and we need her."

"Blythe. She changed her name. She'll be back as soon as I can fetch her. She heard you practicing, and said she would come back very soon. I had to find my way back here, because spaceships scare her."

"Of course; we are afraid of heights. We dent when we fall too far. Blyght already had a dent in her—"

"Don't speak of that to a stranger!" a brass girl told the male brassie.

"So give me some time," Smash said, "and I'll return her. Now I know how to do it."

They were not quite satisfied with this, but let him be. Smash settled down in a niche that moved with the wall, and snoozed.

Chapter 9. Gourmet Gourd

He woke in Xanth, where Tandy had taken away the gourd. "I never know how long to give you," she said. "I'm very nervous about leaving you in there." She lifted the Gap Dragon's Ear. "I kept listening in this, and when it got pretty quiet, I thought maybe it was time to bring you out. I wasn't sure it was you I was listening to, but since your health is relevant to mine—"

Smash took the Ear. He heard a guttural voice, saying, "Mirror, mirror on the wall, pass this fist or take a fall," followed by a tinkling crash.

"It's not quiet now," Smash reported. "Sounds like me talking."

She smiled. "Talk all you want, Smash. You're my mainstay in this strange surface world. I do worry when you're gone."

Smash put his huge, hairy paw over her tiny human hand. "I appreciate that, Tandy. I know it would be bad for you if you got stranded alone in wilderness Xanth. But I am learning to handle things in the gourd, and I am getting stronger."

"I hope so," she said. "We all do need you, and not just for protection from monsters. Chem says there seems to be a mountain range to the north that we can't scale; the dragons are to the east, and the air storm to the south. So we'll have to veer west, back through the Region of Earth—and that volcano is still spewing hot lava."

"We shall just have to wait till the lava stops," Smash said.

"Yes. But we don't know how long that will be—and it

171

will have to cool so we can walk over it. I guess we're here in the melon patch for a while yet."

"So be it," Smash said. He released her hand, lest the inordinate weight of his own damage it. "Did you say these gourds are edible?"

"Oh, yes, certainly. You can eat all you want. We're all full; they're very good, just so long as you don't look in the peephole. Funny thing is, there's no sign of any world in there, no graveyard or anything." She handed him a gourd, peephole averted.

Smash took a huge bite. It was indeed good, very sweet and seedy and juicy. It did seem strange that something that could affect his consciousness could also be such good eating—but, of course, that was the nature of things other than gourds. A dragon could be a terrible enemy—but was also pretty good eating, once conquered.

"That gourd I just looked into—" Smash said between gulps. "Why didn't it return Blythe when she looked?"

"We discussed that while you were out," Tandy said. She was the only one of the girls who remained awake; the others were sleeping, including the brass girl. Smash wondered briefly why a person made of metal needed to sleep, then realized this was no more remarkable than a person of metal becoming animate at the punch of a button. "We concluded that she is merely a representation, like you when you're in the gourd. So she can't cross through by herself; she has to be taken by one of us. Then her pretend-body will vanish here, just as yours vanishes there."

"Makes sense," Smash agreed, consuming another gourd in a few bites. "Did she disappear when I took her aboard the Luna shuttle ship?"

"Yes. You remained, holding nothing. Then she reappeared when we took the gourd away, hugging you—"

"There was no room in that cockpit," Smash explained.

"I understand," she said, somewhat distantly.

"I'm out of the ship now, and back in her building. There won't be any trouble this time."

"That's nice. But please rest before you go back in there," Tandy said. "There is time, while we wait for the lava to stop. And—"

Smash glanced at her. She was mostly a silhouette in the wan moonlight, rather pretty in her pensiveness. "Yes?"

She shrugged. "Take care of yourself, Smash."

"Ogres do," he said, cracking a smile. It seemed to him that she had meant to say something more. But, of course, girls changed their minds readily, especially small girls, whose minds were small. Or whatever.

When he was comfortably stuffed, Smash stretched out among the gourds and slept. Tandy settled against his furry forearm and slept, too. He was aware of her despite his unconsciousness, and found he rather liked her cute little company. He was becoming distressingly un-ogrish at times; he would have to correct that.

As dawn brightened, the lava dulled. The volcano was quiescent. The Siren listened to the Ear and reported silence, which she took to mean that they should wait for further cooling. Periodically she tossed damp fragments of gourd on the nearest hardening lava flow; as long as it sizzled and steamed, the time was not yet right.

"Are you ready to go home, Blythe?" Smash asked the brass girl, knowing the answer. "I'm back in the building."

"Good and ready, ogre," she agreed with alacrity. She turned to the others. "No offense to you folk; I like you. But I don't understand this wide-open land. It's so much more secure in a brass building."

"I'm sure it is, dear," the Siren said, embracing her. "Maybe in due course the rest of us will find our own brass buildings."

"And the way you have to sleep here, instead of getting turned off by a button—that's strange."

"All creatures are strange in their own fashion," Chem said. "And we want to thank you for what you did with the dragons. You may have saved our hides."

"I took no risk," Blythe said. But she flushed copper, pleased.

Then Smash picked Blythe up by her brassiere. "And keep your hand off her knee!" Tandy warned.

Everyone laughed, and he looked into a delicious-seeming gourd.

This time it worked. They were both in the brass building.

The brassies spied them and clustered around. There was

a flurry of welcomings. Blythe was certainly glad to be home.

"Now if you folk can tell me some other way out of here, I will depart," Smash said. "I don't want the spaceship; there must be some land route."

"Oh, there is!" Blythe said eagerly. "I'll show you."

"Haven't you had enough of me?" Smash asked.

"I feel I owe it to you to help you on your way," she said defensively. "I'll show you the way to the paper world."

"As you wish," Smash agreed. "But you helped us considerably, what with the tunneling and such."

Her face clouded, turning leaden. "The dragons wouldn't eat me!"

Smash did not argue the point. Evidently the brass girl had more than one motive for her scene with the dragons.

Blythe led him out a concealed door, into a smaller chamber. Smash had to hunch over to fit in this one. Then the room jerked and moved, causing him to bump into a wall. "This is an elevator," Blythe explained. "It leads to the paper works, but it takes a little while."

"I'll wait," Smash said, squatting down and leaning into a corner so he would not be bumped around too much."

Blythe sat on one of his knees. "Smash—"

He suffered déjà vu. His Eye Queue insisted on running down the relevance immediately, instead of allowing it to be the pleasant mystery nature intended. Tandy had addressed him in much the same way last night. "Yes?"

"I wanted to talk to you a moment, alone," she confessed. "That's why I volunteered to show you the way. There's something you should know."

"Where your dent is?"

"I can't show you that; your knee's in the way. It's something else."

"You know something about the Night Stallion?" he asked, interested.

"No, not that," she said. "It's about Xanth."

"Oh."

"Smash, I'm not part of your world. But maybe I see something you don't. Those girls like you."

"And I like them," he admitted, voicing the un-ogrish sentiment with a certain embarrassment. How was he ever going to find his Answer in life if he kept losing his identity? "They're nice people. So are you."

Again she coppered. "I like them, too. I never knew flesh people before. But that's not what I mean. They—they're not just friends to you. It's hard for me to say, because my own heart's made of brass. They're female; you're male. So—"

"So I protect them," Smash agreed. "Because females aren't very good at surviving by themselves. I'll help as long as they are with me and need protection."

"That, too. But it's more than that. Tandy, especially—"

"Yes, she needs a lot of protection. She hardly knows more of Xanth than you do, and she's not made of metal."

The brass girl seemed frustrated, but she kept smiling. Her little teeth were brass, too. "We talked, some, while you were in the gourd—that's funny, to think of my whole world as a gourd!—and Tandy told us why she left home. I may be violating a confidence, but I really think you ought to know."

"Know what?" Smash asked. His Eye Queue informed him he was missing something significant; that was an annoying part of the curse. A true ogre wouldn't have worried!"

"Why she left home. You see, there was this demon, named Fiant, who was looking for a wife. Well, not a wife, exactly—you know."

"A playmate?"

"You could call it that. But Tandy didn't want to play. I gather a demon is like an ifrit, not nice at all. She refused to oblige him. But he pursued her and tried to rape her—"

"What is that?" Smash asked.

"Rape? You actually don't know?"

"I'm not made of brass," he reminded her. "There's lots I don't know. There is a kind of plant in Xanth by that name that girls shy away from—"

She sighed. "The Siren's right. You are hopelessly naïve. Maybe all males worth knowing are. But, of course, that's why females exist; someone has to know what's what. Look, Smash—do you know the way of a man with a woman?" Her brass face was more coppery than ever, and he realized this was an awkward subject for her.

"Of course not," he reassured her. "I'm an ogre."

"Well, the way of an ogre with an ogress?"

"Certainly." What was she getting at?

She paused. "I'm not sure we're communicating. Maybe you'd better tell me what is the way of an ogre with an ogress."

"He chases her down, screaming, catches her by a rope of hair, hauls her up by one leg, bashes her head against a tree a few times, throws her down, sets a boulder on her face so she can't get away, then—"

"That's rape!" Blythe cried, appalled.

"That's fun," he countered. "Ogresses expect it, and give back little ogres. It's the ogre mode of love."

"Well, it isn't the human mode of love."

"I know. Human beings are so gentle, it's a wonder they even know what they're doing. Prince Dor and Princess Irene have taken four years trying to get around to it. Now, if they had a little more ogre heritage, four seconds might be enough to—"

"Ah . . . yes," she agreed. "Well, this demon tried to—to make ogre love to Tandy—"

"Oh, now I understand! Tandy wouldn't like that!"

"True. She's no ogress. So she left her home and sought help. And the Good Magician told her to travel with you. That way the demon can't get her."

"Sure. If she wants that demon smashed, I'll do it. That's my name."

"That's not exactly what she wants. You see, she does want to marry—someone other than the demon. And she has a lot to offer the right male. So she hopes to find a suitable husband on this journey. But—"

"That's wonderful!" Smash said in the best un-ogrish tradition. "Maybe we'll find a nice human man, just right for her."

"You didn't wait for my but, Smash."

"Your butt?" he asked, looking at her brass posterior. "Where your dent is?"

"But, B U T," she clarified. "As in however."

"However has a dent?"

She paused briefly. "Forget the dent. However she likes you."

"Certainly, and I like her. So I will help her find herself a man."

"I don't think you understand, Smash. She may not want to go with her ideal human man, if she finds him, if she likes you too well first."

He chortled. "Nobody likes an ogre too well!"

The brass girl shook her head doubtfully. "I'm not sure. You are no ordinary ogre, they inform me. For one thing, they told me you're much smarter than most of your kind."

"That's because of the curse of the Eye Queue. Once I get rid of that, I'll be blissfully stupid again. Just like any other ogre. Maybe more so."

"There is that," Blythe agreed. "I don't think Tandy would like you to be just like any other ogre."

The room stopped moving, after a jolt that bounced her off his knee. "Well, here we are at the paper world," she said.

The elevator opened onto a literal world of paper. Green-colored fragments of paper served for a lawn; brown and green paper columns were trees; a flat paper sun hung in the painted blue sky. At least this world had color, in contrast with the monochrome of most of the rest of the gourd.

"This is as far as I go," Blythe said as Smash stepped out. "If it's any comfort, I think that in some ways you're still pretty stupid, even with the Eye Queue."

"Thank you," Smash said, flattered.

" 'Bye, ogre." The door closed and she was gone. Smash turned to the new adventure that surely awaited him.

Paper was everywhere. Smash saw a bird; idly he caught it out of the air in a paw, not to hurt it but to look at it, because it seemed strange. It turned out to be strange indeed; it, too, was made of paper, the wings corrugated, the body a cylinder of paper, the beak a stiffened, painted triangle of cardboard. He let it go and it flew away, peeping with the rasp of stiff paper.

Curious, he caught a bug. It was only an intricate convolution of paper, brightly painted. When he released it, the paper reconvoluted and the bug buzzed away. There were butterflies, also of paper. The bushes and stones and puddles were all colored paper. It seemed harmless enough.

Then a little paper machine charged up. Smash had seen machines during a visit to Mundania and didn't like them; they were ornery mechanical things. This one was way too small to bother him seriously, but it did bother him lightly. It fired a paper spitball at him.

The spitball stung his knee. Smash smiled. The miniature machine had a name printed on its side: TANK. It was cute.

The ogre stomped on. The tank followed, firing another damp paper ball. It stung Smash on the rump. He frowned. The humor was wearing thin. He didn't care to have a dent to match that of the brass girl.

He turned to warn the tank away—and its third shot plastered his nose.

That did it. Smash lifted one brute foot and stomped the obnoxious machine flat. It was only paper; it collapsed readily. But an unexpended spitball stuck to the ogre's toe.

Smash tromped on, seeking whatever challenge this section offered. But now three more of the paper tanks arrived. Burp—burp—burp! Their spitballs spit in a volley at the ogre, sticking to his belly like a line of damp buttons. He stamped all three paper vehicles flat.

Yet more tanks arrived, and these were larger. Their spitballs stung harder, and one just missed his eye. Smash had to shield his face with one hand while he stomped them.

He heard something behind. A tank was chewing up his line of string! That would prevent him from knowing when he crossed his own trail, and he could get lost. He strode back and picked up the tank, looking closely at it.

The thing burped a huge splat of a spitball at him that plugged a nostril. Smash sneezed—and the tank was blown into a flat sheet of paper. Words were printed on it: GET WITH IT, DOPE.

Funny—Smash had never learned how to read. No ogre was smart enough for literacy. But he grasped this message perfectly. This must be another facet of the curse of the Eye Queue. He pretended he did not fathom the words.

He turned again—and saw a much bigger paper tank charging down on him. He grabbed the tip of the cardboard cannon and pinched it closed just as the machine fired. The backpressure blew up the tank in a shower of confetti.

But more, and yet larger, tanks were coming. This region seemed to have an inexhaustible supply! Smash cast about for some way to stop them once and for all.

He had an idea. He bent to scoop through the paper-turf ground. Sure enough, it turned to regular dirt below, with rocks. He found a couple of nice quartz chunks and bashed them together to make sparks. Soon he struck a fire. The paper grass burned readily.

The tanks charged into the blaze—and quickly caught fire themselves. Their magazines blew up in violent sprays of spit. Colored bits of paper flew up in clouds, containing pictures and ads for products and all the other crazy things magazines filled their pages with. Soon all the tanks were ashes.

Smash tromped on. A paper tiger charged from the paper jungle, snarling and leaping. Smash caught it by the tail and shook it into limp paper, the black and orange colors running. He dipped this into a fringe of the fire and used the resulting torch to discourage other paper animals. They faded back before his bright-burning tiger, and he proceeded unhampered. Apparently there was nothing quite so fearful as a burning tiger. If this had been a battle, he had won it.

Now he came to a house of cards. Smash knew what cards were; he had seen Prince Dor and Princess Irene playing games with them at Castle Roogna, instead of getting down to basics the way ogres would. Sometimes they had constructed elaborate structures from the cards. This was such a structure—but it was huge. Each card was the height of Smash himself, with suit markings as big as his head and almost as ugly.

He paused to consider these. At the near side was the nine of hearts. He knew what hearts were: the symbol of love. This reminded him irrelevantly of what the brass girl had told him about Tandy. Could it be true that the tiny human girl liked him more than was proper, considering that ogres weren't supposed to be liked at all? If so, what was his responsibility? Should he growl at her, to discourage her? That did seem best.

He entered the house of cards, careful not to jostle it. These structures collapsed very readily, and after all, this might be the way out of the paper land. He felt he was making good progress through the worlds of the gourd, and he wanted to go on to the last station and meet the Dark Horse.

The inner wall showed the two of clubs. Clubs were, of course, the ogre's favorite suit. There was nothing like a good, heavy club for refreshing violence! Then there was the jack of diamonds, symbolizing the wealth of dragons. His curse of intellect made symbolism quite clear now. He remembered how many of the bright little stones the Dragon Lady had had; this was probably her card. Then there was the two of spades, with its shovel symbol. The suit of farmers.

In the center of the house of cards was the joker. It depicted a handsomely brutish ogre with legs that trailed into smoke. Of course! Smash pushed against it, assuming it to be his door to the next world—and the whole structure collapsed.

The cards were not heavy, of course, and in a moment Smash's head poked above the wreckage. He looked about.

The scene had changed. The paper was gone. The painted sky and cardboard trees existed no longer. Now there was a broad and sandy plain, like that of the nightmares' realm, except that this one was in daylight, with the sun beating down hotly.

He spied an object in the desert. It glinted prettily, but not like a diamond. Curious, Smash stomped over to it. It was a greenish bottle, half buried in the sand, fancily corked. He found himself attracted to it; a bottle like that, its base properly broken off, could make a fine weapon.

He picked it up. Inside the bottle was a hazy motion, as of slowly swirling mist. The cork had a glossy metallic seal with a word embossed: FOOL.

Well, that was the nature of ogres. He was thirsty in this heat; maybe the stuff in the bottle was good to drink. Smash ripped off the seal and used his teeth to pop the cork. After all, he was uncertain how long it would be before he came across anything potable, here in the gourd. But mainly, his action was his Eye Queue's fault; because of it, he was curious.

As the cork blasted free, vapor surged out of the bottle. It swelled out voluminously. Too bad—this was neither edible nor potable, and it smelled of sulfur. Smash sneezed.

The vapor formed a big greenish cloud, swirling about but not dissipating into the air. In a moment, two muscular arms projected from it, and the remainder formed into the head and upper torso of a gaseous man-creature about Smash's own size.

"Who in the gourd are you?" Smash inquired.

"Ho, ho, ho!" the creature boomed. "I be the ifrit of the bottle. Thou has freed me; as thy reward, I shall suffer thee to choose in what manner thou shalt die."

"Oh, one of those," Smash said, unimpressed. "A bottle imp." He now recognized, in retrospect, this creature as the figure on the joker card. He had taken it to be an ogre, but, of course, ogres had hairy legs and big flat feet, rather than trailing smoke.

"Dost thou mock me, thou excrescence of excrement?" the ifrit demanded, swelling angrily. "Beware, lest I squish thee into a nonentitious cube and make bouillon soup of thee!"

"Look, ifrit, I don't have time for this nonsense," Smash said, though the mention of the bouillon cube made him hungry. He had squished a bull into a bouillon cube once and made soup with it; he could use some of that now! "I just want to find the Night Stallion and vacate the lien on my soul. If you aren't going to help, get out of my way."

"Surely I shall destroy thee!" the ifrit raged, turning dusky purple. He reached for the ogre's throat with huge and taloned hands.

Smash grabbed the ifrit's limbs, knotted them together in much the way he had tied the extremities of the ghastlies, and jammed the creature headfirst back into the green bottle. "Oaf! Infidel!" the ifrit screamed, his words somewhat distorted since his mouth was squeezed through the bottle's neck. "What accursed mischief be this?"

"I warned you," Smash said, using a forefinger to tamp more of the ifrit into the container. "Don't mess with ogres. They have no sense of humor."

Struggle as he might, the ifrit could not prevail against Smash's power. "Ooo, ouch!" the voice came muffled from the glass. "OooOOoo!" For Smash's finger had rammed into the creature's gasous posterior.

Then a hand came back out of the bottle. It waved a white flag.

Smash knew that meant surrender. "Why should I pay attention to you?" he asked.

"Mmph of mum genuine free wish," the voice cried from the depths of the bottle.

That sounded promising. "But I don't need a wish about how I will die."

"Mmmph oomph!"

"Okay, ifrit. Give me one positive wish." Smash removed his finger.

The ifrit surged backward out of the bottle. "What is they wish, O horrendous one?" he asked, rubbing his rear.

"I want to know the way to the next world."

"I was about to send thee there!" the ifrit exclaimed, aggrieved.

"The next gourd scene. How do I get there?"

"Oh." The ifrit considered. "The closest be the mirror world. But that be no place for the like of thee. Thy very visage would shatter that scene."

This creature was trying to lull him with flattery! "Tell me anyway."

"On thy fool head be it." The ifrit made a dramatic gesture. There was a blinding flash. "Thou wilt be sorree!" the creature's voice came, fading away with descending pitch as if retreating at nearly the speed of sound.

Smash pawed his eyes, and gradually sight filtered back.

He stood among a horrendous assortment of ogres. Some were much larger than he, some much smaller; some were obesely fat, some emaciatedly thin; some had ballooning heads and squat feet, others the other way around.

"What's this?" he asked, scratching his head, though it had no fleas now.

"This . . . this . . . this . . . this," the other ogres chorused in diminishing echo, each scratching his head.

The Eye Queue needed only that much data to formulate an educated hypothesis. "Mirrors!"

"Ors . . . ors . . . ors . . . ors," the echoes agreed.

Smash walked among the mirrors, seeing himself pacing himself in multiple guises. The hall was straight, but after a while the images repeated. Suspicious, he used a horny fingernail to scratch a corner of one mirror, then walked farther down the hall, checking corners. Sure enough, he came across another mirror with a scratch on it, just where he had made his mark. It was the same one, surely. This hall was an endless reflection, like two mirrors facing each other. One of those endless loops he had been warned about. In fact, now he saw three lines of string: he had been retracing his course. He was trapped.

The ifrit had been right. This was no place for the like of him. Already he was hungrier, and there no food here. How could he get out?

He could smash through a mirror and through the wall behind it, of course—but would that accomplish anything? There were situations in which blind force was called for—but other situations, his Eye Queue curse reminded him obnoxiously, called for subtler negotiation. The trick was to tell them apart. One could not conquer a mirror by breaking it; one could only forfeit the game.

Smash stared into the scratched mirror, and his distorted image stared back. The image was almost as ugly as he was, but the distortion hampered it, making it less repulsive than it should have been. Probably that was why it was snarling.

He turned and contemplated the three strands of string on the floor. He saw where the first one started: it came from another mirror. So he had entered here through a mirror. Surely that was also the way to leave. If he found some means to make another blinding flash, would he be able to step through, as before? But he had no flash-material.

Then he remembered what he had heard in the Gap Dragon's Ear. Could that relate? It had sounded like his voice, talking about a mirror. He decided to try it.

He positioned himself squarely before the mirror. He elevated his hamfist. "Mirror, mirror on the wall," he intoned, imitating his own voice as well as he could. "Pass this fist or take a fall." Then he punched forward.

His fist smashed through the glass and into the wall behind it. The mirror tinkled in pieces to the floor.

Smash leaned forward to peer through the hole in the wall. It opened on another hall of mirrors. Sure enough, there was no escape there; he was caught among the mirrors until he found the proper way out.

He tromped to the next mirror. He raised his fist again and spoke his rhyme. The he punched through, with the same result.

This did not seem to be working. But it was the only clue he had. Maybe when the other mirrors saw what was happening, they would capitulate. After all, this technique had been effective with the shocking doorknobs. The inanimate tended to be stupid, as Prince Dor had shown, but it did eventually learn what was good for it.

The change happened sooner than anticipated. His fist did not strike the third mirror; it passed through without resistance. His arm and body followed it, and he did a slow fall through the aperture.

He rolled on something soft and sat up. He sniffed. He looked. He salivated.

He sat on a huge bed of cake, replete with vanilla icing. Pastries and sweets were all about him, piled high: doughnuts, strudel, éclairs, tarts, cookies, creampuffs, gingerbread, and more intricate pastries.

Smash had been growing hungry before; it had been well over an hour since he had last filled up. Now he was ravenous. But again the damned curse of the Eye Queue made him pause. The purpose of these worlds inside the gourd seemed to be to make him unhappy. This food did not fit that purpose—unless there were something wrong with it. Could it be poisoned? Poison did not bother ogres much, but was best avoided.

One way to find out. Smash scooped up a glob of floor and crammed it in his big mouth. The cake was excellent. Then he got up and explored the region, keeping himself busy while waiting for the poison to act. He had not eaten enough to cause real damage to the gross gut of an ogre, but if he felt discomfort, he would take warning.

He was in a large chamber completely filled with the pastries. There was no apparent exit. He punched experimentally through a wall of fruitcake, but the stuff seemed to have no end. He suspected he could punch forever and only tear up more cake. There appeared to be no reasonable limit to the worlds that fit inside the gourd. How, then, was he to escape this place?

His stomach suffered nothing but the ravages of increasing hunger, so he concluded the food was not poisoned. Still he hesitated. There had to be some trap, something to make him hurt. If not poison, what? There seemed to be no threat, no spitball-shooting tanks, no ifrit, not even starvation from delay.

Well, suppose he fell to and ate his fill? Where would he be? Still here, with no way out. If he remained long enough, stuffing himself at will, he would lose his soul by default in three months. No point in that.

Yet, no sense in going hungry. He grabbed a hunk of angelcake and gulped it down. He felt angelic. That was no mood for an ogre! He chomped some devilsfood, and felt devilish. That was more like it. He gulped some dream pie, and dreamed of smiting the Night Stallion and recovering the lien on his soul.

Wait. He forced himself to stop eating, lest he sink immediately into the easy slough of indulgence. Better to keep hungry and alert, his cursed taskmaster of an Eye Queue told him. What did the Eye Queue care about hunger? It didn't have to eat! But he went along with it for the moment, knowing it would give him no peace otherwise. He would reward himself only for making progress in solving this particular riddle. That was discipline no ordinary ogre could master, infuriating as it was.

Still, time was passing, and he had no idea how to proceed. There had to be *some*thing. After all, it wasn't as if he could simply eat his way out of here.

That thought made him pause. Why *not* eat out? Chew a hole in the wall until he ran out of edibles—which would be another world.

No. There would be too much cake for even an ogre to eat. Unless he knew exactly where a weak spot was—

Weak spot. Surely so. Something that differed from the rest of this stuff.

Smash started a survey course of eating, looking for the difference. All of it was excellent. A master pastry chef had baked this chamber.

Then he encountered a vein of licorice. That was one confection Smash didn't like; it reminded him of manure. True, some ogres could eat and like manure, but that just wasn't Smash's own taste. Naturally he avoided this vein.

Then his accursed, annoying, and objectionable Eye Queue began percolating again. The Eyes of the vine saw entirely too much, especially what wasn't necessarily there. Manure. What would leave manure in the form of a confection?

Answer: some creature in charge of a chamber of confections. The Night Stallion, perhaps. When the Stallion departed, he would leave his token of contempt. Big brown balls of sweet manure.

What exit would the Stallion use? How could that exit be found?

Answer: the trail of manure would show the way. Horses hardly cared where they left it, since it was behind them. They left it carelessly, thoughtlessly, often on the run.

Smash started digging out the licorice. But when he did, the foul stuff melted into other cake, transforming it into licorice, too. That obscured the trail. He had to do something about that.

He cast about, but came up with only the least pleasant solution. He would have to eat it. That was the only way to get rid of it. To consume the manure of the Stallion.

Fortunately, ogres didn't have much pride about what they ate. He nerved himself and bit in. The licorice-cake was awful, truly feculent, but he gulped it down anyway.

Now his gorge was rising violently inside him. Ogres were supposed never to get sick, no matter how rotten the stuff they ate. But this was manure! He ate on.

Smash came to a round hole in the material of the chamber. The dung had led him to it—since this was the exit the Stallion had taken. Smash scrambled through the passage, knowing that if he could just choke down his revolted, revolting stomach a little longer, he would win this contest, too.

He came to a drop-off and tumbled out, spinning and turning in air. Now he was falling through darkness.

That last jolt of weightlessness was too much. His stomach burst its constraints and heaved its awful contents violently out. The reaction sent him zooming backward through space. Smash puked, it seemed, for eons, and worked up a velocity to rival that of the brass spaceship. He hoped he didn't get lost in space beyond the stars.

Chapter 10. Fond Wand

He was retching into the gourd patch. Apparently he had jetted himself right out of the gourd! Chem was using the hardened rind of an empty gourd to scoop the vomit away, making room for more as it flowed voluminously from Smash's mouth.

As he realized where he was, his sickness abated. He looked about.

The girls were in a sorry state. All five of them were spattered. "We decided to get you out of the gourd before it got worse," Tandy said apologetically. "What happened?"

"I ate a lot of horse—er, manure," Smash said. "Instead of cake and pastry."

"Ogres do have unusual tastes," John remarked.

Smash chuckled weakly. "Where's some decent food? I don't want to eat any more gourds, and I'm going to be hungry as soon as I feel better."

"There'll be food at Goblinland," Goldy Goblin said.

"How far is that?"

Chem produced her map. "As I make it, we're close. From what Goldy tells me, the main tribe of goblins is not far from here, as the dragon flies. Just a few hours' walk, except that there's a mountain in the way, so we have to go around—across the Earth works. That complicates it. But I think the lava is cool enough now. We had better get over it before more comes."

"Like hot vomit," Goldy muttered.

Smash looked at the conic mountain. It steamed a little, but was generally quiescent. "Yes—let's cross quickly."

They started across. Goldy knew a little foot-cooling

187

spell used by goblins and taught it to them. It wasn't real magic, but rather an accommodation to the local landscape. Smash's Eye Queue was cynical, suspecting that any benefit from the spell was simply illusion, the belief in cooler feet. Yet his feet did feel cooler.

They had to skirt the volcano's eastern slope. The cone rumbled, annoyed, but was in its off-phase and could not mount any real action.

The ground, however, was rested. It had energy to expend. It shook, making their travel difficult. The shaking became more violent, causing the hardened lava to craze, to crack, to break up, and to form fissures, exposing the red-hot rock down below.

"Hurry!" Chem cried, her hooves dancing on the shifting rocks. Smash remembered that insecure footing made her nervous. Now it made him nervous, too.

"Oh, I wish I could fly again!" John cried, terrified. She stumbled and started to fall into a widening crack.

Chem caught her. "Get on my back," she directed. The fairy scrambled gratefully aboard.

The ground shook again. A fragment turned under the Siren's foot, and she went down. Smash caught her, lifted her high, and saw that her ankle was twisted. He would have to carry her.

Now the volcano rumbled again. It might be in its off-phase, but it wasn't entirely helpless. A new fissure opened in its side, and bright red lava welled out, like fresh blood. It spilled down toward them, shifting channels to orient accurately.

"It's coming for us!" Tandy cried, alarmed. "This land doesn't like us!"

Smash looked northeast. The goblin territory was far across the treacherously shifting rocks. Already the lava plain was humping like a slow ocean swell, as if trying to break free of its cool crust. Smash knew that if much more fragmentation occurred, they would all fall through that crust into the liquid lava below.

"Too far!" Tandy cried despairingly. "We can't make it!"

"North!" Chem said. "It's better to the north!"

They scrambled north, though that horizon looked like a wall of fire. The lava crust broke into big plates that, in turn, fragmented into platelets that slowly subsided under the weight of the party. Red lava squeezed up around the edges and leaked out onto the surface. Meanwhile, the fresh lava from the fissure flowed down to join the turbulent plain, further melting the platelets. There was now no retreat.

"Spread out!" Goldy cried. "Not too much weight on any one plate!"

They did it. The goblin girl was the most agile, so she led the way, finding the best plates and the best crossing places. Tandy followed, glancing nervously back at Smash as if afraid he would be too clumsy. She did care for him; it was obvious, now that Blythe had given him the hint. But that was hardly worth worrying about at this moment. They might all soon perish.

Next in line was Chem, carrying John on her back, her hooves handling the maneuvering well. Then came Smash, holding the Siren in his arms. Her feet had converted back to the tail; evidently that alleviated the pain in her ankle. However, her tail form was also her bare-top form, and the sight of all that juggling flesh made him ravenous again. He hoped he never got so hungry that he forgot these were his friends.

The edges of the plates depressed alarmingly as they took Smash's weight, for it was concentrated in a smaller area than was the centaur's. Once a plate broke under his weight, becoming two saucers, and he had to scramble, dipping a toe in red lava; it hurt terribly, but he ran on.

"Your toe!" the Siren exclaimed. "It's scorched!"

"Better that than falling in," he grunted.

"In case we don't make it," she said, "I'd better tell you now. You're a lot of creature, Smash."

"Ogres are big," he agreed. "You're a fair morsel of creature yourself." Indeed, she had continued to grow more youthful, and was now a sight to madden men. Or so he judged, from his alien viewpoint.

"You're more than I think you know. You could have been where you're going by now if you hadn't let the rest of us impose."

"No. I agreed to take Tandy along, and the rest of you have helped. I'm not sure I could have handled the dragons alone, or gotten out of the gourd."

"You never would have gotten into the gourd alone," she pointed out. "Then you could have avoided the dragons. Would another ogre have taken Tandy along?"

He laughed. He did that a lot since the advent of the Eye Queue, for things he wouldn't have noticed before now evinced humorous aspects. "Another ogre would have eaten the bunch of you!"

"I rest my case."

"Rest your tail, too, while you're at it. If I fall into the lava, you'll have to walk alone."

It was her turn to laugh, somewhat faintly. "Or swim," she said, looking down at the lava cracks.

Now they were at the border. The wall of fire balked them. Goldy stood on the plate nearest it, daunted. "I don't know how much fire there is," she said. "Goblin legend suggests the wall is thin, but—"

"We can't stay here," Tandy said. "I'll find out." And she took a breath and plunged into the fire.

The others stood on separate plates, appalled. Then Tandy's voice came back: "It's all right! Come on through!"

Smash closed his eyes and plunged toward her voice. The flame singed his fur and the flowing hair of the mermaid; then he was on firm ground, coughing.

He stood on a burned-out field. Wisps of smoke rose from lingering blazes, but mostly the ashes were cool. Farther to the north a forest fire raged, however, and periodically the wind shifted, bringing choking smoke and sprinkling new ashes. To the west there seemed to be a lake of fire, sending up occasional mushroom-shaped masses of smoke. To the east there was something like a flashing field of fire, with intermittent columns of flame.

Chem and John landed beside Smash. The fairy was busy slapping out smolders in the centaur's mane. "This is an improvement, but not much of one," Chem said. "Let's get off this burn!"

"I second the motion," Tandy agreed. She, too, had suffered during the crossing; parts of her brown hair had been scorched black. Goldy appeared, in similar condition. None of the girls was as pretty as she had been.

They moved east, paralleling the thin wall of fire. This was the Region of Fire, but since fire had to have something to burn, they were safe for the moment.

Then a column of white fire erupted just ahead of them. The heat of it drove them back—only to be heated again by another column to the side.

"Gas," the Siren said. "It puffs up from fumaroles, then ignites and burns out. Can we tell where the next ones will be?"

They watched for a few moments. "Only where they've been," Chem said. "The pattern of eruption and ignition seems completely random."

"That means we'll get scorched," the Siren said. "Unless we go around."

But there was no way around, for the forest fire was north and the lava flows were beyond the firewall to the south.

Also, new foliage was sprouting through the ashes on which they stood, emerging cracklingly dry; it would catch fire and burn off again very soon. It seemed the ashes were very rich fertilizer, but there was very little water for the plants, so they grew dehydrated. Here in the Region of Fire, there was no long escape from fire.

"How can we get through?" Tandy asked despairingly.

Smash put his Eye Queue curse to work yet again. He was amazed at how much he seemed to need it, now that he had it, when he had never needed it before, as if intelligence were addictive; it kept generating new uses for itself. He was also amazed at what his stupid bonemuscle ogre brain could do when boosted by the Queue and cudgeled by necessity. "Go only where they've been," he said.

The others didn't understand, so he showed the way. "Follow me!" He watched for a dying column, then stepped near it as it flickered out. There would be a little while before it built up enough new gas to fire again. He waited in the diminishing shimmer of heat, watching the other columns. When another died, next to his own, he stepped into its vacated spot.

The other members of the party followed him. "I'll assume this is wit instead of luck," the Siren murmured. Smash was still carrying her, though now she had switched back to legs and dress, in case he had to set her down.

As they moved to the third fumarole, the first fired again. These flares did not dawdle long! Now they were in the middle of the columns, unable to escape unscathed. But

Smash stepped forward again into another dying flame, panting in the stink of it, yet surviving unburned.

In this manner the party made its precarious and uncomfortable way through the fires, and came at last to the east firewall. They plunged through—and found themselves in the pleasant, rocky region of the goblins.

"What a relief!" Tandy exclaimed. "Nothing could be worse than that, except maybe what's inside a gourd."

"You haven't met the local goblins yet," Goldy muttered.

There was a small stream paralleling the wall, cool and clean. They all drank deeply, catching up from their long engagement with the heat. Then they washed themselves off and tended to their injuries. The Siren bound her ankle with a bolt of gauze from a gauze-bush, and Tandy tended to Smash's scorched toe.

"Goldy will find her husband here," Smash said as she worked. "Soon we may find a human husband for you." He hoped he was doing the right thing, bringing the matter into the open.

She looked up at him sharply. "Who squealed?" she demanded.

"Blythe said you were looking for—"

"What does she know?" Tandy asked.

Smash shrugged awkwardly. This wasn't working out very well. "Not much, perhaps."

"When the time comes, I'll make my own decision."

Smash could not argue with that. Maybe the brass girl had been mistaken. Blythe's heart, as she had noted, was brass, and perhaps she was not properly attuned to the hearts made of flesh. But Smash had a nagging feeling that wasn't it. These females seemed to have a common awareness of each other's nature that males lacked. Maybe it was just that they were all interested in only one thing. "Anyway, we'll deliver Goldy soon."

They found no food, so they walked on along the river, which curved eastward, north of the mountain range that separated this land from that of the dragons. The goblins had to be somewhere along here, perhaps occupying the mountains themselves. Goblins did tend to favor dark holes and deep recesses; few were seen in open Xanth, though Smash understood that in historical times the goblins had dominated the land. It seemed they had become less ugly and violent over the centuries, and this led inevitably to a diminution of their power. He had heard that some isolated goblin tribes had become so peaceful and handsome that they could hardly be distinguished from gnomes. That would be like ogres becoming like small giants—astonishing and faintly disgusting.

The river broadened and turned shallow, finally petering out into a big dull bog. Brightly colored fins poked up from the muck, and nostrils surmounting large teeth quested through it. Obviously the main portions of these creatures were hidden beneath the surface. It did not seem wise to set foot within that bog. Especially not with a sore toe.

They skirted it, walking along the slope at the base of the mountain range. The day was getting late, and Smash was dangerously hungry. Where were the goblins?

Then the goblins appeared. An army of a hundred or so swarmed around the party. "What are you creeps doing here?" the goblin chief demanded with typical goblin courtesy.

Goldy stepped forward. "I am Goldy Goblin, daughter of the leader of the Gap Chasm Goblins, Gorbage," she announced regally.

"Never heard of them," the chief snapped. "Get out of our territory, pasteface."

"What?" Goldy was taken aback. She was very fair for a goblin, but it wasn't merely the name that put her at a loss.

"I said get out, or we'll cook you for supper."

"But I came here to get married!" she protested.

The goblin chief swung backhanded, catching the side of her head and knocking her down. "Not here you don't, foreign stranger slut." He turned away, and the goblin troops began to move off.

But Tandy acted. She was furious. "How dare you treat Goldy like that?" she demanded. "She came all the way here at great personal risk to get married to one of your worthless louts, and you—you—"

The goblin chief swung his hand at her as he had at Goldy, but Tandy moved faster. She made a hurling gesture in the air, with her face red and her eyes squinched almost shut. The goblin flipped feet over ears and landed, stunned, on the ground. She had thrown a tantrum at him.

Smash sighed. He knew the rules of interspecies deal-ings. How goblins treated one another was their own busi-ness; that was why these goblins had left Smash and the rest of his party alone. Their personal interplay was rough, but they were not looking for trouble with ogres or centaurs or human folk. Unlike the prior goblin tribe, this one honored the conventions. But now Tandy had interfered, and that made her fair game.

The goblin lieutenants closed on her immediately—and Tandy, like an expended fumarole, had no second tantrum to throw in self-defense. But Chem, John, and the Siren closed about her. "You dare to attack human folk?" the Siren demanded. She was limping on her bad ankle but was ferocious in her wrath.

"You folk aren't human," a goblin lieutenant said. "You're centaur, fairy, and mernymph—and this other looks to be part nymph, too, and she attacked our leader. Her life is forfeit, by the rules of the jungle."

Smash had not chosen this conflict, but now he had to intervene. "These three with me," he grunted, in his stress reverting to his natural ogre mode. He indicated Tandy with a hamfinger. "She, too, me do."

The lieutenant considered. Evidently the goblins were hierarchically organized, and with the chief out of order, the lieutenant had discretionary power. Goblins were tough to bluff or back off, once aroused, especially when they had the advantage of numbers. Still, this goblin hesitated. Three or four females were one thing; an ogre was another. A hundred determined goblins could probably overcome one ogre, but many of them would be smashed to pulp in the process, and many more would find their heads embedded in the trunks of trees, and a few would find themselves flying so high they might get stuck on the moon. Most of the rest would be less fortunate. So this goblin negotiated, while others hauled their unconscious leader away.

"This one must be punished," the lieutenant said. "If our chief dies, she must die. So it is written in the verbal cove-nant: an eyeball for an eyeball, a gizzard for a gizzard."

Smash knew how to negotiate with goblins. It was merely a matter of speaking their language. He formed a huge and gleaming metal fist. "She die, me vie."

The lieutenant understood him perfectly, but was in a

difficult situation. It looked as if there would have to be a fight.

Then the goblin chief stirred, perhaps because he was uncomfortable being dragged by the ears over the rough ground. He was recovering consciousness.

"He isn't dead," the lieutenant said, relieved. That widened his selection of options. "But still she must be punished. We shall isolate her on an island."

Isolation? That didn't seem too bad. Nevertheless, Smash didn't trust it. "Me scratch," he said, scratching his flealess head stupidly. "Where catch?"

The goblin studied him, evidently assessing Smash's depth of stupidity. "The island sinks," he said. "You may rescue her if you choose. But there are unpleasant things in the bog."

Smash knew that. He didn't want to see Tandy put on a sinking island in that bog. Yet he did not have his full strength, and hunger was diminishing him further, and that meant he could not afford to indulge in combat with the goblins at this time. In addition, his Eye Queue reminded him snidely, Tandy *had* attacked the goblin chief, and so made herself liable to the goblins' judgment. The goblins, if not exactly right, were also not exactly wrong.

The goblin lieutenant seemed to understand the struggle going on in the ogre's mind. Goblins and ogres differed from one another in size and intelligence, but were similar in personality. Both sides preferred to avoid the mayhem that would result if they fought. "We will give you a fair chance to rescue her."

"Me dance," Smash said ironically, tapping the ground with one foot, so that the terrain shuddered. "What chance?"

"A magic wand." The lieutenant signaled, and a goblin brought an elegant black wand.

"Me no fond of magic wand," Smash said dubiously. He continued to use the ogre rhymes, having concluded that stupidity, or the appearance of it, might be a net asset.

"All you have to do is figure out how to use it," the goblin said. "Then you can draw on its magic to help the girl. We don't know its secret, but do know it is magic. We will help you figure it out, if you wish."

That was a considerable risk! He had to figure out the

operative mechanism of a wand that had so baffled the goblins that they were willing to help him use it to defeat their decree of punishment. They would have spent days, months, or years on it; he might have minutes. What chance would a smart man have, let alone a stupid ogre? What person of even ordinary intelligence would agree to such a deal?

Why would the goblins risk such a device in the hands of a stranger, anyway? Suppose he did figure out the operation of the wand by some blind luck? He could be twice as dangerous to them as he already was.

Ah, but there was the answer. An ogre was stupid, almost by definition. He could be far more readily conned out of his advantage than could a smart person. Also, the activated wand might be dangerous, acting against the user. Of course they would help him solve its secret; if it destroyed the user, no loss! Only an absolutely, idiotically, calamitously stupid or desperate creature would take that risk.

John sidled up to Smash. "Goblins are cunning wretches," she whispered. "We fairies have had some dealings with them. I think they mistreated Goldy deliberately, to get you into this picklement."

"I'm sure of it," Goldy agreed. A bruise was showing on her cheek, but she seemed otherwise all right. "My own tribe is that way. My father threatened to eat you all, when he doesn't even like ogre or centaur meat, just to force you to take me here."

"It does seem to be an effective ploy," Smash whispered back. "But we would have taken you anyway, had we known you."

If brass girls could blush copper, goblin girls blushed tan. "You mean you folk like me?"

"Certainly we do!" Tandy agreed. "And you helped us cross the lava plates, leading the way. And you told us a tremendous lot about the hypnogourds, so that Smash knows how to save his soul."

"Well, goblins aren't too popular with other creatures," Goldy said, wiping an eye.

"Nor with their own kind, it seems," Tandy said.

"Because the chief hit me? Think nothing of it. Goblin

men are just a little bit like ogres in that respect. It makes
them think they run things."

"Ogres aren't too popular with other creatures, either,"
Smash said. "They beat up their wenches, too."

"This lesson in comparative romance is fascinating,"
John said. "Still, we're in trouble."

"Pick Tandy up and run out of here," Goldy advised.
"That's the only way to deal with our kind."

But Smash knew that the other girls would pay the penalty for that. He had fallen into the goblins' trap; he would
have to climb out of it. His one advantage was that he was,
thanks to the curse of the Eye Queue, considerably smarter
than the goblins thought. "Me try to spy," he told the lieutenant.

"Very well, ogre," the lieutenant said smugly. "Take the
wand, experiment with it, while we place her on the island."

Goblins grabbed Tandy and hustled her into a small
wooden boat. She struggled, but they moved her along anyway. She sent a betrayed look back at Smash, evidently
feeling with part of her mind that he should fight, and he
felt like a betrayer indeed. But he had the welfare of the
entire party in mind, so he had to act with un-ogrish delibera-
tion. This grated, but had to be. If the wand didn't work,
he would charge through the bog and rescue her, regardless
of the fins. Even if the fins proved to be too much for him,
he should be able to toss her to the safe bank before going
under.

They dumped her on an islet that seemed to be mostly
reeds. As her weight settled on it, the structure hissed and
bubbled from below, and slowly lowered toward the liquid
muck surface. A purple fin cruised in and circled the
pneumatically descending isle.

Smash concentrated on the wand while goblins and girls
watched silently. He waved it in a circle, bobbed it up and
down, poked it at imaginary balloons in the air, and shook
it. Nothing happened. "Go, schmoe!" he ordered it, but it
ignored even that command. He bent it between his hands;
it flexed, then sprang back into shape. It was supple and
well made, but evinced no magic property.

Meanwhile, Tandy's isle continued to sink. The purple

fin cruised in tighter circles. Tandy stood in the spongy center, terrified.

But he couldn't watch her. He had to concentrate on the wand. It was evident that his random motions weren't being successful. What was the key?

Eye Queue, find the clue! he thought emphatically. It was high time he got some use from this curse when it really counted.

The Queue went to work. It considered mental riddles a challenge. It even enjoyed thinking.

Assume the wand was activated by motion, because that was the nature of wands. They were made to wave about. Assume that trial-and-error motion wouldn't do the trick, because the goblins would have tried everything. Assume that the key was nevertheless simple, so that the wand could be readily used in an emergency. What motion was both simple and subtle?

A signature-key, he decided. A particular motion no one would guess, perhaps attuned to a particular person. But how could he guess its nature?

Tandy's isle was almost down to muck level, and the circling fin was almost within her reach, or vice versa. Smash could not afford to ponder much longer!

"Goblin man, help if can," Smash called. After all, the goblins wanted to know the secret, too.

"All we know, ogre, is that it worked for the crone we stole it from," the lieutenant replied. "She would point it at a person or thing, and the object would levitate. That is, rise." The goblin thought Smash would not know the meaning of the more complicated term. "But when we tried it—nothing."

Levitation. That would certainly help Tandy! But he needed to get it started in a hurry.

"Crone so smart, how she start?"

"She looped it in a series of loops," the goblin said. "But when we made the same loops, nothing happened."

Tandy's feet were now disappearing into the muck. Only the submerged mass of the isle balked the fin—for now.

"Give poop. What loop?" Smash demanded.

"Like this." The goblin described a partial circle with a tuck in it.

"That looks like a G," John remarked. Apparently fairies were literate, too.

G. A letter of the human alphabet? Suddenly Smash's intellect pounced. What was a signature except a series of letters? A written name? John's own case illustrated the importance of a name; her entire mission was simply to locate her correct one. One could not choose just any name, because only the right one had power. This should apply for wands as well as for fairies, here in Xanth. Maybe it was different inside the gourd, where names could be changed at will. "What name of dame?"

"Grungy Grool," the goblin answered. "She was a witch."

A witch with the initials G G. Suppose the wand tuned in to the signature of its holder? Smash described a big, careful S.

Nothing happened. Holding his disappointment in check, he described a matching O. Smash Ogre—his initials.

Still nothing. The wand remained quiescent in his ham-hand. What now?

Tandy screamed. Her isle was giving way, and she was toppling into the muck.

Smash aimed the wand like an arrow, ready to hurl it at the fin.

Tandy's fall stopped midway. She hung suspended at an angle above the bog, right where Smash was pointing.

"The wand is working!" John cried, amazed and gratified.

Slowly Smash tilted the wand up. Tandy floated, remaining in its power. Of course the activated wand had not moved in his hand before; that wasn't the way it worked. *He* had to move it—to make some other object respond.

"I'm flying!" Tandy cried.

"He made it work!" the goblin lieutenant exclaimed.

Smash guided Tandy carefully to land and set her down. Her feet were muddy and she was panting with reaction, but she was otherwise unharmed. He knew a spunky little girl like her would rebound quickly.

The goblin lieutenant rushed up. "Give me that wand, ogre!"

"Don't do it!" John cried.

But Smash, ever the stupid ogre, blithely handed over the wand. "It is goblin property," he murmured, forgetting to rhyme.

The goblin snatched the wand, pointed it at Smash, and lifted it. Smash did not rise into the air. The wand was not attuned to the goblin. It remained useless to anyone else, exactly as it had been when taken from its witch-owner. Smash had suspected this would be the case.

"But you made it work!" the goblin protested angrily.

"And you tried to turn it against him!" Goldy cried. "Do you call that goblin honor?"

"Well, he's just a stupid ogre," the goblin muttered. "What does he know?"

"I'll tell you what he knows!" Goldy flashed. "He's a lot smarter than—"

"Me smart, at heart," Smash said, interrupting her.

Goldy paused, then exchanged a glance of understanding with him. "Smarter than the average ogre," she concluded.

The goblin lieutenant formed a crafty expression, too subtle for the average ogre to fathom. "Very well, ogre. Teach *her* how to work the wand, if it's not a fluke." He gave the wand to Goldy.

So the goblins figured to get the secret from her. Smash understood perfectly. But he smiled vacuously. "Happily, me teach she."

"Me?" Goldy asked, surprised. "Smash, you don't really want to—"

Smash put his huge mitt on her hand. "You have a mind of your own, chief's daughter," he murmured. "Use it." Gently he moved her hand, making the wand ascribe the letters G G, her initials. Then he stepped back.

"I don't understand," Goldy said, gesturing with the wand.

Three goblins sailed into the air as the moving wand pointed at them.

"She's got it!" the goblin lieutenant exclaimed. "Good enough! Give it here, girl!" He advanced on her.

Goldy pointed the wand at him and lifted it. He rose up to treetop height. "Give what where, dolt?" she inquired sweetly.

The lieutenant scrambled with hands and feet, but

merely made gestures in the air. "Get me down, wretch!" he screamed.

She waved the wand carelessly, causing him to careen in a high circle. "Do what, who?"

"You'll pay for this, you bi—" The goblin broke off as he was pitched, upside down, just clear of the bog. A blue fin cut across and began circling under his nose.

"Smash," Goldy said sweetly, "why don't you and your friends have a good meal while I try to get the hang of this wand? I might need some advice, to prevent me from accidentally hurting someone." And the goblin lieutenant spun crazily, just missing a tree.

"Feed them! Feed them!" the goblin cried. "This crazy sl—young lady goblin will be the death of me!"

"I might, at that, if I don't learn to manage this thing better," Goldy agreed innocently. The wand quivered in her hand, and the goblin did a bone-rattling shake in the air, almost dropping to within reach of the slavering blue fin.

The goblins hastily brought out food. Smash stuffed himself in excellent ogre fashion on strawberry-flavored cavern mushrooms and curdled sea-cow milk while the goblin girl experimented with the wand, lifting first one goblin, then another.

"Let someone else try it!" a goblin suggested craftily. Goldy glanced at Smash, who nodded. Then she handed the wand to the first taker.

The wand went dead again. Several goblins tried it, without result. It occurred to Smash that if one of them should have the initials G G, as was hardly beyond the reach of coincidence, the wand might work—but that never happened. Probably it was not only the key, but the particular person signing it. Another G G goblin would have to make his own G G signature. That was a pretty sophisticated instrument!

"Give me that," Goldy said, taking it back. It still worked for her. Once the wand was keyed to a particular person, it stayed that way. Since the goblins were illiterate, they never would catch on to the mechanism, most likely.

The meal concluded. Smash rubbed his belly and let out a resounding belch that blew the leaves off the nearest bush.

"Well, I can't say it hasn't been fun," Goldy said, offering the wand back to Smash.

Smash refused it, wordlessly.

"You mean I can keep it?" she asked, amazed.

"Keep it," the Siren said. "I think you will have no trouble getting a suitable husband here now. Probably a chief. Whatever you choose."

Goldy considered, contemplating the wand. "There is that. Power is a language we goblins understand somewhat too well." She faced Smash again. "Ogre, I don't know what to say. No goblin would have done this for you."

"He's no ordinary ogre," Tandy said, giving Smash's arm a squeeze. "Keep the wand. Use it well."

"I will," Goldy agreed, and there seemed to be an ungoblinish tear in her eye. "If any of you folk ever have need of goblin assistance—"

"Just in getting out of here," Chem said. "Any information on the geography to the north would be appreciated."

Goldy gestured toward the lieutenant with the wand. "Information?"

Hastily the goblins acquainted Chem with what they knew of the reaches to the north, which wasn't much.

Well fed, the party set out as dusk fell, following the bog to the river, and the river until it petered out. They camped near the firewall, snacking on some leftover mushroom tidbits Goldy had arranged to have packed. They would have to cross the Region of Fire again to get where they were going, as the goblins had assured them that it went right up to the land of the griffins, which beasts were hostile to travelers.

"That was a generous thing you did, Smash," the Siren said. "You could so readily have kept the wand, especially after they tried to trick you out of it and use it against you."

"Goldy had better use for it," Smash said. "Why should an ogre crave more power?"

"One thing I don't understand," John said. "You say you were victimized by the Eye Queue vine. That makes you smarter than an ordinary ogre, whose skull is filled with bone."

"Correct," Smash agreed uncomfortably.

"But that does not account for your generosity, does it?

You have let the rest of us impose on you, and you did something really nice for Goldy, and I don't think another ogre would, not even a smart one. Goblins are like ogres, only smaller and smarter, and they don't do anything for anybody."

Smash scratched his head. Still no fleas. "Maybe I got confused."

"Maybe so," the fairy replied thoughtfully. Tandy and Chem and the Siren nodded, smiling with that certain female knowingness that was so annoying.

Chapter 11. Heat Wave

Smash's Eye Queue would not leave well enough alone; that was its most annoying trait. He greeted the next morning with doubts. "How do we know the griffins are unfriendly?" he asked. "Can we trust the information of the goblins? We do know the fire is dangerous, on the other hand."

"We certainly do!" John agreed. "My wings will never grow back if I keep singeing them! But griffins are pretty violent creatures and they do eat people."

"Let's travel near the firewall," the Siren suggested. "That way we can cross over and risk the fire if the griffins turn out to be too ferocious."

They did that. But soon the bog closed in, squeezing them against the firewall. The colored fins paced them eagerly.

Chem halted. "I think we have to make a decision," she said as she updated her map-image.

"I'll check the other side," Smash said, setting down the Siren. He stepped across the firewall.

He was at the edge of the fumaroles, amidst fresh ashes. Not far north the forest fire continued to rage. There was no safe passage here!

He saw a shape in the ashes. Curious, he uncovered it. It was the burned-out remnant of a large tree trunk, still smoldering. The fall of ashes had smothered it before it finished its own burning. Smash wondered when a tree of this size ever had a chance to grow here. Maybe it had fallen across the firewall from the other side.

Then he had a notion. He put his gloved hamhands on

the charred log and heaved it back through the firewall. Then he stepped through himself. "A boat," he announced.

"A boat!" Tandy exclaimed, delighted. "Of course!"

They went to work with a will, scraping out ashes and burned-out fragments and splinters. Then they launched the dugout craft in the muck. Smash ripped out a sapling to use as a pole so he could shove their boat forward. He remembered traveling similarly with Prince Dor. But this was more challenging, because now he had responsibility for the party.

The colored fins crowded in as the craft slid through the bog. At length Smash became annoyed, and used the tip of his pole to poke at the nearest fin. There was a chomp, and the pole abruptly shortened.

Angry, Smash reached out with a gauntleted hand and caught hold of the offending fin. He heaved it out of the water.

The creature turned out to be fishlike, with strong flukes and sharp teeth. "What are you?" Smash demanded, shaking it. The thing was heavy, but Smash had over half his ogre strength back now and was able to control his captive.

"I'm a loan shark, idiot!" the fish responded, and Smash did not have the wit, until his Eye Queue jogged him snidely later, to marvel that a fish spoke human language. "Want to borrow anything? Prompt service, easy terms."

"Don't do it!" John cried. "You borrow from one of them, it'll take an arm and a leg in return. That's how they live."

"You have already borrowed part of my pole," Smash told the shark. "I figure you owe me. I'll take a fin and a fluke."

"That's not the way it works!" the shark protested. "No one skins sharks!"

"There is always a first time," Smash said. He had a fundamental understanding of this kind of dealing. He put his other hand on the thing's tail and began to pull.

The shark struggled and grunted, but could not free itself. "What do you want?" it screamed.

"I want to get out of this bog," Smash said.

"I'll get you out!" The shark was quite accommodating, now that it was in a bad position. "Just let me go!"

"Don't trust it any farther than you can throw it," John advised.

Smash was not about to. He used one finger to poke a hole in the shark's green fin and passed Chem's rope through it. Then he heaved the creature forward. It landed with a dull muddy splash before the dugout, the rope pulling taut. "That's as far as I can throw it," Smash said.

The shark tried to swim away, but as it moved, it hauled the boat along behind. It was not trustworthy, but it seemed to be seaworthy. Or bogworthy.

"Now you can swim anywhere you want to, Sharky," Smash called to it. "But I'll loose the rope only when we reach the north edge of this bog."

"Help! Help me, brothers!" the shark called to the other fins that circled near.

"Are you helpless?" one called back. "In that case, I'll be happy to tear you apart."

"Sharks never help each other," John remarked. "That's why they don't rule Xanth."

"Ogres don't help each other, either," Smash said. "The same for most dragons." And he realized that he had suffered another fundamental revelation about the nature of power. Human beings helped each other, and thus had become a power in Xanth far beyond anything that could be accounted for by their size or individual magic.

Meanwhile, the loan shark got the message. It was living on borrowed time, unless it moved. It thrust north, and the bog fairly whizzed by. Soon they were at the north bank.

They climbed out, and Smash unthreaded the rope. The shark vanished instantly. No one sympathized with it; it had for once been treated as it treated others.

But now the griffins came. Probably another shark had snitched, so the griffins had been alert for the party's arrival. Since the creatures probably intended no good, Smash stepped quickly across the firewall for a peek at that situation. He found himself in the middle of the forest fire. No hope there!

The great bird-headed, lion-bodied creatures lined up, inspecting the motley group. The monsters were the color of shoe polish. Then they charged.

Smash reacted automatically. He swung his pole, knocking the first griffin back. Then he dived across the firewall, ripped a burning sapling out of the ground, dived back, and hurled the flaming mass at the remaining griffins. The sapling was of firewood, which burned even when green; in a moment the wing feathers of the griffins were burning.

The monsters squawked and hurled themselves into the bog to douse the flames. The colored fins of the sharks clustered close. "You're using our muck!" a shark cried. "You owe us a wing and a paw!"

The griffins did not take kindly to this solicitation. A battle erupted. Muck, feathers, and pieces of fin flew outward, and the mud boiled.

Smash and the girls walked northwestward, following the curve of the firewall, leaving the violence behind. The landscape was turning nicer, with occasional fruit and nut trees, so they could feed as they traveled.

The Siren, rested by her tour in the boat and periodic dippings of her tail, found she could walk now. That lightened Smash's burden.

There were birds here, flitting among the trees, picking at the trunks, scratching into the ground. The farther the party went, the more there were. Now and then, flocks darkened the sky. Not only were they becoming more numerous, they were getting larger.

Then a flight of really large birds arrived—the fabulous rocs. These birds were so big they could pick up a medium-sized dragon and fly with it. Was their intent friendly or hostile?

A talking parrot dropped down. "Ho, strangers!" it hailed them "What melodies bring you to Birdland?"

Smash looked at the parrot. It was all green and red, with a downcurving beak. "We only seek to pass through," he said. "We are going north."

"You are going west," the bird said.

So they were; the gradually curving firewall had turned them about. They reoriented, bearing north.

"Welcome to pass through Birdland," the parrot said. "There will be a twenty per cent poll tax. One of your number will have to stay here."

"That isn't fair!" Tandy protested. "Each of us has her own business."

"We are not concerned with fairness," the poll replied,

while the horrendously huge rocs drifted lower, their enormous talons dangling. "We are concerned with need. We
need people to cultivate our property so there will be more
seeds for us to eat. So we hold a reasonable share of those
who pass."

"A share—for slavery?" Tandy demanded, her spunky
spirit showing again.

"Call it what you will. One of you will stay—or all will
stay. The tax will be paid." And the rocs dropped lower
yet. "Poll your number to determine the one."

Smash knew it would be useless to fight. He might break
the claws of one roc, but another would carry away the
girls. The big birds had too much power. "We'll see," he
said.

Tandy turned on him. "We'll *see*? You mean you'll go
along with this abomination?"

"We don't have much choice," Smash said, his Eye
Queue once again dominating his better ogre nature. "We'll
just have to cross this land, then decide who will remain."

"You traitor!" Tandy flared. "You coward!"

The Siren tried to pacify her, but Tandy moved away,
her face red and body stiff, and hurled an invisible tantrum at Smash. It struck him on the chest, and its impact
was devastating. Smash staggered back, the wind knocked
out of him. No wonder the goblin chief had fallen; those
tantrums were potent!

His head gradually cleared. Smash found himself sitting
down, little clouds of confusion dissipating. Tandy was beside him, hugging him as well as she could with her small
arms. "Oh, I'm so sorry, Smash. I shouldn't have done that!
I know you're only trying to be reasonable."

"Ogres aren't reasonable," he muttered.

"It's just that—one of us—how can we ever callously
throw one to the wolves? To the birds, I mean. It just isn't
right!"

"I don't know," he said. "We'll have to work it out."

"I wish we had the wand," she said.

The Siren came to them. "We do have the Ear," she
reminded them.

"There is that," Tandy agreed. "Let me hear it." She
took the Gap Dragon's Ear and listened carefully. "Silent,"
she reported.

Smash took it from her and listened. For him, too, it was silent. Chem had no better result. "I fear it has gone dead—or we have no future," she said. "Nowhere to go."

John was the last to listen. Her face brightened. "I hear something!" she exclaimed. "Singing—fairies singing. There must be fairies nearby!"

"Well, that's what you're looking for," the Siren said. "Let's see if they're within Birdland. Maybe we can get some advice on how to proceed."

There seemed to be nothing better to do. Smash lurched to his feet, amazed at the potency of Tandy's tantrum; he still felt weak. An ogress could hardly have hit him harder! Yet more than that, he marveled at her quick reversal of mood. She had been almost savagely impetuous—then humanly sorry. Too bad, he mused, she hadn't been born an ogress. That tantrum—it also reminded him a bit of one of his mother's curses.

He shook his head. Foolish fantasy was pointless. He had to clear his reeling noggin, and get moving, and find Tandy a good human-type husband so the demon wouldn't bother her any more. Good Magician Humfrey must have known that there would be a suitable man for her somewhere in this wilderness, a man she would never encounter unless she traveled here. Since Smash was passing this way anyway, it had been easy enough to take her along. The truth was, she was nice enough company, tiny and temperamental as she was. He had not had much company like that before and was becoming acclimated to it. He knew this was un-ogrish; maybe such ridiculous feelings would pass when he got rid of the Eye Queue curse.

They proceeded on, following John, who used the Ear to orient on the fairies. The rocs paced them; they would not be able to depart Birdland without paying their poll toll. One body . . .

Actually, Smash might have a way around that. If he went back into the gourd and fought the Night Stallion and lost, his soul would be forfeit pretty soon, and there would be no point in proceeding north. So in that event, he might as well stay here himself. The only problem was, how would the others survive without him? He had no confidence that they were beyond the worst of the dangers of central Xanth.

As they continued, they saw more and more birds. Some were brightly plumed, some drab; some large, some small; some ferocious of aspect with huge and knifelike beaks, some meek with soft little feathers. There were bright blue-birds, dull blackbirds, and brightly dull spotted birds. There were fat round robins and thin pour-beakers.

They went on. There were ruffled grouse, angrily complaining about things, godwits making profane jokes, sandpipers playing little fifes on the beach, black rails lying in parallel rows on the ground, oven birds doing the morning baking, mourning doves sobbing uncontrollably, goshawks staring with amazement, a crane hauling up loads of stones, and several big old red barn owls filled with hay. Nearby were grazing cowbirds and cattle egrets, and a catbird was stalking a titmouse, tail swishing.

"Birds are funny folk," the Siren murmured. "I never realized there was so much variety."

In due course they came to the palace of the Kingbird. "Better bow good and low," the parrot advised. "His Highness the Bird of a Feather, the ruler of Xanth, First on the Pecking Order, doesn't appreciate disrespect from inferiors."

"Ruler of Xanth!" Chem cried. "What about the centaurs?"

"What about King Trent?" Tandy asked.

"Who?" the parrot asked.

"The human ruler of Xanth, in Castle Roogna."

"Never heard of him. The Kingbird governs."

Smash realized that to the birds, the bird species dominated Xanth. To the goblins, the goblins governed. The same was probably true for the dragons, griffins, flies, and other species. And who could say they were wrong? Each species honored its own leaders. Smash, an ogre, was quite ready to be objective about the matter. When in Birdland, do as the birdbrains did.

He bowed to the Kingbird, as he would have done to the human King of Xanth. To each his own mark of honor.

The Kingbird was reading a tome titled *Avian Artifacts* by Ornith O'Logy, and had no interest in the visitors. Soon Smash's party was on its way again.

They came to a large field filled with pretty flowers. "These are our birdseed plants," the parrot explained. "We have wormfarms and fishfarms and funnybonefarms, and make periodic excursions to Flyland for game, but the bulk of our food comes from fields like this. We are not apt at cultivation—birdshot doesn't seem to do well for us—so we draw on the abilities of lesser creatures like yourselves."

Indeed, Smash saw assorted creatures toiling in the field. There were a few goblins, an elf, a brownie, a gremlin, a nixie, and a sprite. They were obviously slaves, yet they seemed cheerful and healthy enough, acclimated to their lot.

Then Smash had a notion. "John, listen to the Ear again."

The fairy did so. "The waterfall noise almost drowns it out, but I think I hear the fairies close by." She oriented on the sound, going in the direction it got louder, the others following. They rounded a gentle hill, descended into a waterfall-fed gully, and came across the fairies.

They were mending feathers. It seemed some of the birds were too impatient to wait for new feathers to grow, so they had the damaged ones repaired. Only fairies could do such delicate work. Each had a little table with tiny tools, so that the intricate work could be done. And most of them had damaged wings.

"The birds—" Tandy said, appalled. "They crippled the fairies so they can't fly away!"

"Not so," the parrot said. "We do not mutilate our workers, because then they get depressed and do a poor job. Rather, we offer sanctuary for those who are dissatisfied elsewhere. Most of these fairies were cast out of Fairyland."

Tandy was suspicious. She approached the nearest working fairy. "Is this true?" she asked. "Do you like it here?"

The fairy was a male, finely featured in the manner of his kind. He paused, looking up from his feather. "Oh, it's a living," he said. "Since I lost my wings, I couldn't make it in Fairyland. So I have to settle for what I can get. No monsters attack me here, no one teases me for my wing handicap, there's plenty of food, and the work is not arduous. I'd rather be flying, of course—but let's be realistic. I'll never fly again."

Smash saw one fairy down the line with undamaged

wings. "What about him?" he asked. "Why doesn't *he* fly away?"

The fairy frowned. "He has a private complaint. Don't bother him."

But Smash was in pursuit of his notion. "Would it relate to his name?"

"Look," the fairy said, "we aren't trying to aggravate your condition, so why do you bother us? Leave him alone."

John had caught on. "Oh, Smash—I'm afraid to ask!"

"I'm an insensitive ogre," Smash said. "I'll ask." He tromped over to the fairy in question. "Me claim he name," he said in his stupid fashion.

The fairy naturally assumed the ogre was as dull as he was supposed to be. It was all right to tell secrets to stupid folk, because they didn't know enough to laugh. "I am called Joan," he said. "Now go away, monster."

Smash dropped his pretense. "That must be as embarrassing for you as intelligence is for an ogre," he said.

Joan's eyes widened and his wings trembled, causing the cloud pattern on them to roil. "Yes," he agreed.

Smash signaled to John. Diffidently, she approached. "Here is the one who got your name, or one letter of it," Smash said. "Trade him your H for his A, and both of you will be restored."

The two fairies looked at each other. "Joan?" John asked. "John?" Joan asked.

"I suspect the two of you are the same age, and took delivery of your names by the same carrier," Smash said. "Probably the Paste Orifice; it always gums things up. You should compare notes."

Joan reached out and took John's hand. Smash was no proper judge of fairy appearance, but it seemed to him that Joan was quite a handsome young male of his kind, and John was certainly pretty, except for her lost wings. Here in Birdland that particular injury did not count for much.

The two of them seemed almost to glow as their hands touched.

Chem and Tandy and the Siren had joined Smash. "What is that?" Tandy asked. "Is something wrong?"

"No," Chem said. "I've read of this effect, but never hoped to see it. It's the glow of love at first touch."

"Then—" Smash said, in a burst of realization that he had suppressed until this moment. "They were destined for each other. That's why their names were confused. To bring them eventually together."

"Yes!" the centaur agreed. "I think John—I suppose it's Joan now—will be staying here in Birdland."

So the fairy's solution was the group's solution! One of their number would remain—happily. How neatly it had worked out. But of course that was the way of destiny, which was never the coincidence it seemed.

They made their acknowledgments of parting and left their fairy friend to her happy fate. The birds, satisfied, let them go.

Their best route north, the parrot assured them, was through the Water Wing. There were very few monsters there, and the distance to the northern border of Xanth was not great.

They agreed to that route. They had already encountered more than enough monsters, and since the birds assured them there were no fires or earthquakes in the Water Wing, the trek should be easy enough. Besides, the Ear had the sound of rainfall, which suggested their immediate future.

John/Joan hurried up as they were about to cross the border. "Here is a heat wave," she said. "My fiancé had it for when he left Birdland, but now he won't be needing it. Just unwrap it when the time comes."

"Thank you," Smash said. He took the heat wave. It seemed to be a wire curved in the shape of a wave, and was sealed in a transparent envelope.

The girls hugged their friend good-bye, and Smash extended his littlest hamfinger so the fairy could shake hands with him Then they stepped across the border, braced for anything.

Anything was what they got. They were in a drench-pour. Not for nothing was this called the Water Wing by the birds! There was ground underfoot, but it was hard to see because of the ceaseless blast of rain.

Chem brought out her rope, and they tied themselves together again—centaur, Tandy, Siren, and ogre, sloshing north in a sloppy line. Smash had to breathe in through his clenched teeth to strain the water out. Fortunately, the water was not cold; this was a little like swimming.

After an hour, they slogged uphill. The rain thinned as they climbed, but the air also cooled, so they did not gain much comfort. In due course the water turned to sleet, and then to snow.

The poor girls were turning blue with cold. It was time for the heat wave. Smash unwrapped the wire. Immediately heat radiated out, suffusing the immediate region, bringing comfort to each of them. The fairy's present had been well considered, for all that it had been an accident of circumstance.

Slowly the snow stopped falling, but the climb continued. This was a mountain they were on, blanketed with snow. By nightfall they still had not crested it, and had to camp on the slope.

They were all hungry, and Smash was ravenous, so he gave the Siren the heat wave and headed out into the snow to forage. He found some flavored icicles in a crevice-cave and chased a snow rabbit, but couldn't catch it. So he headed back with the icicles; they were only a token, but somewhat better than nothing. They would have to do.

It was colder out here then he had figured. His breath fogged out before him, and the fog iced over and coated him, making him a creature of ice. His feet turned numb, and his fingers, too. He hardly knew where his nose stopped and the ice began; when he snorted, icicles flew out like arrows.

Now he slowed, feeling lethargic. Wind came up, cutting into his flesh, buffeting him about so that he stumbled. He dropped cumbersomely to the ground, his fall cushioned by the snow. He intended to get up, as it was now far downhill to their camp, but it was more comfortable just to lie there for a little longer. His Eye Queue cried warning, but after a while that, too, faded out, and Smash slept.

He dreamed he saw Tandy's father, the soldier Crombie, whirling around in his fashion and pointing his finger. The finger stopped, pointing north. But what was it pointing to? Smash remembered Crombie had said Tandy would lose three things; that must be where it would happen.

Then Smash was being hauled awake. That was much less comfortable than drifting to sleep had been. His extremities hurt, burning like fire and freezing like ice simultaneously; his head felt like thawed carrion, and his belly was roasting as if he were mounted on a spit over a fire. He groaned horrendously, because that was what ogres did when roasted on a spit over a fire.

"He's alive!" a voice cried joyfully.

As Smash recovered more fully, he learned what had happened. He had frozen on the slope. Alarmed at his failure to return, the girls had organized a search party and located him. He was as stiff as ice, because that was what he had become. They had feared him dead, but had put the heat wave on his belly and thawed him. Ogres, it seemed, were freeze-storable.

Now that he was awake, it was time to sleep. They settled down around the heat wave, Tandy choosing to rest her head against Smash's furry forearm. Ah, well, that was harmless, probably. "I'm glad we got you thawed, monster," she murmured. "I'm not letting you out alone again!"

"Ogres do get into trouble," he agreed. It was strange to imagine anyone watching out for him, and stranger yet to imagine that he might need this attention, but it seemed he did, on occasion.

In the night there was a horrendous roar. Smash, dreaming again—he tended to do that when asleep—thought it was an ogress and smiled a huge grimace. But the three girls bolted up, terrified.

"Wake up, Smash!" Tandy whispered urgently. "A monster's coming!"

But Smash, in a dream-daze, hardly stirred. He had no fear of the most horrendous ogress.

The monster stamped near, eyes glowing, teeth gleaming, breath fogging out in dank, cold clouds. It was pure white, and every hair seemed to be an icicle.

"Smash!" Tandy hissed. "It's an abom—abom—an awful Snowman! Help!"

The Snowman looked over them, as pale as a snowstorm. It reached out to grab the nearest edible thing. The girls cowered behind Smash, who was mostly covered by a nice snow blanket, so that little of him showed. This snow was not nearly as cold as that of the rest of the mountain, because this was near the heat wave; he was comfortable enough. But it deceived the Snowman, who caught hold of Smash's nose and yanked.

Ouch! Suddenly Smash woke up all the way. A truly ogrish rage shook him. He reached up one huge, hairy arm and grabbed the snow monster by the throat.

The Snowman was amazed. He had never encountered a worse monster than himself before. He had not known anything like that existed. He did not know how to deal with this situation.

Fortunately, Smash knew how to deal with it. He stood up, not letting go, and shook the hapless monster. "Growr!" he growled, and dropped the creature on top of the heat wave.

There was a bubbling and hissing as the Snowman's posterior converted from ice to steam in one foop. The monster sailed into the air and shot out of there like a gust from a gale. Smash didn't bother to pursue; he knew better than to stray from the vicinity of the heat wave again. He was no Snowman!

"It will be a long time before that creature bothers travelers again," Chem remarked with private satisfaction.

"Yes, we have a worse monster on our side," Tandy said, patting Smash's knee. She seemed to like the notion.

Smash was just glad he had enough of his strength back to handle such things as snow monsters. But soon he would have to meet the Night Stallion and put it all on the line. He had better get the girls beyond these dangerous wilderness regions of Xanth first, just in case.

Once more they settled down to sleep, grouping closely around the heat wave. By morning it had melted them deep into the snow, so that they were in a cylindrical well. There seemed to be no bottom to this layer of snow; was the whole mountain made of it? That could be, since this was the Water Wing, and snow was solidified water.

Smash bashed out a ramp to the surface, and the party resumed the trek. They were all hungry now, but had to be satisfied with mouthfuls of snow.

As they entered the icy ridge of the mountain, the sun melted the remaining clouds and bore down hard on the snow. The snow began to melt. Smash put the heat wave back in its envelope, but soon they were sloshing through slush anyway.

Then the slush turned to water, and the slope became a river flowing over ice. They tried to keep to their feet, but the entire mountain seemed to be dissolving. The treacherous surface gave way beneath them and washed them all helplessly along in the torrent.

Chem seemed to be able to handle herself satisfactorily in the water; and, of course, the Siren assumed her mermaid form and swam like a fish. But Tandy was in trouble because of the sheer rush of water. She could swim well enough in level water, but this was a cataract.

Smash tried to swim to her, but got bogged down himself. He was not really a strong swimmer; he normally waded or whomped through water. But right now he was not at full strength and had been frozen and thawed. This water was becoming too deep and violent for him.

Too much indeed! Smash gulped for air—and got water instead. He coughed and gasped and sucked in a replacement lungful—only to fill up the rest of the way with water.

This was awful! He clawed at his throat, trying foolishly to clear the water while his body struggled for air. But it was no good. The torrent was all about him, finding excellent purchase against his brute body, and he could not breathe.

The agony of suffocation became unbearable. Then something snapped, like the lid of his head, and half his consciousness departed. Smash gave himself up for lost. But it seemed to him that it had been more comfortable to be frozen than to be drowned.

Then he was calm, accepting the inevitable. It was, after all, halfway pleasant doing without air. Maybe this wasn't really worse than freezing. He drifted with the slowing current, relieved, feeling like loose seaweed. How nice just to float forever free.

Then something was tugging fretfully at him. It was the mermaid. She wrapped her arms about one of his and threshed violently with her tail, drawing him forward. But his mass was too much for her. Progress slowed; she needed air herself, with all this exertion. She let him go, and Smash sank blissfully to the depths while she shot up toward the surface.

Slowly he became aware of more tugging, this time on

both arms. He tried to shake himself free, but his arms did not respond. He watched himself being drawn upward from the gloom to the light. There seemed to be two figures drawing him, one on each arm, each with a fish-tail—but maybe he was seeing double.

Smash was not sure how long or far he was dragged; time was compressed or dilated for him. But he became aware that he was on a sandy beach, with a nightmare tromping her hooves on his back. He was mistaken. It was a filly centaur; Chem was treading the water out of his body. The experience was almost as bad as vomiting out all the Stallion manure, after that sequence in the gourd. Almost.

In due course Smash recovered enough to sit up. He coughed another bucket or two of water out of his lungs. "You rescued me," he accused the Siren.

"I tried," she said. "But you were too heavy—until Morris helped."

"Morris?"

"Hi, monster!" someone called from the water.

It was a triton. Now Smash understood why there had seemed to be two merfolk hauling him along. The Siren and Morris the Merman.

"We lost the Ear and the heat wave, but we saved you," the Siren said. "And Chem rescued Tandy."

Now Smash saw Tandy, who was lying face-down on the sand. The centaur was now kneading her back, using hands instead of hooves. "You breathed water, too?" Smash asked.

Tandy raised her head. "Ungh," she agreed squishily. "Did you—float?"

"When I sank," he answered. "If that's what dying is like, it's not bad."

"Let's not talk about death," Chem said. "This is too nice a place for that. I'm already upset about losing the Ear."

"Not more upset about that than I am with me for losing the heat wave," the Siren said.

"Maybe you should have thrown Smash and me back and saved the magic items," Tandy said, forcing a watery smile.

"It was fated that we lose them," Smash said, remembering his dream. "Soldier Crombie said Tandy would lose three things, and our loss is her loss."

"That's true!" Tandy agreed. "But what's the third thing?"

Smash shrugged. "We don't have any third thing to lose. Maybe two covers it."

"No, my father always points things out right. We've lost something else, I'm sure. We just don't know what it is."

"Maybe one of you should stay and look for the lost items," the merman said. He was a sturdy male of middle age, roughly handsome. It was evident that he could not make legs and walk on land the way the Siren could; he was a full triton.

"Maybe one of us should," the Siren said thoughtfully.

After that, it fell naturally into place. This was a pleasant region on the fringe of the Water Wing, where the drainage from the snow mountain became a lake that spread into the mainstream wilderness of Xanth. There was a colony of merfolk here, mostly older, scant of maids. It looked very promising for the Siren.

Chapter 12. Visible Void

The three of them—Smash, Tandy, and Chem—proceeded north to the border of the Void, the last of the special regions of central Xanth. "There is great significance to these five elemental regions," Chem said. "Historically, the five elements—Air, Earth, Fire, Water, and the Void—have always been mainstays of magic. So it is fitting that they be represented in central Xanth, and I'm extremely gratified to get them on my map."

"These have been good adventures," Smash agreed. "But just what is the Void? The other elements make sense, but I can't place that one."

"I don't know," the centaur admitted. "But I'm eager to find out. I don't think this region has ever been mapped before by anyone."

"Now is certainly the time," Tandy said. "I hope it's not as extreme as the others were."

Chem brought out her rope. "Let's not gamble on that! I should have tied us when the snow mountain turned to slush, but it happened so fast—"

They linked themselves together as they approached the line. It was abrupt. On the near side the pleasant terrain of the merfolk's lake spread southward. On the far side was nothing they could perceive.

"I'm the lightest," Tandy said. "I'll go first. Pull me back if I fall into a hole." She smoothed back her slightly scorched and tangled brown hair and stepped across the formidable line.

Smash and Chem waited. The rope kept playing out,

slowly; obviously Tandy was walking, not falling, and not in any trouble. "Is it all right, Tandy?" the centaur called rhetorically.

There was no answer. The rope continued to move. "Can you hear me? Please answer," Chem called, her brow wrinkling.

Now the slack went taut. Chem stood her ground, refusing to be drawn across the line. Smash tried to peer into the Void, but could see nothing except a vague swirl of fog, from this side.

"I think I'd better pull her back," Chem said, swishing her brown tail nervously. It, too, was somewhat bedraggled as a result of their recent adventures. "I'm not sure anything is wrong; maybe she just doesn't hear me."

Chem hauled. There was resistance. She hesitated, not wanting to apply unreasonable force. "What do you think, Smash?"

Smash put his Eye Queue to work, but it seemed sluggish this time. His logic was fuzzy, his perception confused. "I don't—seem to have much of an opinion," he confessed.

She glanced back at him, surprised. "No opinion? You, with your un-ogrish intelligence? Surely you jest!"

"It best me jest," Smash agreed amicably.

She peered closely at him. "Smash—what happened to your Eye Queue? I don't see the stigma on your head."

Smash touched the fur of his scalp. It was smooth; there was no trace of roughness. "No on; it gone," he said.

"Oh, no! It must have been washed out when you nearly drowned! That's the third thing we've lost—your intelligence. That certainly affects Tandy's prospects here. You're back to being stupid!"

Smash was appalled. Just when he needed intelligence, he had lost it! What would he do now in a crisis?

The centaur was similarly concerned, but she had an answer. "We'll have to use my intelligence for us both, Smash. Are you willing to follow my lead, at least until we get through the Void?"

That seemed to make sense to Smash. "She lead, me accede."

"I'll try to haul her back." Chem drew harder on the rope, and, of course, she had the mass to do it. Suddenly it went slack, and the loose end of it slid back across the line.

"Oh, awful!" the centaur exclaimed, dismayed. She switched her tail violently in vexation. "We've lost her!"

"Oh, awful," Smash echoed, since his originality had dissipated with his intellect. What had happened to Tandy?

"I think I'd better step partway across so I can look without committing myself," she decided. "You stay on this side—and don't let me cross all the way. After a minute, if I don't back out, you haul me out, slowly. Agreed?"

"Me agree, assuredly," he said. He was furious at the Eye Queue for deserting him in his hour of need. Of course he had intended to get rid of the curse—but not just yet. Not at the brink of the Void. Now he was liable to do something ogrishly idiotic, and cost his friends their lives. Even his rhyming seemed ludicrous now; what was the point in it? Not until the curse of the Eye Queue had descended on him had he appreciated how stupid a typical ogre seemed—just a hulking brute, too dull to do more than smash things. Indeed, his very name.

The centaur poked her forepart cautiously through the border. It disappeared into the swirl. Smash felt very much alone, though her hindquarters remained with him. He marveled that a human girl as smart and pretty as Tandy could have any interest in him, even as an animal friend. It must have been the Eye Queue that appealed to her, the intelligence manifesting in the oddest of hosts, the sheer anomaly of the bone-headed genius. Her interest would dissipate the moment she discovered what had happened. That, of course, was best; it would free her full attention for her ideal human-type man, whoever and wherever he might be. Yet Smash remained disquieted.

The fact was, he realized now, the curse had had its positive aspect. Like the curse of the moon that human females labored under—one of the things that distinguished them from nymphs—it was awkward and inconvenient, but carried the potential for an entirely new horizon. Females could regenerate their kind; the Eye Queue enabled a person to grasp far broader aspects of reality. Now, having experienced such aspects, he would be returned to his former ignorance.

A minute had passed and gone some distance beyond, and Chem had not backed out. In fact, she was trying to proceed the rest of the way across the line. Smash knew he had to stop that; even if he was now too stupid to perceive the danger in committing oneself to a potential course-of-no-return, he remembered the centaur's orders. "Me take up slack, haul she back," he said, inwardly condemning his ogrish crudity of expression. He might be stupid; did he have to advertise it so blatantly?

That started another chain of thought. Part of the vaunted dullness of ogres was not because of the fact, but because they insisted on the distinguishing characteristic of expression. He could have said, "Because my friend the filly centaur, a decent and intelligent person with a useful magic graphological talent, may be in difficulty, I am required to exert myself according to her expressed wish and draw her gently but firmly back across the demarcation between territories. Then we shall consider how best to proceed." Instead, he had spouted the idiotic ditty in the ludicrous manner of his kind. Surely the Eye Queue vine had been as much of a curse in its untimely departure as in its arrival!

There was resistance. Either Chem didn't want to come back, or something was hauling her forward. Smash drew harder on the rope, but the centaur braced forward, fighting it. Something was definitely amiss. Even an idiot could tell that! Smash was tempted to give one monstrous tug on the rope and haul her back head over tail, as an ordinary ogre would, but several things restrained him. First, her mass was similar to his own; he might lose his footing and yank himself across the line, in the wrong direction. Second, the rope was bound about her humanoid waist, which was delicately narrow; too harsh a force could hurt her. Third, he was not at full strength, so he might not be able to move her effectively even if properly anchored.

Then the rope went slack. Chem, too, was proceeding unfettered into the Void.

Smash dived for her disappearing rump, his ogrish action preceding his inadequate thought. He was too late. She crossed the line. Only her tail flicked back momentarily, as if flicking free a fly.

Smash caught the tail and worked his way along it, hand over hand. Her forward impetus hauled him right up to the line; then he got his balance, dug his toes in, and brought the centaur and himself to a halt.

Now he exerted what remained of his power and drew her back. It sufficed; slowly her rump reappeared. When he got her hind legs across, he shifted his grip carefully, picked up her two feet, and wheelbarrowed her backward. She could not effectively resist, with her feet off the ground.

At last he got her all the way across. She was intact. That relieved one concern. "Tell why she untie," he grunted, not letting her go.

Chem seemed dazed, but soon reorganized herself. "It's not what you think, Smash. It's beautiful in the Void! All mist and fog and soft meadows, and herds of centaurs grazing—"

Smash might be stupid, but not that stupid. "She still in daze. Centaurs no graze."

Her eyes rounded, startled. "Why, that's right! Sea cows graze. Water-horses graze. Black sheep graze. Centaurs eat in human fashion. What am I thinking of?"

Perhaps she had seen a herd of grazing animals and jumped to a conclusion. But that was of little moment at the moment. "That is dandy. Where is Tandy?"

"Oh, Tandy! I didn't see her." Chem was chagrined. "I crossed the line to seek her and was so distracted by the beauty of the region that I forgot my mission. I'm not usually that flighty!"

True enough. Chem was a filly with all four hooves on the ground. She was less aggressive than her father Chester and less imperious than her mother Cherie, but still had qualities of determination and stability that were to be commended. It was entirely unlike her to act in an impetuous or thoughtless manner.

Now something else occurred to Smash. There were various kinds of magic springs in Xanth that trapped the unwary. Some caused a person to fall in love with the first creature of the opposite sex he or she saw; that was how the species of centaur had originated. Some caused a person to turn into a fish. Some healed a person's wounds instantly and cleanly, as if they had never been. Had the group encountered one of those before, John the Fairy would have been able to restore her lost wings. And some springs caused a person to forget.

"She get wet, she forget?" he asked, wishing he could voice his concern more eloquently. Damn his bonehead!

"Wet?" Chem was perplexed. "Oh—you mean as in a lethe-spring? No, I didn't forget in that fashion, as you can see, and I'm sure Tandy didn't. For one thing, there was no spring nearby, certainly not within range of the rope. It's something else. It's just such lovely land, so pleasant and peaceful, I simply had to explore it. Nothing else seemed important, somehow. I knew that farther in there would be even more wonder, and—" She paused. "And I just couldn't step back. I realize that was very foolish of me. But I'm sure that place is safe. No monsters or natural hazards, I mean."

Smash remained doubtful. Tandy was gone, and Chem had almost been gone. It had been no simple distraction of mind that kept her there; she had untied her safety rope and resisted his pullback with all her might. Yet she seemed to be in full possession of her faculties now.

Tandy must have been similarly seduced. She now was wary of the easy paths leading to tanglers and ant-lion lairs, but would not have experienced this particular inducement. Instead of being an easy access path to a pleasant retreat, this was an entire landscape that lured one in. Was that why it was called the Void—because no one ever returned from it, so that nothing was known about it?

If that were so, how could they leave Tandy to its merciless mercy? She needed to be rescued immediately!

"As I see it," Chem said, "we shall have to go in and look for Tandy and try to bring her out. We risk getting trapped ourselves—not, I think, by some monster, but by the sheer delight of the region. We won't *want* to leave." She flicked her tail, perturbed. "I realize this is a lot to ask of you now, Smash, but do you have any opinion?"

How ironic! If the curse had stayed with him just a little longer, he could have marshaled its formidable power and expressed an eloquently cogent and relevant thought that might completely clarify their troubled course. Something like: "Chem, I suggest you employ your three-dimensional holographic map-projection to chart the Void as we explore

it, so that not only will we be able to orient more specifi-
cally on Tandy's most likely course, we shall also have no
difficulty finding our way out again." But the curse had
left him, so that he had become too stupid to think of that,
let alone express it. All that actually came out was, "Make
map, leave trap."

"Map? Trap?" she asked, her brow furrowing. "I do
want to chart the Void, as I do everything, but I don't see
how—"

Sure enough, he had not gotten through. He tried again.
"Find way, no stay."

"Use my magic map to find our way out?" She brightened. "Of course! We can't get lost if I keep it current. I'll
mark a dotted line; then we can follow it back if there is
any problem. That's a very good idea, Smash." She said it
comfortingly, as one would to a dull child. And, of course,
intellectually, that was what he was. What he had been
when infected by the weed of smartness was of no present
relevance; he had to accept the reality, depressing as it now
seemed. He was not, and never would be, inherently intelligent. He was, after all, an ogre.

That would definitely solve one problem, he thought.
Tandy might have taken a certain girlish fancy to him—
but it had been the enhancement of his intellect provided
by the Eye Queue that appealed to her. Now that he was
back to normal, she would properly regard him as the animal he was. That was certainly best—though, somehow, he
was too stupid to appreciate the nicety of it fully. He had,
in fact, been somewhat puffed up by her attention, unde-
served as it was, and had rather enjoyed her company, the
flattery of her uncritical nearness. He did not relish the
prospect of going his way alone again. But of course he
had no choice. An ogre went the ogre's way.

"Let's try it," Chem said, coiling her rope. "Let's keep
each other in sight, and call out any special things we see.
Our object is to locate Tandy and then to bring us all out
on the north side of the Void. Do you agree?"

"Good stratagem, centaur femme," he agreed inanely.

She smiled briefly, and he saw how nervous she was.
She was afraid of what they were about to encounter in the
Void, pleasant though it seemed. She knew their perspec-

tives would change the moment they crossed the line, and that they might never return. "Wish us luck, monster."

"Luck, Chem, pro tem," he said.

They stepped across the line together.

Chem had been correct. The landscape was even, slightly sloping down ahead, with low-hanging clouds cruising by. The ground was covered with lush turf that seemed innocent and had a fragrant odor, with pretty little flowers speckled through it. Certainly there was no obvious danger. And that, he feared, was the most obvious danger of all.

Now Chem generated her magic map. The image appeared in the air by her head. But this time it expanded enormously, rapidly overlapping the terrain they stood on, so that the features of the Land of Xanth in image passed by them both. Mountains, lakes, and the Gap Chasm—apparently her map was not affected by the forget-spell on the Gap, an item of possible significance—rushed by them. Then trees and streams became large enough to be seen individually, and even occasional animals, frozen as recorded yet seeming to move because of the expansion of the map. "Hey, it's not supposed to do that!" she protested. "It's turning life-size!"

Obviously the map was careering out of control. Smash wondered why that should happen here. If only he had his Eye Queue back, he would be able to realize that this was surely no coincidence, and that it related in some fundamental way to the ultimate nature of the Void. He might even conjecture that the things of the mind, whether animated in the form of a map or remaining inchoate, had considerable impact on the landscape of the Void. Perhaps the interaction between the two created a region of animated imagination that could be a lot of fun, but might also pose considerable threats to sanity if it got out of control. Perhaps no purely physical menace lurked within the Void, but rather, the state of mental chaos that might prevail when no aspects of physical reality intruded upon or limited the generation of fanciful imagery. But naturally a mere stupid ogre could in no way appreciate the tiniest portion of such a complex conjecture, so Smash was oblivious. He hoped this foolish oblivion would not have serious consequences. Ignorance was not necessarily bliss, as any smart creature would know.

Chem, confused by her map's misbehavior, turned it off.
Then she tried it again, concentrating intently. This time it
expanded from its point source, then contracted to pinpoint
size, gyrating wildly, until it steadied down around the size
she wanted it. She was learning new control, and this was
just as well, for lack of discipline might be extraordinarily
troublesome here.

"See, there are the grazing centaurs," Chem said, pointing ahead.

Smash looked. He saw a tribe of grazing ogres. Again, if
only he had retained the curse of intelligence, he might
have comprehended that another highly significant aspect
of this region was manifesting. Chem perceived one non-
sensical thing, and he perceived another. That suggested
that the preconceptions of the viewer defined in large part
what that viewer saw; there was not necessarily any objective standard here. Reality, literally, was something else. In
this case, perhaps, a herd of irrelevant creatures was grazing, neither centaurs nor ogres.

If this were so, he might have continued his thought,
how could they be certain that anything they saw here was
not a kind of illusion? Tandy could be lost in a world of
altered realities and not realize it. Since Chem and Smash
also were in altered states of perception, the problem of
locating Tandy might be immensely more complicated than
anticipated. But he, a dull ogre, would merely blunder on,
heedless of such potential complications.

"Something funny here," Chem said. "We know centaurs don't graze."

"It seem a dream," Smash said, trying vainly to formulate the concept he knew he could not master without the
curse of intellect.

"Illusion!" Chem exclaimed. "Of course! We're seeing
other creatures that only look like centaurs." She was
smart, as all centaurs were; she caught on quickly.

But she didn't have it all yet. "Me no see centaur she,"
he said clumsily.

"You see something else? Not centaurs?" Again her
brow furrowed. "What do you see, Smash?"

Smash tapped his own chest.

"Oh, you see ogres. Yes, I suppose that makes sense. I

see my kind, you see yours. But how can we see what is really there?"

This was far too much for him to figure out. If only he had his Eye Queue back, he might be able to formulate a reversal of perspective that would cancel out the mind-generated changes and leave only the undisturbed truth. Perhaps a kind of cross-reference grid, contrasting Chem's perceptions with his own, eliminating the differences. She saw centaurs, he saw ogres—obviously each saw his own kind, so that was suspect. Both saw a number of individuals, so there the perceptions aligned and were probably accurate. Both saw the creatures grazing, which suggested they were, in fact, grazing animals, equine, caprine, bovine, or other. Further comparison on an organized basis, perhaps mapping the distinctions on a variant of Chem's magic map, would in due course yield a close approximation of the truth, whatever it might be.

Of course, it might be that there was nothing. That even their points of agreement were merely common fancies, so that the composite image would be that illusion that was mutually compatible. It just might be, were the fundamental truth penetrated, that what remained in the Void was—nothing. The absence of all physical reality. Creatures thought, therefore they existed—yet perhaps even their thinking was largely illusion. So maybe the thinkers themselves did not exist—and the moment they realized this, they ceased to exist. The Void was—void.

But without his mental curse he wouldn't see any of that, and perhaps this was just as well. If he were going to imagine anything, he should start with the Eye Queue vine! But he would have to use it cautiously, lest the full power of his enhanced intellect succeed only in abolishing himself. He needed to preserve the illusion of existence long enough to rescue Tandy and get them out of the Void, so that their seeming reality became actual. "Me need clue to find Eye Queue," he said regretfully.

Chem took him literally, which was natural enough, since she knew he now lacked the wit to speak figuratively. "You think there are Eye Queue vines growing around here? Maybe I can locate them on my map."

She concentrated, and the suspended map brightened.

Parts of it became greener than others. "I can't usually place items I haven't actually seen," she murmured. "But sometimes I can interpolate, extrapolate from experience and intuition. I think there could be such vines—here." She pointed to one spot on her map, and a marker-glow appeared there. "Though they may be imaginary, just ordinary plants that we happen to see as Eye Queues."

Smash was too stupid to appreciate the distinction. He set off in the direction indicated by the map. The centaur followed, keeping the map near him so he could refer to it at need. In short order he was there—and there they were, the dangling, braided eyeball vines, each waiting to curse some blundering creature with its intelligence and perception.

He grabbed one and set it on his head. It writhed and sank in immediately. How far had he sunk, to inflict so eagerly this curse upon himself!

His intelligence expanded, much as the centaur's map had. Now he grasped many of the same notions he had wished to grasp before. He saw one critical flaw in the technique of using a cross-reference grid to establish reality: turned on his own present curse of intelligence, it would probably reveal his smartness to be illusion. Since Smash needed that intelligence to rescue Tandy, he elected not to pursue that course. It would be better to use the devices of perspective to locate Tandy first, then explore their unreal mechanisms when the loss of such mechanisms no longer mattered. It would also be wise not to ponder the intricacies of his own personal existence.

What would be the best way to find her? If her footprints glowed, it would be easy to track her. But he was now far too smart to believe that anything so coincidentally convenient could exist.

The centaur, however, might be deceivable. "I suspect there could be some visible evidence of the passage of outsiders," he remarked. "We carry foreign germs, alien substances from other magic regions. There could be interactions, perhaps a small display of illumination—"

"Smash!" she exclaimed. "It worked! You're smart again!"

"Yes, I thought it might."

"But it's illusion. The Eye Queue is only imaginary! How can it have a real effect?"

"What can affect the senses can also affect the mind," Smash explained. She had seemed so smart a moment ago. Now, from the lofty vantage of his restored intelligence, she seemed a bit slow. Certainly it was stupid of her to attempt to explain away his mental power, for that would put them right back in the morass of incompetence. He had to persuade her—before she persuaded him. "In Xanth, things are mostly what they seem to be. For example, Queen Iris's illusions of light enable her to see in the dark; her illusion of distant vision enables her to see people who are otherwise too far away. Here in the Void, in contrast, things are what they seem not to be. It is possible to finesse these appearances to our advantage, and to generate realities that serve our interests. Do you perceive the footprints?"

She looked, dismayed by his confusing logic. "I—do," she said, surprised. "Mine are disks, yours are paw-prints. Mine glow light brown, like my hide; yours glow black, like yours." She looked up. "Am I making any sense at all? How can a print glow black?"

"What other color befits an ogre?" he asked. He did not see the prints, but did not remark on that. "Now we must cast about for Tandy's prints." He cracked the briefest smile. "And hope they do not wail."

"Yes, of course," she agreed. "They must originate where we crossed the line: that's the place to intercept them." She started back—and paused. "That's funny."

"What's funny?" Smash was aware that the Void was tricky and potentially dangerous. If Chem began to catch on to its ultimate nature, he would have to divert her in a hurry. Their very existence could depend on it.

"I seem to be up against a wall. It's intangible, but it balks me."

A wall. That was all right; that was a physical obstacle, not an intellectual one, therefore much less dangerous. Much better to wrestle that sort of thing. Smash moved to join her—and came up against the wall himself. It was invisible, as she had suggested, but as he groped at it he began to discern its rough stones. It seemed to be fashioned of ogre-resistant stuff, or maybe his weakened condition prevented him from demolishing it properly. Odd.

His Eye Queue had another thought, however. If things in the Void were not what they seemed to be, perhaps this was true of the wall. It might not exist at all; if he could succeed in disbelieving in it, he could walk through it. Yet if he succeeded in abolishing a wall this tangible by mental effort, what then of the other things of the Void, such as the Eye Queue? He might do best not to disbelieve.

"What do you perceive?" Chem asked.

"A firm stone wall," he said, deciding. "I fear we shall find it difficult to depart the Void." He had thought that intellectual dissolution, or the vacating of reality, might cause the demise of intruders into the Void; perhaps it was, after all, a more physical barrier. He would have to keep his mind open so as not to be trapped by illusions about these illusions.

"There must be a way," she said with a certain false confidence. She suspected, as he did, that they could be in worse trouble right now than they had been when the Gap Dragon charged them or the volcano's lava flows began breaking up under them. Mental and emotional equilibrium was as important now as physical agility had been then. "Our first job is to catch up with Tandy; then we can tackle the problem of departure."

At least she had her priorities in order. "Certainly. We can intercept her footprints by proceeding sidewise. We now have a notion why she did not return. This wall must be pervious from the edge of the Void, impervious from the interior. A little like a one-way path through the forest."

"Yes. I always liked those one-way paths. I don't like this wall quite as well." Chem proceeded sidewise, following the wall. She did not see it or really feel it, yet it balked her effectively. Meanwhile, Smash did not see the glowing footprints, but knew they would lead the two of them to Tandy. There seemed to be more substance to these illusions than was true elsewhere. The illusions of Queen Iris seemed very real, but one could walk right through them. The illusions of the Void seemed unreal, yet prevented penetration. Would they really all dissipate at such time as he allowed himself to fathom the real nature of the Void?

If nothing truly existed here, how could there be a wall to block escape? He kept skirting the dangerous thoughts!

Soon Chem spied Tandy's footprints—bright red, she announced. The prints were headed north, deeper into the Void.

They followed this new trail. Smash checked every so often and discovered that the invisible wall paced them. Any time he tried to step south, he could not. He could only go north, or slide east or west. This disturbed him more than it might have when he was ogrishly stupid. He did not like traveling a one-way channel; this was too much like the route into the lair of a hungry dragon. The moment he caught up to Tandy, he would find a way to go back out of the Void. Maybe he could break a hole in the wall with a few hard ogre blows of his fist.

Yet again his Eye Queue, slanted across with an alternate thought. Suppose the Void were like a big funnel, allowing people to slide pleasantly toward its center and barring them from climbing out? Then the wall would not necessarily be a wall at all, merely the outer rim of that funnel. To smash it apart could be to break up the very ground that supported them, and send them plunging in a rockslide down into the deeper depth. No percentage there!

How could he arrange to escape the trap and take his friends with him? If no one had escaped before to give warning, that was a bad auspice for their own chances! Well, he intended to be the first to emerge to tell the tale.

Could he locate a big bird, a roc, and get carried out by air? Smash doubted it. He distrusted air travel, having had a number of uncomfortable experiences with it, and he certainly distrusted birds as big as rocs. What did rocs eat, anyway?

What else was there? Then he came up with a notion he thought would work in the Void. This would use the properties of the Void against the Void itself, rather than fighting those properties. He would try it—when the time came.

"There's something ahead," Chem said. "I don't know what it is yet."

In a moment they caught up to it. It was an ogress—the beefiest, fiercest, hairiest, ugliest monster he had ever seen, with a face so mushy it was almost sickening. Lovely!

"What's another centaur doing here?" Chem asked.

Instantly the Eye Queue analyzed the significance of her observation. "That is another anonymous creature. We had better proceed cautiously."

"Oh, I see what you mean! Do you think it could be a monster?" The centaur, delicately, did not voice the obvious fear—that the monster could have consumed Tandy. After all, it stood astride her tracks.

"Perhaps we should approach it from opposite sides, each ready to help the other in case it should attack." He wasn't fully satisfied with this decision, but the thought of harm to Tandy made the matter urgent.

"Yes," Chem agreed nervously. "As I become acclimated to this region, I like it less. Maybe one of us can draw near her and the other can hide, ready to act. We can't assume a sleek centaur filly like that is hostile."

Nor could they afford to assume the ugly ogress was *not* hostile! They had to be ready for anything. "You hide; I will approach in friendly fashion."

The centaur proceeded quietly to the west, and in a moment disappeared. Smash gave her time to get properly settled, then stomped gently toward the stranger. "Ho!" he called.

The hideous, wonderful ogress snapped about, spying him. "Who you?" she grunted dulcetly, her voice like the scratching of harpies' talons on dirty slate.

Smash, aware that she was not what she seemed, was cautious. Names had a certain power in Xanth, and he was already below strength; it was best to remain anonymous, at least until he was sure of the nature of this creature. "I am an inquiring stranger," he replied.

She tromped right up to him and stood snout to snout, in the delightful way of an ogress. "Me gon' stir he monster," she husked in the fascinatingly unsubtle mode of her apparent kind, and she clinked him in the puss with one hairy paw.

The blow lacked physical force, but Smash did a polite backflip as if knocked heels over head. What a romantic come-on! He remembered how his mother knocked his father about and stepped on his face, showing her intimidating love. How similar this ogre-she was!

Yet his Eye Queue cautioned caution, as was its wont. This was not a real ogress; she might just be roughing him up for a meal. She might not be nearly as friendly as she seemed. So he did not reciprocate by smashing her violently into a tree. Besides, there was no suitable tree handy.

He used un-ogrish eloquence instead. "This is a remarkably friendly greeting for a stranger."

"No much danger," she said. "He nice stranger." And she gave him a friendly kick.

Smash was becoming much intrigued. He was sure this was no ogress, but she was one interesting person! Maybe he should hit her back. He raised his hamfist.

Then a third party appeared. This was another ogress. "Don't hit her, Smash!" she cried. "I just realized—"

"Smash?" the first ogress repeated questioningly. She seemed amazed.

"We must all describe exactly what we see," the second ogress said. She, too, was no true ogress, for her speech did not conform—unless she had blundered into some Eye Queue vines—but that hardly seemed likely. "You first, Smash."

Confused by this development, he obliged. "I see two attractively brutal ogresses, each with a face mushier than the other, each hunched so that her handpaws reach almost down to her hindpaws. One is brown, the other red."

"And I see two centaurs," the second ogress said. "A black stallion and a red mare."

Oho! That would be Chem, seeing her own kind. Once she had separated from him, her own perceptions had taken over, so that she saw him falsely.

"I see a handsome black human man and a pretty brown human girl," the first ogress said.

"Then you are Tandy!" Chem exclaimed.

"Tandy!" Smash repeated, amazed.

"Of course I'm Tandy!" Tandy agreed. "I always was. But why are you two dressed up like human people?"

"We each perceive our own kind," Chem explained. "Each person instinctively generates his or her own reality from the Void. Come—take hands and perhaps we can break through to reality."

They took hands—and slowly the alternate images dissipated, and Smash saw Chem in her ruffled brown coat and Tandy in her tattered red dress.

"You were awful handsome as a man," Tandy said

sadly. "All garbed in black, like a dusky king, with silver gloves." Smash realized that his orange jacket had become so dirty it was now almost indistinguishable from his natural fur. "But why did you fall down when I tried to shake your hand?"

The Eye Queue provided the insight to cause him embarrassment. "I misunderstood your intent," he confessed. "I thought you were being friendly."

"I *was* being friendly!" she exclaimed indignantly. "You were the first human being I was able to get close to in this funny place. I thought you might know some way out. I can't seem to go back myself; I bang into an invisible hedge or something. So I wanted to be very positive, and not scare you away. After all you might have been lost too."

"Yes, of course," Smash agreed weakly.

"But you acted as if I'd hit you, or something!" she continued indignantly.

"This is the way ogres show affection," Chem explained.

Tandy laughed. "Affection! That's how human beings fight!"

Smash was silent, horribly embarrassed.

But Tandy would not let it go. "You big oaf! I'll show you how human beings express affection!" And she grabbed Smash's arm, pulling him toward her with small human violence. Bemused, he yielded, until his head was down near hers.

Tandy threw her arms around his furry neck and planted a firm, long, hot-blooded kiss on his mouth, moving her lips against his.

Smash was so surprised he sat down. Tandy followed him, still pressing close, locking his head to hers. He fell all the way back on the ground, but she stayed with him, her brown hair flopping forward to cover his wildly staring eyes as she drove home the rest of the kiss.

At last she released him, as she needed a breath. "What do you think of that, ogre?"

Smash lay where she had thrown him, unable to make sense of the experience.

"He's overwhelmed," Chem said. "You gave him an awfully stiff dose for his first such contact."

"Well, I've wanted to do it for a long time," Tandy said. "He's been too stupid to catch on."

"Tandy, he's an ogre! They don't understand human romance. You know that."

"He's an ogre with Eye Queue. He can darned well learn."

"I'm afraid you're being unrealistic," the centaur said, talking as if Smash were not present. Perhaps that was the case, mentally. "You're a spunky, pretty human girl. He's a hulking jungle brute. You can't afford to get emotionally involved with a creature like that. He just isn't your type."

"And just what is my type?" Tandy flared defiantly. "A damned demon intent on rape? Smash is the nicest male creature I've met in Xanth!"

"How many male creatures have you met in Xanth?" the centaur inquired.

Tandy was silent. Of course her experience had been quite limited.

Smash at last essayed a remark. "You could visit a human village—"

"Shut up, ogre," Tandy snapped, "or I'll kiss you again!"

Smash shut up. She was not bluffing; she could do it. She still had her arms looped around his neck, since she lay half astride him, holding him down, as it were.

"You have to be realistic," Chem said. "The Good Magician sent you out with Smash so the ogre could protect you while you searched for a husband. What good will it do you to find the destined man, as John and the Siren and maybe Goldy did, if you foolishly waste your love on an inappropriate object? You would be undermining the very thing you seek."

"Oh, phooey!" Tandy exclaimed. "You're right, centaur, I know you're right, centaurs are always right—but oh, it hurts!" A couple of hot raindrops fell on Smash's nose, burning him with an acid other than physical. She was crying, and he found that even more confusing than the kiss. "Ever since he rescued me from the gourd and got me back my soul—"

"I'm not denying he's a good creature," Chem said. "I'm just saying, realistically—"

Tandy turned ferociously on Smash. "You monster! Why couldn't you have been a *man*?"

"Because I'm an ogre," he said.

She wrenched one arm clear of him and made as if to strike his face. But her hand did not touch him.

The Void spun about him, dimming. Smash realized she had hit him with another tantrum. That, ironically, was more like ogre love. Why couldn't she have been an ogress?

An ogress. Now, his mind shaken by the double whammy of kiss and tantrum, Smash floated, half conscious, and realized what he had been missing. An ogress! He, like every member of his party, could not exist alone. He needed a mate. That was what had brought him to Good Magician Humfrey's castle. That had been his unasked Question. How could he find his ideal mate? Humfrey had known.

And of course there would be ogresses at the Ogre-fen-Ogre Fen. That was why the Good Magician had sent him to seek the Ancestral Ogres. He would be able to select one who was right for him, knock her about in ogre fashion, and live in brutal happiness ever after, exactly as his parents had. It all did make sense.

He drifted slowly to earth as the horrendous impact of the tantrum eased. "Now I understand—" he began.

"I warned you, oaf," Tandy said. She leaned over and plastered another big kiss on him.

Smash was so dazed that he almost grasped the nature of the kiss, this time. Perhaps it was the effect of the Void, making things seem other than they were. It was as if she were punching him in the snoot—and with that perception she became much more alluring.

Then she broke, and the odd perspective ended. She became a girl again, all soft and pretty and nice and wholly inappropriate for romance. It was too bad.

"Oh, what's the use," Tandy said. "I'm a fool and I know it. Come on, people; we have to get out of this place."

"That may not be readily accomplished," Chem said. "We can travel in deeper, or edge sideways, but we can't back out. I'm sure it's like a whirlpool, drawing us ever inward. What we shall find in the center, I hesitate to conjecture."

"Oblivion," Tandy said tightly. She, too, had caught on.

"A maw," Smash said, climbing unsteadily to his feet.

"This land is carnivorous. It gives us respite only because it doesn't need to consume us instantly. It has herds of grazing creatures to eat first. When it gets hungry, it will take us."

"I fear that is so," the centaur agreed. "Yet there must be some way for smart or creative people to escape it. There is so much illusion here, maybe we could fool it."

"So far, it's been fooling us, not we it," Tandy said. "Unless we can wish away that wall—"

But Smash's Eye Queue had been cogitating on this problem, and now it regurgitated a notion—the one he had flirted with before. "If we could escape into another world, one with different rules—"

"Such as what?" Chem asked, interested. "Have you got something on your hairy mind?"

"The hypnogourd."

"I don't like the gourd!" Tandy said instantly.

"And the fact is, even if we all entered the gourd, our bodies would remain right here," the centaur pointed out. "The gourd is a trap itself—but if we did get out of it, we'd still be in the Void. A trap within a trap."

"But the nightmares can go anywhere," Smash said. "Even to Mundania—and back."

"That's true," Tandy agreed. "They can go right through walls, and I think some can run on water. So I suppose they could run through the Void, and out again. They're not ordinary mares. But they're very hard to catch and hard to ride, and the cost—" She smiled ruefully. "I happen to know."

"They would help us if the Night Stallion told them to," Smash said.

"Oh, I forgot!" Tandy exclaimed. "You still have to fight the Night Stallion! You sacrificed your soul for me—" She clouded up. "Oh, Smash, I owe you so much!"

The centaur nodded thoughtfully. "Smash placed his soul in jeopardy for you, Tandy. I can appreciate how that would affect you. But I'm not sure you interpret your debt correctly."

"I was locked into that horror, deprived of my soul!" Tandy said. "I had no hope at all. The lights had gone out on my horizon. Then he came and fought the bones and

smashed things about and brought out my soul, and I lived
again. I owe my everything to him. I should give back my
soul—"

"No!" Smash cried, knowing that she could endure no
worse horror than the loss of her soul again. "I promised to
protect you, and I should have protected you from the
gourd, instead of splashing in the lake. I'll fight this
through myself."

Chem shook her head. "I do see the problem—for each
of you. I wish I perceived the answers as clearly."

"I have to meet the Stallion anyway," Smash said. "So
when I have conquered him, I'll ask him for some mares."

"That's so crazy it just might work!" Chem said. "But
there's one detail you may have overlooked. We have no
hypnogourds here."

"We'll use your map again," he said.

The centaur considered. "I must admit it worked for
your Eye Queue replacement vine, and our situation is desperate enough so that anything's worth trying. But—"

"Replacement?" Tandy demanded.

"Chem will explain it to you while I'm in the gourd,"
Smash said. "Right now, let's use the map to locate a gourd
patch."

The centaur projected her map and settled on a likely
place for gourds while Tandy watched skeptically. Then the
party went there, though the way took them deeper into the
Void.

And there they were—several nice fat hypnogourds with
ripe peepholes. Smash settled himself by the largest. "You
girls get some rest," he advised. "This may take a while.
Remember, I have to locate the Stallion first, then fight
him, then round up the mares."

Tandy grabbed his hamhand in her two delicate little
hands. "Oh, Smash—I wish I could help you, but I'm terrified to go into a gourd—"

"*Don't* go in a gourd!" Smash exclaimed. "Just stay close
so you don't get walled off from me and can't bring me out
in an emergency," he said gruffly.

"I will! I will!" Tandy's eyes were tear-bright. "Oh,
Smash, are you strong enough? I shouldn't have hit you
with that tantrum—"

"I like your tantrums. You just rest, and wait for the nightmares, by whatever route they come."

"I know I'll see nightmares," she said wanly.

Smash glanced at Chem. "Keep an eye on her," he said, disengaging his hand from Tandy's.

"I will," the centaur agreed.

Then Smash put his eye to the peephole.

Chapter 13. Souls Alive

He found himself emerging from the cakewalk onto a vast empty stage. He landed gently. There was no vomit. There was a new scene.

The floor was metal-hard and highly polished; his feet left smudge marks where they touched. The air was half lit by a glow that seemed inherent. There was nothing else.

Smash peered about. It occurred to him that if the Night Stallion were here, he could spend a long time looking, as this place seemed infinitely extensive. He had to narrow its compass, somehow.

Well, he knew how to do that. He started tromping, unreeling his string behind him. He would crisscross this region for as long and as far as it took him.

Smash advanced. The string became a long line, disappearing in the distance behind. It divided the plain into two sections.

This could take even more time than he had judged, he realized. Since the girls were waiting outside the gourd in the Void and would not be able to go in search of food or water, he wanted to get on with it quickly. So he needed some way to speed things up.

He cudgeled his Eye Queue again. How could he most efficiently locate a creature that didn't want to be located?

Answer: what about following its trail?

He applied his eye to the floor. Now that he concentrated, he saw the hoofprints. They crossed his projected line, coming from the right rear and proceeding to the left front. There would be no problem following that!

But his curse, in its annoying fashion, caused him to

242

question the simplicity of this procedure. The hoofprints were suspiciously convenient, crossing his line just at the point he thought to look, almost as if they were intended to be seen. He knew that tracking a creature was not necessarily simple, even when the prints were clear. The trail could meander aimlessly, looping about, getting lost in bad terrain. It could become dangerous if the quarry knew it was being tracked—and the Dark Horse surely did know. There could be tricks and ambushes.

No, there was no sense playing the game of the Night Stallion. The trail was not to be trusted. It was something set up to delude an ordinary ogre. Better to force the Stallion to play Smash's game—and if the Horse did not know of Smash's hidden asset of intelligence, that could be a counter ambush. A smart ogre was quite different from a stupid one.

Smash stomped on, following his straight line, halving the territory. This should also restrict the range of the Stallion, since it could not go any place Smash had already looked—as he understood the rules of this quest—and therefore could not cross the line.

Yet the territory still seemed to be infinitely large. He might tromp forever and never come to the far side. For that matter, he hadn't started at the near side, either; he had simply appeared within the range and begun there. He also realized that halving the total territory did not necessarily cut the area remaining to be searched. Half of infinity remained infinity. Also, unless he knew which half the Stallion was in, he had gained nothing; he could spend all his time searching in the wrong half, his failure guaranteed.

Smash pondered. His Eye Queue was really straining now, and probably the eyeballs of it were getting hot in their effort to see the way through infinity. One thing he had to say for the curse: it certainly tried to help him. It never really opposed its will to his own; it sought instead to call his attention to new aspects of any situation encountered, and to provide more effective ways of dealing with problems. He had discovered how useful that was when he had tried to function without its aid. Now he needed it again. How could he figure out a sure, fast way to proceed?

The vine came up with a notion.

Smash put the ball of string into his mouth and bit it in half. He now had two balls, each smaller than the first but magically complete. He took the first and rolled it violently forward.

The ball zoomed straight on, unrolling, leaving its straight line of string. Since it had an infinite length, it would proceed to the infinite end of the plain. Infinity could be compassed by infinity; even an ordinary ogre might grasp that! This process would complete the halving of the Stallion's range.

Now Smash set his ear to the floor and listened. Yes—his keen ogre hearing heard a faint hoofbeat in the distance, to the forward right. The Stallion was up there somewhere, moving clear of the rolling string. Now Smash had the creature partially located. He had done something unexpected, forced his opponent to react, and gained a small advantage.

Smash bit the remaining ball in half and shaped the halves into new balls. He hurled one to the east, establishing a pie-section configuration that trapped the Stallion inside. Then he listened again, determining in what quadrant the creature lurked, and pitched another half-ball in a curve. This wound grandly around behind the Stallion's estimated location, cutting off its retreat. For, though Smash had not tromped personally wherever the string went, the string remained his agent and surely counted. He was using a sort of leverage, and the Horse could not cross his demarcation, lest the animal break its own rule of being only in the last place Smash looked.

He put his ear to the floor again. The beat of hooves had ceased. The Stallion had either gotten away or stopped running. Since the former meant a loss for Smash, he did the expedient thing and decided on the latter. He had at last confined his target!

Smash stomped into the string-defined quadrant. If the Stallion were here, as he had to be, he would soon be found.

In due course Smash spied a blotch on the horizon. He stomped closer, alert for some ruse. The blotch grew as he approached it, in the manner that distant objects did, since they did not like to appear small from up close. It took the form of an animal, perhaps a lion. A lion? Smash didn't want that! He refused to have a mundane monster foisted off on him in lieu of his object. "If it's a lion, it's a Stallion!" he muttered—and of course as he said it, it was true. A single, timely word could make a big difference.

It was a huge, standing, wingless horse, midnight black of hide, with eyes that glinted black, too. This was surely the Night Stallion—the creature he had come to settle with, the ruler of the nightmare world.

Smash stomped to a halt before the creature. He stood taller than it, but the animal was more massive. "I am Smash the Ogre," he said. "Who are you?" For it was best to be quite certain, in a case like this.

The creature merely stood there. Now Smash saw that there was a plaque set up at its forefeet, and the plaque said: TROJAN.

"Well, Trojan Horse," Smash said, "I have come to redeem the lien on my soul."

He had expected the animal to charge and attack, but it did not move or respond. It might as well have been a statue.

"How do I do this?" Smash demanded.

Still no response. Evidently the creature was sulking, angry because he had caught it.

Smash peered more closely at the Stallion. It certainly seemed frozen! He tromped forward and put out a ham-hand to touch it.

The body was metal-cold and hard. It was indeed a statue.

Had he, after all, located the wrong thing? That would mean he had been deceived by a decoy and would have to do his search all over again. Smash didn't like this notion, so he rejected it.

He looked at the floor. Behind the statue were hoofprints. The thing might be frozen now, but it had not always been. Probably its present stasis was merely another device to interfere with Smash's quest. This was one devious beast!

Well, there was one way to take care of that. He stood before the Stallion and hoisted a hamfist. "Deal with me, animal, or I will break you into junk."

The midnight orbs seemed to glitter ominously. Trojan did not like being threatened!

Smash found himself alone, on a lofty, windy, rainswept pinnacle.

He looked around. The top ledge was just about big enough for him to stretch out on, but almost featureless. The flat, slick rock terminated abruptly at the edge, plunging straight down to a smashing ocean far below. There were no plants, no food, no structures of any kind—just the tug of the wind and the roar of the ocean beneath.

The Night Stallion had done this, of course. It had spelled him to this desolate confinement, getting rid of him. So much for fair combat.

The storm swirled closer. Storms really liked to get a person stranded in a situation like this! A bolt of lightning crackled down, striking the pinnacle. A section of rock peeled off in a shower of sparks and collapsed, falling with seeming slowness to the distant water.

Smash stood at the steaming brink and watched the tiny splash. The rock had been a fair chunk, massive, yet from this vantage it looked like a pebble.

This was a really nice vacation spot for an ogre. But he didn't want a vacation; he wanted to fight Trojan. How could he get back into the action?

Now his perch was too small to stretch out on. About a quarter of it had fallen. The wind intensified, taking hold of his fur, trying to move him off. He wanted to travel, but not precisely this way! What kind of a splash would he make?

Rain splatted in passing sheets, making the surface doubly slick. The water coursed around his feet, digging under his calloused toes, trying to pry him from the rock so that he would be carried with it as it flowed over the brink in a troubled waterfall. Such a drop did not hurt water, but his own flesh might be less fortunate.

A huge wave surged forward, below, taking dead aim at the base of the rock column. The wave smashed in—and the entire column trembled. More layers of stone peeled and fell. For a moment Smash thought the whole thing was coming down, but about half of it withstood the violence and held its form. However, it was obvious that this perch would not endure much longer.

Smash considered. If he stood here, the column would soon collapse, dropping him into the ravenous ocean. He was an ogre, true, but he lacked his full strength; he would probably be crushed between the tumbling rocks in the water. If he tried to climb down, much of the same thing would happen; the column would collapse before he got below. Ogres were tough, but the forces of nature operating here were overwhelming; he had no realistic chance.

He saw that the ocean waves developed only as they got close to the tower. His Eye Queue concluded that this meant the water was much deeper away from this structure, because deep water didn't like to rouse itself from its stillness. That meant that region was safe to plunge into.

Good enough. He hated to leave this pleasant spire, but discretion urged the move. He leaped off the brink, sailing out in a clumsy swan dive toward the deep water.

Then he remembered he couldn't swim very well. In a calm lake he was all right; in a raging torrent he tended to drown.

He eyed the looming ocean, surging deep and dark. It was no mere torrent; it was an elemental monster. He had no chance at all. Too bad.

He faced the horse-statue. There was no tower, no ocean. It had all been a magic vision. A test, perhaps, or a warning. Obviously he had wiped out. He felt weak; he must have lost a chunk of his soul.

But now he knew how it worked. The Night Stallion did not fight physically; the creature simply threw turbulent visions at him, the way Tandy threw tantrums and curse-fiends threw curses. The ocean tower had been sort of fun. So were those tantrums, he realized; when Tandy hit him with one of them . . . But that was nothing to speculate on right now.

"Try it again, horseface!" he grunted. "I still want my soul back."

The Stallion's dark eyes flashed malignantly.

And Smash stood in the center of a den of Mundane lions—real lions this time, not stal-lion or ant-lions. He felt abruptly weaker; this must be a Mundane scene, beyond the region of magic, so that his magic strength was gone.

The lions snarled like mammalian dragons, lashed their tufted yellow tails, and stalked him. There were six of them: a male, four females, and a cub. The females seemed to be the most aggressive. They began sniffing him, trying to determine how dangerous he might be and how edible.

Ordinarily, Smash would have liked nothing better than to mix with a new crowd of monsters in sublime mayhem. Ogres lived for the joy of bloody battle. But two things militated against his natural inclination—his Eye Queue and his weakness. According to the pusillanimous counsel of the first, it was best to avoid combat when the outcome was uncertain; and according to the second, the outcome was highly uncertain. He would do better, his cowardly intelligence informed him, to flee immediately.

But two things were wrong with that course. There was no place to flee to, because he was in a walled arena with wire mesh over the top, so he could not escape, and the lions had him surrounded anyway. He would have to fight, unless he could bluff them.

He tried the bluff. He raised his hamfists, though they were unprotected by his centaur gauntlets, and bellowed defiance. This was a stance that would frighten almost any creature of Xanth.

But the lions were not creatures of Xanth. They were from Missouri, Mundania. They had to be shown. They pounced.

Ordinarily, Smash would have been able to mince the mere six monsters with so many blows of fists, feet, and head. But with his strength reduced to Mundane normal, all he could handle was one. While he was pulping that one, the other five were chomping him.

In a moment they had bitten through the hamstring tendons of his arms and legs, making his hamhands and hamfeet useless. They chomped through the nerve channel of his neck, making his head slightly less functional than before. He was now mostly helpless. He could feel, but could not move.

Then they gnawed at him, taking their time, one female on each extremity, the male clawing out his belly for the tasty guts. The pulped cub roused itself enough to commence work on Smash's nose, biting off small bites so as not to choke on its meal. It hurt horribly as the monsters chewed off his hands and feet and delved for his kidneys, and it wasn't much fun when the cub scooped out an eyeball, but Smash didn't scream. Noise seemed pointless at this point. Anyway, it was hard to scream properly when his tongue was gone and his lungs were being chewed out. He knew that when the beasts got to his vital organs, sensation would end, so he waited.

But the lions were sated before then, for Smash was a lot of creature. They left him, delimbed and eviscerated, and piled themselves up for a family snooze. Now the flies appeared, settling in swarms, and every bite was a new agony. The sun shone down through the mesh, cooking him, blazing into his other eye, which paralysis prevented him from closing. Soon he was agonizingly blind. But he still felt the flies crawling up his nose, looking for new places to bite and lay their maggots. It was going, he knew, to be an exceedingly long haul.

How had he gotten himself into this fix? By challenging the Night Stallion to recover his soul and to obtain help to rescue Tandy and Chem from the Void. Was it worth it? No, because he had not succeeded. Would he try it again? Yes, because he still wanted to help his friends, no matter how much pain came.

He was back before Trojan, whole of limb and gut and eye. It had been another test case, and obviously he had lost that one, too. He should have found some way to destroy the lions, instead of letting them destroy him. But it seemed he still had most of his soul, and perhaps the third trial would enable him to win the rest of it back.

"I'm still game, master of nightmares," he informed the somber statue.

Again the eyes flashed cruelly. This creature of night had no sympathy and no mercy!

Smash was standing at the base of a mountain of rocks. "Help!" someone cried. It sounded like Tandy.

How had she gotten here? Had she disobeyed his instruction and entered the gourd, following his string to locate him? Foolish girl! Smash looked about, but found no one.

"Help!" she cried again. "I'm under the mountain!"

Smash was horrified. He had to get her out! There was no passage, so he started lifting and hurling away the boulders. He had most of his strength now, despite his prior losses, so this was easy enough.

But there were many boulders, and somehow Tandy's voice always came from under the highest remaining pile. Smash was making progress leveling the mountain, but still had far to go. He was tiring.

Gradually the pile of rocks behind him loomed higher than the pile before, but the cries continued to come from beneath. How had she gotten herself in so deep? He no longer had the strength to hurl the boulders away, but had to carry them with great effort. Then he could no longer lift them, and had to roll them.

At last the mountain had been moved, and the ground was level. But now the voice came from deep below. This was, in fact, a pit the size of an inverted mountain, filled with more boulders—and Tandy was at the bottom.

His body was numb with fatigue. It was a labor just to move himself now. In this respect his agony was worse than it had been in the lions' den, for there all he had to do was lie still and wait. Now he had to cudgel his reluctant muscles to perform, inflicting the torture of exertion on himself. But he kept going, for the job remained to be done. He shoved and heaved and slowly rolled the boulders out.

The deeper he got, the worse the chore became, for now he had to shove the boulders up out of the deepening pit. Still her voice cried despairingly from below. Smash staggered. A boulder slipped from his falling grasp and rolled down to the lowest point. He lumbered after it, hearing her faint sobs. She seemed to be fading as fast as he was!

But his strength had been exhausted. He could no longer move the boulder far enough, strain as he might. Still trying, he collapsed, and the big stone rolled over him.

Again he faced the Night Stallion, his strength miraculously restored. He realized that Tandy had never been there in the vision, only her voice, used to goad him into an impossible effort.

"I'm still going to save my soul and my friends," Smash said, though he dreaded whatever the Dark Horse would throw at him next. Tandy might not have been literally below that mountain of rocks, but his success in these endeavors had a direct bearing on her fate, so it was the same thing. "Trojan, do your worst."

The evil eyes flashed horrendously, darkening the entire area.

Smash was in a compound with assorted other creatures. It was a miserable place, stinking of poverty, doom, and despair. Jets of bright fire shot from cracks in the ground, preventing escape. Harpies and other carrion birds wheeled above, watching for food.

"Slop time!" a guard called, and dumped a pail of garbage into the compound. A gnome, an elf, and a wyvern pounced on the foul refuse. But before they got more than a few stinking scraps, the harpies swooped down in a squadron and snatched it all away, leaving only a pile of defecation in its place. The prisoners squabbled among themselves in angry frustration. Smash saw that all were emaciated; they had not been getting enough food. Small wonder, with those harpies hovering!

What was to be his torture this time? For Smash realized now that these scenes were supposed to be extremely unpleasant, even for an ogre; each was awful in a different way. As he considered, the sun moved rapidly across the pale sky, as if time were accelerating, for normally nothing could prevail on the sun to hurry its pace one bit. Smash's hunger accelerated, too; it took a lot of food to maintain a healthy ogre.

"Slops!" the guard called, and dumped the pail. There was another scramble, but the wyvern wasn't in it. That noble little dragon was now too far gone to scramble. In any event, the harpies got most of the slop again. Smash felt a pang; even garbage looked good now, and he had gotten none. Of course he wouldn't touch anything a harpy had been near, anyway; they spoiled ten times as much as they ate, coating their discards with poisonous refuse. Harpies were the world's dirtiest birds; in fact, real birds refused to associate with these witch-headed monsters.

The wyvern belched out a feeble wisp of fire and collapsed. Smash crossed over to it, moved by un-ogrish compassion. "Anything I can do for you?" he asked. After all, it took one monster to understand another. But the wyvern merely expired.

Immediately the other prisoners converged, working up what slaver they could; dragon meat was a lot better than starvation. Affronted by the notion of such a fine fighting animal being consumed so indelicately, Smash hefted a fist, ready to defend the body. But the vultures descended in a swarm, gouging the corpse to pieces from every side so swiftly that Smash could do nothing; in moments, nothing but bones was left. His efforts, perhaps pointless from the beginning, had been wasted. Smash returned to his place.

The sun plopped behind a distant mountain, throwing up a small shower of debris that colored the clouds briefly in that vicinity. It really ought, he thought, to be more careful where it landed! The stars blinked on, some more alertly than others. The nocturnal heavens spun by, making short work of the night.

By morning Smash was ravenous. So were his surviving companions. They eyed one another covertly, judging when one or the other might be unable to defend himself from consumption. When the guard came with the slops, the gnome stumbled forward. "Food! Food!" he croaked.

The guard paused, eying the gnome cynically. "Are you ready to pay?"

"I'll pay! I'll pay!" the gnome agreed with uncomfortably guilty eagerness.

The guard reached through the bars of fire and into the gnome's body. He hauled out the gnome's struggling soul, an emaciated and bedraggled thing that slowly coalesced into a pallid sphere. The guard inspected it briefly to make certain it was all there, then crammed it indifferently into a dirty bag. Then he set the pail of slop down and waved the hovering harpies away. They screamed epithets of protest, but obeyed. One, however, so far lost control of herself as to loop down close to the tantalizing garbage. The guard's eyes glinted darkly, and the harpy screeched in sudden terror and pumped back into the dingy sky, dropping several greasy feathers in her haste. Smash wondered what it was that had so cowed her, for harpies had little respect for anything and the guard was an ordinary human being, or reasonable facsimile thereof.

The gnome plunged his head into the bucket and greedily slurped the glop. He guzzled spoiled milk, gulped apple and onion peels, and crunched on eggshells and coffee grounds in a paroxysm of satiation. He had his food now; he had paid for it.

The guard turned to gaze at Smash. There was a malignant glitter in the man's eye. Smash realized that he was, in fact, an aspect of the Night Stallion, on his rounds collecting more souls.

Now Smash understood the nature of this trial. He resolved not to purchase his sustenance at that price. If he lost his soul here, he lost it everywhere, and would not be able to help Chem and Tandy escape. But he knew that this would be the most difficult contest yet; each time the Stallion came, Smash would be hungrier, and the pail of slops would lure him more strongly. How could he be sure he would hold out when starvation melted his muscles and deprived him of willpower? This was not a single effort to be made and settled one way or the other; this was a dragging-out siege against his hunger—and the hunger of an ogre was more terrible than his strength.

The sun shoved rapidly across the welkin, looking somewhat undernourished and irritated itself. It kicked innocent clouds out of the way, burning one, so that the cloud lost continence and watered on the ground below. It was an evil day, and Smash's hunger intensified. He had to escape before he succumbed.

He got up, dusted off his bedraggled and filthy hide, and approached the burning barrier. These jets were unlike those of the firewall in Xanth or the jets of the Region of Fire, for they were thicker and hotter than the first and steadier than the second. But perhaps he could cross them. Certainly he had to try.

He held his breath, closed his eyes and charged across the barrier of flames. After all, he had done this in the real world; he could survive a little additional scorching.

He felt the sudden, searing heat. His fur curled and frizzled. This was worse than he had anticipated; his hunger-weakened body was more sensitive to pain, not less. Then the fire passed. He screeched to a halt on singed toes and opened his clenched eyelids.

He was in the prison chamber, the bars of flame behind him. He had blackened stripes along his fur, and his skin smarted—but it seemed he had gotten turned about. What a mistake!

He turned, gulped more air, screwed his orbs shut again, and leaped through the burning bars. Again the pain flared awfully. This time he knew he hadn't turned; he had been in midair as he crossed the flame.

But as he unscrewed his vision, blinking away the smoke from his own eyelashes, he found himself still in the cell. Apparently it was not all that easy to escape. He had to go by the rules of the scene.

Nevertheless, he readied himself for a third try, because an ogre never knew when to quit. But as he oriented on the bars, he saw the guard standing just beyond them, with a glittering gaze. Suddenly he did know when to quit; he turned about and went back to his original spot in the compound and squatted there like a good prisoner. He didn't want to go near the Dark Horse until this struggle was over.

The sun plunged. Another poor creature yielded his vital soul to the Stallion in payment for food. Two more perished of starvation. Smash's firewounds festered, and his fur fell out in stripes. His belly swelled as his limbs shriveled. He became too weak to stand; he sat cross-legged, head hanging forward, contemplating the tendons that showed in high relief on his thighs where the hair had fallen out. He did not ask for food, though he was now being consumed by his own hunger. He knew the price.

Slowly, while the days and nights raced across the sky, he starved. He realized, as he sank into the final stupor, that when he died, the Stallion would have his soul anyway. Somehow he had misplaced this one, too.

Once more he stood before the Stallion statue. Still he had some of his soul, and would not yield. Apparently there was a limit to how much of a soul could be taken as penalty for each loss, and ogres were ornery creatures. "I'll fight for my soul as long as any of it remains to fight for," Smash declared. "Bring on your next horror, equine."

The eyes glinted. Then the Night Stallion moved, coming alive. "You have fought well, ogre," it said, speaking without difficulty through its horse's mouth. "You have won every challenge."

This was completely unexpected. "But I died each time!"

"Without ever deviating from your purpose. You were subjected to the challenge of fear, but you evinced no fear—"

"Well, ogres don't know what that is," Smash said.

"And to the challenge of pain, but you did not capitulate—"

"Ogres don't know how," Smash admitted.

"And to the challenge of fatigue—"

"How could I stop when I thought my friend was caught?"

"And to the challenge of hunger."

"That was a bad one," Smash acknowledged. "But the price was too high." His Eye Queue curse had made him aware of the significance of the price; otherwise he almost certainly would have succumbed.

"And so you blundered through, allowing nothing to sway you, and thus vacated the lien on four-fifths of your soul. Only one more test remains—but on this one depends all that you have gained so far. You will win your whole soul here—or lose it."

"Send me to that test," Smash said resolutely.

The Stallion's eyes flickered intensely, but the scene did not change. "Why did you accept the lien on your soul?" the creature asked.

Smash's Eye Queue warned him that the eye-flicker meant he had been projected to another vision and was being tested. Since the scene had not changed, this must be a different sort of test from the others. Beware!

"To save the soul of my friend, whom I had promised to protect," Smash said carefully. "I thought you knew that. It was your minion of the coffin who cheated her out of it."

"What kind of fool would place the welfare of another before his own?" the Horse demanded, ignoring Smash's remark.

Smash shrugged, embarrassed. "I never claimed to be other than a fool. Ogres are very strong and very stupid."

The Stallion snorted. "If you expect me to believe your implication, you think *I'm* a fool! I know most ogres are stupid, but you are not. Why is that?"

Unfortunately, ogres were not much given to lying; it was part of their stupidity. Smash had been directly asked; he would have to answer. "I am cursed with the Eye Queue. The vine makes me much smarter than I should be and imbues me with aspects of conscience, aesthetic awareness, and human sensitivity. I would rid myself of it it I could, but I need the intelligence in order to help my friends."

"Fool!" the Stallion roared. "The Eye Queue curse is an illusion!"

"Everything in the gourd and in the Void is illusion of one sort or another," Smash countered. "Much of Xanth is illusion, and perhaps Mundania, too. It might be that if we could only see the ultimate reality, Xanth itself would not exist. But while I exist in it, or think I do, I will honor the rules of illusion as I do those of reality, and draw on the powers my illusory Eye Queue provides as I do on those my real ogre strength provides."

The Stallion paused. "That was not precisely what I meant, but perhaps it is a sufficient answer. Obviously your own intelligence is no illusion. But were you not aware that the effect of the Eye Queue vine is temporary? That it wears off in a few hours at most, and in many cases provides, not true intelligence, but a vain illusion of it that causes the recipient to make a genuine fool of himself, the laughingstock of all who perceive his self-delusion?"

Smash realized that the creature was indeed testing him another way—and an intellectual test was most treacherous for an ogre. "I was not aware of that," he admitted. "Perhaps my companions were too kind to think of me in that way. But I believe my intelligence is real, for it has helped me solve many problems no ordinary ogre could handle, and has broadened my horizons immeasurably. If this be illusion, it is tolerable. Certainly it lasted me many days without fading. Perhaps it works better on ogres, who can hardly be rendered more foolish than they naturally are."

"You are quite correct. You are no ordinary ogre and you are smart enough to give me a considerable challenge. Most creatures who place their souls in peril do so for far less charitable reasons. But, of course, you are only half-ogre."

Naturally the Lord of Nightmares knew all about him! Smash refused to lose his temper, for that surely was what the Stallion wanted. Lose temper, lose soul! "I am what I am. An ogre."

The Stallion nodded as if discovering a weakness in Smash's armor. He was up to something; Smash could tell by the way he swished his tail in the absence of flies. "An ogre with the wit and conscience of a man. One who makes the Eye Queue vine work beyond its capacities, and makes it work again even when the vine itself is illusory. One who maintains a loyalty to his responsibilities and associates that others would fain define as entirely human."

"I also made the gourd work in the Void, when it was illusory," Smash pointed out. "If you seek to undermine my enhanced intelligence by pointing out that it has no basis, you must also concede that your testing of me has no basis."

"That was not precisely my thrust. Similar situations may have differing interpretations." He snorted, clearing his long throat. "You have mastered the four challenges without fault and are now entitled to assume the role of Master of Challenges. I shall retire from the office; you shall be the Night Ogre."

"The Night Ogre?" Smash, despite the Eye Queue, was having trouble grasping this.

"You will send the bad images out with your night ogresses and collect the souls of those who yield them. You will be Master of the Gourd. The powers of the night will be yours."

"I don't want the powers of the night!" Smash protested. "I just want to rescue my friends."

"With the powers of the night, you can save them," the Stallion pointed out. "You will be able to direct your night creatures to bear them sleeping from the Void to the safety of the ordinary Xanth jungle."

But Smash's Eye Queue, illusory though it might be, interfered with this promising solution. "Would I get to return to the world of the day myself?"

"The Master of Night has no need to visit the day!"

"So you are prisoner of the night yourself," Smash said.

"You may capture the souls of others, but your own is hostage."

"I can go to the day!" the Stallion protested.

Again the Eye Queue looked the horse's gift in the mouth. It was full of dragon's teeth. "Only if you collect enough souls to pay your way. How many does it take for an hour of day? A dozen? A hundred?"

"There is another way," the Stallion said uncomfortably.

"Surely so. If you arrange a replacement for yourself," Smash said. "Someone steadfast enough to do the job according to the rules, no matter how unpleasant or painful or tedious it becomes. Someone whom power does not corrupt."

The Dark Horse was silent.

"Why is it necessary to send bad dreams to people?" Smash asked. "Is this only a means to jog them from their souls?"

"It has a loftier rationale than that," the Stallion replied somewhat stiffly. "If no one ever suffered the pangs of conscience or regret, evil would prosper without hindrance and eventually take over the world. Evil can be the sweet sugar of the soul, temptingly pleasant in small doses, but inevitably corrupting. The bad dreams are the realizations of the consequence of evil, a timely warning that all thinking creatures require. The nightmares guard constantly against spiritual degradation—that same corruption you have withstood. Take the position, ogre; you have earned it."

"I wish I could help you," Smash said. "But my life is outside the gourd, in the jungles of Xanth. I am a simple forest creature. I must help my friends survive the wilderness in my own fashion, and not aspire to be more than any ogre was ever destined to be."

The Stallion's eyes dimmed. "You have navigated the final challenge. You have avoided the ultimate temptation of power. You are free to return to Xanth with your soul intact. The lien is voided."

Suddenly Smash felt completely strong again, his soul restored. "But I need help," he said. "I must borrow three of your nightmares to carry my party out of the Void."

"Nightmares are not beasts of burden!" the Stallion protested, scraping the ground with a forehoof. It seemed this creature, if not actually piqued by Smash's refusal to take over the proffered office, was still less cooperative than he might have been. When one scorned an offer of any nature, one had to bear the penalty.

"The nightmares alone can travel anywhere, even out of the Void," Smash said, knowing he had to find some way to gain the assistance he needed. "Only they can help us."

"They could if they chose to," the Horse agreed. "But their fee is half a soul for each person carried."

"Half my soul!" Smash exclaimed. "I don't have enough for three!"

"Half *a* soul, not necessarily your own. But it is true you do not have enough. Nightmare rides come steep."

Smash realized that he was right back in the dilemma he thought he had escaped. He had placed his soul in jeopardy to rescue Tandy from the gourd; now he would have to do it again to rescue Tandy and Chem from the Void. But if he rescued both, he himself would be lost, for the Eye Queue informed him that two halves of a soul amounted to the whole soul.

Of course, he could rescue only Tandy, the one he had agreed to protect. But he could not see his way clear to leave Chem in the Void. She was a nice creature with a worthy mission. She did not deserve to be deserted. And he had more or less agreed to protect her, too, when her brother Chet had delivered her to him at the brink of the Gap Chasm. "I will pay the price," he said, thinking of the gnome begging for slops.

"Do you realize that you could rescue them and retain your soul by becoming the Master of Night?" the Stallion asked.

"I fear I must go to hell in my own fashion," Smash said regretfully. The Horse obviously thought him a smart fool, and his Eye Queue heartily endorsed the sentiment, but somehow his fundamental ogre nature shied away from the responsibility for damning others. Better to be one of the damned.

"Even in sacrifice, you are ogrishly stupid," the Stallion remarked with disgust. "You are obviously unfit for duty here."

"Agreed," Smash agreed.

"Go negotiate directly with the mares," the Horse

snorted. "I'll have no part of this." His eyes flared with their black light.

Then Smash found himself on the plain of the mares. The dark herd charged toward him, circling him in moments, as was their wont. Then they recognized him and hesitated.

"I need two of you to carry my friends to safety," he said. "I know the price."

"Naaaay!" one cried. Smash recognized her as the one he had tried to befriend, the one who had carried Tandy to the Good Magician's castle. That had been involuntary, without a fee—until the coffin had claimed a double fee retroactively. Obviously none of that payment had gone to the mare; it had been a gyp deal all around. But she certainly knew how to carry a person. He was sorry he had not been able to figure out what she wanted from Xanth.

"I must rescue Tandy and Chem," Smash said. "I will pay the fee. Who will make the deal?"

Two other mares volunteered. Smash wasn't sure what use they would have for the halves of his soul, but that was not much of his business. Maybe half souls were bartering currency within the gourd, accounting for status in the nightmare hierarchy. "S.O.D.," he said, cautioned by his Eye Queue. "Soul on Delivery."

They nodded, agreeing. "Can you find them?" he asked. When they nodded naaay, he realized he would have to go with them, at least to where the girls were. "Well, we'd better introduce ourselves," he said. "I am Smash the Ogre. How shall I know the two of you?"

One of the two struck the ground with a forehoof. She left a circular impression in the dirt, with little ridges, dark spots, and pockmarks. Smash peered at it closely, struck by a nagging familiarity. Where had he seen a configuration like that before? Then he grasped it; this was like a map of the moon, with the pocks like the cheese holes. One of the dark areas was highlighted, and he saw that there was lettering on it: MARE CRISIUM.

"So you're the mare Crisium," he said, making the connection. "Mind if I call you Crisis?"

She shrugged acquiescently. Smash turned to the other. "And who are you?"

The other stomped a forehoof. Her moon-map was high-lighted in another place: MARE VAPORUM.

"And you're the mare Vaporum," he said. "I'll call you Vapor."

The befriended mare now came forward, nickering, of-fering to carry him. "But I have no soul left over to pay you," he protested. "Besides, you're far too small to handle a monster like me."

She walked under him—and suddenly he found that he had shrunk or she had grown, for now he was riding her comfortably. It seemed nightmares had no firmly fixed size.

"Then tell me your name, too," he said. "You are doing me an unpaid favor, and I want to know you, in case I should ever be able to repay it. I never did discover what you wanted from Xanth, you know."

She stamped her hoof. He leaned down over her shoul-der, hanging on to her slick black mane that flowed like a waterfall, until he was able to read her map. It was high-lighted at a large patch labeled: MARE IMBRIUM.

"You I will call Imbri," he decided. "Because I don't know what your name means."

The three mares galloped across the plain, leaving the herd behind. Little maps of the moon formed the trail wherever their feet touched. It made him hungry to think about it. Too bad the maps weren't real, with genuine cheese!

Soon they passed through a greenish wall and out into the Void. It was the rind of the gourd, Smash realized. They were large and the gourd was small—but somehow it all related. He kept trying to forget that size and mass hardly mattered when magic was involved.

They looped once around—and there was the brute ogre, staring into the gourd's peephole. Until this moment, Smash had not quite realized that his body had not accom-panied him inside. He had known it, of course, but never truly *realized* it. Even his Eye Queue had never come to grips with the seeming paradox of being in two places at the same time.

Then he spied Tandy and Chem. They were asleep; it was night, of course, the only time the nightmares could go abroad.

"We'll have to wake them," Smash said, then paused. "No—a person has to be asleep to ride a nightmare; I remember now. Or disembodied, like me. I'm really asleep, too. I'll put them on you asleep." He dismounted and went to pick Tandy up.

But his hands passed right through her. He had no physical substance.

He pondered. "I'll have to wake myself up," he decided. "Since my soul is forfeit anyway, I should be able to stay near the nightmares. They aren't going to depart before they get their payment." It was a rather painful kind of security, however.

He went to his body. What a hulking, brutish thing it was! The black fur was shaggy in some places, unkempt in others, and singed from his experiences with the firewall in yet others. The hamhands and hamfeet were huge and clumsy-looking. The face was simultaneously gravelly and mushy. No self-respecting creature would be attracted to the physical appearance of an ogre—and, of course, the monster's intellect was even worse. He was doing Tandy a favor by removing himself from her picture.

"Come on, ogre, you have work to do," he grunted, putting out a paw to shake his shoulder. But his hand passed through himself, too, and the body ignored him, exactly like the stupid thing it was.

"Enough of this nonsense, idiot!" he rasped. He put a hamfinger over the peephole. He might be insubstantial in this form, but he was visible. The finger cut off the view. The effect was similar to the removal of the gourd.

Suddenly Smash was back in his body, awake. The phantom self had vanished. It existed only when he peered into the gourd, when his mental self was apart from his physical self.

The three mares stood watching him warily. Ordinarily, they would have fled the presence of a waking person, but they realized that this was a special situation. He was about to become one of them.

"All right," he said quietly, so as not to wake the girls. "I'll set one girl on each of you volunteers. You carry them north, beyond the Void, and set them down safely. Then you split my soul between you. Fair enough?"

The two mares nodded. Smash went to lift Chem, gently.

She weighed as much as he, but he had his full strength now and could readily handle her mass. He set her on Crisis. Chem was bigger than the mare, but again the fit was right, and the sleeping centaur straddled Crisis comfortably.

He lifted Tandy next. She was so small he could have raised her with one finger, as he had Blythe Brassie, but he used both hands. With infinite care he set her on Vapor.

Then he mounted his own mare, Imbri, who had come without the promise of payment. Again the fit was right; anybody could ride any nightmare, if the mare permitted it. "I wish I knew what you want from Xanth," he murmured. Then he remembered that this was irrelevant; he would not be returning to Xanth anyway, so could not fetch her anything.

They moved on through the Void, traveling north. This was the easy part, descending into the depths of the funnel, and Smash saw that the center of the Void was a black hole from which nothing returned, not even light. This the mares skirted; there were, after all, limits.

They galloped as swiftly as thought itself, the mares as dark as the awful dreams they fostered. Smash now had a fair understanding of the origin and rationale of those dreams; he did not envy the Dark Horse his job. If it was bad to experience the dreams, how much worse was it to manufacture them! The Stallion had the burden of the vision of evil for the whole world on his mind; no wonder he wanted to retire! What use was infinite power when it could be used only negatively?

They climbed the far slope of the funnel, leaving the brink of the dread black hole behind, unobstructed by the invisible wall, in whatever manner it existed. In another moment they were out of the Void and into the night of normal Xanth.

Smash felt a horrible weight departing his shoulders. He had saved them; he had gotten them out of the Void at last! How wonderful this normal Xanthian jungle seemed! He looked eagerly at it, knowing he could not stay, that his soul was now forfeit. The mares had delivered, and it was now his turn. Perhaps he would be allowed to visit this region on occasion, in bodiless form, just to renew the awareness of what he had lost, and to see how his friends were doing.

They halted safely beyond the line. Smash dismounted and lifted Chem to the ground, where she continued sleeping, feet curled under her, head lolling. She was a pretty creature of her kind, not as well developed as she would be at full maturity, but with a nice coat and delicate human features. He was glad he had saved her from the Void. Someday she would browbeat some male centaur into happiness, exactly as her mother had done. Centaurs were strong-willed creatures, but well worth knowing. "Farewell, friend," he murmured. "I have seen you safely through the worst of Xanth. I hope you are satisfied with your map."

Then he lifted Tandy. She was so small and delicate-seeming in her sleep! Her brown hair fell about her face in disarray, partly framing and partly concealing her features. He deeply regretted his inability to see her through her adventure. But he had made a commitment to the Good Magician Humfrey, and he was honoring that commitment in the only fashion he knew. He had seen Tandy through danger, and trusted she could do all right now on her own. She had fitted a lot of practical experience into this journey!

In a moment, he knew, he would not care about her at all, for caring was impossible without a soul. But in this instant he did care. He remembered how she had kissed him, and he liked the memory. Human ways were not ogre ways, of course, but perhaps they had a certain merit. Through her he had gleaned some faint inkling of an alternate way of life, where violence was secondary to feeling. It was no life for an ogre, of course—but somehow he could not resist returning the favor of that kiss now. He brought her to his face and touched her precious little lips with his own big crude ones.

Tandy woke instantly. The two mares jumped away, afraid of being seen by a waking person not of their domain. But they did not flee entirely, held by the incipient promise of his soul.

"Oh, Smash!" Tandy cried. "You're back! I was so worried, you stayed in the gourd so long, and Chem said she thought you weren't ready to be roused yet—"

Now he was in trouble. Yet he was obscurely glad. It was better to explain things to her so that she would not think he had deserted her. "You are free of the Void, Tandy. But I must leave you."

"Oh, no, Smash!" she protested. "Don't ever leave me!"

This was becoming rapidly more difficult. Separating from her was somewhat like departing the Void—subtly awkward. "The mares who carried you out of the Void, in your sleep—they have to be paid."

Her brow furrowed, in the cute way it had. "Paid how?"

He was afraid she wouldn't like this. But ogres weren't much for prevarication, even in a good cause. "My soul."

She screamed.

Chem bolted awake, snatching up the rope, and the mares retreated farther, switching their tails nervously. "What's the matter?"

"Smash sold his soul to free us!" Tandy cried, pointing an accusing finger at the ogre.

"He can't do that!" the centaur protested. "He went to the gourd to win back his soul!"

"It was the only way," Smash said. He gestured to the two mares. "I think it is time." He looked behind him, locating Imbri. "And if you will kindly carry my body back into the Void afterward, so it won't get in anyone's way out here—"

The three mares came forward. Tandy screamed again and threw her arms about Smash's neck. "No! No! Take my soul instead!"

The mares paused, uncertain of the proprieties. They meant no harm; they were only doing their job.

Tandy disengaged herself and dropped to the ground. Her dander was up. "My soul's almost as good as his, isn't it?" she said to the mares. "Take it and let him go." She advanced on Crisis. "I can't let him be taken. I love him!"

She surely did, for this was the most extreme sacrifice she could make. She was deathly afraid of the interior of the gourd. Smash understood this perfectly; that was why he couldn't let her go there. But if she refused to let him go in peace, what was he to do?

Chem interceded. "Just exactly what was the deal you made, Smash?"

"Half my soul for each person carried from the Void."

"But three were carried, weren't they?" the centaur

asked, her fine human mind percolating as the fog of sleep dissipated. "That would mean one and a half souls."

"I am returning with the mares," Smash said. "I don't count. Imbri carried me as a favor; she's the one who carried Tandy to the Good Magician's castle a year ago. She's a good creature."

"I know she is!" Tandy agreed. "But—"

"Imbri?" Chem asked. "Is that an equine name?"

"Mare Imbrium," he clarified. "The nightmares come out only at night, so they never see the sun. They identify with places on the moon."

"Mare Imbrium," she repeated. "The Sea of Rains. Surely the raining of our tears."

So that was what the name meant; the education of the centaur had clarified it. Certainly it was appropriate! Imbri was reigning over, or reining in, the rain of tears. But it could be said in her favor that she had not done anything to cause those tears. She had charged no soul.

"Not *my* tears!" Tandy protested tearfully. "Smash, I won't let you go!"

"I have to go," Smash said gently. "Ogres aren't very pretty and they aren't very smart, but they do do what they agree to do. I agreed to see the two of you safely through the hazards of Xanth, and I agreed to parcel my soul between the two mares who delivered you from the Void."

"You have no right to sacrifice yourself again for us!" Chem cried. "Anyway, it won't work; we'll perish alone in the wilderness of northern Xanth."

"Well, it seemed better to get you to Xanth instead of the Void," Smash said awkwardly. Somehow the right he thought he was doing seemed less right, now. "Near the edge of Xanth the magic begins to fade, so it's less dangerous."

"Ha!" Tandy exclaimed. "I've heard the Mundane monsters are worse than the Xanth ones!"

"It may be less dangerous only if you accompany us," Chem said. She considered briefly. "But a deal's a deal; the mares must be paid."

"I'll pay them!" Tandy offered.

"No!" Smash cried. "The gourd is not for the like of you! It is better for the like of me."

"I don't think so," Chem said. "We have all had enough

of the gourd, regardless of whether we've been inside it. But there are three of us. We can pay the mares and retain half a soul each. Three fares, so Smash can be free, too."

"But neither of you has to give any part of her soul for me!" Smash objected.

"You were doing it for us," the centaur said. "We can get along on half souls if we're careful. I understand they regenerate in time."

"Yes," Tandy said, grasping this notion as if being saved from drowning. "Each person can pay her own way." She turned to the nearest mare, who happened to be Crisis. "Take half my soul," she said.

Chem faced the second, Imbri. "Take half of mine."

The mare of Rains hesitated, for she had not expected to be rewarded, and she had not carried Chem.

"Take it!" the centaur insisted.

The mares, glad to have the matter resolved, galloped past their respective donors. Smash saw two souls attenuate between girls and mares; then each one tore in half, and the mares were gone.

Smash was left standing by the third mare, Vapor. He realized that he could not do less—and of course Vapor was supposed to have a half soul. In fact, she had been promised half of his. Now she would get it, though she had not carried him. "Take half of mine," he said.

Vapor charged him. There was a wrenching and tearing; then he stood reeling. Something awfully precious had been taken from him—but not all of it.

Then he saw the two girls standing similarly bemused, and he knew that something even more precious had been salvaged.

Chapter 14. Ogre Fun

In the morning they woke, having suffered no bad dreams. The nightmares were not about to venture near them now, for that might give them the opportunity to change their minds about their souls. Also, what dreams could they be served, worse than what they had already experienced?

Xanth was lovely. The green trees glistened in the fading dew, and flowers opened. White clouds formed lazy patterns around the sun, daring it to burn them off, but it ignored their taunts. The air was fragrant. Mainly, it was a joy to be alive and free. Much more joy than it had been before Smash discovered that such things were by no means guaranteed. He had died in a great dark ocean, under the teeth of lions, under a rock he was too fatigued to move, and of starvation in prison. He had won back his soul, then given it up again. Now he was here with half his soul and he really appreciated what he had.

For some time they compared notes, each person needing reassurance because of the lingering ache of separated souls. But gradually they acclimated, finding that half a soul was indeed much better than none.

Smash tested his strength—and found it at half-level. He had to use both hands instead of one to crush a rock to sand. Until the other half of his soul regenerated, he would be only half an ogre in that respect. But this, too, seemed a reasonable price to pay for his freedom.

"I think it is time for me to go my own way," Chem said at last. "I think I have had about as much of this sort of adventure as I can handle. I have it all mapped; my survey is done. Now I need to organize the data and try to make sense of it."

"Magic doesn't have to make sense," Smash said rhetorically.

"But where will you go?" Tandy asked.

The centaur filly generated her map, with all of northern Xanth clearly laid out, their travel route neatly marked in a dotted line. "It is safe for my kind around the fringes of Xanth," she said. "Centaurs have traded all along the coasts. I'll trot west to the isthmus, then south to Castle Roogna. I'll have no trouble at all." Her projected route dotted its way down the length of northern Xanth confidently. She seemed to have forgotten her protestation of last night about how they would perish without Smash's protection, and Smash did not remind her of it. Obviously it had been his welfare, not her own, she had been concerned with.

"I suppose that's best," Tandy said reluctantly. "I really liked the company of all you other creatures, but your missions are not my mission. Just remember, you're not as strong as you should be."

"That's one reason I want to get on home," Chem said. "I'd recommend the same for both of you, but I know your destiny differs from mine. You have to go on to the Ogre-fen-Ogre Fen, Smash, and take what you find there, though I personally feel that's a mistake."

"Me make mistake?" Smash asked. The things of the Void had faded in the night, since they had left it, and now he found it easier to revert to his normal mode of speech. There was no hypnogourd and no Eye Queue vine, so he was not smart any more.

"Smash, you're half human," Chem said. "If you would only give your human side a chance—"

"Me no man, me ogre clan," he said firmly. That faith had brought him through the horrors of the gourd.

She sighed. "So you must be what you must be, and do what you must do. Tandy—" Chem shook her head. "I can't advise you. I hope you get what you want, somehow."

The two girls embraced tearfully. Then the centaur trotted away to the west, her pretty brown tail flying at half-mast as if reflecting the depressed state of her soul.

"I'm as foolish as you are," Tandy said, drying her eyes,

so that the blue emerged again like little patches of sky. "Let's get on to the Fen before night, Smash."

They moved on. Smash, now so near his destination, found himself strangely uneasy. The Good Magician had told him he would find what he needed among the Ancestral Ogres; Humfrey had not said what that would be, or whether Smash would like it.

Suppose he didn't like what he needed? Suppose he hated it? Suppose it meant the denial of all that he had experienced on this journey with the seven girls? The Eye Queue had been a curse, and surely he was well rid of it—yet there had been a certain covert satisfaction in expressing himself as lucidly as any human being could. Facility of expression was power, too, just as was strength of muscle. The gourd had been a horror—yet that, too, had had its fine moments of exhilarating violence and deep revelation. These things were, of course, peripheral, no concern of a true ogre—but he had felt something fundamentally good in them.

He struggled through his annoying stupidity as he tromped on toward the Ogre Fen. Exactly what had made his journey so rewarding, despite its nuisances and problems? Not the violence, for he could have that any time by challenging stray dragons. Not the intelligence, for that was no part of an ogre's heritage. Not the exploration of the central mysteries of Xanth, for ogres were not very curious about geography. What, then?

As the day faded and the sun hurried down to the horizon so as not to be caught by night, Smash finally broke through to a conclusion. It wasn't a very original one, for ogres weren't very original creatures, but it would do. He had valued the camaraderie. The seven girls had needed him, and had treated him like a person. His long association with the human beings and centaurs of Castle Roogna had acclimated him to company, but this time he had had the wit to appreciate it more fully, because of the Eye Queue curse. Now he was cursed with the memory of what could not be again. Camaraderie was not the ogre way.

At dusk they reached the dismal fringe of the Ogre-fen-Ogre Fen. The swampy marsh stretched out to the east and north as far as the eyeball could peer, riddled with green gators and brown possums and other half-fanciful denizens. Were the Ancestral Ogres also here?

"Look!" Tandy cried, pointing.

Smash looked. There were three ironwood trees braided together. That was a sure signal of the presence of ogres, since no other creature could do such a thing.

"I guess you'll get what you want tomorrow," Tandy said. "You'll meet your tribe." She seemed sad.

"Yes, me agree," he said, somehow not as overjoyed as he thought he should be. His mission was about to terminate; that was what he wanted, wasn't it?

He twisted a coppertree into the semblance of a shelter for her and spread a large leaf from a table tree over it. In the heyday of his strength he could have done better, but this would have to do for tonight. But it didn't matter; Tandy didn't use it. She curled up against his furry shoulder and slept.

What was her destiny? he wondered before he crashed into his own heavy slumber. He now understood that she was looking for a human husband and was destined to find one on this journey—but time was running out for her, too. He hoped whoever she found would be a good man who would appreciate her spunky qualities and not be bothered by her tantrum-talent. Smash himself rather liked her tantrums; they were a little like ogre love taps. Perhaps his first inkling of liking for her had been when she threw a tantrum at him. She wasn't really a bad-tempered girl; she just tended to get overly excited under extreme stress. There had been some of that on this journey!

Too bad, he thought again, that she couldn't have been an ogress. But, of course, ogresses didn't have magic tricks like tantrums, or cute little ways of expressing themselves—like kissing.

He shook his head. He was getting un-ogrishly maudlin! What could an ogre know of the refined raptures of human love? Of the caring that went beyond the hungers of the moment? Of the joy and sacrifice of helping the loved one regardless of the cost to oneself? Certainly not himself!

Yet there was something about this foolish, passionate, determined girl-human creature. She was so small she was hardly a good morsel for a meal, yet she was precious beyond the comprehension of his dim ogre wit. She had shown cunning and courage in catching and riding a nightmare to escape her amorous demon, and other excellent qualities had manifested since. He would miss her when she found her proper situation and left him, as had the other girls.

He thought to kiss her again, but the last time he had tried that, she had awakened instantly and things had gotten complicated. He wanted her to complete her sleep in peace this time, so he desisted. He had no business kissing a human girl anyway—or kissing anything, for that matter.

A drop of rain spattered on her forehead. No, not rain, for the night was calm and the nightmare of Rains was nowhere near. It was a tear, similar to the ones she had dropped on him when she had so angrily demonstrated how human beings expressed affection. A tear from his own eye. And this was strange, because no true ogre cried. Perhaps it was her own tear, recycled through his system, returning to her.

Carefully he wiped away the moisture with a hamfinger. He had no right to soil her pretty little brow with such contamination. She deserved much better. Better than an ogre.

The tromp of enormous, clumsy feet woke them in the morning. The ogres were coming!

Hastily Smash and Tandy got up. Smash felt a smidgen stronger; perhaps his soul had grown back a little while he slept. But he was nowhere near full strength yet. Knowing the nature of his kind, he worried some about that.

The Ogres of the Fen arrived. Small creatures scurried for cover, and trees angled their leaves away. No one wanted trouble with ogres! There were eight of them—three brutish males and five females.

Smash gazed at the ogresses in dim wonder. Two were grizzled old crones, one was a stout cub, and two were mature creatures of his own generation. Huge and shaggy, with muddy fur, reeking of sweat, and with faces whose smiles would stun zombies and whose frowns would burn wood, they were the most repulsive brutes imaginable. Smash was entranced.

"Who he?" the biggest of the males demanded. His voice was mainly a growl, unintelligible to ordinary folk; Smash could understand him because he was another ogre. Smash himself was unusual in that he could speak comprehensibly; most ogres could communicate verbally only with other ogres.

Suddenly Smash was fed up with the rhyming convention. What good was it, when no one who counted could understand it anyway? "I am Smash, son of Crunch. I come to seek my satisfaction among the Ancestral Ogres, as it is destined."

"Half-breed!" the other ogre exclaimed. "No need!" For Smash's ability to talk unrhymed betrayed his mixed parentage.

Smash had never liked being called a half-breed, but he could not honestly refute it. "My mother is a curse-fiend," he admitted. "But my father is an ogre, and so am I."

One of the crones spoke up, wise beyond her years. "Curse-fien', human bein'," she croaked.

"Half man!" the big male ogre grunted. "We ban!"

"Might fight," the child ogress said, eyes lighting.

It was true. An ogre could establish his place in a tribe by fighting for it. The male grunted eagerly. "He, me!" He naturally wanted to be the first to chastise the presumptuous half-breed.

"What are they saying?" Tandy asked, alarmed by the increasingly aggressive stances of the Fen Ogres.

It occurred to Smash that she would not approve of a physical fight. "They merely seek some ogre fun," he explained, not telling her that this was apt to be roughly similar to the fun the lions of the den had had with him. "Fun in the Fen."

She was not fooled. "What ogres call fun, I call mayhem! Smash, you can't afford any trouble; you're only at half-strength."

There was that. Fighting was fun, but getting beaten to a pulp was not as much fun as winning. If anything happened to him here, Tandy would be in trouble, for these ogres were not halfway civilized, as Smash himself was. It was galling, but he would have to pass up this opportunity. "No comment," he said.

The ogres goggled incredulously. "Not hot?" the male ogre demanded, his hamfists shuddering with eagerness to pulverize.

Smash turned away. "I think what I want is elsewhere after all," he told Tandy. "Let's get away from here." He tried to keep the urgency suppressed; this could get difficult in a moment. At least he was not caged in, the way he had been with the lions.

The male made a huge jump, landing directly before Smash. He poked a hamfinger at Smash's soiled orange centaur jacket. "What got?" he demanded. This was not curiosity but insult; any creature in clothing was considered effete, too weak to survive in the jungle.

Smash raged inwardly at the implication, but had to avoid trouble. He stepped around the ogre and went on north, toward the Fen.

But again the male leaped in front of him. He pointed at Smash's steel gauntlets, making a crudely elaborate gesture of pulling dainty feminine gloves on his own hairy meat hooks. The humor of ogres was necessarily crude, but it was effective on its level. Smash paused.

"Me swat he snot!" the ogre chortled, aiming a wood-sundering blow at Smash's head. Smash lifted a gleaming fist of his own, defensively.

"No!" Tandy screamed.

Again Smash had to avoid conflict. He ducked under the blow in a gesture that completely surprised the ogre and continued north, inwardly seething. It simply wasn't an ogre's way to accept such taunts and duck away from a fight.

Now one of the mature females barred his way. Her hair was like the tentacular mass of a quarrelsome tangle tree that had just lost a battle with a giant spider web. Her face made the bubbling mud of the Fen seem like a clear mirror. Her limbs were so gnarled she might readily pass for a dead shagtree riddled by the droppings of a flock of harpies with indigestion. Smash had never before encountered such a luscious mass of flesh.

"He cute, cheroot," she said.

That was a considerable come-on for an ogress. Since there were more females than males in this tribe, there was obviously a place for Smash here, if he wanted it. Good Magician Humfrey had evidently known this, and known that Smash needed to settle down with a good female of his own kind. What the aging Magician had overlooked was

the fact that Smash would arrive at half-strength, and that
Tandy would not yet have found her own situation. Thus
Smash could not afford to accept the offer, however
grossly tempting it might be, because he could not fight
well and could not afford to leave Tandy to the ogres' mer-
cies. For a female went only to the winner of a fight between males. So once again he avoided interaction and continued on north.

Then the male ogre had an inspiration of genius for his
kind. "Me eat complete," he said, and grabbed for Tandy.

Smash's gauntleted fist shot forward and up, catching
the ogre smack in the snoot. The gauntlet made Smash's
fist harder than otherwise and increased the effect of its
impact. The creature rocked back, spitting out a yellow
tooth. "Delight!" he cried. "He fight!"

"No!" Tandy yelled again, despairingly. She knew as
well as Smash did that it was too late. Smash had struck
the ogre, and that committed him.

Quickly the other ogres circled him. Tandy scooted to a
beerbarrel tree, getting out of the way.

Smash had never before fought another ogre and wasn't
quite sure how to proceed. Were there conventions? Did
they take turns striking each other? Was anything barred?

The ogre gave him no chance to consider. He charged,
his right fist swinging in a windmill motion, back and up
and forward and down, aimed for Smash's head. Smash
wished he had the Eye Queue so that he could analyze the
meaning of this approach. But dull as he was now, he simply had to assume that it meant anything went.

Smash dodged, ducked down, caught the ogre's feet, and
jerked them up to head height. Naturally the ogre flipped
back, his head smacking into the ground with a hollow
boom like thunder, denting a hole and shaking the bushes
in the neighborhood. The watching ogres nodded; it was a
good enough counter, starting things off. But Smash knew
that he had substituted guile for force, to a certain extent,
finding a maneuver that did not require his full strength;
he could not proceed indefinitely this way.

The ogre bounced off his head, somersaulted backward,
and twisted to his big, flat feet. He roared a roar that
spooked a flock of buzzards from a buzzard bush and sent
low clouds scudding hastily away. He charged forward

again, grabbing for Smash with both heavy arms. But Smash knew better than to wait for an ogre hug. His orange jacket would protect him from most of its crushing force, but he would not be able to initiate much himself. He jumped high, stomping gently on the ogre's ugly head in passing.

The stomp drove the ogre a small distance into the ground. It was the first motion of the figure called the Nail. The ogre had to extricate his feet one by one, leaving deep prints. Now he was really angry. He turned, fists swinging.

Smash parried with one arm, using a technique he had picked up at Castle Roogna, then sent his gauntleted fist smashing into the ogre's gross mid-gut. It was like hitting well-seasoned ironwood, in both places; his parrying arm was bruised, and his striking fist felt as if it had been clubbed. This ogre was stupid, so that his ploys were obvious and easily avoided, but he was also tough. Smash had held his own so far only because he was less stupid and had the protection of his centaur clothing. If jacket and gauntlets failed him—

The ogre caught Smash's parrying arm in a grip of iron or steel and hauled him forward. Smash parried again by placing his free fist against the ogre's snoot and shoving. But he quickly became aware of his liability of half-strength; the other ogre could readily outmuscle him.

Worse, the ogre also became aware of this. "Freak weak," he grunted, and lifted Smash into the air. Smash twisted trying to free himself, but could not. Now he was in for it!

The ogre jammed him down on his feet, so hard it was Smash's turn to sink into the ground. He shot a terrible punch at Smash's chest—but now the jacket did protect Smash from most of the effect. Centaur clothing was designed to be impervious to all stones, arrows, pikes, teeth, claws, and other weapons; an ogre's fist was, of course, more than it was designed to withstand, but the jacket was much better than nothing. Meanwhile, Smash countered with another strike to the ogre's face, beautifying it by knocking out another tooth. He had good defense and good offense, thanks to the centaurs—but otherwise he remained treacherously weak.

The ogre windmilled his fist again, this time holding

Smash in place so that he could not escape the blow. The fist sledgehammered down on the top of his head, driving Smash another notch lower. He tried to parry but could not; the ogre countered his counter. Another hammer blow landed on his noggin, driving him down yet more. This was the Nail again—and this time Smash was the Nail.

"Don't hurt him!" Tandy screamed, coming down from her tree. "Eat me if you must, but let Smash be!"

"No!" Smash cried, knee-deep in the ground. "Run, Tandy! Ogres don't honor deals about food!"

"You mean he'll destroy you anyway, after—?"

"Yes! Flee while you can, while they're watching me!"

"I can't do that!" she protested. Then she screamed, for the child ogress, larger than Tandy, had pounced on her.

Tandy threw a tantrum. Once more her eyes swelled up, her face turned purple, and her hair stood out from her head. The tantrum struck the little ogre, who fell, senseless, to the ground. Tandy retreated to her tree, for it took her some time to recharge a tantrum. She was now as helpless as Smash.

The ogre had paused, watching this byplay. The typical ogre was too stupid to pay attention to two things at once; he could not watch Tandy while pounding Smash. Smash, similarly, had been too dull to try to extricate himself while watching Tandy, so had not taken advantage of his opportunity. Now the ogre resumed his effort, completing the figure of the Nail. Smash had somehow left his arms by his sides, and now they, too, were caught in the ground, pinned. He knew he would never have allowed himself to get into this situation if he had retained his Eye Queue! Almost any fool would have known better.

Knocks on the head were not ordinarily harmful to ogres, because there was very little of importance in an ogre skull except bone. But the repeated impacts did serve to jog loose a few stray thoughts, flighty fancies not normally discovered in such territory. Why had Tandy tried so foolishly to help him? It would have made far more sense for her to flee, and she was smart enough to have seen that. Of course her loyalty was commendable—but was largely wasted on an ogre. As it was, both would perish. How did that jibe with the Good Magician's Answers? Two people dead . . .

One answer was that the Magician had grown too old to practice magic any more, had lost his accuracy of prophecy, and had unwittingly sent them both to their doom. It was also possible that the Magician was aware of his inadequacy and had sent them to the wilds of interior Xanth in order to avoid giving real Answers. He could have suspected, in his cunning senility, that they would never return to charge him with malpractice.

No, Smash remained unwilling to believe that of Humfrey. The man might be old, but the Gorgon had invigorated him somewhat, and he still might know what he was doing. Smash hoped so.

Soon the ogre had him waist-deep in the ground, and Smash could not retaliate. He lacked the strength. Yet if he had not yielded up half his soul, someone would have had to remain in the Void, and that might not have been much of an improvement over the present situation.

Still the blows descended, until he was chest-deep, and finally neck-deep. Then the ogre began to tire. Instead of using his fist, he gave his big horny feet a turn. He stomped on Smash's head until it, too, was buried in the packed dirt.

The figure of the Nail was complete. Smash had been driven, like a stake, full-length into the ground. He was helpless.

Satisfied with his victory, the ogre stomped toward the beerbarrel tree where Tandy hid. Smash heard her scream in terror; then he heard a fist crash into the trunk of the tree. He heard beer swish out from the punctured barrel and smelled its fumes as it coursed across the ground toward him. He was in a dent in the ground formed by the ogre's pounding; he would soon be drowned in beer, if he didn't manage to drink it all, and Tandy would be dipped in beer and eaten by the victor.

Then he heard the patter of Tandy's feet coming toward him. She was still being foolish; she would be much easier to catch here. The earth about his face became moist as the beer sank in, and he heard it splashing when her feet struck it. He hoped her pretty red slippers didn't get soiled. Meanwhile, the ground shuddered as the other ogre tromped after her, enjoying the chase.

Then she was over Smash, scraping out the ground about

his head with her feeble little human hands, uncovering his buried eyes. Foaming beer from the tree swirled down, blearing his vision but softening the dirt somewhat so she could better excavate. But this was useless; she could never hope to extricate him herself, and already the ogre was looming over her, amused at the futility of her effort.

"Smash!" she cried. "Take my half soul!"

In Smash's dim, beer-sotted mind, something added up. One half plus one half equaled something very much like one. Two half souls together—

He saw her half soul dropping toward him, a hemisphere like a half-eaten apple, bisected with fair precision. Then it struck his head, bounced, and sank in, as the Eye Queue had done. He became internally conscious of it as it spread through him. It was a small, sweet, pretty, innocent but spunky fillet of soul, exactly the kind that belonged to a girl like her. Yet as it descended and joined with his big, brutish, homely, leathery ogre half soul, it merged to make a satisfying whole.

At this point, in the Night Stallion horror visions, this would have been the end. But here in real life, with a full soul pieced together, it just might be the beginning. Smash felt his strength returning.

The ogre lifted Tandy into the air by her brown tresses. He slavered. Smash's sunken orbs perceived it all from their beer-sodden pit in the ground.

The girl tried to throw a tantrum, but she was mostly out of the makings. She was terrified rather than angry, her tantrum-energy had recently been expended, and she had no soul. Her effort only made the ogre blink. He opened his ponderous and mottled jaw and swung her toward his broken teeth.

Smash flexed. He had a full soul, of sorts, now; his strength was back. The ground buckled about him. One hamhand rose up like the extremity of a zombie emerging from a long-undisturbed grave, dripping beer-sodden dirt. It caught the hairy ankle of the ogre.

Smash lifted. He was well anchored in the ground, so all he needed was power. He had it. The ogre rose into the air, surprised. But he did not let Tandy go. He continued to bring her to his salivating maw. First things first, after all.

Smash brought the foot belonging to the ankle he held to

his own mouth. He opened his own dirt-marbled jaws. They closed on the ogre's horny toes. They crunched, hard.

Folklore had it that ogres were invulnerable to pain because they were too tough and stupid to feel it. Folklore was in error. The ogre bellowed out a blast of pain that shook the welkin, making the sun vibrate in place and three clouds dump their water incontinently. He dropped Tandy. Smash caught her with his other hand, after ripping it free of the ground with a spray of dirt that was like a small explosion. He set her gently down. "Find shelter," he murmured. "It could become uncomfortable in this vicinity."

She nodded mutely, then scooted away.

Smash spit out three toes, watching them bounce across the dirt. He waved the ogre in the air. "Shall we begin, toadsnoot?" he inquired politely.

The ogre was no coward. No ogre was, since an ogre's brain was too obtuse to allow room for the circuitry of fear. He was ready to begin.

The battle of ogre *vs.* ogre was the most savage encounter known in Xanth. The very land about them seemed to tense expectantly, aware that when this was over, nothing would be the same. Perhaps nothing would be, period. The landscape of Xanth was dotted with the imposing remnants of ancient ogre fights—water-filled calderas, stands of petrified trees, mountains of rubble, and similar artifacts.

The ogre began without imagination, naturally enough. He drove a hamfist down on Smash's head. This time Smash met it with his open jaws. The fist disappeared into his mouth, and his teeth crunched on the scarred wrist.

Again the ogre bellowed, and the sun shook in its orbit and the clouds soaked indecorously. One downpour spilled onto the sun itself, causing an awful sizzle.

The ogre wrenched his arm up—and popped Smash right out of the ground in the process, for naturally Smash had not let go. Beer-mud flew outward and rained down on the watching ogres, who snapped at the blobs automatically.

The ogre slammed his two fists together hard. Since one fist was inside Smash's mouth, this meant Smash's head was getting doubly boxed. Vapor shot out of his ears. He spit out the fist, since he was unable to chew it properly, and freed his head.

Now the two combatants faced each other, two hulking monsters, the one covered with dirt and reeking of beer, the other minus two teeth and three toes. Both were angry—and the anger of ogres was similar to that of volcanoes, tornadoes, avalanches, or other natural calamities—apt to destroy the neighborhood indiscriminately.

"You called me half-breed," Smash said, driving a gauntleted fist into the other's shoulder. This time the blow had ogre force; the ogre was hurled sidewise into the trunk of a small rock-maple tree. The tree snapped off, its top section crashing down on the ogre's ugly head.

He shrugged it off, not even noticing the distraction. "He go me toe," he said, naming his own grievance, though unable to count beyond one. He fired his own fist at Smash's shoulder. The blow hurled Smash sidewise into a rock-candy boulder. The boulder shattered, and sugar cubes flew out and descended like hailstones around them.

"You tried to eat my friend," Smash said, kicking the ogre in the rear. The kick sent the monster sailing up in a high arc, his posterior smoking. Then, to make sure the ogre understood, Smash repeated it in ogrish: "He ea' me she."

The ogre landed bottom-first in the Fen, and the water bubbled and steamed about him. He picked himself up by hauling with one hamhand on the shaggy nape of his neck, then stomped the bog so that the mud flew outward like debris from a meteoric impact and ripped a medium-sized hickory tree from its mooring on an islet. The tree came loose with an anguished "Hick!" and hicked again as the ogre smashed it down across Smash's head, breaking it asunder. Smash felt sorry for the ruined tree, probably because of the influence of the sweet girl's half soul he had borrowed.

The two ogres faced each other again, having now warmed up. There was a scurrying and fluttering in the surrounding jungle as the creatures of the wild who had remained before now fled the scene of impending violence. There were also ripples in the swamp and the beat of dragons' wings, all departing hastily. None of them wanted any part of this!

Now that Smash had his full strength and had interacted with the other ogre, it was his judgment that he was the stronger of the two and the smarter. He believed he could beat this monster—and it was necessary that he do it to protect Tandy. But a lot of battle remained before the issue would be resolved.

Smash leaned forward, threw his arms around the ogre, picked him up, and charged toward the dense, hard walls of a big walnut tree. The ogre's head rammed right through the wood and was buried inside the wall-trunk, his body dangling outside.

Then there was a chomping sound. The ogre was chewing his way out, despite his missing teeth. Soon his snout broke through the far side of the wall, then chomped to the left and right. He spit out wall-nuts as he went, and they formed little walls around the tree where they fell. Then the tree crashed to the ground, its trunk severed. The ogre returned to the fray.

He ripped a medium rosewood tree from the ground and hurled it at Smash. Smash threw up a fist to block it, but the trunk splintered and showered him with splinter-roses.

Smash, in turn, swung a fist through a sandalwood trunk, severing it. He grabbed the loose part and hurled it at the ogre, who blocked it. This time there was a shower of sandals and other footwear.

The ogre took hold of a fat yew tree, twisting it around and around though it bleated like a female sheep, until the trunk separated from the stump. "Me screw with yew," he grunted, ramming the twisted trunk at Smash's face.

"That is un-ogrammatical," Smash said. "Ogres always say he or she, not you." But he ripped off a trunk of sycamore and used it to counter the thrust. "Syc 'em!" he cried, bashing at the yew. "Syc 'em more!" he cried, bashing again. And because this was the nature of that tree, it sycked 'em more.

Both trunks shattered. Trunks were really better for containing things than for fighting. Some trunks were used for trumpeting. Still, these were the most convenient things to use for this battle.

The ogre tromped into the deeper forest to the south, where larger trees grew. He chopped with both fists at a big redwood trunk. Smash stomped to a bigger bluewood and began knocking chips out of it with his own fists. Soon both trees came crashing down, and each ogre picked one up.

The other ogre was the first to swing. Smash ducked, and the redwood whistled over his head and cracked into a sturdy beech tree. The encounter was horrendous. The red was knocked right out of the redwood, and the sand flew from the beech. A cloud of red-dyed sand formed, making a brief but baleful sandstorm that swirled away in a series of diminishing funnels, coating the other trees.

Now Smash swung his bluewood. The ogre ducked behind a butternut tree. The trunk clobbered the tree. Blue dye flew out, and butter squished out. Blue butter descended in a gooky mass, coating everything the red sand had missed, including a small pasture of milkweed plants. Blue buttermilk formed. All the spectator ogres turned from dry red to dripping blue. It did improve their appearance. *Anything* was better than the natural hue of an ogre.

The ogre bent to rip out a boxwood tree. This time Smash was faster. He sliced off a section of trunk from a cork tree and rammed that at the exposed posterior. The cork shoved the ogre right into the box, where he was stuck bottom-up, corked.

Now the ogre was really angry. He bellowed so hard the box exploded and the cork shot up toward the sun with a loud Bronx cheer. When it hit the sun it detonated, and a foul cloud eclipsed the orb, turning a clear day to the smoggiest night ever to clog the noses of the jungle. Creatures began coughing and choking all around, and a number of plants wilted as the stench spread out like goo.

In the cloying darkness, the ogre retreated. He had had enough of Smash's full strength. But Smash was not through with him. He pursued, following the ogre into the deepest jungle by the sound of his tromping.

Something struck Smash's arm, temporarily numbing it. It was an ironwood bar. In the dark the ogre had harvested another tree and had hurled it from ambush. Some might consider this to be a cowardly act, but ogres did not know the meaning of cowardice, so it must have been some other kind of act. Ogres did comprehend cunning, so perhaps that was it.

Smash picked up the bar, started to twist it into a harmless knot, reconsidered and started to hurl it violently back, reconsidered again, and hung on to it. It would make a decent spear.

He listened, trying to locate the ogre. He heard the *sproing!* as another ironwood sapling was harvested. He charged that spot—and tripped over a fallen log. Naturally the log splintered into a storm of toothpicks that shot out like shrapnel, making pincushions of the surrounding vegetation. Smash lost his balance. He windmilled an arm and a leg.

Now the ogre knew Smash's location more accurately. The other spear came whistling at him as if it had not a care in the world and caught his outflung foot. That smarted! Smash rolled back, got his feet properly under him, limped, and struck back where his keen ogre hearing indicated the other ogre was.

Unfortunately, he had not realized that dirt remained in his ears, from the time he was spiked into the ground. His blow was countered, being off target, and the other bar clonked him on the side of the head.

This turned out to be a serendipitous blessing, for the clonk knocked out most of the dirt. Now he could hear properly! He reoriented and swung hard and accurately at the other—and missed, for the other was retreating.

The smog was beginning to clear. Smash pressed forward, striking repeatedly at the dim shape before him. The counterings grew fewer and weaker as the enemy retreated. Smash accelerated—and the figure ducked aside, put out a foot—and Smash tripped over it and stumbled headlong into a drop-off.

In midair he realized he had been tricked. The ogre, familiar with the terrain while Smash was not, had led him to the cliff. Smash should have been more suspicious of the sudden, seeming weakness of his opponent. But of course, without his Eye Queue, he was no smarter than any other ogre.

He landed on a bed of sharp gravel. Something yiped. Great yellow eyes opened. A jet of flame illuminated the area. Smash got a clear view of his situation.

Oops! He had fallen directly into a dragon's nest! This was the lair of a big surface dragon, open to the day because such a monster feared nothing, not even ogres. The dragon wasn't here at the moment, but its five cubs were.

In a moment all of them were up and alert. They were large cubs, almost ready to depart the nest and start consuming people for themselves. They were all as massive as Smash, with coppery snouts, green metal neck scales, and manes of silvery steel. Their teeth glinted like stars, and their tongues slurped about hungrily. As the light returned, all recognized him as an enemy and as prey. What a trap this was!

The ogre looked over the brink of the pit. "Ho ho ho ho!" he roared thunderously, causing the nearby trees to shake. "Me screw he blue!" For Smash stood on blue diamonds that made up the nest, which he had taken for gravel. All dragons liked diamonds; they were pretty and hard and highly resistant to heat. Because dragons hoarded diamonds, the stones assumed unreasonable value, being very rare elsewhere. Smash understood this extended even to Mundania, though he wasn't sure how the dragons managed to collect the stones from there.

Dragons were not much for ceremony. All five pounced, blasting out little jets of flame that incinerated the vegetation around the nest and heated the diamonds at Smash's feet, forcing him to jump.

Smash, angry at himself for his stupidity in falling into this mess—imagine being outwitted by a dull ogre!—reacted with inordinate, i.e., ogrish, fury. He just wasn't in the mood to mess with little dragons!

He put out his two gauntleted hands and snatched the first dragon out of the air. He whipped it about and used it to strike the second in mid-pounce. Both dragons were knocked instantly senseless. Weight for weight, no dragon was a match for an ogre; only the advantage of size put the big dragons ahead, and these lacked that.

Smash hurled both dragons at the other ogre, who stood gloating, and grabbed for two more. In a moment both of these were dragging, and the dragging dragons were hurled up to drape about the ogre.

The fifth dragon, meanwhile, had fastened its jaws on Smash's legs. They were pretty good jaws, with diamond-hard teeth; they were beginning to hurt. Smash plunged his fist down with such force that the skull caved in. He ripped the body away and hurled it, too, at the other ogre.

The smog had largely cleared, perhaps abetted by the breeze from Smash's own activity. Now an immense shadow fell across them. Smash looked up. It was the mother dragon, so huge her landbound bulk blocked off the light of the sun. Not all big dragons were confined to Dragonland! It would take a whole tribe of ogres to fend her off—and the tribe of the Ogre-Fen Ogres would certainly not do that. Smash had been tricked into this nest because the other ogre knew it would be the end of him.

But Smash, having cursed the darkness of his witlessness, now suffered a flashback of dull genius. "Heee!" he cried, pointing a hamfinger at the other ogre.

The dragoness looked. There stood the ogre, in midgloat, with the five limp, little dragon cubs draped around his body like so much apparel. He had been so pleased with his success in framing Smash that he had not thought to clear the debris from himself. The liability of the true ogre had betrayed him—his inability to concentrate on more than one thing at a time. Naturally the dragoness assumed that he was the guilty creature.

With a roar so horrendous that it petrified the local trees and caused a layer of rock on the cliff to shiver into dust, several diamonds to craze and crack; and a blast of fire that would have vaporized trees and cliff face, had the one not just been converted from wood to stone and the other not just powdered out, she went for the guilty ogre.

The ogre was dim, but not that dim, especially as a refracted wash of fire frizzled his fur. While the dragoness inhaled and oriented for a more accurate second shot, he flung off the little dragons and dived into the nest-pit, landing snoot-first in the diamonds. The contrast was considerable—the sheer beauty of the stones versus the sheer ugliness of the ogre. It looked as if he were trying to eat them.

Smash hardly paused for thought. At the moment, the dragoness was a greater threat to his health than the ogre. He wrestled a boulder out of the pit wall and heaved it up at the dragoness, while the other ogre struggled to his feet, shedding white, red, green, blue, and polka-dot diamonds. The dragoness turned, snapped at the boulder, found it inedible, and spit it out.

Smash realized that the other ogre had disappeared. He

checked, and saw a foot in a hole. The boulder he had thrown had blocked a passage, and the ogre was crawling down it, leaving Smash to face the fire alone. Smash didn't appreciate that, so he grabbed the foot and hauled the ogre back and out. Several more diamonds dropped from crevices on the creature's hide—black, yellow, purple, plaid, and candy-striped. In a moment Smash had the ogre in the air, swinging him around by the feet in a circle.

The dragoness was pumping up for a real burnout blast. Such an exhalation could incinerate both ogres in a single foop. She opened her maw, letting the first wisps of super-heated steam emerge, and her belly rumbled with the gathering holocaust.

Smash let go of the ogre, hurling him directly into the gaping maw, headfirst.

The dragon choked on her own blocked fire, for the ogre's body was just the right size to plug her gullet. The ogre's feet, protruding slightly from the mouth, kicked madly. Then the ogre's broken teeth started working as he chewed his way out. The dragoness looked startled, uncertain how to deal with this complication.

Smash wasn't sure how this contest would turn out. The dragoness' fire was bottled, and her own teeth could not quite get purchase on the ogre in her throat, but she did have a lot of power and might be able to clear the ogre by either coughing him out or swallowing him the rest of the way. On the other hand, the ogre could chew quite a distance in a short time. Smash decided to depart the premises with judicious dispatch.

But where could he go? If he scrambled out of the nest, the dragoness might chase after him, and he would be more like a sitting duck than a running ogre, in the open. If he remained—

"Hssst!" someone called. "Here!"

Smash looked. A little humanoid nymph stood within the hole left by the boulder.

"I was raised in the underworld," she said. "I know tunnels. Come!"

Smash looked back at the dragoness, who was swelling with stifled pressure, and at the kicking ogre in her throat. The former was about to fire the latter out like a missile. He had sympathy for neither and was fed up with the

whole business. What did he want with ogres anyway? They
were dull creatures who crunched the bones of human folk.

Human folk. "Tandy!" he cried. "I must save her from
the ogres!"

The nymph was disgusted. "Idiot!" she cried. "I am
Tandy!"

Smash peered closely at her. The nymph had brown
hair, blue eyes, and a spunky, upturned little nose. She was
indeed Tandy. Odd that he hadn't recognized her! Yet who
would have expected a nymph to turn out to be a person!

"Now get in here, you oaf!" she commanded. "Before
that monster pops her cork!"

He followed Tandy into the tunnel. She led him along a
curving route, deep down into the ground. The air here
turned cool, the wall clammy. "The dragon mines here for
diamonds that my mother leaves," she explained. "There
would be terrible disruption in Xanth if it weren't for her
work. The dragons would go on a rampage if their diamonds ran out, and so would the other creatures if they
couldn't get their own particular stones. It certainly is nice
to know my mother has been here! Of course, that could
have been a long time ago. There might even be an aperture to my home netherworld here, though probably she
rode the Diggle and left no passage behind."

Smash just followed, more concerned about escaping the
dragon than about the girl's idle commentary.

There was a sound behind them, like a giant spike being
fired violently into bedrock. The dragoness had no doubt
disgorged the ogre from her craw and now was ready to
pursue the two of them here. Though the diameter of the
tunnel was not great, dragons were long, sinuous creatures,
particularly the wingless landbound ones, who could move
efficiently through small apertures. Or she could simply
send a blast of flame along, frying them. Worse yet, she
might do both, pursuing until she got close, then doing
some fiery target practice.

"Oh, I'm sure there's a way down, somewhere near,"
Tandy fussed. "The wall here is shallow; I can tell by the
way it resonates. I've had a lot of experience with this type
of formation. See—there's a fossil." She indicated a glowing thing that resembled the skeleton of a fish, but it squiggled out of sight before Smash could examine it closely.

Fossils were like that, he knew; they preferred to hide from discovery. They were like zombies, except that they didn't generally travel about much; they just rested for eons. He had no idea what their purpose in life or death might be. "But I can't find a hole!" Tandy finished, frustrated.

Smash knew they had to get out of this particular passage in a hurry. He aimed his fist and smashed a hole in the wall. A new chamber opened up. He dropped through, carefully lifting Tandy down.

"That's right!" she exclaimed. "I forgot about your ogre strength! It's handy at times."

A rush of fire flowed along the tunnel they had quitted. They had gotten out just in time!

"This is it!" Tandy cried. "The netherworld! I haven't been in this section before, but I recognize the general configuration. A few days' walk, and I'm home!" Then she reconsidered. "No, there isn't any direct connection. The— what's that thing that cuts Xanth in half? I can't remember—"

"The Gap Chasm," Smash said, dredging it out of his own fading memory. In his ogre personality, he was too stupid to forget things as readily as Tandy could.

"Yes. That. That would cut off this section from the section I live in, I think. Still—"

She led him through a dark labyrinth, until the sounds of the enraged dragon faded. They finally stood on a ledge near cool water. "She'll never find us here. It would douse her fire."

"I hope you'll be able to find our way out. I'm lost." Ogres didn't care one way or the other about the depths of the earth, but did like to be able to get around to forage for food and violence.

"When the time is right," she said. "Maybe never."

"But what of our missions?" Smash demanded.

"What missions?" she asked innocently.

Then Smash remembered. She no longer cared about seeking fulfillment. She had given up her soul.

Chapter 15. Point of View

But in a moment he realized this was not serious. "I have your half soul," he said. "Take it back." He put his huge paw on his head and drew out the fillet. It adhered to his own soul, with which it had temporarily merged; evidently the two souls liked each other, different as they were. At last her soul rested in his palm.

Then he moved the faintly luminous hemisphere to her head and patted it in. The soul dissolved, flowing back into her. "Oh, that feels so good!" she exclaimed. "Now I know how much I missed my soul, even the half of it!"

Smash, back to his own half soul, suddenly felt tired. He sank down on the rock where he was resting. It was dark here, but he didn't mind; it was easy to rest in this place.

Tandy sank down beside him. "I think my soul feels lonely," she said. "It was half, and then it was whole with yours, and now it's half again, with maybe the better half missing."

"Yours is the better half," he said. "It's cute and spunky and sensitive, while mine is gross and stupid."

"But strong and loyal," she said. "They complement each other. A full person needs strength *and* sensitivity."

"An ogre doesn't." But now he wondered.

She found his hamhand with her own. "Okay, Smash, I remember our missions now. I wanted to find a good husband, and you—"

"Wanted a good wife," Smash finished. "I didn't know it, but the Good Magician evidently did. So he sent me where I could find one. But somehow the notion of sharing the rest of my life with an ogress no longer appeals. I don't know why."

"Because true ogres and ogresses are brutes," she said. "You really aren't that kind, Smash."

"Perhaps I wasn't when I had the Eye Queue curse. But when I lost it, I reverted to my natural state."

"Are you sure your natural state is brutish?"

"I was raised to be able to smash ironwood trees with single blows of my horny fist," he said. "To wrestle my weight in dragons and pulverize them. To squeeze purple bouillon juice from purple wood with my bare hands. To chew rocks into sand. To—"

"That's impressive, Smash. And I've seen you do some of those things. But are you sure you aren't confusing strength with brutishness? You have always been very gentle with me."

"You are special," he said, experiencing a surge of unfamiliar feeling.

"Chem told me something she learned from a Mundane scholar. Chem and I talked a lot while you were in the gourd, there in the Void, because we didn't know for sure whether we would ever get free of that place. The scholar's name was Ichabod, and he knew this little poem about a Mundane monster resembling a tiger lily, only this one is supposed to be an animal instead of a plant."

"I have fought tiger lilies," he said. "Even their roots have claws. They're worse than dandy-lions."

"She couldn't remember the poem, exactly. So we played with it, applying it to you. 'Ogre, ogre, burning bright—' "

"Ogre's don't burn!"

"They do when they're stepping across the firewall," she said, "trying to fetch a boat so the rest of us can navigate past the loan sharks. That's what reminded Chem of the poem, she said. The flaming ogre. Anyway, the poem tells how they go through the jungle in the night, the fiery ogres, and are fearfully awful."

"Yes," Smash said, becoming pleased with the image.

"We had a good laugh. You aren't fearful at all, to us. You're a big, wonderful, blundering ball of fur, and we wouldn't trade you for anything."

"No matter how brightly I burn," Smash agreed ruefully.

He changed the subject. "How were you able to function without your soul? When you lost it before, you were comatose."

"Partly, before, it was the shock of loss," she said. "This time I gave it away; I was braced, experienced."

"That shouldn't make much difference," he protested. "A soul is a soul, and when you lose it—"

"It does make a difference. What a girl gives away may make her feel good, while if the same thing is taken by force, it can destroy her."

"But without a soul—"

"True. That's only an analogy. I suppose I was thinking more of love."

He remembered how the demon had tried to rape her. Suddenly he hated that demon. "Yes, you need someone to protect you. But we found no man along the route, and now we are beyond the Good Magician's assignment without an Answer for either of us."

"I'm not so sure," she said.

"We're drifting from the subject. How did you survive, soulless? Your half soul made me strong enough to beat another ogre; you had to have been so weak you would collapse. Yet you didn't."

"Well, I'm half nymph," she said.

"Half nymph? You did seem like a nymph when—"

"I always thought of myself as human, just as you always thought of yourself as ogre. But my mother is Jewel the Nymph. So by heredity I'm as much nymph as girl."

"What's the difference?" He knew there was a difference, but found himself unable to define it.

"Nymphs are eternally young and beautiful and usually none too bright. They are unable to say no to a male for anything. My mother is an exception; she had to be smart and reliable to handle her job. She remains very pretty, prettier than I am. But she's not as smart as I am."

"You are young and beautiful," Smash said. "But so is Princess Irene, and she's a human girl."

"Yes. So that isn't definitive. Human girls in the flush of their young prime do approach nymphs in appearance, and have a number of nymphal qualities that men find appealing. But Irene will age, while true nymphs won't. She loves, while nymphs can't love."

"Can't love?" Smash was learning more than he had ever expected to about nymphs.

"Well, my mother does love. But as I said, she's a very special nymph. And my father Crombie used a love-spell on her. So that doesn't count."

"But some human people don't love, so that is not definitive, either."

"True. It can be very hard to distinguish a nymph from a thoughtless human girl. But one thing is definitive. Nymphs don't have souls."

"You have a soul! I am absolutely certain of that! It's a very nice little soul, too."

He could feel her smile in the dark. Her body relaxed, and she squeezed his paw. "Thank you. I rather like it myself. I have a soul because I'm half human. Just as you do, for the same reason."

"I never thought of that!" Smash said. "It never occurred to me that other ogres wouldn't have souls."

"They're brutes because they have no souls. Their strength is all magic."

"I suppose so. My mother was a variety of human, so I inherited my soul from her."

"And it gave you strength to make up for what you lost by being only half ogre."

"Agreed. That answers a mystery I was never aware of before. But you still haven't explained how you—"

"Functioned without a soul. Yes. It was simply a matter of how I thought of it. You see, human beings have always had souls; they have no experience living without them. Other creatures never had souls, so they have learned to cope. My mother copes quite well, though I suppose some of my father's soul has rubbed off on her." Tandy sighed. "She's such a good person, she certainly deserves a soul. But she *is* a nymph, and I am half nymph. So I can function without a soul. All I had to do, once I realized that, was to think of myself as a nymph. It made a fundamental difference."

"But I think of myself as an ogre—yet I have a soul."

"Maybe you should try thinking of yourself as a man, Smash." Her hand tightened on his.

"A man?" he asked blankly. "I'm an ogre!"

"And I'm a girl. But when I had to, I became a nymph.

So I was able to operate without sinking into the sort of slough I did before, in the gourd. I was able to follow your fight, and to step in when I needed to."

"A man!" he repeated incredulously.

"Please, Smash. I'm a half-breed, like you. Like a lot of the creatures of Xanth. I won't laugh at you."

"It's impossible! How could I ever be a man?"

"Smash, you don't talk like an ogre any more. You're not stupid like an ogre any more."

"The Eye Queue—"

"That vine faded a long time ago, Smash! And the one you got in the Void—that never existed at all. It was sheer illusion. Yet it made you smart again. Did you ever consider how that could be?"

It was his turn to smile in the dark. "I was careful not to think that one through, Tandy. It would have deprived me of the very intelligence that enabled me to indulge in that chain of thought, paradoxically."

"You believe in paradox?"

"It is an intriguing concept. I would say it is impossible in Mundania, but possible in Xanth. I really must explore the implications further, when I have leisure."

"I have another hypothesis," she said. "The Eye Queue was illusion, but your intelligence was not."

"Isn't that a contradiction? It's illogical to attribute an effect as significant as intelligence to an illusion."

"It certainly is. That's why I didn't do it. Smash, I don't think you needed the Eye Queue vine at all, ever. Not the illusory one *or* the original one. You always had the intelligence. Because you're half human, and human beings are smart."

"But I was never smart until the Eye Queue made me so."

"You were smart enough to fool everyone into thinking you were ogrishly stupid! Smash, Chem told me about the Eye Queue vine. Its effect wears off in hours. Sometimes its effect is only in self-perception. It makes creatures think they're smart when they aren't, and they make colossal fools of themselves without knowing it. Like people getting drunk on the spillage from a beerbarrel tree, thinking they're being great company when actually they are disgusting clowns. My father used to tell me about that; he

said he'd made a clown of himself more than once. Only
it's worse with the vine."

"Was I doing that?" Smash asked, mortified.

"No! You really *were* smart! And it didn't wear off, until you lost the vine in the flood. And it came back the
moment you got a new vine, even though you only imagined it. Doesn't that suggest something to you, Smash?"

He pondered. "It confirms that magic is marvelous and
not entirely logical."

"Or that you became smart only when you thought you
ought to be smart. Maybe the Eye Queue showed you how,
the first time. After that you could do it any time you
wanted to. Or when you forgot to be stupid."

"But I'm not smart now," he protested.

"You should listen to yourself, Smash! You've been dis-
coursing on the nuances of paradox and you've been talking in a literate fashion."

"Why, so I have," he agreed, surprised. "I forgot I had
lost the Eye Queue."

"Precisely. So where does your intelligence come from
now, ogre?"

"It must be from my human half, as you surmise. Like
my soul. I just never invoked it before, because—"

"Because you thought of yourself as an ogre, until you
saw what ogres really were like and started turning off
them. Now you are sliding toward your human heritage."

"You see it far more clearly than I do!"

"Because I'm more objective. I see you from the outside.
I appreciate your human qualities. And I think the Good
Magician Humfrey did, too. He's old, but he's still savvy. I
ought to know; I cleaned up his castle for a year."

"It didn't looked cleaned up to me. I could hardly find a
place to stand."

"You should have seen it before I cleaned it up!" But
she laughed. "Actually, I didn't touch his private den; even
the Gorgon leaves that alone. If anyone ever cleaned up in
there, no one would know where all his spells and books
and things were. He's had a century or so to learn their
locations. But the rest of the castle needs to be kept in
order, and they felt the Gorgon shouldn't have to do it,
since she's married to him now, so I did it. I cleaned off the
magic mirrors and things; some of them had pretty smart

mouths, too! It wasn't bad. And in that year I came to understand that behind the seeming absent-mindedness of Humfrey there lies a remarkably alert mind. He just doesn't like to show it. He knew all about you, for example, before you approached the castle. He had you marked a year in advance on his calendar, right to the day and hour of your arrival. He watched every step of your progress. He chortled when you came up against those ogre bones; he'd gone to a lot of work to get those set up. That man knows everything he wants to know. That's why he keeps the Gorgon in thrall, instead of she him; she is in complete awe of his knowledge."

"And I thought he was asleep!" Smash said ruefully.

"Everyone does. But he's the Magician of Information, one of the most powerful men in Xanth. He knows everything worth knowing. So he surely knew how much of a mind you had and crafted his Answer accordingly. Now we know he was correct."

"But our missions—neither is complete! He didn't know we would fail, did he?"

She considered, then asked, "Smash, why did you fight the other ogre?"

"He annoyed me. He insulted me."

"But you tried to avoid trouble."

"Because I was at half-strength and knew I'd lose."

"But then you slugged him. You knocked out a tooth."

"He was going to eat you. I couldn't allow that."

"Why not? It's what ogres do."

"I had agreed to protect you!"

"Did you think of that when you struck him?"

"No," Smash admitted. "I popped him instantly. There was no time for thought."

"So there was some other reason you reacted."

"You're my friend!"

"Do ogres have friends?"

He considered again. "No. I'm the only ogre who ever had friends—and they were mostly human friends. Most ogres don't even like other ogres."

"Unsurprising," she said. "So, to protect me, twice you risked your soul."

"Yes, of course." He wasn't certain of the point of her comment.

"Would any true ogre have done that?"

"No true ogre. Of course, since ogres don't have souls, they would never be faced with the choice. But still, if they did have souls, they wouldn't—"

"Smash, doesn't it seem, even to you, that you have more human qualities than ogre qualities?"

"In this circumstance, perhaps. But in the jungle, alone, it would be otherwise."

"Why did you leave the jungle, then?"

"I was dissatisfied. As I said before, I must have needed a wife, only I didn't know it then."

"And you could have had a nice brute of an ogress, with a face whose full glare would have made the moon rot, if you'd reacted more like an ogre. Are you sorry you blew it?"

Smash laughed, becoming more conscious of her hand on his. "No."

"Do ogres laugh?"

"Only maliciously."

"So you've thrown away the Answer you worked so hard for, you think. Are you going back to the lonely jungle now?"

Strangely, that also did not appeal. The life he had been satisfied with before seemed inadequate now. "What choice do I have?"

"Why not try being a man? It's all in your viewpoint, I think. The people at Castle Roogna would accept you, I'm sure. They already do. Prince Dor treated you as an equal."

"He treats everybody as an equal." But Smash wondered. Would Prince Dor have been the same with any of the Ogre-Fen Ogres? This seemed questionable.

Then something else occurred to him. "You say I was able to make the illusory Eye Queue vine work in the Void because I always did have human intelligence, so there was no paradox?"

"That's what I say," she said smugly.

"Then what about the gourd?"

"The gourd?" she asked faintly.

"That was illusory, too, in the Void, and it had nothing to do with my human nature, yet it also worked."

"Yes, it did," she agreed. "Oh, Smash, I never thought of that! But that means—"

"That illusion was real in the Void. That what we thought was there really *was* there, once we thought it, such as gourds and glowing footprints. So there is no proof I'm smart without the vine."

"But—but—" She began to sniffle.

Smash sighed. He hated to see her unhappy. "Nevertheless, I admit to being smart enough now to find the flaws in your logic, which, paradoxically, proves your case to that extent. Probably we're both right. I have human intelligence, and the Void makes illusion real." He paused, yet again aware of her hand on his. What a sweet little hand it was! "I have never in my life thought of myself as a man. I don't know what it could accomplish, but at least it might be a diversion while we wait for the dragoness to stop searching for us."

Her sniffles abated magically. "It might be more than that, Smash," she said, sounding excited.

Smash concentrated. He imagined the way men were: small and not very hairy and rather weak, but very smart. They used clothing because their natural fur didn't cover the essentials. They plucked shoes from shoe trees and socks from hose vines. He had a jacket and gloves; that was a start. They lived in houses, because wild creatures could otherwise attack them in their sleep. They tended to congregate in villages, liking one another's company. They were, in fact, social creatures, seldom alone.

He imagined himself joining that company, walking like a man instead of tromping like an ogre. Resting on a bed instead of on the trunk of a tree. Eating delicately, one bite at a time, chewing it sedately, instead of ripping raw flesh, crunching bones, and using sheer muscle to cram in whatever didn't conveniently fit in his mouth. Shaking hands instead of knocking for a loop. But the whole exercise was ridiculous, because he knew he would always be a huge, hairy, homely monster.

"It isn't working," he said with relief. "I just can't imagine myself as—"

She set her other hand on his gross arm. Now he felt the touch of her soul, her half soul, for he was attuned to it after borrowing it. There seemed to be a current of soul traveling along his arm between her two tiny hands. He had rescued that soul from the gourd, and it had helped rescue him from the ogres.

He also remembered how quick she had always been in his defense. How she had kissed him. How she had stayed with him, even when he went among the ogres, even when she lacked her soul. Suddenly he wanted very much to please her.

And he began to get the point of view. He felt himself shrinking, refining, turning polite and smart.

Suddenly it opened out. His mind expanded to take in all of Xanth, as it had when he first felt the curse of the Eye Queue. This time it was no curse; it was self-realization. He had become a man.

Tandy's hands remained on his arm and hand. Now he turned to her in the dark. His eyes saw nothing, but his mind more than made up the difference.

Tandy was a woman. She was beautiful in her special fashion. She was smart. She was nice. She was loyal. She had a wonderful soul.

And he—with the perspective of a man he saw her differently. With the mind of a man he analyzed it. She had been a companion, and he realized now how important that had become to him. Ogres didn't need companions, but men did. The six other girls had been companions, too, and he had liked them, but Tandy was more.

"I don't want to go back to the jungle alone," he murmured. His voice had lost much of the ogre guttural quality.

"I never thought you belonged there, Smash." Oh, how sweet she sounded!

"I want—" But the enormity of the notion balked him.

It didn't balk Tandy, however. "Smash, I told you before that I loved you."

"I have human perception at the moment," he said. "I must caution you not to make statements that are subject to misinterpretation."

"Misinterpretation, hell!" she flashed. "I knew my mind long before you knew yours."

"Well, you must admit that an ogre and a nymph—"

"Or a man and a woman—"

"Half-breeds," he said, half bitterly. "Like the centaurs, harpies, merfolk, fauns—"

"And what's wrong with half-breeds?" she flared. "In Xanth, any species can mate with any other it wants to, and some of the offspring are fine people. What's wrong with Chem the Centaur? With the Siren?"

"Nothing," he said, impressed by her vehemence. Moment by moment, as she talked and his manhood infiltrated the farthest reaches of his awareness, he was warming to her nature. She was small, but she was an awful lot of small.

"And the three-quarter breeds, almost identical to the humans, like Goldy Goblin and Blythe Brassie and John the Fairy—"

"And Fireoak the Hamadryad, whose soul is the tree," he finished. "All good people." But he wondered passingly why, since nymphs were so nearly human, they didn't have souls. Obviously there was more to learn about the matter.

"Consider Xanth," she continued hotly. "Divided into myriad Kingdoms of people and animals and in-betweens. We met the Lord of the Flies and the Prince of Whales and the Dragon Lady and the Kingdoms of the goblins, birds, griffins—"

"And the Ancestral Ogres of the Fen," he said. "All of which believe they dominate Xanth."

"Yes." She took a breath. "How can Xanth be prevented from fragmenting entirely, except by interaction and crossbreeding? Smash, I think the very future of Xanth depends on the half-breeds and quarter-breeds, the people like us who share two or more views. In Mundania, no species breeds with another—and look at Mundania! According to my father's stories—"

"Awful," he agreed. "Mundania has no magic."

"So their species just keep drifting farther apart, making that land more dreary year by year. Xanth is different; Xanth can reunify. Smash, we owe it to Xanth to—"

"Now I understand what men object to in women," Smash said.

She was startled. "What?"

"They talk too much."

"It's to fill in for inactive men!" she flared.

Oh. He turned farther toward her in the dark, and she met him halfway. This time there was no confusion at all about the kiss. It was a small swatch of heaven.

At last they broke. "Ogre, ogre," she murmured breathlessly. "You certainly are a man now."

"You're right. The Good Magician knew," he said, cuddling her close to him. In the dark she did not seem tiny; she seemed just right. As with riding the nightmares, things were always compatible. He had known Tandy was very feminine; now this quality assumed phenomenal new importance. "He sent me to the ogres—to find you."

"And he sent me to find you—the one creature rough enough to drive off the demon I fled, while still being gentle enough for me to love."

Love. Smash mulled that concept over. "I cried for you last night," he confessed.

"Silly," she teased him. "Ogres don't cry."

"Because I thought I would lose you. I did not know that I loved you."

She melted. "Oh, Smash! You said it!"

He said it again. "I love you. That's why I fought for you. That's why I bargained my soul for you."

She laughed, again teasingly. "I don't think you know what love is."

He stiffened. "I don't?"

"But I'll show you."

"Show me," he said dubiously.

She showed him. There was no violence, no knocking of heads against trees, no screaming or stomping. Yet it was the most amazing and rewarding experience he had ever had. By the time it was done, Smash knew he never wanted to be anything but a man and never wanted any woman but her.

They found another way out of the netherworld, avoiding the lurking dragon, and trekked south along the east coast of Xanth. Smash, by the light of day, was smaller than he had been, and less hairy, and hardly ugly at all. But he didn't really mind giving up his previous assets, because the acquisition of Tandy more than made up for them. She sewed him a pair of shorts, because men wore them, and he did rather resemble a man now.

They traveled quietly, avoiding trouble. When this threatened to rankle his suppressed ogre nature, Tandy would take his hand, and smile up at him, and the rankle dissipated.

The trip took several days, but that didn't matter, because it was sheer joy. Smash hardly noticed the routine Xanth hazards, since most of his attention was on Tandy. Somehow the hazards seemed diminished, anyway, for news had spread among the griffins, birds, dragons, goblins, and flies that Tandy's companion was best left alone, even if he didn't look like much. It seemed that a certain ogre of the Fen had staggered out of the jungle with a headache, and though he had not given any details, it was evident that he had been roughly treated by the stranger he had fought. Even the crossing of the Gap, which Smash had almost forgotten until he encountered it again, was without event. The Gap Dragon, reputed to have a sore tail, stayed clear.

At length, they drew near the entrance to Tandy's home region. The route was through a chasm guarded by a tangle tree. It was a big, aggressive tree, and Smash knew he could not overcome it. So he drew on his human intelligence and harvested a number of hypnogourds, intending to roll them down to the tree. If it made the mistake of looking in a single peephole—

But as they carried two gourds from the patch, a cloud of smoke formed before them. This coalesced into a dusky demon.

"Well, my little human beauty," the demon said to Tandy, switching his barbed tail about. "You were lost, but now are found. I shall have my will of you forthwith." He advanced on her, grinning lasciviously.

Tandy screamed and dropped her gourd, which shattered on the ground. "Fiant!"

So this was the demon who sought to rape her! Smash set his own gourd down carefully and stepped forward. "Depart, foul spirit!" he ordered.

The demon ignored him, addressing Tandy instead. "Ah, you seem more luscious than ever, girl-creature! It will be long before I tire of you."

Tandy backed away. Smash saw that she was too frightened even to throw a tantrum. The demon had come upon her so suddenly she had not been able to brace emotionally for the assault.

Smash interposed himself between demon and girl. "Desist, Fiant," he said.

The fat demon put out a hand and shoved him. Smash tripped on a stone and tumbled to the ground ignominiously. The demon stepped on his stomach and advanced on Tandy. "Pucker up, cutie; your time has come at last."

Smash was becoming perturbed. Tandy might believe in crossbreeding as the hope of Xanth, but she had not chosen to do it with the demon. As she had explained, there was a considerable difference between what was given voluntarily and what was forced. Smash scrambled to his feet and hurried after Fiant, catching him on the shoulder.

The demon swung about almost carelessly, delivering a brain-rattling slap across Smash's cheek. Smash fell back again, reeling.

Now Fiant shot out a hand and caught Tandy by the hair. She screamed, but could not pull away.

Smash charged back into the fray—only to be met with a careless straight-arm that nearly staved in his teeth. Now the demon deigned to notice him, momentarily. "Get lost, lout, or I'll hurt you."

What was this? Fiant seemed to be stronger than Smash!

The demon drew Tandy in to him by the hair, reaching with the clawed fingers of his other hand to rip off her blouse.

Smash charged again, fists swinging. He caught the demon on his pointed ear.

This time Fiant became annoyed. "You seem to be a slow learner, creep." He loosed the girl, spun about, and struck Smash with a lightning-fast one-two combination punch on chin and stomach. Smash went down, head fogging, gasping for breath. "No man can stand against a demon," Fiant said arrogantly, and turned again to Tandy.

But the brief respite had given her a chance to work up some spunk. She dived for Smash. "Take my soul!" she cried, and he felt its wonderful enhancement infusing him. He had forgotten how weak he was with only half a soul.

Then she was yanked away by the hair. Fiant held her

up, her feet dangling. "No more Mr. Nice Guy," he said. "Off with your skirt." On the trip down, Tandy had remade the tatters of her red dress into a good skirt, and completed her wardrobe and Smash's by sewing material from cloth bushes.

Smash leaped up and tackled the demon. Now he had his strength! But Fiant poked two fingers at his eyes. Painfully blinded, Smash fell to the ground again. He had a full soul again; why couldn't he prevail?

It was Tandy who came up with the answer. "Smash, you're too much of a man now!" she cried from her dangle. "Too gentle and polite. Try thinking of yourself as an ogre!"

It was true. Smash had spent several days becoming manishly civilized. As Fiant had said, no man was a match for a demon.

But an ogre, now . . .

Smash thought of himself as an ogre. It wasn't hard. He had spent his life indulging in just such thinking; the old thought patterns were strong. He visualized the ground trembling at his stomp, trees being ripped from their moorings, boulders being crushed to sand by single blows of horny fists.

Hair sprouted on his arms. Muscles bulged horrendously. His height jumped. His orange jacket, which hung on him loosely, abruptly became tight. His shorts split apart and fell off. His hands swelled into hams. His bruised eyeballs popped into awful ogre orbs. *Ogre, ogre . . .*

Smash put one hamfinger to the ground and lifted his whole body into the air; then he flipped neatly to his rock-calloused feet. He roared—and the leaves of the nearest trees swirled away. So, unfortunately, did Tandy's clothes, such as remained; they were not constructed for hurricane winds.

She swung in dainty nudity by her hair. "Go get him, ogre!" she cried, and kicked the demon on the nose.

Fiant looked at Smash—and gaped. Suddenly he faced a monster far worse than himself. He dropped the girl and turned to flee.

Smash bent down, hooked his fingers in the turf, and yanked. The turf came toward him in a rug, dumping the demon on his horns. Smash took one tromp forward and launched a mighty kick at Fiant's elevated rump. The kick should have propelled the demon well toward the sun.

But Smash's foot passed right through Fiant. Smash, thrown off balance by the missed kick, did a backward flip and whomped on his head. That hardly mattered to an ogre, but it gave the demon a chance to get organized.

Fiant realized that the ogre could not really hurt him, thanks to his ability to dematerialize at will. This restored his courage marvelously. Bullies always got brave when the odds were loaded on their side. He got up, strode toward Smash, and punched him in the gut. It was a good, hard blow—but now Smash shrugged it off as the trifle it was and countered with a sweep of his arm that was so swift and fierce it caused a contrail behind it.

But this blow, too, passed through the demon without effect.

"He's dematerializing!" Tandy cried. "You can't hit him!"

Unconvinced, Smash plunged his fist at the demon's head from above. This blow should have driven the demon halfway into the ground. Instead, it passed the entire length of Fiant's body without impediment and struck the bare rock beneath, where the rug of turf had been removed. The rock cracked apart and powdered into sand, naturally. Then Smash rammed a straight punch at Fiant's belly— and only succeeded in sundering the tree behind him. Smash was tearing up the landscape to no avail.

But the demon could hit Smash, by rematerializing his fists just before they struck. The blows didn't really hurt, but Smash was annoyed. How could he pulverize a creature who could not be hit back?

He tried to grab Fiant. This worked slightly better. The demon's body was as diffuse as smoke to his touch, but Smash's spread hamhands had more purchase, and he was able to guide the smoke as long as he handled it carefully. Unfortunately, the demon's fists remained material, and they now beat a brutal tattoo on Smash's face. His nose and eyes were hurting anew.

"Use your mind, Smash!" Tandy called.

Smash held the demon in place, enduring the facial bat-

tering while he put his natural Eye Queue intellect to work.
What would deal with such a demon once and for all? It
would not be enough merely to drive Fiant off; he had to
fix it so the demon could never again bother Tandy. If
Tandy had a notion how he should proceed, why hadn't she
simply screamed it out?

Because if the demon heard, he would act to negate it.
Smash had to do whatever it was by surprise.

He glanced at Tandy—and saw her sitting on the gourd
he had carried. Suddenly he understood.

He snapped at the demon's fists, using his big ogre teeth.
"Oh, no, you don't, monster!" Fiant exclaimed. "You can't
get me that way!" Sure enough, he punched Smash on the
tongue, and when Smash's teeth closed on the fist, it dematerialized and withdrew unhurt.

But meanwhile, Smash was carrying the demon toward
the gourd. When he got there, he slowly tilted Fiant down
toward the peephole Tandy had been sitting on. The demon
was about to face the gourd. If Fiant saw it too soon, he
would strike it and shatter it, ruining the ploy.

Fiant, intent on punching Smash's snout into a pulp, did
not spy the gourd until he was abruptly face to face with it.
"No!" he cried, realizing what it was. He jammed his eyes
closed so he could not look, and dematerialized.

"Yes!" Smash grunted. He shoved the demon headfirst
at the gourd. Because Fiant was dematerialized, he passed
right through the peephole, headfirst. Suddenly Smash remembered the bottle ifrit inside this same gourd. Wasn't
the gourd another kind of container? "You want to force
your way into something? This is a good place." Smash fed
the rest of the demon through, arms, torso, legs, and feet,
until all of him was gone.

"Let him find his way out of *that*!" Tandy cried jubi-
lantly. "Oh, this really serves him right!"

Smash put his ear to the peephole. He heard a faint,
angry neighing, as of an aroused stallion, and a startled
scream. It seemed the demon could not dematerialize very
effectively in a world where everything was already imma-
terial. Then the beat of hooves faded away in the internal
distance.

Smash smiled. As Tandy had suggested, it would be long
before the demon found his way out of that situation!

He drew forth Tandy's fillet of soul and handed it back to her. Suddenly he felt his full strength return, and saw Tandy brightening similarly. Their two half souls had been returned!

Smash realized what it was. The nightmares had made a fair exchange for the two halves of Fiant.

Smash straightened up, keeping his eye averted from the peephole. He squinted at Tandy, perceiving her disheveled but pert nudity. "Ogre confess, like she dress," he said.

"Oh, you're a sight for sore eyes yourself!" Tandy said in nurselike fashion, wiping Smash's battered face. "And sore nose, too! But do you know something? I love you just as much in the ogre view."

He kissed her then, using his sore lips, not caring what point of view it might be. Love was, after all, blind.

About the Author

Piers Anthony is the name of a hopelessly Mundane character who has difficulty taking About-the-Author notes seriously. He was born in England, moved to Spain, had his sixth birthday aboard the ship that brought him and the former King Edward VIII of England to the New World, and took three years to get through first grade because he couldn't learn to read. Naturally he grew up to be a writer whose interest was in islands, peninsulas, Kings, and illiteracy. His early problems in math still manifest in his tendency to crowd five or six novels into a trilogy. He now lives in the backwoods of Florida with his brown-eyed wife, blue-eyed daughters, and brown-eyed horses and dogs. The old railroad tracks that cut through the hill in sight of their house bear a suspicious resemblance to the Gap Chasm; the drooping live oaks with their Spanish Moss are reminiscent of tangle trees, and if the local sugar sand isn't very sweet, at least it is excellent for miring vehicles. The Land of Xanth is real for those who understand it. Those who don't believe in it are relegated to Mundania: it serves them right.

Piers Anthony lost count of his novels when they approached the number of his years of age. His first was written in 1956 and was never published. His second, *Chthon*, was published in 1967. Now he turns them out at the rate of about three a year. The first Xanth revelation, *A Spell for Chameleon*, won the August Derleth Fantasy Award for best novel of 1977. But the real success of Xanth is indicated by the fact that it has generated more fan mail than any other series by this author, from people ranging in age from nine to (censored). Xanth is spreading; a tangle tree was recently spotted in Colorado, and nightmares have ranged even farther out.